Spy
MOM

HYPERION

NEW YORK

Spy
MOM

The Adventures of Sally Sin

★

BETH McMULLEN

ISBN: 978-1-4013-1270-1

Hyperion books are available for special promotions and premiums. For details contact the HarperCollins Special Markets Department in the New York office at 212-207-7528, fax 212-207-7222, or email spsales@harpercollins.com.

FIRST PAPERBACK EDITION

10 9 8 7 6 5 4 3 2 1

SUSTAINABLE FORESTRY INITIATIVE

Certified Fiber Sourcing
www.sfiprogram.org

THIS LABEL APPLIES TO TEXT STOCK

We try to produce the most beautiful books possible, and we are also extremely concerned about the impact of our manufacturing process on the forests of the world and the environment as a whole. Accordingly, we've made sure that all of the paper we use has been certified as coming from forests that are managed, to ensure the protection of the people and wildlife dependent upon them.

CONTENTS

Original
S█N

A Sally Sin Adventure

Beth McMullen

For Mike

1

know I'm not crazy. I know this because it said so in my file, which I stole out of Director Gray's office on a drunken dare from a guy who eventually disappeared in Somalia. Somewhat emotionally detached, the file said, and loose with the truth, yes, but in the eyes of the Agency, these were positive attributes. A red star at the top of the file corresponded to a note stuck to the inside cover. *Refer to Simon?* the note said. The question mark has always troubled me. They were never sure I could cut it.

So how to explain what I'm doing right now. Gardening? Searching for a lost contact lens? Seeing if there is a stranger crawling around under my shrubs waiting to sneak into my house and strangle me with a length of piano wire?

It is Tuesday morning, the San Francisco sun is shining and the fog is starting to recede back toward the ocean. It's as regular as any other morning except that on this morning rather than sitting at my kitchen table sipping a scalding cup of coffee, here I am in the backyard crawling around on my knees under the juniper trees, muttering to myself like one of the local shopping-cart pushing, bottle-collecting loonies.

"There is no evidence here," I whisper. I am holding tightly to a brightly painted set of Matryoshka dolls, shaking them as if to make a point to my invisible audience. If I were really thinking, I would have picked up the cast-iron frying pan, still warm from this morning's pancakes. Cast iron is generally accepted to be a better choice of weapon than a bunch of Russian nesting dolls. I continue to crawl forward under the scrubby trees.

"There are no tracks, no shell casings, no cigarette butts or discarded coffee cups. You are simply having a paranoid attack that, most likely, a hit of caffeine will alleviate. Now get up and go back in the house." Yet from my position here in the garden, I can't help but notice that the palm tree in my perfectly landscaped backyard is situated in just such a way as to allow direct spying in through my kitchen window. Someone with skills could even figure a way into the house from here. How could I not have noticed this?

My neighbor Tom, a British gentleman who always looks slightly past his "use by" date, watches me from his own backyard, a curious expression on his face.

"Problems with the trees, Lucy?" he asks as I crawl out, pulling twigs and needles from my unwashed hair.

"Yes. Well, no, actually. I thought I heard a cat." Oh please. "It sounded like it was in trouble. Lost maybe?"

"No cats here," Tom says. He looks left and then right with an exaggerated turn of his bald head. "None that I've seen anyway."

"Well, thanks for checking. Gotta go. Left a child inside unattended. You know how that can end up."

Tom stares at me blankly. I guess not. I start to pull the debris from my hair, trying not to look too particularly crazed on this fine morning. And then I see it, off to the side of the back stairs. Five years ago I would have known immediately the height, weight, eye color, and sexual orientation of the owner of this footprint. But today, I am not sure. Is it my husband's footprint, the washing machine repairman, the woman who comes to read the meter? I haven't a clue. But I have that sinking feeling it is not supposed to be here.

I head up the stairs throwing Tom a half-assed wave over my shoulder. I know he is still watching me and will continue to watch me until I disappear into the house. Sometimes I think everyone knows and that I should hang a neon sign outside my bedroom window that says: YES, YOU ARE ALL RIGHT. THINGS ARE NOT AS THEY APPEAR TO BE.

I have left Theo for one minute too long. Covered in applesauce, he's trying, with great enthusiasm, to bite the cat's tail. The cat is howling to be let go. Theo is howling in delight. And I swear that not ten minutes ago I heard someone crawling around under my house. But I am not crazy. My file said as much. Tomorrow, however, everything might change.

2

My name is Lucy Parks Hamilton and in addition to being paranoid, un-showered, emotionally detached, and a liar, I am also a stay-at-home mom. Ten years ago, I would have met the idea that I would be going on playdates and walking around with streaks of snot on my shoulder with absolute indignation. Nowadays it's possible for me to wear the same pair of jeans for seven days in a row and not get too worked up about it.

My son Theo is three. He attends Happy Times Preschool twice a week for three hours. During these long three hours, I could be doing things. I could be folding laundry or shopping for food or writing my autobiography. I could even get a haircut or wash the car. But no. I have to sit where I can see the bright yellow door of the Happy Times Preschool. And that happens to be by the windows at the third table to the left in the Java Luv, a small coffee shop across the street and about half a block away from the school. The folks at the Java Luv are all very pleasant and are in complete agreement with one another that I'm a little weird. Or perhaps a lot weird.

"Good morning, Lucy," the barista, a guy named Leonard covered in spiderweb tattoos, greets me. "Read any good books lately?" He laughs because it's become something of a joke. I sit in the same seat at the same table and do nothing more than stare out the window. I never pull out a well-worn best seller or peck away on my laptop or socialize or pick my cuticles or anything. I just sit and watch that yellow door. So I guess they are right about me. Strange.

But I do have a purpose. I am here to make sure that no one goes into Theo's school who does not belong there. I want to know that my son is exactly where he is supposed to be until the moment I can retrieve him. Some people might say I have developed overprotective tendencies. They have not seen what I have seen.

When Theo and I are together, we spend a lot of time engaged in potty talk to varying degrees.

"Mommy, I have to pee. I have to pee NOW," he'll shout at the top of his lungs.

"But honey, we went not ten minutes ago. Can we at least finish getting our groceries and go to the potty after that? Again?"

"I go right here," he'll announce and squat down on the ground of whatever unfortunate store I've chosen to patronize on that day.

"Okay, let's go. Let's hurry!"

After a dozen such close calls, I discovered my son is simply a potty tourist, interested in visiting potties the world over. Let me tell you, it gets old pretty fast.

When we're at home and not crowded into the restroom du jour, we read Dr. Seuss. *The Cat in the Hat, Green Eggs and Ham, Horton Hears a Who.* Lately, in my head, everything is conducted in a pleasant ultra-violent singsongy Seussian.

Is there a door in that store?

A big door.

A big purple door.

Go through the big purple door in the big store and perhaps on the other side you will meet a s'more all covered in red gore.

And so on. My brain is atrophying. I can feel it. But I'm not entirely sure how to stop its slow slide into mush.

We sing. I can sing "The Wheels on the Bus" and "Old MacDonald" in several different keys and octaves. Occasionally I'll throw out a verse in Urdu or Czech or Tagalog for practice. Yes, Theo looks at me funny, but I'm willing to bet I'm the only mom in the 'hood who can do so.

It turns out I am a fabulous multitasker, at least in my own mind. I can dress Theo with one hand and arrange playdates with the other. I can simultaneously shower, play cowboys and horses, tie shoes, and make scrambled eggs. Occasionally the shoes end up in the eggs. Or in my hair. But nobody's perfect, right?

I do laundry, separating the darks from the whites from kid clothes and using a different detergent and water temperature for each load. I make organic applesauce and fix toys and spend so much time crawling around on my knees playing cars or dinosaurs that my knees now have more calluses than skin. I go to Whole Foods and squeeze the fruits and vegetables like we're longtime lovers, spending perfectly useful minutes in the perfectly useless pursuit of the perfect melon. It is important, although I couldn't tell you exactly why. I cook healthy meals with whole grains and fish and green vegetables. The fact that I wash them down with half a bottle of expensive red wine doesn't trouble me in the least. I often find myself in conversations that seem to go like this:

"So what do you do all day?"

"I'm a stay-at-home mom. I take care of my son."

"Oh. Well. I think I need to go and stick a needle in my eye."

End of conversation. It's a bum rap. Being a mother is hard. And I feel like I have a few data points in the "hard" category.

I am thirty-six years old. I am fairly tall, with indistinct, brown, shoulder-length hair that could certainly benefit from a few highlights. I have blue eyes that some people say are so intense they find it unnerving. And I can still kill an adult male twice my weight with one precisely placed punch in the chest. This is not something I tell the other moms at the playground. It simply doesn't come up all that often.

"Hey, Lucy, I hear you used to be a spy. Got any extra wipes in that bag? Or maybe an AK-47 lifted off some rebel in Afghanistan? Or a small drop of poison I could slip into my husband's Manhattan because I swear he's screwing the nanny?" Like I said, it really doesn't come up too often. And in reality, this motherhood thing hasn't been so good for the old termination skills. I'm a little rusty in all areas except, it seems, paranoia. My paranoia is still largely intact.

So these are the things that I do as a stay-at-home mom. Play, clean, shop, feed, sleep, play some more, repeat. There is no denying I am a long way from where I used to be.

Places that included Cambodia, Vietnam, Budapest for a short while, Croatia, Nepal, Slovenia—but that was for a vacation with the guy who disappeared in Somalia—a number of desolate locations in Africa, Tibet, and more of China than I care to remember, and several places I'm still not at liberty to comment on but let's just say the weather was terrible. In those days, I was not Lucy Parks Hamilton, wife of William Wilton Hamilton III, mother of Theodore Hamilton. Back then I was Agent 26, aka Sally Sin, of the United States Agency for Weapons of Mass Destruction.

The Agency, as you already know if you read the papers, is comprised of a bunch of analysts sitting around trying to figure out who has what, when they are going to use it, and on whom. And for the most part that's true. But there is a single line on page 415 of the USAWMD budget that reads, simply, Operations—Additional. And that's where we lived, a small group of spies trained to ferret out elusive information, the one missing piece of the puzzle. And on occasion we were called upon to disarm those individuals or groups who had become a little too proud of their personal stash of Armageddon. Oftentimes these folks would decide, logically of course, that blowing up all of Cleveland because the guy who cut them off in traffic had a Cleveland Cavaliers bumper sticker was perfectly reasonable. Agency policy required us to disagree, although there are plenty of people who don't see the point of Cleveland anyway. But that's another story. The covert agents of the USAWMD are out there every day trying to stop the bad things from happening by whatever means possible. Sometimes it works and sometimes it doesn't. Most people remember the times when it doesn't.

There weren't twenty-six agents. I have no idea how many there were but I think it was less than twenty-six. However, my boss, Simon Still, seemed to think I looked like Agent 26.

"Hey, Sally Sin, Agent Twenty-six, I got something for you," he'd yell through the labyrinth that comprised our office space.

"Agent who?"

"Twenty-six."

"Who are agents one through twenty-five?"

"I'm not at liberty to disclose that information."

"So how am I supposed to know that I'm really Agent Twenty-six?"

"You're starting to annoy me, Agent Twenty-six."

"Sorry, sir. It won't happen again."

And Agent 26 wasn't nearly as bad as Sally Sin, which was a joke from the computer game that started this whole mess in the first place. We'll get to that in a minute.

My husband, Will, once made a ton of money as an investment banker. But then he had a transformative experience while visiting the Fresh Kills landfill in Staten Island. As he stood staring out over the two thousand acres of waste, he says he began to hyperventilate and not only because of the stink. He started to see himself and everyone he knew swimming through an ocean of decomposing medical waste and old toys and rotten grapefruits. It must have been quite an image because days later he quit his seven-figure job and decided he had no choice but to dedicate his life to saving the planet. And I mean that literally. He managed to come up with enough seed money to start his own investment fund to support the development of green energy. Will speaks with a certain reverence about solar cells and geothermal energy, and if he catches me absentmindedly putting a piece of paper in the garbage rather than in the recycle bin, the pain is acutely visible on his face. He is a good person and he expects me to recycle with the same enthusiasm that he does. So I try. Honestly, I do.

"Honey, this is a tree," he says, gingerly removing the piece of newspaper from the garbage can. "It can be turned into so many other things, like egg cartons for instance. But you need to give it a chance to go on and do good in the world."

When I first met Will I thought he might be another hippie throwback talking the talk but finding the walk part kind of inconvenient and opting instead for a quick trip to Starbucks. But not Will. As it turns out, he is the first person I have ever met who truly believes a single individual can make all the difference. It's humbling.

Despite my poor recycling habits and my inability to under-stand the complexities of trading carbon credits, he seems to like me anyway. I'm not exactly sure how that happened, but I try not to question my good fortune too much. And, of course, Will loves Theo to pieces and buys him all sorts of exciting sustainable wooden toys. In the interest of marital harmony, we both ignore the fact that I occasionally slip the kid a Matchbox car made in China. I do try and remember to recycle the packaging, however.

We live in a modest house in San Francisco, California, with a roof covered in solar cells. The amount Will paid for the house still makes my throat dry, but Theo likes it here. He can play outside in February and rarely has to wear shoes. He is beautiful and I'm not saying that simply because I'm his mother. People approach us on the street wanting only to touch his silky blond hair. This, as you might guess, doesn't go over particularly well with me. Remember the paranoia I mentioned earlier? In addition to the blond hair, he has my blue eyes and a dimple in his chin like his dad.

My local friends want to know what it is I do when I'm not with Theo. They want to know how I spend those hours that I'm not playing cars or dinosaurs or reading *Where the Wild Things Are* for the eight thousandth time. I don't tell them about my coffee shop vigil. I don't tell them I stare at the front door of Theo's preschool waiting for bad guys to appear and mess up my perfectly happy existence. My goal in this stage of my life is to fly under the radar. Being that weird is definitely not under the radar. And how would I explain that I occasionally slip out to Donovan's Dojo, patronized exclusively by ex-cons and cops, to kick the shit out of a bunch of people who think my name is Amy and that I did time for armed robbery? Or that in a lockbox in my closet, buried under some sweaters, is a .45 caliber Colt Commander that I have used to kill people? And that sometimes I take it out and look at it to remind myself of what that was like.

So I deflect the invitations to lunch or coffee with as little fan-fare as I can manage and focus on Theo. He is, after all, the reason I am here in San Francisco and not dead in the desert in Yemen or crawling around in the jungles of Myanmar. And the truth is I like it here, the clean smell of the air, the soft pink of the evening sky. It is all so peaceful and orderly. After nine years with the USAWMD, I appreciate peaceful and orderly in a way I never did before.

Part of being Agent 26 meant no one from my life—past, present, or future—could know I was Agent 26. My official story is that after I graduated from college I went to work for the government as an analyst for the USAWMD. I sat at a desk, in a row of other people sitting at similar desks, and I read documents. When I was done, I summarized what I read in five hundred words or less and passed it on down the line. I can fill in the agonizing details if pressed, but if you present it correctly no one ever asks a follow-up question. It's really too boring for the average citizen to consider. So we talk about something exciting, like the weather.

The unofficial story is more interesting. In college I was always broke. To collect enough money for the necessary survival items—beer, cigarettes, pot, what have you—I would volunteer at the graduate psychology school to take various screenings and tests, earn a few bucks, and help the struggling grads gather up enough data to come up with yet another expert conclusion, such as: If you eat too much, you may become fat. Clever.

It was my senior year, well into the deep freeze of a northeast winter, when I found myself in an overheated classroom filling out a psychological survey about fear. What made me afraid? What did I do when I was afraid? Did I feel like fear was something I could control? The second instrument, as the grads called the questionnaires, wanted to know how I felt about moral ambiguity. Was having an affair always wrong? If you kill someone for a good reason, is it still wrong? If you back over the neighbor's cat, do you confess? The third one was a series of mathematical questions where you had three seconds in which to give your answer. Even at the time, I knew it was about pressure and not math. Will the test-taker crack and run screaming out of the room? But that sort of thing never bothered me and my blood pressure stayed as level as a football field.

The final part of the study involved playing a computer game. We had to give ourselves a code name and run through a scenario, which required that the player make a lot of choices based on dubious information. I chose Sally Sin as my code name, thinking it was funny. I regret that now, but how was I to know it would actually matter?

So I got my twenty dollars and left the building, bracing myself for the freezing winds and slippery sidewalks. I made it as far as the convenience store before the man in the dark coat and sunglasses caught up to me. Even then he seemed strangely out of place. Jeez, I thought, who is this guy? An engineering professor? A tragically unhip visitor from another planet, like the South or something?

"You shouldn't smoke," he said, suddenly standing next to me at the checkout window. I barely looked up as I dug around in my knapsack for enough loose change to cover the pack of cigarettes on the counter. Growing impatient, my new friend in the cashmere overcoat and shiny black shoes slapped a five down next to the box.

"Didn't you earn twenty bucks not ten minutes ago?" he asked.

"Yes, but I don't want to break it yet."

The man shook his head in apparent disgust.

"Thanks," I said, gesturing toward the five on the counter. "I'll pay you back. After I break the twenty."

"Please, keep your pennies."

"Nice glasses," I said, starting to walk out of the store. The man followed closely behind. "Do you work for the FBI?" Thinking back, I'm lucky he didn't flatten me for being snotty.

Instead, the man gave a quick laugh, more like a snort really. "NSA, actually, but I'm doing a favor for USAWMD."

"A lot of letters there," I said. My attention was already turned to peeling the cellophane wrapper from the pack of cigarettes.

"Listen," he said, taking my arm, "like I mentioned, I'm doing a favor so let me make it quick. We'd like to speak with you about your career plans. We think we might be able to offer you a chance to have some adventures and earn a pretty good living at the same time. If that sounds appealing, let us know. Enjoy your smokes." He slipped a card into my pocket and disappeared out the door.

The card read "John D. Smith, Recruitment, USAWMD." It had a phone number and a note that said to call anytime. I put the card back into the pocket of my down jacket and headed home.

I was a good student, exceptional only in the area of foreign language. After learning high school Spanish from the textbook before the teacher even figured out all of our names, I had yet to encounter a language I couldn't master with a minimum of focus and a couple of weeks. When I joined the Agency, I spoke normal languages like French, Spanish, and German. When I left, I spoke things like Mandarin, Arabic, Kurdish, Hungarian, Azerbaijani, Portuguese, Hindi, Vietnamese, Urdu, Persian, Korean, Nepali, and the list goes on.

I liked the fact that I could speak French like a Parisian and German like a Berliner, but it never occurred to me that it could be useful for anything but vacations. Four years into college and I still had no idea what I wanted to do when I grew up other than get as far from the cold northeast wind as possible. I thought about being a writer but had nothing all that interesting to say. I thought about being a lawyer but didn't know any lawyers who would admit to liking it. So I resigned myself to trudging along, waiting for that *Eureka, I've found it!* moment, which showed no signs of surfacing.

Five days after graduation, packing up my tiny college apartment with no clue as to where I was going and what I was going to do when I got there, I came across the business card of John D. Smith. And so, having nothing to lose and a possible job in a troubled economy to gain, I called him. That a total stranger claiming to work for the NSA followed me into a convenience store and offered me a job didn't alarm me in the least. Not a single lightbulb went on in my fuzzy twenty-something head. It never occurred to me that this was anything but completely normal.

I met with John D. Smith in a coffee shop. He had on a navy blazer and a white shirt even though it was 90 degrees and humid outside. He seemed pleased to see me. He called me Smokey the Bear and I had to deliver a long explanation about how I only smoked during finals, because of the stress and all. He laughed, saying something about how he already knew that and continued to call me Smokey the Bear. Later, after several years with the Agency, I would develop a perverse hatred of nicknames, code names, pet names, and any name not written expressly on one's birth certificate, not that I was able to use that one either.

"So what would the job be?" I asked.

"Well, you'd have to come to Washington for a while, after which you might visit . . . other places. And there would be a lot of reading and studying and giving your opinion."

Giving my opinion was something I was good at. I accepted his offer without even asking about the pay, and headed to D.C. six days later.

For a month, I read files on Cambodia, a place I could barely find on the map. There were sketchy pictures of what looked like a massacre, newspaper clips I couldn't decipher, and personal reports from people who were still there or had been there. After completing my required reading, I was asked what I thought about Cambodia.

"It seems like a nice place to visit, but I wouldn't want to live there," I said.

"In other words," John Smith prompted.

"They're fucked," I said. He snorted. His snorting was starting to get under my skin.

"But why are they fucked?" he asked.

"Because no one will take responsibility for the slaughter of millions of people. There has been no reckoning. And there always has to be a reckoning. Someone has to pay for the blood. The situation will never be stable otherwise. You know, that whole justice thing."

I found out later that they had been watching me for that month, not so much interested in my silly opinion of the Cambodian holocaust, but rather in what I ate for dinner, if I crossed against the light, if I flossed every day or every other. They followed me to and from the office, to the movies, to the dry cleaners, on one lame date with an accountant, to the grocery store. They even followed me into the locker room at the gym. Wherever I went, my shadow followed. Of course, I had no idea. All of that following and being followed and following someone following someone else contributed to the development of my acute sense of paranoia, which is why I was crawling around under the shrubs this morning while my sweet little boy was inside coating himself in applesauce and trying to bite the cat's tail. Some things never go away.

After those first few months, I was invited to spend some time with Simon Still, a mysterious figure who floated in and out of the USAWMD offices from time to time. He was of average height, thin, pale, with hair that might have been blond at some point. He always wore a white Panama hat and dark glasses and bore an odd resemblance to David Bowie, circa 1985.

It was not that I didn't like Simon exactly. But he made me uncomfortable, like a pair of jeans that are a little too tight and pinch your thighs when you try to sit down. He took me for a walk on the Mall and explained in a very Simon-like way what was going on.

"Okay, Sally Sin, here's the deal. Did you watch all those spy movies when you were a kid? With agents and double agents and James Bond and all of that horseshit? Yes? Good. Well, it's all true. Actually, Hollywood dumbs it down a bit for mass consumption. Being a real spy is much sexier in real life than it is on TV."

I had no idea what he was talking about, but I remembered Sally Sin.

"How did you know about Sally Sin?" I began. But before the words got all the way out of my mouth, I suddenly understood something.

"Those tests were not for grad work?" I asked.

"You *are* as brilliant as they say you are, Ms. Sin. No. Of course they weren't for grad work. They were an agency screening. You'll be pleased to know that out of several thousand tests administered, only three people passed. Plus your language thing, that put you over the top."

I'll admit I was impressed, but at the same time a little freaked out. "Who else made the cut?" I asked, thinking immediately of the guy in the cubicle next to mine with the terrible mustache, and the woman from upstairs with the paisley scarves.

"Tsk, tsk," Simon said, "that is for me to know and for you never to know, if you get my meaning."

He continued, "So here you are. Do you want to be a spy for USAWMD or not? Do you want to track down bad guys, call in the cavalry, walk away a hero time and time again? Only you can decide. Of course, if you decide not to, we'll have to kill you." He paused for a second too long. "Just kidding. Naturally. So what do you think?"

Me? A spy? This was ridiculous.

When I was little I would play spy in the old barn out back. I'd tip a few dusty hay bales up on end, creating a series of obstacles that I'd navigate around, pulling my imaginary gun like in the *Charlie's Angels* reruns I was addicted to, as I went around each hay bale corner. Somewhere out there in the maze of hay was a nameless, faceless bad guy. While I created elaborate scenarios about whom I was rescuing, the villain was always vague. I could never summon up an image of his face.

I could play this game for hours, until the hay started to itch my nose and make my skin red.

But to be a real spy? I looked up at the Lincoln Memorial. Simon did this on purpose, posed his question right here in front of this great and courageous man. Do it for your country, Lincoln seemed to be saying, looking down on small, inconsequential me. Do it because your country needs you now. Step up. Be a hero.

But in the end, I said yes because it was easier than looking for a new job. Perhaps being a spy was what I was meant to do. There was certainly nothing else of interest happening in my life.

And for nine years I faithfully executed the duties of my job. These duties included dropping into foreign countries in the middle of the night, and I do mean dropping. Speaking languages that still cramp my tongue. Being places that I shouldn't have been, taking pictures of things I shouldn't have been taking pictures of. Pretending to be any number of individuals. Possessing an ability to sleuth under duress. Staying alive. Delivering the goods, mechanical, chemical, human, or otherwise, again and again and again. And I was good at my job. Not the best there ever was, but good enough.

3

Reentering the house, I realize the applesauce is not only in Theo's hair and on the cat, but there is also a thin veneer coating the walls and the table. Theo sits with the jar between his legs, a blue plastic spoon deep in the applesauce, making "mmmm" sounds as he licks his hands and arms. I feel a slight involuntary twitch in my left eyelid. He's only three, I remind myself. It's only applesauce.

"Mommy, what's outside? Do I have pea school today? Do we have more applesauce?" Sometimes I feel like my brain is no longer elastic enough to follow a preschooler's train of thought.

"No school today. No more applesauce. And nothing was outside, sweetie. Mommy thought she heard something, that's all. But it was nothing, probably just a cat."

"Probably just a cat," Theo repeats. "Just a cat. Cat." He rolls the word around in his mouth, tasting it like only a child can. Then he digs into the remaining applesauce with his still chubby fingers to retrieve the spoon. "You eat some?" he offers. He holds the spoon out to me.

"Of course," I say, sitting down on the floor next to him, ignoring the mess. "I'd love some." He spoons the sauce directly into my mouth very carefully. Theo has Will's power of concentration, of being able to block out the whole world and see only the task at hand. I, on the other hand, can have ten things running simultaneously through my head, which is not always a good thing. For example, I can't let go of the possibility that someone was in my backyard. And if that is true, what do they want? And whenever my mind goes in this general direction, I always end up thinking, does this have anything to do with Simon Still?

. . .

That I met William Wilton Hamilton III at all is Simon's doing. He's the one who sent me to Hawaii in the first place. It was supposed to be Stanley, but he turned up on the banks of the Zambezi and that was that.

With an afternoon to kill in the lovely tropics, I went scuba diving. The last time I'd been diving was in the Caribbean, there specifically to blow up a smuggler's yacht and his cache of FN Five-seven pistols pilfered from Dublin. Normally at the Agency we stuck to big weapons, the kind known to level entire cities, but sometimes we dabbled in the small stuff. In this case, the guns in question were purchased illegally with U.S. funds, given to Peruvian rebels, sold to the IRA, and, shortly thereafter, stolen by the smuggler with the boat. The intent was to bring them back into the States and sell them for a tidy profit on the black market. Ah, the circle of life. There was a reporter sniffing around, which might have led to some embarrassing moments for the sitting government. Call Simon. He can take care of it.

I was willing to bet that the last time most of my fellow divers were under water they were admiring the clown fish and giant brain corals and things. But no matter.

Anyway, I climbed aboard thinking nothing more than how nice it would be to pretend to be a normal person for a few hours, and there he was.

The first thing I noticed was how the skin around his eyes crinkled when he smiled and the easy way he lounged, with his wetsuit unzipped to the waist, on the stained boat cushions. He seemed so comfortable in his skin, so relaxed. His laughter greeted me as I climbed aboard and it was real laughter, without even a hint of bitterness. It had been a long time since I'd heard that sound. Suddenly my own skin felt old and worn. And for a second I was just unbelievably tired.

The dive master, studying his clipboard like the Rosetta Stone, announced that this guy and I were the only solo divers on the trip and therefore would have to "buddy up."

I should probably take a minute and explain something here. My dive instructor at the Agency was a retired Navy SEAL. Somewhere off of the Washington coast, he sat me down, explained the basics, and dropped me, fully geared up, over the side of the boat into the 50-degree Pacific Ocean. All in about forty-five minutes. There was no buddy system, no classroom training, no checkout dives. There was nothing more than me, the freezing water, and whatever strange Agency task had brought me there. So this whole buddy thing was news to me. But I'd happily play along if it meant I could spend the afternoon swimming with this man.

"Will Hamilton," he said, extending his hand across the rocking boat.

"Sounds like you intend to be president," I said. I gripped his hand a little too tightly, desperate not to fall over and make an utter fool of myself.

"No. I definitely inhaled." His voice was rich and creamy, like homemade chocolate pudding. "But don't tell anyone. So, buddy, done much diving?"

I shrugged. "Some."

"Favorite places?"

I noticed his dive gear was well worn, familiar. Mine was well worn, rental. He appeared only moderately concerned that his as-signed dive buddy didn't have any experience. How to explain?

"Oh, um, warm water mostly, I guess." I sounded like an idiot. I thought about taking a moment to drown myself.

"Great. Well, we'll take good care of each other," he said, a ques-tioning smile lingering on his lips. And I'm mortified to report I actually blushed. I studied my pruned feet until the flush left my cheeks.

"Yes, we will," I said. Even then it felt like more. Now if you had asked me under normal circumstances if I believed in love at first sight, I would have accused you of being a sentimental fool with, at best, a tenuous grip on reality. Yet there I was, feeling a little queasy. And I was pretty sure it wasn't the rocking boat.

Under the water we moved well together. He pointed out an eel and a stingray, and I managed the disappearing backside of a turtle. Back on board, I marveled at how good he looked wet and was actually approaching giddy when he sat next to me for the return journey. As the ride ended and the boat pulled into the pier, he asked me if I'd like to meet him for a cocktail. He was here for a convention. Or something like that. I nodded dumbly. Of course I would.

We never actually had the cocktail.

Later, wrapped only in the Egyptian cotton sheets of my fancy hotel bed, listening to the waves crashing on the beach, Will told me about growing up rich and privileged in Los Angeles, the son of a television producer.

"It was basically the best childhood that money could buy. I was the only kid, with older parents, and they could not give me enough. Surf lessons, golf lessons, private schools, skiing in Zermatt, sailing in the British Virgin Islands. You know, the list goes on."

"Sounds nice."

"Doesn't it? Except it sucked. Because it was all to keep me out of their hair. They basically wanted to sit on the beach and occasionally wave to me as I went off with yet another instructor or babysitter or whatever. They wanted me to look good at dinner but not to say too much. And if I was going to have opinions, it would be better if they lined up nicely with their own."

"So it felt kind of empty?" I asked, thinking that sounded like the right thing to say.

"Completely. The pathetic part is I kept right on doing what they wanted me to do until not that long ago. Then everything changed. I saw the garbage."

When he asked me what I did, I told him about my dull desk job as a nuclear analyst for the United States Agency for Weapons of Mass Destruction. I could see his eyes glaze over as I dazzled him with statistics about how many nuclear warheads were actually unaccounted for at the time. I'll give him credit though. He did try.

"That sounds really interesting," he said, stifling a yawn.

Yes. Thrilling. Really. "It's not bad. It pays the bills and I like to read."

"And writing, too. You must do some writing."

"Yes. Some." There was a long pause.

"So do you think you might want to go diving again tomorrow?"

The next morning, before the sun was up, as William Hamilton slept soundly at my side, I called Simon Still.

"I've been doing this for nine years," I said quietly into the phone. "I'm tired, Simon."

"You're tired?" He didn't even try to hide his disgust. "Take a nap then, Sally."

"No. I mean tired as in my soul is tired. Does that make any sense?"

"None whatsoever. Get your soul a prescription and let's not talk about it anymore."

"I think I want to quit." There was a long pause.

"Quitting," Simon said, "is not always as easy as it sounds."

"I think I want a normal life."

"You are assuming, my dear Sally, that there is such a thing as a normal life."

I glanced over at Will, his blond hair covering his eyes, snoring slightly. From the dark recesses of my mind, a voice echoed. What makes you think he wants you, Sally? What makes you think you will ever see him again? My only answer was that I had no idea. But it didn't matter. I had already started down the road.

"I think there is," I said.

"What name did you give him, Sally? Lucy, Maggie, Susan, Elizabeth, Allison? Don't think you can run from it. It will always find you."

He didn't have to add the last part. I got it. But still.

"Lucy," I said. "Lucy Parks."

"Well, I always kind of liked that one. We'll talk about this when you get back to the office." He didn't ask me if I was going to finish the job. He knew I would. Simon Still knew me better than anyone at that time in my life. It is a point in my favor that I no longer believe that to be true.

I climbed out of bed, pulled on the thick hotel robe, slipped into the fuzzy hotel slippers, and padded a few steps down the hallway to room 437. In the pocket of the robe was a key card for that very room, exactly as I'd arranged. A little money goes a long way with those making minimum wage and being forced to wear horrible uniforms.

Inside, the occupant, known to us at the Agency as Conan the Rastafarian, slept soundly next to a very young woman I knew not to be his wife. Conan was not a bad guy really, but he'd gotten a little too ambitious for our comfort level lately. He wanted to be the boss, and we, the Agency, did not want that to happen. So, to curb his career ambitions, we would simply turn his friends into his enemies and let nature take its course.

I was looking for a catalog of sorts of the weapons Conan was peddling, things like FIM-9 Stinger Missiles and HIMARS truck-mounted, multiple rocket launchers, mostly behind the backs of his partners. I'd been told he carried the catalog on a memory stick attached to his key chain.

I didn't worry about Conan and his date waking up. I'd also arranged for their room service to have a little something extra in it, something to help them sleep.

I quickly got to it, digging through his bags, his briefcase, the heels of his shoes. I found the keys and the memory stick in the room's safe, along with some photographs of the beautiful young woman that she'd probably regret when she finally woke up. I slipped the stick into Conan's laptop to verify it was what I wanted, stopping briefly to download all of his contact information onto it just for kicks. You never knew who might turn up on such a list. For example, in Conan's contacts I saw a senator from the Midwest who would surely be supporting the USAWMD the next time the director went to Capitol Hill to ask for funding. While I was pondering what that conversation might sound like, a thickly muscled and thoroughly tattooed arm wrapped around my neck.

"I need a double dose, missy," Conan growled into my ear. "You should know that by now." He tightened his grip on my neck. Usually these sorts of turns for the worse served only to focus me. But at that moment all I could see was Will's sleeping face a few doors down.

"Shit," I squeaked out, with what little air I had left.

"What did you say?"

"I said 'shit.' Is it possible that I could fall in love with someone? Me?"

"I'm trying to kill you and you're talking about love? What sort of fucked-up outfit do you work for?"

It was a good question, but not one I had time to answer. While Conan proceeded to strangle me, I grabbed his laptop with two hands and swung it with as much force as I could muster up over my head. When it met his skull it made a sickening crunching sound, which I hoped was his head, not just the machine. He moaned, releasing me for long enough that I was able to turn. One knee up, hard, in the groin, and down went Conan. I rolled him on his stomach and pulled both his arms up behind his back with the intention of handcuffing him.

But he was heavy, strong, and not all that interested in going down quietly. He bucked me off of his back. I slammed into the media center and watched the hotel flat-screen wobble precariously above my head. As I scrambled away from the falling TV, Conan got back on his feet. He then proceeded to run at me, shoulders down, like a really angry football player. To this day, I think his intention was to ram me right through the plate glass window and on into eternity. He had speed. He was mad. After all, I'd drugged him. But in the end I simply stepped aside and watched as Conan the Rastafarian flew right out his window like a baby albatross taking its first flight. I did not look down to see what sailing out of a twentieth-story window looked like on the other end. But I can tell you it made a very unpleasant sound.

Quickly, I dug the memory stick out of what remained of the laptop and slipped out of the room. There would be a commotion. I wanted to be tucked into my bed by the time it started.

Back in my room, I kicked off my slippers and climbed in beside a still sleeping Will. He rolled over and flung an arm across my waist.

"Did you go somewhere?" he asked.

"No," I said. I didn't mention that I had just killed somebody. Not on purpose, but I didn't think that mattered. Simon was going to be mad.

"Mmm," Will gurgled, falling back to sleep. I giggled, feeling all of a sudden high and reckless.

By the time I got back to Washington and my small, sparsely furnished apartment, I was halfway out the door of the USAWMD. Simon Still tried to convince me otherwise.

"Does this guy know that while he was sleeping you pushed a perfectly nice thug out of a hotel window?" he asked, not looking up from my report on Hawaii.

"No, sir. Of course not. And he wasn't nice. And I didn't push him."

"Any relationship you enter under false pretenses is doomed to failure. And your whole life is pretense."

"Thanks for pointing that out."

"What are you going to do without the Agency?" he asked. "Have tea parties? Pick out paint and tiles for the bathroom? Take your soul out for restorative walks along the beach?"

"No," I said. "Maybe I'll go and see a movie, subscribe to a magazine, cook a meal, have only one passport. Maybe I'll get a goldfish."

"A pet?" he laughed, unable to hide his bitterness. "Let's be honest here, Sally. You won't like being a private citizen. It's a lot harder than it looks."

But I did mean it. I was done wandering around the globe looking for people who A) wanted to blow up the United States, B) wanted to blow up friends of the United States, or C) my personal favorite, people who wanted to blow me up directly.

By my thirty-third birthday I was married to Will and the mother of Theo. When he was born I received an e-mail from Simon

Still, the first communication we'd had since I left the Agency eighteen months earlier.

"Good luck," it read. "You thought Cambodia was hard . . ."

I'd like to say he was wrong, but there are days when I clearly remember the Cambodian jungle as a cakewalk.

4

Overall, I like to think I'm not bad at being a regular person, a mom, someone whose opinion in the grand scheme of things is not given much value. I try to keep my mouth shut because Lucy Parks Hamilton has no background and I really would prefer it if no one goes digging around trying to find out who I am.

But once in a while I screw up. For example, The Green Fund's annual Christmas party. One of Will's wiseass investors, who can't possibly be more than eighteen years old from the looks of him, says I have a great ass. But he says it in Hungarian because who the hell speaks Hungarian? Even the Hungarians don't want to speak Hungarian because there are way too many letters.

"You should keep those thoughts to yourself," I say back to him in Hungarian, with a wink. "I could kill you in seven different ways using only my hands."

He is so surprised he drops his champagne glass. I pluck it out of the air a second before it hits the fashionable concrete floor. I smile demurely when Will asks me what is going on. "Nothing," I say. "I'm having a lovely chat with this fine young gentleman here."

"How did you do that?" the man asks, as I hand him back his glass.

"What? Speak Hungarian?"

"No. The glass. Yes. The Hungarian." He blushes. "I'm sorry. I think I've had too much to drink."

"I don't speak Hungarian. I don't know what you are talking about."

"But I . . . didn't you . . . you caught my glass though, right?"

"Yes, but in English."

The man looks bewildered. I stare at him blankly. He wanders off, muttering to himself, clutching the half-full glass like a baby bottle.

I like my life. I'd be the first to admit that sometimes the repetition makes me start to doubt my sanity. But at the end of the day it makes sense to me. I get up in the morning to the sounds of Theo singing about the space shuttle or trains or his windup shark bathtub toy. We have breakfast: coffee for me, juice for him, oatmeal for everyone and all over the place. We play with toys, build giant towers out of blocks and knock them down, maybe read a few books. We go out to the park, to the zoo, to the ocean. Theo likes the beach and the zoo the best so we spend a lot of time there. He tells me he is ready to surf. I tell him the water is really cold and he really ought to learn how to swim first. He gives me that look like I'm a complete idiot. I've thought about dropping Simon Still an e-mail suggesting he study why children are impervious to cold. It is a skill that could be useful for stints in Siberia.

We take music classes, swimming classes, art classes. Theo does great but I spend my time checking out the other moms and nannies, convinced that my clothes are all wrong. Clearly my years of mucking around in foreign relations left me with little or no fashion sense.

Theo has a big heart. He is constantly on the lookout for signs of pain and discomfort in other creatures.

"Mommy," he says, staring into the lion cage at the zoo, "that lion is hungry. Can he come for ice cream?" The lion stands back beyond the protective moat. I pull Theo a little closer. The lion licks his lips, slowly, patiently. I can see him thinking, calculating, planning. I've seen that same look in the eyes of certain individuals with less than my best interests at heart.

I begin to lead Theo toward the penguins, benign and small. "I'm sure he is hungry," I say, "but the zookeepers will be by shortly to feed him. Besides, I don't think lions like ice cream."

Theo ponders this. "How would he hold the cone? And rainbow sprinkles or chocolate? Too hard for the lion maybe."

I nod in agreement, casting one last look back at the hungry lion, and we continue our tour.

I'm friendly with other moms, but not so friendly that we're spilling our guts to each other over double-shot lattes at the Java Luv. I want my life to stay peaceful, which means making sure no one gets overly curious about me. Will says I'm too introverted, but the truth is I'm scared. Now I have something to lose.

Today is a day like any other, except for the imaginary person in the backyard and my brain feeling like it is on fast-forward. The sun is warm, the sky blue. Theo is on the floor playing with a battery-free windup bamboo toy car while I scrub the applesauce from the floors and walls.

"Can you play with me?" he asks.

"No, I'm cleaning the applesauce."

"Can you play with me?" he asks again. I marvel at his selective deafness.

"No, I can't. When I am done cleaning I can play with you." The eyelid starts to twitch again. It feels like a butterfly has hatched in there right on my eyeball.

"Why are you cleaning? Why?"

"Because you put applesauce on the walls. Remember?"

"Oh. Well, when you are done, okay?"

I agree to the terms. Theo turns his attention back to the car in question. He especially likes to send it crashing off the dining room table onto the heirloom Oriental rug, a wedding gift from Will's parents. I've been told in agonizing detail of the rug's provenance, its long journey from places in China that my father-in-law finds difficult to pronounce. I don't have the heart to tell him that the story that came with his rug is most likely false. I've been to these places. They are nothing like he describes.

But Theo loves it. Every time his car hits the rug and explodes in spinning tires and smashing glory, he yells out, "Oh man, look at that," and I can't help but laugh.

My husband leaves the house at 6 A.M. every weekday and occasionally on weekends too. He comes home twelve hours later looking as energized as when he left, bursting with stories about solar farms and wind turbines. I, on the other hand, look like I've been run over by a bus, my reserve of nurturance sucked completely dry.

There are times when Will comes bouncing through that doorway and I want nothing more than to hurl a sustainably farmed cantaloupe melon at his head because it has to be his fault. It has to be his fault that I have spent my day picking up Cheerios and wiping noses and making inane conversation about fuzzy red monsters and dump trucks. And yet other times my heart leaps at the very sight of him. Now I can't say for sure if that feeling is the result of still being in love with him or panic at what I have done to my life. Perhaps a little of both.

Will travels a lot. He doesn't like it, he says. It's hard for him to be away from us. Plus air travel really kills his carbon footprint. I can't tell you exactly how many trees have been planted in an attempt to make ours a carbon-neutral household, but suffice it to say it's a lot. Sometimes, late at night, I catch him looking at me curiously, like there is something he wants to ask but he can't quite put his finger on it.

Our affair was fast and furious, undertaken with the same lack of respect for consequences that landed me with the Agency in the first place. Will tracked me down in D.C. two weeks after we left Hawaii with promises to see each other again soon, which I'd naturally assumed were false. I'd wanted to believe I could fall in love with this man and he could fall in love with me and we could live happily ever after. But the fact that not a single active USAWMD agent had a personal life was not entirely lost on me. It was a Friday night and Will called my personal cell phone, on which I'd received possibly one call ever, every five minutes until I finally relented and picked up.

"I'm here in your city with no friends and no plans, so I really could use your help," he said. He claimed the reason for his visit was business, but I'm inclined to believe he made up the business part of it. Something was happening and neither of us could deny it.

I met him for dinner and, after a few cocktails, I couldn't come up with a convincing enough reason not to let him into my apartment. I didn't tell him that he was maybe the second person to step foot through the door. Will wanted to say something nice about my place, but I could see he was shocked by its sparseness. For the first time, I was embarrassed by where I lived, by the bare walls and the dead cactus.

"I travel a lot for work," I said with a shrug. "I'm, um, not usually home."

He nodded. "Of course," he said. "You travel." He rallied to the cause. "You are a minimalist. Not addicted to the constant acquisition of more stuff. I love it. You are anti-materialistic. So rare."

Who would have thought my ugly and empty apartment could actually be a turn-on? We spent the next forty-eight hours in bed, ordering out for food and bottles of wine. When Monday rolled around Will went back to California and I got on a plane for London to meet with a contact who swore he had mind-blowing information for me that could only be delivered in person. I didn't want to go. For the first time, my heart wasn't in it. I was doodling Mrs. William Hamilton on my cocktail napkin all the way across the Atlantic. And it didn't help that my source was more interested in shooting me than in giving me valuable information.

"Focus, Sally," Simon berated me afterward. "Do you want to wake up dead tomorrow? You walked right into his trap like an amateur."

"But you are the one who set up the meeting," I pointed out.

"Who cares about the details? You were sloppy."

I called Will the minute my plane touched the ground back in Washington.

"God, Lucy, I thought you vanished or decided you hated me. Didn't you get any of my messages? I didn't know what to do."

"I missed you too," I said and actually meant it. "I really did."

"Come to California."

"I might be able to get out there for a few days next week. How does that sound?"

"No, I mean come to California forever. I think I'm in love with you."

Well, that stopped me dead in my tracks. Saying it out loud made it real. It also made for a fine mess.

"Really?" I asked.

"Yes. Lucy, come to California, move into my house, and marry me. If you don't I think I might die."

"You shouldn't kid around like that. I might take you seriously."

"I am serious, Lucy," he said. "I've never been more serious in my life."

The next day I met Simon Still at yet another crowded coffee shop. I wanted to ask him why not a nice Italian place or maybe sushi? But I didn't think the timing was the best.

"I can't keep doing this forever, can I?" I asked. "At some point I need to have a real life. Maybe this is that time." Lately it seemed like I spent most of my time dodging bullets. My luck was running out. My karma was compromised. And I wasn't sure if I wanted to die just yet.

"Why not?" Simon asked. "I intend to do it until someone kills me. If I'm old when that happens, great, if not, oh well."

I sat back with my piping hot coffee and stared at Simon. He looked a little ragged around the edges, tired, but it was hard to remember a time when he didn't look that way. Having the safety of the world in your hands is hard work. Other than the fact that he was born in the West, I knew nothing about him. Did he have parents, siblings, a cat? Did he sleep with men or women or whomever happened to be free when he blew into town? And what town was that, where did he live? Who washed his socks? What did he do for fun? Did he know how to have fun? And I knew suddenly, sitting there, that I didn't want to be Simon Still. I didn't want to find myself twenty years down the road in the same sad empty apartment with no friends, no family, nothing but a history of crazy stories that I could never tell anyone anyway. I took his hands in mine.

"I feel like I've known you forever," I said, "so I think you'll understand that I'm serious when I say this. I want out."

He pulled his hands back as if I had burned him, put on his sunglasses, and pushed back from the table.

"The one thing you never understood," he said, "is that in order to save humanity, you cannot be a part of it. Consider yourself out." Then he stood up and walked away without even a glance back.

And it was almost that easy. When your job doesn't exist, quitting it is not that complicated. I met with two men I'd never seen before and they gave me the ground rules for being an ex-USAWMD agent.

1. You were never here.
2. We were never here.
3. We're still not here.
4. During this period you worked for USAWMD Analyst Bureau. There are tax records, etc., to back up your story, if you should need them.
5. Hand in your passports, all of them. You will be given a clean U.S. passport with whatever name you intend to use printed on it. We recommend you don't return to the one you started with.
6. Watch your back. You never know when someone might recognize you.

But they weren't done yet. There was a number seven, kind of quietly added on at the end. We reserve the right to call on you if your expertise is required. And if we do, you must call back. I agreed. It wasn't as if any of this was really up for debate.

So Theo is tossing his car off the table and I'm standing at the sink rinsing out dish towels covered in applesauce. It makes a sticky, paste-like substance that has now migrated up my forearms. My hair hangs in my face, but I don't dare tuck it behind my ears. Adding the applesauce slop to it would surely not improve my situation.

And just like that, the phone rings. Not my cell phone or any of Will's three work lines. Not the fax machine. But the regular old landline. It is not my natural inclination to answer it because no one I know actually ever calls me on that phone. I'm not even sure why we have it. But now it is ringing. On this beautiful San Francisco morning, my house phone is ringing.

"Hello," I say, "Hamilton residence."

"Hello there, Sally," comes down the line. I'm not exactly surprised to hear Simon Still on the other end. But that doesn't mean I don't almost choke at the sound of his voice.

"Hello, Simon," I say. "Where are you? Have you been in my backyard recently?"

"I can't say, you know that."

"Of course," I say, remembering the long list of things a USAWMD agent can't do.

"How can I help you?" I ask.

"Coffee, three o'clock, that place you always go to in your neighborhood."

You see? I'm not paranoid. They really are watching me.

"I can't. I have the baby."

"He's not a baby anymore, Lucy. He's three," Simon says impatiently. "Bring him."

"What is this about?" I ask.

"A simple chat," he answers and hangs up on me with no further details.

I hold the phone in my hand. It feels a little hot, but that is probably because I am sweating. Theo clings to my jeans. I fight the urge to swat him away like a mosquito.

"Mommy," he says, "pick me up, pick me up, pick me up." I hoist him up and he wraps his arms around my neck, buries his face in my hair, and starts chewing. Theo likes to chew on my hair. When I ask him why, he rolls his eyes and gives me a long "Mommy." It's my hair. How could I possibly not know?

"Who was on the phone? Daddy?"

Definitely not Daddy. If Daddy knew who was on the phone, he'd blow a fuse.

"No. It was an old friend of Mommy's," I say. The idea of Simon Still and Theo occupying the same space for even the length of a cup of coffee makes my mouth dry.

In the beginning, I thought about filling Will full of martinis and confessing all. I would tell him about Sally Sin and the long nights I spent in the Cambodian jungle, stepping carefully between land mines, hoping like hell not to make a mistake. I'd tell him about Budapest and a man I almost fell in love with who turned out to be oh so very bad. I'd tell him about train rides through Vietnam that seemed to last forever, the lonely endless days traveling from place to place to place, blending in and disappearing, pretending I didn't exist. I'd tell him about the fear that each day might very well be my last. I had a keen sense of wanting to stay alive even if I had no idea what for. I might even tell him about Ian Blackford.

But as time slipped by, the possibility of confessing my multitude of sins became more remote. And here I was four years later, and telling him was no longer an option. I couldn't risk ruining Theo's life for secrets I could silently continue to keep.

Simon Still calling me on the house phone, however, made things more complicated. I put Theo back on the floor, with a mouthful of my hair.

"I want to go on the swing in the park on the hill. I want to go fast. I want to go high," he chants, bouncing up and down.

I want to run away. I want to go fast. I want to go far.

"Okay, playground it is," I say, distracted. "Let's get ready."

Theo tears down the hallway. Getting ready for him means collecting about one hundred of his favorite toys and dragging them all into the car and to the park. For me, it includes sippy cups of juice, snack packs of crackers, blueberry yogurt, bananas, napkins, water, jackets, sunscreen, hats, wipes, extra kid shirt and pants, cell phone, wallet, car keys, stroller, and finally travel coffee mug, full. This is all to go two miles down the road to play in the sand and swing on the swings. I used to travel for twelve months at a stretch with nothing more than a toothbrush and a change of underwear.

Theo comes toward me hauling today's spoils. We have tractors, sticker books, a bucket, two shovels, a stuffed pumpkin, and the puzzle people, as we call them, which are really the set of beautifully crafted Matryoshka dolls that I was using as a weapon earlier. The littlest doll in this set has a small rattle inside that Theo adores. I shake the big doll and hear the rattle inside.

"Are you sure you want to bring these? I don't want you to lose them and be sad about it."

"I *have* to bring them. They go on top of the sand mountain." How is it a person this small can sound exasperated? The dolls go into the bag.

We load everything into the car, a Toyota Prius that any self-respecting spy would have exactly nothing to do with. It appeared one day in my garage, replacing my 350 horsepower silver Audi S6, the one indulgence I'd allowed myself post-agency. I kind of loved that car. After I drove it from Washington, D.C., to San Francisco I couldn't resist cruising over the Bay Bridge and right into an aftermarket outfitter in Oakland. Used to servicing the hip-hop community, they couldn't understand why I'd want Kevlar Second Chance panels in the doors and Chroma-Flex bullet resistant film in the windows.

"Someone trying to kill you, lady?" the mechanic asked.

"You never know," I said, handing over my cash.

"What do you think?" Will asked, stroking the wee car parked in my spot.

"About what?" I asked, ignoring the obvious.

"Listen, I wasn't feeling right about your car. It's a gas guzzler, killing the planet. This one gets fifty miles to the gallon! Can you believe that?"

"What . . . did . . . you . . . do . . . with . . . my . . . car?" I thought seriously for a moment about beating him senseless. But that wouldn't bring my car back.

"You're mad, aren't you? Okay, so I probably should have asked you before I traded it in, but this was the last one on the lot. Isn't that great? A small fuel-efficient car that is actually flying out of the dealerships. I am so excited about this, Lucy. You have no idea."

I tried to calm down. I counted backward from one hundred. I rolled my neck, popping out the kinks. I cracked all of my fingers, one by one.

"I liked my car," I said slowly, deliberately.

"I know. It's hard. But we all need to sacrifice for the good of the future, right?"

"No! Who cares about the future?" I kicked the wheel of the little car for emphasis. Will gasped.

"Lucy, no need to take out your anger like that. You might hurt it."

"It's a car, Will. It doesn't have feelings." I kicked it again to prove my point.

And the look on his face, one of sheer horror at my inability to grasp how important this was for the greater good, made me start to giggle. And once I started, I couldn't stop. And neither could he. And then he did some things to me on the hood of that car that made me glad it couldn't talk.

We head to the park. It's a nice park, as parks go, with a playground funded by the local people who are all very rich. So the equipment is new and innovative and clever and you can be fairly confident that the swings aren't going to suddenly detach from their chains and send your kid orbiting into outer space.

The usual crowd is assembled. It's divided equally between nannies and moms. The nannies sit on one side speaking Spanish. The moms sit on the other side speaking Californian. They are an interesting group. There is Claire, an investment banker who, after going through four nannies, decided the only one who could raise Owen correctly was her. She has taken motherhood to a whole new level of intensity. Last Christmas, her gingerbread house had a master suite with a walk-in closet with fifteen tiny pairs of gingerbread shoes on a minuscule shelf. She never raises her voice or expresses any frustration with Owen. However, I think he subconsciously realizes that his mommy is a little scary and, in his case, good behavior is simply a form of self-preservation.

There is Belinda, who favors long, flowing skirts and Birkenstocks. Three-year-old Amanda has free will, Belinda has told us, so why shouldn't she be allowed to act on it? Amanda, as a result, is a holy terror. She once held a boy facedown in the sand until he promised to give her all of his Halloween candy, and it was only July. Belinda used to be a suit-wearing, office-going editor of a weekly business journal. I have a hard time imagining it, but apparently it's true.

There's Sam, as in Samuel, grandfather of Carter and part-time child care provider. We have never met Carter's mother or father. The park is obviously not their thing. Sam provides a much needed dose of testosterone in our den of estrogen. He does a good job keeping us from turning into a bunch of clucking hens, at least on the days that he and Carter join us in the park.

And there is Avery, my best mom friend. I didn't actually know people could be this nice. In my experience, the nice people were always after something. Even in states of extreme sleep deprivation, I've never heard Avery say an unkind word about anyone. Her daughter is the most refined three-year-old I've ever met. She meets us at the playground gate.

"Hello, Mrs. Hamilton," she says.

"Hello, Sophie," I answer.

"Come on, Theo," she says, taking my little boy by the hand and leading him off into the mess of kids rolling around in the sand like puppies.

Avery is sitting on a bench. She waves me over and I join her.

"I think Sophie is going to grow up to be a cruise director or a CEO. She likes to boss people around," she says.

"At least she is polite about it so you don't resent that you are being told what to do. Besides, Theo will go with anyone, provided she or he has long hair and doesn't object to him taking the occasional bite of it."

Avery laughs. "So what's new?"

Well, I want to say, I just got this phone call from my old boss, from back when I used to be a spy, see? It seems he wants to have a chat. Now, that would be all well and good except members of the USAWMD don't pay social calls. They generally have no friends and no lives, so social calls aren't necessary. Anyway, I'm retired but now he wants to see me and I don't know why, but I'm pretty sure I'm not going to like it.

Instead, I say nothing is new. Things are quiet. The usual. We watch the kids play. They are building a tower out of sand and water, and Theo's recycled plastic adventure people and the Matryoshka dolls are BASE jumping from the top.

Sometimes I have flashbacks. Normally, in my memory, I'm pretty good at keeping my nine years with the USAWMD down to a constant yet dull hum. But sometimes a certain smell, say the exhaust from a passing bus or the way someone is walking down the street, will bring it all back into razor-sharp focus. Watching Theo and Sophie and Owen, I remember Simon Still bleeding in a back alley in Budapest.

"I'm going to die," he said. I knelt over him, covering his wounds as best I could with my knockoff designer scarf. "You know what to do when an agent dies, don't you?"

"I didn't read that part of the manual, Simon. Sorry. So I guess I'm going to have to leave you here on the street, let the rats have at you."

He smiled through his pain. "Bitch," he said. "I might really die."

"Stop being a baby," I said, his blood soaking through my fingers. "Nobody dies from a gunshot wound."

"I can't even laugh at that," he said.

"Who wants to kill you?" I asked, tossing aside the bloody scarf. I pulled off my jacket, covered the bullet holes, and leaned on the whole mess as hard as I dared. Simon groaned.

"Everyone."

"But no one knows we're here. We're not even supposed to be here," I said. I tried to ignore the blood soaking through my jacket, forming little pools around my hands. "We're supposed to be in Madrid."

"Doesn't matter," Simon said through gritted teeth. "Get used to it."

I called for an ambulance and got Simon to a local hospital. They wanted an explanation. I shouted at them hysterically in French until they couldn't stand it anymore and gave up. After they patched him up, the doctor, very slowly in very elegant French, explained to me that they needed to keep him for several days on account of the large bullet holes in his chest, but that was out of the question. In the end, I simply wheeled him out the back door when no one was paying attention and onto a transport back to the States.

When I finally came home after a useless three weeks in Budapest, Simon was back to work, still a little pale and moving slowly.

"We were not even supposed to be there," I reminded him again. I'd had a lot of time to think about what happened while I was wandering around Budapest eating cucumber salad and accomplishing nothing. "We were supposed to be in Madrid."

Simon ignored me, rearranging the yellow and pink Post-it notes on his desk. Now, a smart person would have accepted his silence on the matter and moved on. But not me. No. I had to keep at it.

"Do you think there is a rat?" I asked, which turned out to be the wrong question altogether.

Simon made that clear by sending me to Yemen for the worst assignment I'd ever had. Sand reminds me of Africa. Hostile acts, like throwing innocent recycled plastic adventure people and cute Russian dolls off of sand towers, remind me of Africa.

"You look like you've seen a ghost," Avery says, bringing me quickly back to the present and San Francisco and the sun and the playground.

"No," I say. "I was thinking about something from a long time ago." She gives me that look, the same one that Will sometimes throws in my direction. It's the one that says I know you are not telling me the whole truth.

"Are you coming to yoga tonight?" Avery asks, changing the subject.

"Oh right. Yoga. Yes. I hate it but I'm coming."

"Good."

We sit on the bench some more, watching the kids. Eventually, Theo comes over and begs for snacks and juice, and the kids sit in a merry circle and trade food and end up wearing much more than they eat. It's just another normal morning in my normal life, and if I didn't have to see Simon Still in less than an hour, it would be a good day all around.

5

Simon Still sits at a table in the Java Luv. He is wearing a white fedora, dark sunglasses, and a raincoat, although it hasn't rained in months. It surprises me that he is waiting. Simon never arrives first. I stand outside, watching him through the big glass windows. For nine years, I considered him my mentor, the shoes I wanted to fill, if in a nicer color. However, I never deluded myself into believing he considered me anything more than your standard-issue amoeba. In profile his chin sags a bit more, but the rest of him looks the same. His eyes lock onto mine and I smile. He does not. I have Theo by the hand and he is joyously singing a tune about his toy car, which he clutches in the other hand. I see Simon run his eyes over my boy and I want to break his neck. There is no obvious reason for this; he hasn't done anything yet. But I have not a single doubt in my mind that he will.

I take a deep breath and push the door open. The strong smell of coffee, usually so inviting, is suffocating today. I move through the crowd, navigating my singing son in front of me. Simon doesn't stand up. He gives me a slight nod of acknowledgment, and for the second time in less than five minutes I want to kill him.

"Simon Still," I say.

"Sally Sin," he says.

"Lucy, if you don't mind."

"Of course." He nods. "Lucy. That's what it says on your passport, must be true. And this must be Theodore Wilton Hamilton, correct?"

"Yes. Say hi to the nice man, Theo," I prompt.

"Nice man? Well, that's a new one," Simon says.

"Hi," Theo says. "Do you want to play cars?"

"No. I don't want to play cars. I have some quick business with your mother after which I'm sure she will play cars with you. That is her job now, you know."

Theo looks disappointed. He is used to people cooing over him and smiling and enthusiastically playing whatever silly games he can dream up.

"Oh," he says, looking at me for guidance in these uncharted waters.

"Can you sit here in the chair like a big boy for Mommy? Only for a few minutes and after we'll get an ice cream?" Okay. So I'm not above bribery, but I challenge you to find me one mother who is.

"I guess so," Theo says, crawling under the table with his car. On the chair, under the chair, it's all the same when you're little.

I focus on Simon. "What do you want?" I ask. My tone is harsher than I intend. I fill my lungs with fresh air, close my eyes. All the yoga I do ought to be good for something, right? I start again.

"It's good to see you, Simon. You look well. Healthy."

"I've been in South America." I don't ask him why or where. "It's good to see you too, Mom." There is a sneering quality to his voice that I don't like, but short of pitching a cup of scalding coffee in his face, my hands are tied.

"What brings you to sunny California?" I ask, hoping to get down to business before Theo grows bored and starts tugging on people's shoelaces.

"I wanted a cup of coffee and who better to have it with than Sally Sin? Sorry," he corrects himself, "Lucy. No more Sally."

I try to read him but it's impossible. Simon Still is not the best there ever was either but he is damn close. He gives nothing away—not a sign, not a gesture, nothing. So I go the direct route.

"As much as I'd like to believe that is true," I begin, "I know that it's not. So I will ask you again. Why are you here, Simon?"

"That's Mr. Still to you," he says in a tone that sets my teeth on edge. "Just kidding. Your boy is in the garbage can."

Theo has, in fact, crawled into the recycle bin and is mucking around the dirty bottles and cans. I can hear him talking to himself.

"Theo, baby, come out of there," I coax, "please?"

"No, Mommy. I like it in here. I like the cans."

"Theo, now," I say. I can feel Simon's eyes boring holes in my back. This is a test and I'm failing. I reach in and grab Theo and he begins to shriek and flail, pounding on me with his three-year-old fists.

Once he is locked down in my version of the human straitjacket, I return to the table. But I can't sit down because I'm holding on very tightly to my son, who is about ready to blow.

"We need to take this conversation outside," I say. Simon raises an eyebrow. He doesn't say anything but I know what he is thinking. This is what you traded in a life of adventure and romance and chasing bad guys for? Brilliant choice. And you're so good at it. Really.

I wrestle Theo into his stroller and give him a chocolate chip cookie. This takes the edge off his fit. We walk down the street.

"I've always liked San Francisco. It's very . . . gay and happy," Simon comments. And despite all my efforts to hate him and what he is about to do to my life, I laugh.

"You've not changed at all," I say. "You're still not funny."

"You have, my dear. You've changed in a great many ways." I don't ask for specifics. We'd be out here on the street all day and we have exactly the length of one chocolate chip cookie to complete our business.

"What's going on, Simon? You have to tell me eventually, right? So let's get it over with."

"We find ourselves in a situation that requires your assistance," he says.

"Why? It seems hard to believe you don't have ten Sally Sins in your current clutches."

"No," he says, "there was only one Sally Sin." And for a second I swear he sounds wistful, but I wouldn't bet my life on it. "The situation is delicate. It involves Ian Blackford."

Talk about flashbacks. Every good spy needs a nemesis. Think about where James Bond would be without Dr. No, Auric Goldfinger, and Tee Hee, not to mention Jaws. He'd be just another good-looking guy in an expensive suit driving a nice car. A nemesis, by definition, heightens your senses, makes you grow eyes in the back of your head, adds an edge to every move you make. Of course, most spies go through a life of snooping with nary a nemesis in sight. And that's not altogether bad because in most cases your nemesis is trying very hard to kill you. So while it makes life interesting, it can also bring it to a premature end. My nemesis wasn't trying to kill me exactly, just torture me with the unexpected.

"Ian Blackford is dead," I say.

"Well, that's why it's delicate," Simon responds. From the look on his face, I know what is coming and I don't like it one bit.

Ian Blackford's name was on everyone's lips when I joined the Agency. He actually *had* been the best there ever was. Everyone agreed. Ian Blackford had magical powers. He singlehandedly averted nuclear war no less than ten times. The sad thing is I'm not kidding. But that wasn't why everyone was talking about him. All evidence pointed to the fact that Ian Blackford had turned, gone to the dark side, committed treason, done a really bad thing. It seemed that the money was too tempting for an underpaid, underappreciated government employee. So Ian Blackford went from being a star of the USAWMD to being a premier international illegal arms dealer in the blink of an eye. Everyone tried to catch him. Us, the CIA, Mossad, Interpol, even the FBI, although their attempt was kind of weak. But he was too good, as elusive as a cloud, sharp as a knife. If you bit him too hard, he'd bite back and it was sure to hurt. The story was that Blackford had offed two agents sent in after him and the USAWMD director was furious. Of course, I didn't know the dead agents and I had never met the Agency's director so, for me, it was nothing more than part of the lore.

And Ian Blackford would have remained simply that for me, a story, a myth, a cautionary tale, had he not gone and started kidnapping me over and over again.

My second assignment as an agent for the USAWMD put me in Madrid helping Spanish authorities translate Arabic documents that named a number of terror suspects. I'm not sure even now why the Spanish didn't use their own translator, but at the time I didn't have the confidence to ask such things. After a night of lying on my single bed in a little cave-like hotel room, I decided to go out. Everyone in Madrid was out. Staying in made me stand out, I reasoned. I needed to go out to blend in. My training said that blending in was all important. Don't ever want to look out of place or be pegged as odd. It's a sure way to get killed. So I planted myself on a stool in a cramped, smoky bar and drank a few glasses of sangria, ate some tapas, and generally soaked up the atmosphere, trying to figure out ways to look more Spanish. Impossible, I thought. Americans can never properly imitate the laissez-faire that the Spanish have elevated to an art form. No one around me was talking about stock options or the market or their new $120,000 Mercedes that can parallel park itself and do the occasional load of laundry. They talked about dancing and music and clothes and a possible cigarette ban. A gorgeous man with black hair and blue eyes took a seat next to me and ordered more sangria. I knew he wasn't Spanish but his accent was flawless. After a while I asked him if he was Canadian.

"No," he answered, "I'm from all over." He was staring at me, a slightly confused look on his face. "And you are not at all what I expected. Not at all."

What? At almost the exact second those words flowed from his perfect lips my world started to bob and weave and buckle. I knew immediately that I had screwed up. Never let anyone buy you a drink. Whatever he put in my sangria was working its magic.

"Stand up," he said.

"I can't," I said. I felt so weak I thought I might collapse right there on the filthy floor.

"Of course you can," he said. "You are trained to act under duress. This is duress. I drugged you. So get up and come on."

I wanted to ask him how he knew me and what I was about, but I couldn't move my lips. The hardest thing I've ever done was get up off that bar stool and walk out into the night in front of my captor. And I include childbirth on that list.

Once outside, the man with the black hair and the blue eyes swept me up in his arms and carried me off down the street. To the innocent bystander, it probably looked achingly romantic. And it might have been had it not actually been a kidnapping. He walked carrying all 135 pounds of me for what seemed like forever. When I eventually retraced the route, it was only five blocks. But that's still a lot of weight, especially when it's dead weight. I passed out cold almost immediately and came to some time later to find myself locked in the marble bathroom of a luxurious hotel suite.

I tried to stay quiet, figure out my options. But my head was pounding so hard I could barely think. Under the sink, in the third drawer, was a note.

"Take this. It will help." On top of the note was a single pill with no brand or identifying letters.

"Right," I said to my reflection in the huge mirror. "After you drug me and kidnap me and lock me in a bathroom I'm supposed to trust you and pop that thing in my mouth? How fucking stupid do you think I am?"

I could hear Simon's voice in my head. "Very stupid. You did everything wrong."

I took the pill, if only to shut Simon up.

Ten minutes later I felt substantially better and began investigating a way out. It didn't take me long to conclude there was none, so I sat down on the toilet to reflect on my short yet exciting career with the USAWMD.

"Sad," I said. "I might have been pretty good at it."

"At this?" Mr. Kidnapper, standing in the open bathroom door, asked. "Not until you learn a few ground rules. Didn't Simon teach you anything?"

"Who are you? Is this another test?"

"No, this is officially a hostage situation. You're the hostage." A Walther P99 dangled at his side, but I could see even from my perch on the toilet seat that his finger was on the trigger, ready and waiting. "My name is Ian Blackford. Heard of me?"

Ian Blackford? *The* Ian Blackford? This was getting weirder by the minute.

"Yes," I said, trying not to panic, "I've heard of you. Once or twice." Suddenly I couldn't remember if I was supposed to diminish the captor or build him up. And all that stuff about trying to create a psychological bond, make him feel empathy, seemed ridiculous as I sat on a toilet, held prisoner by a turncoat.

"What have you heard?"

"Oh, things," I said, trying to dodge.

"As long as you're here, you might as well tell me what things. So maybe now is a good time to start talking?"

In all the chatter about Blackford I'd heard back at the office, it was never once mentioned that the man made James Bond look like a slob. Ian Blackford filled the bathroom door, his arms crossed over his broad chest. He was tall and fit, but that was all secondary to the black hair and those blue eyes, in such contrast, so startling.

"Do you dye your hair?" I asked suddenly.

"What?" I caught him off guard. One little unimportant useless point for me. Go team.

"Is your hair really that black?"

"That's none of your business."

"Sorry," I said, "I was curious."

"Curiosity will get you killed," he said in a tone that scared me more than I cared to admit. With that he slammed the bathroom door and I heard it lock from the outside.

"Nice work, Einstein," I muttered to my reflection in the bathroom mirror.

I didn't have a watch so I have no idea how much time passed while he made his point that I was not to ask him about his hair color. I learned the lesson pretty fast, but I estimate he kept me in there for the better part of three hours.

When Ian Blackford finally unlocked the bathroom, he invited me out into the main room of the suite for lunch. I made a promise to myself that I would do nothing but answer his questions. I certainly wouldn't ask him for any more personal information. And I would definitely not comment on his very thin skin when it came to his hair.

"I ordered you a few things. Are you hungry?" On the table before him was what looked like the entire room service menu.

"Yes, thank you," I said, thinking if he was going to toss me out a window it might as well be on a full stomach. Blackford paced behind me as I inelegantly stuffed my face. He ran the dull edge of a steak knife back and forth across the palm of his hand. I kept one eye glued on the knife and one eye glued on the food. It wasn't easy.

Blackford continued pacing around the hotel suite like a caged tiger with OCD. I crammed some more ham in my mouth to keep it quiet. Finally he stopped directly behind me, tapping the knife rhythmically against his hand. It took me a minute before I realized he was waiting for me to tell him how his betrayal was playing back on the home front.

"Okay, well, I haven't been with the Agency for that long really," I began. "I'm not even sure why they wanted me, but that's another story. What have they been saying about you? Honestly? That you're a traitor, that you let them down. They've been trying to catch you ever since it became obvious that . . . well, you know."

"Know what?" he prompted. It was almost as if he needed to hear me say it for it to finally be true.

"That you turned. That you did the worst thing a spy can do." I waited for him to plunge the steak knife between my shoulder blades, but he didn't so I went on. "You went willingly into the arms of the enemy." I'll admit that I was taking some poetic license, but the idea was the important part. And for a split second I thought I saw regret flash in those arctic blue eyes. But it did not last.

"I brought you here to kill you," he said matter-of-factly. "It seemed to be the only reasonable response. An eye for an eye. But you really have no idea who you are, do you? Not even a suspicion."

He studied the knife, thinking. "Unexpected. But it makes me think I might let you live. For now."

And with that he threw the knife. It floated in the air, rotated, and stuck fast dead center in the bathroom door. I had no idea what he was talking about, but it didn't matter. Apparently he wasn't going to stick that knife in me and that was all I really cared about.

"Yes, sir," I gulped. "Thank you, sir."

He reached over me to get the other knife from the table. He was so close I could feel his warm breath on the back of my neck. I shivered.

"They also said you were the best there ever was. It's cliché, I know, but that's what they said."

"I was," he said. "But things change. You'll see."

I won't turn, I wanted to say. I might end up living in a corrugated tin shack in western Montana, writing insane rambling letters to the editor of the local paper, but I won't turn.

"I'm pretty sure that when I get back I'm going to get fired anyway, so I probably will never make it to the point of disillusionment," I said.

Ian Blackford smiled then, and if the smile hadn't been laced with cynicism it might have stopped my heart. I tried to swallow the piece of bread in my mouth. It stuck like paste in my throat. He hurled the second knife and planted it in the door, a centimeter below the first one.

"Ask Simon to teach you to throw knives. It's never actually useful but it can be a good way to pass the time. And Simon is the best. He'll stab you in the back from halfway around the world." I didn't answer. Instead, I sat quietly at the table like a schoolgirl, waiting for what was going to happen next. A good spy would have had a plan by then, some elaborate way to escape the hotel and rush to safety, stopping along the way to learn how to throw knives. But not me. I was simply reciting the parts of the Hail Mary that I could remember and hoping for the best.

Suddenly Blackford spun my chair from the table so we were face-to-face. "So here is the new plan. When you get back to Washington, make sure they know I got to you. Make sure Gray knows I got to you. It was a pleasure meeting you, Sally Sin. I'll see you again someday."

He didn't need to ask me twice. I stood bolt upright and in three giant steps was out the door and in five more was on my way down the stairs. I hit the street running, in the first direction that occurred to me.

Theo is about to finish his cookie. I have nothing else to bribe him with. I look at Simon, waiting for the inevitable next sentence.

"It appears Ian Blackford is not actually dead. It appears he is still very much alive. And it appears he is up to his old tricks with someone local. Someone here."

The cookie is gone.

"Well, doesn't everybody just love a resurrection," I say.

"Mommy, I have to poop," Theo bellows. "I really have to poop. I have to poop now!"

Simon looks alarmed. Put him in a room full of armed terrorists and he's right as rain. Expose him to a partially toilet-trained toddler and he freaks.

"We have to go to my car. This way, quick," I say. Simon does as he's told, staying close at my heels. I pop the trunk of my Prius and pull Theo's plastic potty from a bag.

"What are you doing?" Simon asks, his voice oddly high-pitched.

"You heard the kid," I said. "We don't mess around with these sorts of things."

"Doesn't your coffee shop have a bathroom?" His eyes grow wide with realization followed by horror.

"He won't go there."

"I won't even ask."

"It's better that you don't."

I wrestle Theo out of his stroller, pull his jeans and Thomas the

Train underwear down, and plop him on the plastic potty. Simon averts his eyes. Theo starts to sing. He won't use the potty unless he can sing. I don't exactly know what the song is, something about rain and butterflies I think. It's a sweet song.

"This is really happening to you," I say to Simon, who stands with his back to the trunk of my car, a disgusted hand over his mouth. "But now we have a few minutes to finish that conversation we were having."

"I don't know how you do this. Honestly. Where was I?"

"Ian Blackford. Alive. You know, little things like that."

"Right. We were watching this professor here at the University on an anonymous tip. Well, not exactly watching, more like monitoring. We knew nothing about him other than he is a quirky genius of some sort in the field of analytical chemistry, so at the very least it seemed like a good time to fill in some blanks in case the guy ever decided to go rogue on us." Simon Still pauses, as if reflecting upon a very bad memory. "And out of nowhere, in waltzes the very dead Ian Blackford."

"Wow. That must have been a surprise."

"Yes. We were a little surprised, as you put it."

"And the Blind Monk?" I ask, before I can stop myself. "He must play some role in this tale of woe."

Simon's shoulders tighten almost imperceptibly. He furrows his brow. The crease is deep. A person could get lost in there and never be heard from again.

"Information is on a need-to-know basis, Lucy. I don't think you need to know."

"Well, as much as I'm enjoying this dialogue," I say, "I fail to see what any of this has to do with me."

My baby continues to sing gleefully on his potty. "I'm almost done," he announces.

I look at Simon. "You'd better hurry."

"I put three analysts to task answering one question. And that question was, what is Ian Blackford's weakness? Where do we stick the knife if we want to kill him? My analysts spent three hundred man-hours on it and came up with only one. You. We need you to lure Blackford out. He'll show himself for you."

That's not quite how I thought of it, but whatever you say.

"What makes you so sure?"

"I am sure. You can trust me."

I think about it for a minute and don't like the conclusion I reach. "No," I say finally, "forget it." I turn back to Theo, but Simon grabs my arm.

"There is no choice here, Lucy," he says.

"There is always a choice. What are you going to do, arrest me?"

"He knows where you are," Simon says. Just like that.

I pretend I didn't hear what he said because I don't want to have heard what he said. So he says it again.

"Somehow Blackford got into our records and was able to figure out where you were and under what name."

"Tell me you are making a very bad joke. Please. My records? Are you fucking kidding me?" There is a note of hysteria in my voice. It sounds like it belongs to someone else.

"What's fucking, Mommy?" Theo chimes from his potty. Can this get worse?

"Nothing, honey," I say, helping him stand up. "It's an ugly word that big people say sometimes when they're mad."

"Are you mad at me?" he asks.

"No, baby."

"Are you mad at the man who won't play cars?" Theo has a memory like an elephant. Simon will always be the man who wouldn't play cars. If he lives to be one hundred, Theo will never forget this slight. I get him cleaned up and his pants back on and his hands wiped and the little plastic potty hermetically sealed in a garbage bag.

"No," I say again, strapping Theo into his car seat, Simon leaning on my hood. "I'm not getting involved."

"It's too late for that. You are involved. Help us and we can protect you and your family."

"And finally get your guy. That's what this is really about, isn't it? You want bait. You don't give a shit if this professor lights up the sky with nuclear fireworks so long as you finally nail Blackford. So let me ask you, Simon, did Blackford suddenly find my records in his carry-on? Did a little birdie whisper in his ear? You were banking on him not being able to stay away from me, weren't you? I can't believe I ever *liked* you." I shove Simon out of my way, get in the car, and peel out from the parking place as well as you can in a hybrid. I see him in the rearview mirror shaking his head, looking after me.

6

an Blackford kidnapped me again on my seventh mission, but I'd gotten better and gave him a run for his money. In the end, however, I walked right into his trap, so to speak. He simply waited for me in my hotel room. I'd changed locations no fewer than six times, so I'm not sure how he stayed ahead of me but there he was, sitting in a straight-back chair, lights off, right foot tapping a gentle rhythm on the floor.

"How come," I asked, "you always seem to know exactly where I am? It's a little uncanny."

A slow smile crept across his face. "Sorry, Sally," he said and like a Vulcan he pinched some nerve in my neck and I collapsed in a heap at his feet. I woke up hours later on a foul-smelling couch in a drafty communist-style apartment building in Zagreb, Croatia, my head pounding and my neck sore.

"Are you planning on killing me this time?" I asked, thinking I might as well know what was in store. Blackford sat perched on the edge of the single window in the perfectly square apartment.

"Perhaps. Haven't decided yet," he said.

"Great. Thanks." I pulled myself up into a seated position and leaned back against the wall. "That makes me feel so much better."

"I have a message I want you to deliver."

"So I guess you are not going to kill me?"

"I told you. I haven't decided yet."

"But if I'm dead how can I deliver a message?"

Blackford grimaced. "Please, Sally. Can you stop talking?"

I nodded.

"How's the head?"

"My head is terrible," I said. "Feels like Jell-O. You knocked me out."

"I know. I'm good at knocking people out, that sort of thing. My third-grade teacher told me to do what I was good at, so there you have it. Blame it on Mrs. Pearson."

Don't tell me things about yourself, I thought, holding my aching head in my hands. *I don't want to know you.*

"What's the message?" I asked, hoping he might hurry up and deliver it and let me go on my merry way.

"Tell Gray this is his last warning. If he doesn't back off in Libya, the consequences could be bad."

And here is what I wanted to say: Gray? You mean the guy who runs the place, the one you sent a message to the last time you snatched me? Well, let me tell you what happened after that. Nothing. Nothing happened. Gray does not even have a phone number, near as I can tell. And if he did he would certainly not be taking calls from me. I might as well be a worm for all he cares.

But instead I answered, "Okay. I will tell Director Gray to stop getting in your way in Libya. Is that the whole message?"

"What? That's not good enough? Then let me elaborate. Tell him I will start eliminating those agents who show up in my shadow. Up until now, my nostalgia for the USAWMD has kept me from doing so, but my patience is wearing thin and they are becoming more of a nuisance than I'm inclined to tolerate." He focused those blue eyes on me and my heart pushed its way into my throat. "I kill, Sally Sin, Agent Twenty-six. That's what I do. And I'm very good at it. Do we understand each other?"

"Yes," I said. "I understand perfectly."

He sat down next to me, our legs not twelve inches apart, on the mildewed old couch.

"Competition is tough out there, as I'm sure you can imagine. So I don't need the Agency fucking up any more of my deals." He sounded like we could have been talking about the weather or politics or the Red Sox. "And as long as you're here, there is something I want you to tell me, something about the Agency."

The way he put it you would think I had popped in to borrow a cup of sugar and now he couldn't get rid of me, which wasn't really

how it felt from where I was sitting. And what could I possibly tell
him that he didn't already know? I was basically a subhuman life-
form at the Agency, so green that most people wouldn't even give me
the time of day, let alone state secrets. All the rungs of the ladder
were still above my head. But even if, by accident, I did know something, I'd have to let him kill me before I could give him any Agency
intelligence. And I didn't fancy dying in a dusty old apartment
building with this lunatic. I sighed. Blackford laughed. Naturally.

"Don't worry, Sally Sin, I'm not going to make you give up any
of your prized tidbits of useless information. You can go. Live another day. I assume you can find your way home." Insulted or not,
I was out the door in no time.

Simon didn't like the message I had nor did he like the fact that I
kept getting myself kidnapped. He also told me that if I tried to
pass the message on to Gray as I'd been instructed, he'd send me to
Siberia. He stepped up the pursuit of Ian Blackford, but that didn't
seem to have much of an impact. It did, however, lead to several
uncomfortable situations that were hard to explain to the bosses.

So we kept stumbling along, tripping over our own feet, until
one rainy Monday word came from deep in Sudan that Blackford
was dead. The Blind Monk had finally gotten to him through some
unsatisfied militiamen. He was shot at close range in the head. In
fact, the range was so close that there was no head left. But several
reliable European allies confirmed that it was without a doubt Ian
Blackford, dead as a doornail.

Simon gathered us in his office. He glowed like a woman in her
second trimester. It was the happiest I had ever seen him, before or
since. Standing on his swivel chair, trying hard not to fall off, he
clapped his hands to draw our attention.

"Blackford," he said, spreading his arms as if to take flight, "is
dead."

"Dead," he said again in case we somehow missed it the first
time. "Now go back to work. Do something useful." And we were
dismissed.

As I walked toward my empty little office, all I could think was, *Wait a minute. Nothing interesting ever happens on a Monday. This is impossible.* In the background, Simon Still was chanting "Blackford is dead, Blackford is dead" over and over again as if he were insane. I waited for relief to rush in, for the tension in my neck to suddenly vanish. But instead of relief, I felt like a helium balloon two days after the circus leaves town, smaller and duller and forgotten. Blackford was dead and I was alive. Somehow I'd always seen it ending up the other way around.

But like I said, nothing that interesting ever happens on a Monday. And in this case, apparently, I was right.

I pull into my driveway and hit Will's Colnago custom-made road bike, parked precariously near where my front bumper usually goes. The uncomfortable sound of crunching metal is the final straw.

"Shit!" I scream. "Double shit!" I pound my steering wheel with my fists.

And from the backseat I hear, "Mommy, what is double shit? Double shit, double shit, double shit," Theo gleefully cries.

I try not to smile, but it's hard. "Theo, Mommy said another naughty word. It's best not to say it, okay?"

He smiles, widely, happily, such a well-adjusted little boy, and shouts out "Fucking! Double shit!" as loud as he can.

I haul him out of his car seat. Now he is dancing around the garage, singing a song of pure obscenity. At that moment my neighbor Tom chooses to appear on the sidewalk right outside my garage.

"Lovely song, Lucy," he says, pointing at Theo, as if I don't know what is happening right in front of me.

"Yes," I say, exasperated. "We're working on the follow-up. It's called 'Go Fuck Yourself.'"

And to my surprise, Tom laughs. He grabs one of the bags of toys wedged into my trunk. "Let me help you."

We climb up the front steps to the house. Tom carries the toys into the kitchen and puts them on the table. It occurs to me he has never been in my house before.

"Do you want some coffee?" I offer. He nods. "Always."

For the moment, Theo has stopped singing and is now pulling impatiently at my leg.

"Yogurt pop, Mommy. Yogurt pop, yogurt pop, yogurt pop." I lean over to the freezer, Theo still attached to my pants, and pull out a frozen yogurt. He snatches it from my hands and takes off down the hallway.

"Theo," I call after him, "don't you want me to open it?" But he's gone. I shrug and set about getting some coffee for Tom. He settles in at the kitchen table. The nesting dolls are sitting on the tabletop. Tom picks them up, turns them slowly in his manicured hands. A little pile of sand tumbles out onto the floor.

"These are lovely," he says. "An amazing example of the craft. Where did they come from?"

"I don't know," I reply honestly. "Someone sent them as a present when Theo was born, but with no note and no indications on the box about where they came from. I think they must have been hand delivered. They're nice though, aren't they?"

Tom carefully extracts each smaller doll and lines them up on the table. He gives the tiny one a shake.

"Interesting. They are probably quite valuable. They look old. Anyway, some of your mail ended up in my box," he says, pulling a few envelopes from his jacket pocket. He looks around my kitchen with an odd expression. "I've never been in here before. That seems strange. And you've never been in my house either, now that I think about it. How can that be? Tell me about yourself, neighbor." He means it in a friendly way. He wants to know the people whose walls touch his. It's only natural.

But as I stand with my back to him, pouring coffee, I feel a familiar tingling in my spine that always seems to show up right before I get into serious trouble. I clear my throat and turn back toward Tom, who is staring at me intently.

"Oh, I'm not very interesting," I say. "This is pretty much the whole picture."

"If you say so," he says, taking the coffee. I lean against the counter, sizing him up. Mid-fifties, bald, bad teeth, gay, short with a slight paunch that I imagine was not always there. He has visitors, mostly younger men with a lot of hair. They stumble home with him after midnight, drunk, laughing. And they are always different. We are all hiding something. I take a slow sip of coffee.

"What is it you do, Tom, when you are not delivering my mail?" I ask. I've discovered, after years of informal field-testing, that the best way to distract a person is to invite him to talk about himself. People love to talk about themselves. They can go on for hours. It can be rather painful but, in some situations, no doubt worth the price. Is it really that weird that I don't know what my neighbor, a man whom I regularly can hear singing in the shower, does for a living? Probably, but in a city you can still get away with that.

"I'm a reporter, actually," he says, "for the BBC, but semiretired now. I do the occasional stateside human interest story when they ask. And some travel items when I can get away with it."

It's an effort but I manage to not spit my coffee out all over Tom and my kitchen. I'm living next to a reporter? Is this some sort of cosmic joke?

"I used to cover politics and the military, but as I got older I wanted to slow down a bit and I thought parking it here might be fun for a while. Looks like I'm never leaving." As I'm about to thoroughly lose my composure, Theo appears, covered in strawberry yogurt, now melted.

"More," he demands.

"No," I say with as much conviction as I can muster.

"Shit," he mutters and trudges off down the hallway.

I look at Tom, who is trying not to look shocked, and we both start laughing.

7

I f you watch enough television and movies, you'd naturally assume that to become a covert agent for the USAWMD you'd have to undergo months of intense physical and mental preparation. You'd imagine cruel runs in the rain and mud carrying backpacks full of rocks and bricks and things. Maybe you'd envision mile-long swims in a stormy cold ocean at night. Or perhaps being forced to find your way out of the deep, dark woods with nothing more than an orange and a Popsicle stick. Probably you'd expect some jujitsu training where the master is kicking your ass back and forth across the room, all the while pontificating about how you will never be any good unless you let go of the past and focus on the future.

Well, forget all that stuff. After I accepted Simon Still's invitation to become a spy and save the world, I went back to sitting in my cubicle, reading documents, and making summaries. I wanted to ask when the spying thing started or, at the very least, when the training began. But already I was developing the acutely paranoid view of the world that is necessary for a spy to stay alive. I wanted to ask what was going on, but didn't trust anyone to know what I knew or needed to know. A few weeks passed in that fashion, my anxiety level pushing slowly up into the red zone. Did I dream the conversation with Simon? Was I having some sort of mental breakdown? When I was this close to having myself checked out by a psychiatrist, Simon appeared at my desk—the first time I'd seen him since our talk on the Mall.

"Come with me," he said. I scrambled up from my desk and followed at his heels like a well-behaved golden retriever.

"Got any plans?" he asked in the elevator, which was delivering us into the bowels of the building.

"For right now? Or do you mean, like, plans for the future?" I asked.

Simon gave me a look, one intended to make me wither on the vine. Suddenly, I felt about twelve inches tall.

"No," I said softly. "No plans."

We got off our elevator and walked down a long, white corridor to another elevator. There Simon punched in a series of codes and placed his palm on a sensor for a fingerprint scan. After a moment, the elevator opened its black jaws and in we went. Our journey continued downward. I said nothing. Simon said nothing. Finally, after one more elevator and three more long, empty hallways, we entered a circular lobby with several closed doors off of it, like petals on a daisy.

"Welcome to the USAWMD Underground," Simon said. He opened one of the doors and invited me to step inside. I expected an office, something with burgundy leather club chairs and deep, rich carpets, with decanters of good whisky on a polished cherry side-board. What I saw was quite the opposite. Simon's office consisted of several beat-up metal file cabinets and a folding card table serving as a desk. The walls were bare, the phone unplugged from its jack. The carpet was gray industrial, but slightly gritty-looking, as if it had never been vacuumed. There was an empty, obviously old, coffee cup on the floor near the trash can. The fluorescents hummed overhead, bathing everything in a sickly green light.

"Nice," I commented.

"We prefer our agents to be out in the world doing something useful rather than sitting around at home picking their noses. So we make it unpleasant to sit, if you get my meaning."

Suddenly I missed my cubicle upstairs with at least a distant view of the outside world.

"What's through that door?" I asked, pointing to another door opposite where we stood. Simon opened it to reveal yet another daisy.

"That one is yours," he said, pointing to one of the closed doors. "Don't look so excited."

On my new desk was a packet of information containing a passport with a strange name but my face and some details about a guy named Peter Bradley in Auckland, New Zealand, who, I was told, was suspected of being part of the Blind Monk's network.

"Your job here is to follow Peter to the best of your ability. Record his activities. Plain and simple. Under no circumstances are you to interact with him. Understood?"

"Yes," I said, starting to sweat a little, "but is that it?"

"What did you expect?" Simon said. "The Director likes to say you're either born with it or not. This is the fastest way to find out. Maybe later we'll teach you how to kill someone. Your flight leaves tonight. Don't miss it. And don't call me. I don't want to hear from you until you are back."

"What if I get in trouble?"

Simon gave me the withering look again. And all that was left of my bravado, which wasn't much, seeped right through the soles of my shoes, sucked up by the greedy gray carpet.

"Don't," he said. "Now, why don't I show you the way out so you don't end up lost down here for the next one hundred years?"

"Wait!" I blurted. "One more question."

"What?" Simon Still was already leaving.

"Who is the Blind Monk?"

Simon sighed. "Hasn't anyone taught you anything?" I guessed not.

The Agency had been looking for the Blind Monk for years by the time I showed up at the USAWMD Underground. Of course, the man in question wasn't blind and he wasn't a monk, but he did use both blind and monk for cover on occasion. He was, in reality, a high-level, illegal arms dealer hailing, we believed, from Tibet. His focus was purchasing all the component parts for a nuclear device and selling it as a do-it-yourself bomb product. Kind of like paint-by-numbers for the mass-destruction set. And he was pretty good at it. We'd collected several of the bombs he'd been instrumental in providing and they were the real deal. As a result, the

Blind Monk was toward the top of the Agency's Most Wanted list, which existed mostly in Simon Still's head.

The Blind Monk was also not a very nice man, which was particularly insulting when he was playing the part of a deeply religious person. It has to be a little shocking to be strangled by a man wearing the saffron robes of a Buddhist monk. You would never expect it. Also, to give credit where credit is due, he was highly creative when it came to dispatching people he found annoying. In addition to the aforementioned strangling, his methods of choice might include drowning, shooting, decapitating, burning, tossing off the rooftops of very high buildings, backing over in cars—both big and small (the cars, that is)—and neck-breaking. And when he grew bored, he would experiment with something different like leaving his victim in a freezer unit until the unfortunate soul attained Popsicle status. Rumor had it that the Blind Monk had started out as a front for a far more sinister terrorist than himself but he soon grew tired of taking orders and buried his mentor alive somewhere deep in the Himalaya.

And as it turned out, he was the perfect foil for a new and cocky Agent Ian Blackford. Word was that the minute Blackford showed up down in the daisy, the Blind Monk was all his. Sometimes timing is everything. Blackford chased the Blind Monk around the globe dozens of times, but never quite managed to close the deal. Which really fed the rumor mill. Ian Blackford was supposed to be invincible. It was generally accepted that he knew everything. So why was it he never got it together enough to shoot the Blind Monk and call it good? That remained a fine, and unanswered, question.

I grabbed the file off of what was now my desk and quickly followed after Simon, thinking he might be right about me wandering around this sub-basement circle of hell forever.

To say I was scared would be an understatement. I was moving one degree closer to this Blind Monk character and I didn't want to end up dead before I even really started. But I also felt a buzz in that fear, an adrenaline rush I'd never experienced before. Having less than three hours until my plane took off, I raced back to my empty apartment to throw some things in a knapsack and head off into professional oblivion. Only when I was zipping my toothbrush into a plastic bag did I notice that my hands were shaking.

"Am I going to die?" I asked my reflection in the bathroom mirror. "Is this it?" I stared at my face. There was something new there, something twitchy and alert. As scared as I was of Peter Bradley and the Blind Monk, of the Agency and Simon Still and everything I didn't know and hadn't learned, one thing was clear as a bell. I liked it.

I found out later that I was not supposed to be sent to New Zealand to follow Peter Bradley, a notorious gunrunner known for his generally psychotic behavior in addition to his connection to the Blind Monk. It was supposed to be a guy named Thomas Kin. But I never met Thomas because he was dead at the time and I was the only agent around to fill in. It took me a few years to work up some good old-fashioned resentment at having been thrown to the wolves in that fashion. But I survived. And I guess in the long run that was the only thing that mattered.

8

Theo is playing on the floor. He's removed all the cushions from the living room couch and has assembled a makeshift fort from which he announces he plans to attack me.

"If you attack me, who is going to make your dinner?" I ask. I am met with silence.

So instead, I ask if I'm allowed into the complex with my lowly security clearance. After giving my request some consideration, he pushes one of the pillows away and clears a path for my entry.

"This is a very nice fort," I comment, folding myself up like a pretzel to fit inside.

"Is that man with no hair gone?"

"Tom? He's our neighbor. And yes, he's gone."

"Good."

"Why? You don't like him?"

"I want to play," he pouts.

"Well, he's gone now. What do you want to play?"

"Fort." I'm not sure how one goes about playing fort exactly, so I sit in my knot and wait for my charming son to give me some direction. He seems to have forgotten I'm there, suddenly intent on pushing all his Matchbox cars through one of the cracks in his fortress. I study his profile, his little snub nose, blue eyes, broad straight forehead, and pursed lips as he concentrates on the cars. Such a life this kid leads. So protected. Everyone loves him. Even his grandparents, despite the fact that they find me confusing.

• • •

A short while after my arrival in San Francisco, Will decided it was time for me to meet his parents. He looked about as excited by this prospect as one might get when facing a root canal.

"I have to warn you up front, they are kind of hard to handle. They think my career change is a delayed rebellion, that everything in my life must be, somehow, a reaction to them. Can you believe that shit? They are that self-centered."

"I think I can handle it," I said.

"I haven't even seen them in over a year. My own parents."

"It can happen."

When we pulled up to the gates of their palatial Hollywood Hills estate, Will turned a strange shade of gray and it went steadily downhill from there. They were expecting a woman named Laura, the girlfriend whose tenure ended with my arrival in San Francisco.

Laura was a somebody, a graduate of Stanford Law, a partner at Morrison & Foerster. She was tall, thin, blonde, knew what shoes to wear and what handbag to carry, as well as the best places to vacation if you wanted to be seen but not bothered. She came from Greenwich, Connecticut, and made sure you knew it, even if that fact was meaningless to you.

I was most definitely not Laura. And there were lots of furrowed brows and sidelong glances as Rose Marie Wales Hamilton and William Wilton Hamilton II got used to that idea. They were halfway home when Will announced we were planning on getting married and, well, let me tell you, that very quickly put them in full retreat. Will and I were home in time for breakfast on Saturday morning.

On our second attempt to connect with the elder Hamiltons, I quietly retired to the stone infinity pool to admire the spectacular view and generally stay out of harm's way. I was reading a magazine, sipping tart lemonade served by a nameless uniformed housekeeper, and trying not to listen to the conversation going on in the living room behind me.

"I checked her out, William," William II said, "and it's like she almost doesn't exist. There are years of tax returns from some low-level government job but nothing else. Not a thing. She never went out to dinner on a credit card or bought a pair of jeans or had a bank account. Nothing. And everyone leaves a paper trail, son. Everyone."

There was a brief pause as this news sank in. I shrank down in my chair, not all that excited for what would come next.

"You did what? You hired Marty to investigate my fiancée? Have you lost your mind?"

"No. I have your best interests at heart."

"Bullshit, you do. She doesn't fit into your wet dream of what a daughter-in-law should be and it drives you crazy."

"Now William, no need to be vulgar," Rose Marie chimed in. "We simply expected something a little different. A person from . . . somewhere. What ever happened to that nice girl you were with be- fore?" Her voice, like nails on a chalkboard, made me involuntarily cover my ears.

"You guys," Will practically hissed, "you sit up here on your hill, with your Cadillac Escalade and your heated pool and your beef flown in from Japan, and you think you can judge me and my choices? You are destroying the planet. I'm just getting married."

With that Will stormed out of the kitchen, grabbed me by the arm, and stuffed me into the rental car. Three hours later we were back in San Francisco. The abrupt departure was becoming a habit.

"Sorry about all of that," Will said as our plane touched down lightly in the San Francisco fog.

"Not a problem," I said, "I think I understand."

Will turned pale. "Did you hear?"

I nodded. "I really liked the part about the Caddy."

"I am so sorry."

"Are you sure you aren't doing this to piss them off?" It seemed like something I had to ask.

"You?"

"Yes. Am I the ultimate 'fuck you' to your parents?"

Will was so mad that I would suggest such a thing that he didn't speak to me until after dinner. But sometimes I still wonder if his attraction was due partly to the fact that I was the worst thing his parents could imagine. A person from nowhere.

Needless to say, we didn't see Rose Marie or William II until our wedding, a hot, dry day in Napa Valley. Held at the winery of Will's college roommate, it was everything a girl could dream of, had a girl been dreaming of such things, of course. I wanted a quick trip down to City Hall, maybe a nice meal out, and twenty-four hours of uninterrupted sex, but Will had different ideas. He wanted to give me the whole enchilada, even if I hadn't asked for it.

"I want you to have the fairy tale," he said. "I want you to have everything you want, now and forever."

It was hard to say no. So I plotted and planned a wedding, which included one hundred fifty of Will's closest friends and exactly none of mine.

Now, even if Will was marrying me to stick it to his parents, it was impossible for him to ignore what his father had suggested. It led to some strange conversations, such as:

"So you lived off the grid?" he'd ask.

"What? Grid?"

"You know. You didn't use credit cards, you kept your cash in a safe-deposit box, didn't own a car or property or anything."

"I had a really nice bicycle."

"Was it because you worked for the government? You probably saw some scary things."

Yes. Some.

"Well, I think it takes a lot of guts to live like that," he'd continue.

"Sure," I'd say. "So gutsy." Now at the time, in my mind, I hadn't actually lied. I had simply said nothing. Bit by bit, Will filled in my backstory with little or no input from me.

Add to the mix my dead parents, and some compassion gene in Will magically turned on and he felt terrible that I'd had this little orphan Annie childhood and he wanted to make it all better. Thus the princess wedding.

Maybe in the end it's nothing more than another example of love and denial, twisted up together like a pretzel. Not all that unusual if you consider the human condition.

So then, what is the real story? Everyone must come from somewhere and I am no exception to this rule. I grew up on a farm in upstate New York, surrounded by acres of corn and milk cows named Bessie and Moo. It was an idyllic existence in the beginning. During the summer, I'd roll out of bed in my nightgown and bare feet, grab a few still-warm biscuits and a glass of fresh milk from the kitchen table, and go sit on the porch. Watching the farm hustle and move all around me, I'd plot my day. Maybe I'd get Luke from next door and we'd fish for trout in the river with our dime-store poles. Or go swimming in Black Lake. Or ride our bikes down the endless dirt road that seemed to go nowhere. Or go searching for fossils in the dried-out streambed that ran by Luke's farm. The possibilities were endless. As I was only eight years old, I was not called upon to help on the farm. And because we lived in the middle of nowhere, I was allowed to run amok, unquestioned. I had the long, endless days of childhood summer all to myself and everything was a wonder to behold.

I would come flying into the house in the early evening, hair a mess, damp from swimming, covered in dirt and mud, a huge grin on my face, and throw myself into my chair at the big, oak dining room table. My parents would look at me and shake their heads. What are we raising here, a wild animal? I'd dig into my food— meat, potatoes, vegetables, and bread straight out of the oven—as if I hadn't eaten in a month. After dinner, I'd help clean up the kitchen, we'd play cards or watch TV, and I'd go to bed. The next day I'd wake up and do it all over again.

The winters in upstate New York are another situation entirely— long, cold, and gray. It is safe to say nothing good ever happened in an upstate New York winter. I like to believe it was the bleakness that made the annual winter visits from the man in the dark blue overcoat stand out in my memory. Or maybe it was the fact that he was the only person ever invited into our house.

The first time he came I opened the door despite my mother yelling that she'd get it. I flung it open and there he stood, tall, slightly stooped, a thick wool cap on his head, and the overcoat, much too fancy for our neck of the woods. He was covered with new snowflakes that were quickly melting into shiny little spots on the blue wool. I stepped back to let him in but he didn't move, staring at me, a slight twitch evident at the corner of his mouth.

"Come in, please," I said in my most adult voice. And the man in the snow-covered coat seemed to exhale my name as if it had been caught in his throat for years.

At that moment, my mother came flying out of the kitchen, pulling off her apron on the way. She grabbed me by the upper arm, too hard. Her fingers would leave bright red marks on my pale skin.

"What did I just tell you about answering the door?" she hissed.

"Not to," I answered, my eyes welling up with hot, humiliated tears. How could she, in front of this perfect stranger? The man removed his cap and stepped over the threshold.

"It's okay," he said. He continued to stare at me as I slid, uncomfortable now, behind my mother's skirt.

"Sir?" my mother said, trying to draw his attention back to her. The man shook his head as if to clear it.

"Yes. Of course. I didn't expect her to be so . . . lovely." He gave me one last pained glance and followed my mother down the hallway.

From my room I could hear them downstairs, talking quietly and urgently. I was not yet old enough to yearn for the name of this man, the details of their conversation, a connection to the great big world outside my window. That would come later.

Not your average farmers, my parents would travel every February, when activity on the farm was slow, to New York City for a long weekend of good restaurants, opera, museums, and a hotel room with crisp cotton sheets and a fluffy white comforter. It appeared to be the one extravagance of two people who worked dawn to dusk every other day of the year. One February, while driving home during an ice storm, they were hit by an out-of-control tractor-trailer and both of them were killed instantly.

Later I learned the truck driver was drunk and had fallen asleep at the wheel of his fifteen-ton rig. After two years with the Agency, I made a discreet inquiry and found him. He lived alone in a dead and depressing corner of the city of Utica, New York. When I showed up at his door, intent on extracting some revenge, I learned a valuable lesson. Sometimes letting a person continue to live is a far worse punishment than killing him. Releasing this broken and pathetic man from life would have been a gift, and I was not there to bestow such a kindness. I left him in his dark apartment, which smelled like mildew and sweat, to rot away his remaining days.

When I came back to Washington, Simon Still wanted to know why I didn't do it. I tried not to express surprise that he knew what I was up to. I shrugged.

"It wasn't worth it," I said. "What's done is done."

He gave me a cold look. "You lack a certain killer instinct, Sal," he said. "Someday that is going to get you into trouble."

The farm was sold and all of my parents' assets were placed in a trust for me. I used the money to pay for college. In the years in between I lived with an aunt and uncle in Vermont. It wasn't bad. It wasn't good. It wasn't really anything but killing time, waiting to see what came next.

All of this would have been available for Will II's investigator, but he was missing a crucial piece of information: my name. Lucy Parks never lived in upstate New York. She lived in Connecticut somewhere and probably had pink wallpaper and a fluffy rug covered in hand-embroidered butterflies. She was the kind of girl who would have ended up married to an entrepreneur with his own investment fund, living in San Francisco, obsessing over the amount of omega-3 her child is getting in his diet. She makes total sense. The girl from the farm, the one who used to run down the gravel driveway with no shoes, chasing the dogs, she is gone.

But no story, at least in real life, is ever quite so tidy. One night in an empty bar on the Lower East Side of New York, Simon, well into his fourth scotch, leaned in close to me.

"Don't you ever wonder," he slurred, "how it is you came to be here?" A drink or two behind him but not altogether sober, I asked him what the hell he was talking about.

"Here in this bar or here on this planet? You'll have to be more specific."

Simon tried to focus his swimming eyes on me.

"You're so good at deflecting, aren't you? Must run in the family." He paused long enough to toss back the last of his drink, slam down the glass, and position his hat just so on his head. When he tried to stand up, I had to steady him to keep him from falling on the floor. He grabbed onto my arm and pulled me in so our faces were inches apart. His breath was heavy and sour and I tried to pull back.

"Do you think you were plucked from obscurity by John Smith, NSA, because you were so smart? Nothing is ever that simple. I've known canned tuna with more curiosity than you."

With that he pushed me away and stumbled out into the cold New York night.

Most people, anyone sane or curious or even human for instance, would have gone after him and demanded an explanation. But not me. No. I stayed right there on my rickety bar stool and sucked on the sticky sweet cherry from my drink. Then I ordered another.

Simon had a way of finding the most tragic thing in your life and exploiting it. Although I would rather have been set on fire than tell him about how I always felt a little bit disconnected from everyone around me, he knew. My past was gray, existing only in my memory, and Simon found that irresistible.

Our wedding, Will's and mine, was beautiful. It was held on the patio of a faux Italian villa in Napa Valley, surrounded by stunning English gardens and hills covered with grape vines. The English gardens upset Will. "All that water!" But he got over it and by midafternoon everyone was drunk on the house wine and dancing up a storm. Even my new in-laws seemed to have thawed a bit, welcoming me into their family with a hint of tension behind their eyes. When the party finally ended, my father-in-law was propped up against the bar. He grabbed me as I walked past.

"Who are you?" he slurred. "Everyone leaves a paper trail."

I smiled, making my eyes as cold as possible. "It would be better for you if you let this go," I said. With that, his fingers slid from my arm and his face lost some of its rosy glow. He would not remember this incident later, which was good for me. Sometimes I overreact.

I was happy to survive the wedding more or less intact, but that was not enough for my darling new husband. Will wanted some sort of great adventure for our honeymoon.

"How about Thailand?" he suggested, standing in the travel section of our local bookstore, months before our wedding.

"No, bad weather that time of year," I said. Have you ever lived through a monsoon in the jungle? It's horrible.

"Cambodia?"

I looked at him over the top of the book I was holding. "Tell me you're kidding."

"It's supposed to be amazing, off the beaten path. Time to go is now," he quoted from the open travel book in his hands.

"No."

"Jeez, Lucy, where is your sense of adventure?" At which point I started laughing in a high-pitched, slightly insane sort of way. I'd never traveled on my clean passport. I'd never traveled for pleasure. I had no idea how it was done. And I was paranoid that the minute I stepped outside of the borders of my own country, bullets would start to whiz by over my head. Hard to relax in that frame of mind.

"Laos? China? Nepal? Bhutan?"

"Aren't honeymoons supposed to involve a lot of sex and cocktails and things?"

"Typically."

"So why do you want to go to a place where there is a better than average chance that you will end up sleeping on a bed of rocks with all of your clothes on?"

"That is a good question."

"Think about it. Where are your priorities?" I asked.

Will put down his travel book and walked toward me. "My priorities are in order," he said, as he slid his hands under my shirt. Pulling me into the enclosure of his jacket, he undid my bra and pulled both it and my shirt off over my head. He unbuttoned his own shirt so our skin could touch. Standing half naked amid the dark stacks of our favorite bookstore, I found myself sighing with pure pleasure.

"Do you think this is a good idea?" I whispered.

"I'm showing you my priorities," he said, maneuvering me backward toward the single cramped bathroom with the drippy faucet. Once inside, under the harsh fluorescent light, he took off the rest of my clothes, lifted me onto the dirty sink, and had his way with me. We spent our honeymoon on the very civilized Caribbean island of Anguilla. I promised him adventure, excitement, and near-death experiences for our next vacation. Which I have tried very hard to avoid.

9

Before we get too far along, I should probably explain how I first came to meet the Blind Monk. It is not a love story.

After I survived following Peter Bradley in New Zealand without getting caught or killed, the Blind Monk became my hot property. Mind you, I didn't ask for preferential treatment when it came to men with particularly bad intentions, but all things Monk suddenly started to flow downstream in my direction, leaving me drenched and cold.

The agents trapped down in the daisy with me couldn't believe their good fortune.

"You really stepped in it, Sally," they'd laugh.

"Better you than me."

"Simon must be trying to kill you."

"Now, had Blackford managed to off the guy before he went rogue, things would be different. Remember to thank him for the inheritance next time he snatches you!"

So of course when word came in that the Blind Monk was masquerading as a masseur in a place catering to western tourists off of Sukhumvit in Bangkok, presumably not to give massages, Simon barely let me finish my morning coffee before we were on a plane heading east. During the flight, Simon sat beside me, drumming his fingers, tapping his foot, fiddling with the TV controls, spinning the gold ring he wore on his right ring finger around and around.

"Will you stop it?" I finally begged. "You are starting to drive me crazy. Wouldn't it be better if you went home and let me handle this? You don't seem centered."

Simon glared at me. "I'm very centered. And you would not be able to handle the Blind Monk on your own. He's a tricky character. Takes a seasoned agent to go up against someone of his caliber."

I rolled my eyes. "Simon, it's not as if I just got off the boat, you know?" He ignored me.

"There is a chance that there might be other players involved too. People of interest to us."

"Who?"

"I'll tell you on a need-to-know basis."

"I need to know now."

"No, you don't."

"Blackford," I said, matter-of-factly.

"Definitely not Blackford," Simon said.

"You're lying."

"And you're insubordinate."

"I do what I can."

"Go to sleep."

"I can't. You keep fidgeting around over there and it's really annoying."

"Learn to ignore it."

"Fine." I pulled my eyeshade down and reclined my seat. I could still feel the vibrations of Simon's aerobics, but eventually I fell asleep anyway.

Bangkok in November is not altogether unpleasant, if you don't mind your days being extremely hot, humid, and gritty. The air was thick with pollution hanging in a haze over the city as we left the airport and headed into town. The view outside never seemed to change. The half-finished buildings never got any closer to being done, the construction cranes long gone to China. As we whizzed along on the toll road designed for visitors with cash, I could see the locals sitting in mile after mile of stopped traffic on the parallel free route, their cars belching gray smoke into the toxic mix outside. Our cab driver tried to convince us to go immediately to his cousin's shop for custom-made suits and dresses, but shut up after I explained in Thai how we weren't here as tourists but with a United

Nations agency looking into the exploitation of Thai children in the custom clothing sector. We stopped briefly at Simon's favorite Bangkok guesthouse to drop off our few belongings. He was greeted like a member of the family who's been gone for a while. He explained that he'd been promoted and had not been spending quite as much time on the road as he used to. That was news to me.

"Such good work you do, sir," the owner said, leading us to our rooms. "So nice you find pretty girl to travel with." The very thought turned my stomach, but I didn't say anything.

Simon followed me into my room and shut the door. He sat down on my thin mattress, propped himself up comfortably on my single pillow, and started to do that thing he was always doing with his fingers. Here is the church, here is the steeple, open the doors and see all the people. You know that one, right? Whenever Simon was contemplating throwing you to the wolves, he'd start in with that routine. It was fascinating to watch, his fingers and hands moving as if independent from the rest of his body. This was not going to be good for me.

"The Blind Monk knows me, obviously, but he doesn't know you, at least not yet," Simon said, fingers moving furiously. Church, steeple, people, church, steeple, people. "So you will be the lead here. But I don't want you to do anything. Go to his place and get a massage and see what you can see, nothing more. We'll figure out a plan after we know a few things. There are sure to be at least half a dozen of his men around so don't make any moves. You are another American tourist on vacation. Is that understood? Remember every little detail that you see. The Blind Monk's strength is in the details."

I nodded my head, thinking a massage sounded kind of nice, considering the circumstances.

"I'll be watching you from the coffee shop across the street. If he tries to kill you, of course, feel free to defend yourself."

"Gee, thanks for the permission."

The Blind Monk's massage parlor was known for being straight. If you wanted a prostitute for a little extra behind the curtain, you'd have to take your business down the road, although not very far.

I asked at the front desk how long I'd have to wait for the Blind Monk himself to do my massage and was told about an hour, which was perfect, allowing me time to sit unobtrusively and watch what was going on.

The place was jumping with clients, mostly western, coming and going from behind a flowing curtain covering the door to the massage stations. Most emerged with happy, dopey expressions on their faces, floating out the front entrance with a sublime disinterest in the chaos that awaited them out there. There were two large Thai men behind the counter with the receptionist. They didn't seem to be doing anything but sitting there and I assumed they were the Blind Monk's bodyguards. There were also several female masseuses that came in and out to collect clients. Nothing else of interest transpired.

Eventually the Blind Monk himself emerged from behind the curtain. He was so enormous that his monastic robes strained across his shoulders and barely covered his knees. I could see the silky dark hair cascading down his calves, coming to a hard stop at his ankles. His hands were roughly the size of frying pans and he rubbed them together like he was about to sit down before a grand feast. I just hoped it wasn't me.

He filled the space behind the small counter, dwarfing the very men meant to protect him. Dark sunglasses hid his perfectly functioning eyes. He gestured that I was to follow him, which I did.

Behind the curtain were about six massage stations, small cubicles divided by curtains, with raised platforms covered in dense straw mats. I was invited to change into the flowing pajamas typical to Thai massage.

For the first hour everything went fine. I was actually feeling pretty good. The perpetual tingly tightness in my neck began to disappear beneath the aggressive hands of the Blind Monk. I was so relaxed that I didn't much notice the brief pause in my massage and the totally wrong stillness that followed. I raised my head off of the mat.

"Are we all done?" I asked, feeling a little bit dizzy. Looking left and right, I realized I was now the only one in the back room. All the other massage stalls were empty. Uh-oh. I rolled over and sat up to face the Blind Monk flanked by his goons from behind the desk. They made a strange sight. The Blind Monk could almost rest his elbows on their heads. I smiled, trying to contain my urge to giggle.

"I am so pleased you came right to me rather than me having to chase you all over the world," the Blind Monk said in perfect English. "You are as lovely as everyone says. A shame, but Blackford has brought this on himself. Your demise will send the exact message to him that I intend." Before I had time to think of a clever retort, he pushed me back onto the massage mat, took my right arm, and pulled it back and up toward the base of my neck until I shouted out with the pain.

"I don't know what you're talking about," I said, weakly.

"Speak Thai," the Blind Monk demanded, adding a little more pressure to my arm.

"But you're speaking English!" I squeaked through the searing flash in my shoulder.

"Doesn't matter what I do. We are in Thailand, are we not? You Americans, you all think the world should bend to your whim and speak English. So you speak Thai."

"I would love to speak Thai," I said in English. "But I can't even say hello. I am not who you think I am." This made him pull a little harder on my arm. I groaned.

"I said speak Thai!"

"I'll speak fucking Greek if you want me to. I still don't know why we are having this conversation!"

"You are Sally Sin of the United States, are you not?

"Who?"

"Your acting, it does not convince me. But I have a way to find out if you are Sally Sin or not."

I didn't really want to hear it but figured he was going to tell me anyway.

"Put her in the cage," the Blind Monk announced. He pulled a little bit harder on my arm. I could feel my shoulder reaching its limits. "If Blackford shows up to rescue her, we know she is Sally Sin and we kill her. If Blackford doesn't show up to rescue her, well, we kill her anyway." The Blind Monk laughed at his own joke. His two bodyguards joined in although I doubted they understood anything he was saying in English.

With that he gave my arm a final twist. And when my shoulder released my arm, popping it clean out of its socket, I passed out.

Later, Simon Still berated me for passing out over something as mundane as a dislocated shoulder. He reminded me that passing out was only acceptable if I was dead. Still, it hurt like hell and when I woke up in a wire cage attached to a rusty-looking crane dangling over the Chao Phraya River, it didn't feel much better. The cage was about twenty feet above the water, suspended on a thin chain that looked like it could go at any moment.

Through the cloud of pain, I remembered what the Blind Monk said about killing me to piss off Blackford. The very thought made me groan. And where the hell was Simon? What happened to his watching me from across the street? This was turning out to be a bad afternoon all around.

There is a technique for relocating your shoulder. It hurts. A lot. Especially if you are trying to do it while sitting in a cage designed for a small dog over a fast-running, filthy river.

I lay on the bottom of the cage, with my legs bent into my chest, my agonizing arm flat alongside my body. I bent my elbow so my hand was now at a right angle to my body.

"Fuck!" I screamed, the pain blurring my vision for a few seconds. "I hate this job!" I lay my forearm across my chest and rotated it back out, keeping my upper arm stationary. I started to sweat, the drops leaving a cold trail as they rolled down my forehead. Slowly, I attempted to coax the wayward shoulder back into its socket. I repeated the process, the whole time cursing Simon Still and his inept planning. Finally, a pop followed by a wave of relief and pure nausea. I rolled over on my side and threw up through the mesh bottom of the cage. Great. Things were really looking up.

After a few minutes I sat up as best I could in my cramped cell and assessed my situation. My shoulder and arm throbbed with the trauma of the dislocation. I craved a drink of water, only made worse by the river flowing beneath me.

"So here I am," I said out loud to nobody but the fishes. "Not likely that anyone is going to rescue me, right?" The water was silent. "No, not likely." I shifted my weight, trying to ease the pressure on my shoulder, pushed up against the side of the cage.

But before I could get too comfortable, the bottom of the rusty old thing gave out. I heard the slightest scraping sound and then I dropped twenty feet into the muddy brown Chao Phraya. The Chao Phraya looks like a relatively calm river. At any given time, it's so crowded with boats and ferries and people floating on wooden pallets that you'd think it was an easily navigable waterway. But at certain times of the year it flows with purpose, fast and reckless, belying its calm surface.

This was one of those times. To say my sudden plunge into the water surprised me would probably be an understatement. As I hit, I held my weak arm to my body to lessen the shock of the impact. I shot downward like a missile about ten feet before the desperate flapping with my good arm stopped my descent. Then I paddled toward the surface, breaking through with a gasp. The water tasted of metal and gas in my mouth. The shoreline rushed by. I tried to swim toward it but my arm wouldn't cooperate and it was all I could do to stay afloat.

Strange. I never thought I'd die by drowning. Maybe getting pushed off a cliff or run over by a bus or something, but drowning never occurred to me. I thought for a second I might cry. There were things I wanted to do in my life. I wasn't exactly sure what they were but I knew they were out there. And if I were dead I'd never figure them out.

Flipping onto my back, I started to kick deliberately with my feet and pull with the good arm.

At first, all I could hear was a faint buzz under water. It grew into a whine, getting louder as the engine drew closer. A Jet Ski.

I picked my head up enough to see it coming right for me. I ducked under the water fast and despite the pain started to swim like hell toward the shore. When I opened my eyes, it looked like I was swimming through a huge cup of tea, my orange hands cutting through the dirty water in front of me.

The engine whine faded into the distance but soon headed back in my direction. I dove again, watching it pass inches above my head.

I heard a splash and one of the Jet Ski passengers plunged into the water. The man was in a wet suit, with a mask, swim fins, and a small tank of compressed air. Definitely not a level playing field, in my opinion.

Beneath me I could see the dark hulk of what had to be a collapsed pier. Rusted steel beams protruded out of the slabs of concrete, now covered in a thick layer of soft green seaweed. I took a deep breath and swam down toward the pier. The man was right at my heels, breathing comfortably while my lungs burned. I slipped a foot under one of the bent steel rods sticking out of the concrete. The man grabbed my good arm, trying to pull me toward him and the surface. I resisted, instead pulling him down toward me.

We rotated in the water around each other, doing a strange sort of ballet. As we turned, I pushed him backward with all of my strength onto a protruding rusty beam with a nasty point. It pierced him like a knife. In his shock the regulator fell out of his mouth. I snatched it and sucked the air into my empty lungs, my eyes on the verge of popping out of my head. Trying to breathe normally, I swam through the cloud of blood, not toward the surface but toward the shore, leaving my skewered victim without even a glance back.

I climbed out of the water a good ways downriver from where I had started, collapsing on the dirty street in an exhausted heap. Simon Still stood nearby, his white suit immaculate despite the dust.

"You look terrible, Sal," he said. "Hope your tetanus is up to date."

I could barely lift my head, the taste of Chao Phraya and blood still polluting my mouth.

"I hate you," I said quietly, rolling over in the dirt.

"No, you don't." Simon lit a cigarette and blew a perfect smoke ring in my direction.

"Yes," I confirmed, "I really do. Thanks for your help."

"Well, I couldn't exactly barge in there and save you, now could I? Then we both would have ended up in that cage. And that would have been a real calamity."

"You saw me in the cage?"

"I was all prepared to free you when you fell in the river," he said, matter-of-factly. "Which actually worked out quite nicely, don't you think?"

I tried to stand up, my legs wobbly. "I killed someone," I said. Simon caught me under the arm. I could see the dirt jump hungrily from my body to his clean white cuff. He made a face.

"Yes. But I expect that whomever you killed would have killed you first, given the chance. The ends justify the means. Almost always."

"Shouldn't we be getting out of here?" I asked. Simon studied his watch, as if the answers to all the universe's most perplexing questions were provided there. He looked left and right like he was waiting for someone.

"Well, this has turned out to be a complete loss. But on the positive side, I'd say we have about half an hour before the Blind Monk figures out you killed one of his men and escaped. So we have time for some curry if we eat quickly. I'm starved." He let go of my arm and marched away down the street. I sank back to my knees.

"Come on, Sally! Time's a-wasting!"

On my knees in the dust, I suddenly understood something very clearly. This was not about the Blind Monk. If it had been, we would have stormed into his massage parlor like we were serious. But we didn't. Because the man we were really after was Ian Blackford. Simon Still expected that Blackford would show up to save me, drawn like a moth to a flame. Did Simon Still himself tip off the Blind Monk to my arrival? Did my own boss give me up? I pushed that thought out of my head as fast as I could. I couldn't let it be possible and survive.

So that was the first time Simon attempted to use me as bait to draw out Blackford. Which might help you understand why I am not all that excited to try it again.

10

Theo, exhausted from building forts and knocking them down, is sleeping in my arms as I move slowly back and forth in an antique rocking chair. He smells like sunshine and strawberry yogurt. I bury my nose in his hair and inhale. It is times like these that I can forget the boredom of motherhood, the longing for something exciting to happen, the little voice in my head that wants to know if I did the right thing all those years ago. Right now none of that matters. Right now I am happy.

I run my fingers down the soft, pale skin of his arm. He stirs slightly and changes position, muttering something about cats. I should put him in his bed, go downstairs, and fold laundry. I should go downstairs and figure out what's for dinner. I should go downstairs and work out how to fix this mess I'm in. But I can't let go of him yet. We continue to rock slowly, back and forth. When he does wake up, I'll take him to the playground for another hour. He'll run around until he's sweaty and red-cheeked. And I'll sit on the benches, chatting with the other moms and nannies, pretending that what they all see is really my life.

Another fifteen minutes pass. Finally, I lift Theo gently into his bed. He rolls over, sighs, and slips back into a deep sleep. I stand in his doorway and float again into the past.

The fifth time I went to Cambodia for the Agency, it was to follow a man named Sovann who was suspected of acquiring too much black market nuclear materials for his own good. Your average global citizen was allowed a certain amount of what we called "restricted" materials, but if you got to stockpiling the stuff in your backyard we got interested. It's only fair. To make things worse, it looked like Sovann intended to sell his stockpile to the Blind Monk, and that was making everyone a little uncomfortable.

By the time I crossed into Cambodia we were at a fairly high level of discomfort. Intelligence told us the Blind Monk all but had his shopping bags out, ready to fill them with uranium and plutonium and switches and detonators and all the other goodies Sovann had for sale. This was usually a pretty good sign that a transaction was in the cards. Money was going to change hands and really bad stuff would be transferred really bad people.

My mission, loosely defined as always by Simon, was to watch Sovann. Basically, I was to confirm that Sovann was indeed going to make a deal with the Blind Monk, after which we'd move in and take down the lot of them. Or so I thought.

You might wonder, as I did, why they would send me, being as the Blind Monk had expressed an interest in killing me the last time we met.

"Sally, who else am I going to send? Glenn?"

"He's dead," I said.

"Exactly. Now stop asking questions to which you already know the answer." I didn't know the answer but assumed I was not to seek further clarification.

My train ride from Thailand to Cambodia came to an end in a Thai town called Aranyaprathet. I stood up, feeling all the vertebrae in my spine pop and crack. I rolled my shoulders a few times, grabbed my knapsack, and followed the streams of people off of the train. Outside, the air was hot and wet but the smell of this place, so foreign and yet so familiar, was always a thrill. I took a deep breath and started toward the band of idling tuk-tuks, one of which would gladly shuttle me the three or four miles from the train station to the actual border crossing. I chose an older man as a driver, a man who didn't look like his eyesight was too great. Not so good for driving but excellent for not remembering my face. As I settled myself in the little trailer attached to his motorbike, a man the size of a mountain hauled himself into the small remaining space next to me.

"Hello there. Name's Roger. Mind if I join you?" he said in a crisp British accent.

I shrugged, not sure of the proper etiquette for kicking this intruder out of my tuk-tuk.

"Great." He wiggled into the narrow spot, popping me up out of my seat and onto the edge of the cab in the process.

"Thanks. Great," he repeated. "You are headed to the border, aren't you?"

I gave him a tight smile. "Yes." I could feel the heat radiating off his enormous bulk. The sweat began to run freely down my face and back, but my arms were trapped. I blinked my eyes to clear the salty water from my field of vision. This was not starting out well.

We bounced along slowly for about ten minutes until the Thai border stations were visible, all sound drowned out by the roaring of our driver's motorbike. Roger made a great show of handing the driver 100 baht although I'd negotiated a rate of half that, and then refusing my offer of half the fare. I slipped it to the driver as Roger turned away. The driver rewarded me with a condescending shake of the head.

Now while Aranyaprathet is relatively civilized, Poipet on the Cambodian side is not. The air there even tastes different, slightly wild and acidic. Behind Roger, I marched through the Thai border station. The guards barely looked up as they stamped my fake passport and handed it back to me.

On the other side, in the no-man's-land between the two border stations, was a strip of run-down hotels and casinos. Outside the ramshackle hotels, the touts shouted and called to me, promising me riches beyond compare. A chance at another chance, they said. I kept my head down and kept walking. My new friend Roger fell in beside me.

"Quite a place," he said, swabbing his face with a crusty red bandana. He was breathing hard, the thick air causing a slight wheeze on his exhale.

"Give it a few years and it will be a mall anchored by Target on one end and Home Depot on the other," I said. My companion laughed.

"Thanks for sharing your ride back there," he said, offering me his hand while we continued to walk. I shook it briefly. It was damp with sweat.

"Camilla. Nice to meet you. On holiday?"

"Yes. Well, no actually. I'm a scientist. I'm looking for some . . . particular . . . flowers."

Up went my radar. He was having trouble with his cover story.

"What sort of flowers?" I asked.

"Purple ones, actually. Actually, yes, purple ones might be the best way to describe them."

"Wow. Good for you," I said. "I'm going to the temples to have a transcendental experience myself."

He laughed before he realized I might be serious. We arrived at the Cambodian crossing. On the other side, I could see Rangsey waiting patiently for me atop a rusted minibike. I, of course, had a plan for crossing the border. It did not include Roger. I gave Rangsey a small shrug, telling him this might take a few minutes. He went back to tapping away on his cell phone.

The border guards were sitting at a table, faces buried in huge bowls of hot soup, one hour into their four-hour lunch break, all border traffic at a standstill. Tiny Cambodian women and girls were running back and forth to a makeshift kitchen at the back of the guards' shack, bearing big steaming bowls of kuyteav and platters of banh chiao accompanied by bottles of cold beer. You'd think these guys did something other than sit in a booth and accept bribes from people all day.

"I am always bothered by this sort of thing in developing countries," Roger said. He took a seat outside the shack to wait with all the others.

"Maybe I'll see you in Siem Reap," I said, continuing to walk toward the guards.

"Wait," Roger called after me. "Where are you going?"

The pile of American dollars I deposited among the soup bowls was not insignificant, the sort of wad of cash that even these corrupt guards could appreciate. Underneath the cash was my passport with a photo that looked like me, but actually wasn't, and an official vaccination record that may or may not have been real.

"Something for after lunch," I said in Cambodian, without looking directly at any of them. I gestured to my passport, open to the fake visa, ripe for stamping. A few grunts and slurps and mutterings among the group. One of them put down his spoon long enough to attend to my passport. He slid it back toward me, slick with soup and oil from his meaty hands.

"Proceed."

I nodded, adjusted my backpack, and walked around the small sawhorse blocking the official way into Cambodia. I wanted to look back at Roger, but I didn't dare. Calling attention to myself was stupid, but I was in a rush.

The drivers of the new minibuses and bikes, the tuk-tuks, and the broken-down cars swarmed around me like bees, offering up the world. I pushed through them to where Rangsey was waiting.

Without a word, I hopped on the back of the bike and he took off.

Easy, right? Sometimes having the United States as my personal banker made my job less difficult. Other times throwing money around did nothing more than piss off the very person I intended to bribe.

Rangsey took off at full speed down the Khao San Road, which is taking some poetic license with the word "road." Deep gullies and potholes the size of pickup trucks scarred the hard-packed earth. You would think a driver, at least one with any sense of self-preservation, would navigate slowly and carefully, like the captain of a ship moving through a shallow reef system at night. But to my dismay, I discovered that in Cambodia there are two speeds: stop or "pedal to the metal" as my driver Rangsey informed me the first time we met. I clung to his thin chest for dear life.

I met Rangsey during my first mission to Cambodia. I was as green as an agent could be but I had my pride. When one of the notorious Phnom Penh child pickpockets took a whack at me, I gave chase as if my life depended on it. Rangsey was fast but not quite fast enough. When I caught him, he was clutching one of my many fake passports, panting.

"This is useless," I said quietly, taking the passport from his small hands.

"No," he said, shaking his head. "I can sell it. Food for my sister, for Ary."

"Do you really have a sister?"

He nodded. "She's sick. Land mine." From his pocket he pulled out a mangled photo of a girl, missing an arm. I had no idea at the time if he was trying to con me, but something in his eyes made me want to find out.

"How old are you?"

"Ten."

"Take me to where you live."

His eyes grew wide with fear. "You're not in trouble," I reassured him. "I want to meet your sister."

Keeping up with him wasn't easy as he sped through the labyrinth of dusty streets in his bare feet. His house was a few flimsy pieces of plywood tied with string. A tattered tarp covered the dirt floor. In one corner was a girl missing an arm, sleeping on a straw mat. Ary was a little older than Rangsey. When she saw me, her face went dark with suspicion.

"Who have you brought here, Rangsey?" Ary whispered. He shrugged and looked down at his feet.

"It's okay," I said. "He's done nothing wrong."

"You speak Cambodian?" the girl asked.

"Some," I said. And she smiled, a huge grin, full of life in this depressing shantytown on the outskirts of a wild city.

I sat down on the dirty tarp and learned that both parents were dead, one of gunshots and one of what sounded like AIDS. A land mine took her arm during a desperate attempt to steal rice from a nearby field.

I drew a decent salary from the USAWMD, and other than the rent on an apartment with no furniture, I spent none of it. It sat there in my bank waiting for a rainy day. Maybe this was my rainy day.

"If I help you, maybe you can help me," I said. They glanced briefly at each other and settled their eyes on me, keeping them deliberately blank. Offers of help in their world usually came with strings attached.

"I'm going to have to visit here from time to time for my work and will need someone reliable to drive me around. Do you drive, Rangsey?"

An indignant look from the young boy. Everyone drives here, even the toddlers.

"If I buy you a motorbike, you can taxi for people when I'm not here but use it for me when I am here. I'll arrange for money so you can keep the bike in decent shape. How does that sound?"

Ary's face hardened at the offer. "Why do you do this?" she asked.

"I don't know," I said, honestly. "I guess I just want to. You can trust me."

I could see her at that moment making a deal with fate, deciding to believe me when all her experience to this point had been to the contrary. Rangsey, thoughts of his own motorbike clouding his vision, looked desperately from Ary to me and back again.

"Thank you," she said in a tiny voice. "We won't let you down."

"No, I don't imagine you will," I said, giving this wisp of a child a small hug.

I took Rangsey out and bought him a used bike, not too flashy but solid. I arranged for him to use the bike shop when he needed to do repairs. I told the owner that I'd make him disappear if he didn't honor our agreement and I think he believed me. I didn't disclose to Rangsey or his sister the nature of my work. There are some who would believe that I'd actually endangered the lives of these two unfortunate souls. But I was not one of them. I didn't see the alternative, the life they were already living, as being less dangerous than hanging around with me.

Every month I arranged for money to be sent to a market near their house for food. I didn't want to give them cash directly, making them objects of undesirable attention. I also sent them to an American doctor working for a local NGO. A nice fat donation to his cause and he agreed to keep an eye on the two children in my absence.

When I got home, mission accomplished, Simon Still was sitting in my apartment, feet up on the coffee table, reading my mail.

"Too involved, Sal," he said. He did not even bother to look up.

"I've been flying for about a hundred hours," I pointed out. "Can't this wait until tomorrow?"

"No," he said, standing abruptly, my junk mail and flyers scattering across the floor. "You don't get involved with the locals. You don't save them. You use them. Do you understand the difference?"

I nodded slowly.

"Are you sure? Because it certainly didn't look like it over there in Phnom Penh."

"Yes, I understand."

"Well, you had better, Sally Sin. If you get involved, you end up dead. Got it?"

I nodded again, looking at the ground.

"It's for your own good. Don't you have any interest in living to see thirty?"

I continued to nod my head, knowing already that I would defy his orders. Simon kept me out of Cambodia for two years as punishment for my humanitarian leanings. But when I finally showed up again, there was Rangsey, exactly as we'd arranged. And he'd been there every time since.

Rangsey and I didn't talk until we stopped for tea, about halfway to our destination of Siem Reap, home to Angkor Wat. By this point in the ride, I was so rattled I felt like my molars were about to fall out of my head.

"Next time, I think I'll fly," I said, sipping my scalding hot tea.

"Flying is not so low profile, Sally."

"I know, I know. But this road. I'm growing to hate this road."

Rangsey laughed. "You have no sense of adventure."

"Then I clearly picked the wrong profession, wouldn't you agree?"

Rangsey looked serious for a moment. "You be careful of Sovann and Blind Monk. They are very dangerous, even for Cambodia."

I waved him off. "It's not like I'm going to sit down and have a meal with them. I need to poke around a little, ask some questions. When I'm done, I'll disappear back into the jungle."

"You hate the jungle," Rangsey reminded me.

"I didn't mean that literally," I said.

"It's wet," he continued, "there are huge bugs. Not to mention the land mines. Can't forget about the land mines."

"Okay," I said, "enough with the jungle. You made your point. Tell me what you know."

As Rangsey got older, I started using him as an ear to the ground. His information was always right as opposed to the information I got at my desk in Washington. That intelligence was never attached to anyone. It was written in short spurts, with no punctuation, and more often than not it was wrong. The Agency demanded to know if you were using your own sources in addition to what they provided you because they liked to take liberties with those sources for their own purposes. But I knew better than to mention Rangsey to Simon Still. Chances were we'd both end up in Outer Mongolia for the rest of our natural lives. Or something equally appealing.

"The Blind Monk is here for the grand opening of The Grand Event, Siem Reap's latest luxury addition to hotel alley. Word is that Blind Monk is one of the hotel's investors, but I don't know anything about his partners. Probably Chinese."

I nod. "Busy guy."

"But that is not all. The Blind Monk is here to check up on his hotel investment, yes, but also to do some business with Sovann, who has some bombing materials hidden in a warehouse in the jungle."

"Nuclear stuff?"

"Yes, what you said. Nuclear stuff."

"Anything new you can you tell me about Sovann?"

"He's still the same wee little man. Still not too friendly. But he has become a big deal in Cambodia. Lots of people owe him. Kind of like that Godfather movie. You see that one? Very good, I think."

"You've got a real talent for this, Rangsey."

He beamed.

"But don't do anything foolish," I added.

"No," he said, "I don't do anything like what you would do."

"Gee, thanks."

"Oh, there is one more thing. Someone else is here too. Everyone is talking about the man with the blue eyes and the black hair."

I leaned back in my chair. Fucking fabulous.

"Sally? You okay? Bad information?"

"No," I said, patting Rangsey's hand. "Great information. Bad Ian Blackford."

II

I am crawling around on the living room floor picking up the drift of children's books before Maria the cleaning lady arrives, lest she sweep them into her giant trash bag and toss them out with the rest of the junk. When Will first suggested I ought to have someone come in and clean the house, I didn't know whether to be relieved or insulted.

"It's not like I don't clean the house," I said.

"I hate to say this, Lucy, but you don't clean the house. And neither do I. So let's agree that we both don't clean the house. Okay?"

I nodded. I wasn't confident I could accurately explain that having a strange person walking around inside my house with a broom and a bottle of Seventh Generation Disinfecting Multi-Surface Cleaner might not be so good for my paranoia. How was I to know that her intentions were solely to make my stainless-steel refrigerator gleam like a hotel mirror?

"Okay. I agree on the cleaning thing. But what if she, you know, isn't who she says she is or something?"

"That's kind of paranoid, don't you think, Lucy?"

You have no idea.

But I eventually agreed to the deal because I was not that good at cleaning toilets and it seemed no one had bothered to change the sheets on our bed for over a month.

I hear Maria's key rattling around in the lock and I go still, my body ready for some sort of ambush, even if my mind knows I'm not at any real risk from a five-foot-tall grandma.

"Hello, Mrs. Lucy. You here?"

"In the living room, Maria, trying to put away the rest of the books."

Maria joins me on the floor. "Why don't you leave them? I finish here."

"Are you sure?"

She nods, muttering in Spanish, something about how she thinks I'm kind of a kook, but not necessarily in a bad way.

I leave her with the books, but today I don't go far because today, it appears, anything can happen. Lingering outside the door, I pretend to be engrossed in my cell phone when really, I'm scrolling up and down my contacts list, which contains about ten numbers on a good day. It's true that Maria seems innocent enough, but who is to say that she isn't an Agency plant, put here to spy on me, ready to be activated at any moment? She carries an impossibly large, worn brown tote bag that is so heavy she can barely manage my front steps. Come to think of it, I've never seen her take anything out of that cavernous sack. Which means it's completely within the realm of possibility that Maria could, at any moment, whip out a fully loaded Uzi and start taking hostages. Or maybe pull out a hand grenade and roll it into my kitchen, which would really make a mess of things.

Maria glances up from the floor.

"You go drink some coffee, Mrs. Lucy. Yes?"

I grumble something about taking a call, humiliated that my cleaning lady thinks I'm crazy. And I head toward the kitchen, but I still can't quite get there. That brown tote bag is too big for me to really relax.

On a certain level, I am embarrassed that I have someone picking up my books, washing my dishes, and folding my laundry. I have not gotten used to the feeling of uselessness that sometimes goes along with being a full-time mother, the feeling that you aren't doing much more than waiting for the next stage of child development to show up so you will have something new to obsess about. Is it enough to raise your child? Should I be cleaning my own house and making a pot roast? Have I simply become a consumer of resources with nothing to contribute? Oh the horror. But then again, back when I used to have an impact on things, that impact wasn't always positive. No, I'd be the first to admit that Siem Reap turned into an unmitigated disaster.

After a few dreadful hours rattling around on the back of Rangsey's motorbike, we finally arrived in Siem Reap. Rangsey dropped me off at a guesthouse and waved good-bye. I had no idea where he slept and didn't ask. Such a question would seem too forward somehow.

In my room, I lay down on the bed and closed my eyes, trying to get my body to accept that it was no longer on the road from hell. The noise from the vibrating motorbike still rang in my ears, but it didn't stop me from hearing my room lock being picked. Fast. I didn't even bother to sit up.

"Are you going to kill me this time?" I asked, not moving, my eyes shut tight against how my simple mission was starting to resemble a three-ring circus.

"Perhaps. I haven't decided yet."

"You always say that."

"One day you will ask me and the answer will be yes." And the way he said it, I knew he was telling the truth. "So why don't you tell me what you are you doing out here in this nasty jungle, Sally?"

"Sightseeing."

"And I'm the fucking King of Siam."

"You are definitely not the King of Siam. He was bald."

"That was a joke."

"It wasn't a very good one."

"Maybe I should have killed you in Madrid."

I finally sat up and there he was, blue eyes twinkling like Santa Claus on Christmas Eve. I shuddered and looked away. This never seemed to get any easier. Might as well cut to the chase.

"Are you trying to start a war with the Blind Monk?" I asked. There was no other reason I could come up with, no matter how far-fetched, to explain his being here. He was preparing to throw a monkey wrench into the Blind Monk's carefully executed deal with Sovann.

Blackford stood across the room from me, his feet planted, his shoulders loose. He had the nerve to look relaxed, but his face was dark. I'd managed to irritate him already.

"When did you decide you could ask me questions?"

"When you picked my lock!" I blurted, suddenly angry at his intrusion. "Doesn't the violation of my privacy entitle me to ask a few questions?"

Blackford glared at me. "Go ahead. One question."

"Are you here to start a war with the Blind Monk?"

"Start a war? Where have you been, Sally? The Blind Monk and I are already at war. We're enemies. Traditionally, enemies try to eliminate each other." He smiled, and I swear he sounded gleeful about the prospect of a battle among titans. Couldn't they just go outside and beat each other up like civilized men?

"Let me put it another way. Are you going to jump-start this war by trying to buy Sovann's stash out from under the Blind Monk?" Almost as soon as the question passed my lips, I knew I'd gone too far.

"Sorry, Sal. I said one question and besides, that's strategy and that remains confidential. My advice is for you to shove off. Maybe finish out your holiday in Phnom Penh. Take those straggly kids of yours out for a proper meal or something."

At the mention of Rangsey and Ary, I felt an unfamiliar surge in my blood pressure. I never understood it until I held Theo for the first time, that do or die mother instinct that silences all rational thoughts around it.

"Never mind the kids," I said.

Blackford grinned. It wasn't a nice grin.

"Look at Sally getting all worked up. Nice. Listen, you and I both know that if I wanted those little urchins in a ditch outside the city limits, it would be done before we even finished this rather hostile and unpleasant conversation."

In a split second, I flew across the room and had Blackford by the neck. It was an amateur move. He could have easily killed me, but

I wasn't thinking. I was acting. I tightened my grip, but he kept grinning.

"Crazy Sally. I always knew you had it in you."

With one quick motion of his arm, he tossed me aside as if I were weightless. I landed hard against the door. This would hurt later. Blackford stood over me, a blank look on his face.

"Don't ever try something like that again. It will end badly for you."

I didn't move, too scared to get up from the floor.

"I'd like you to leave Siem Reap," he said, his voice flat. "And I don't want to ask you twice."

With his foot, he shoved me out of the way, opened the door, and disappeared down the hallway.

I crawled over to my knapsack and pulled out my cell phone.

"Blackford is here," I whispered when Simon answered. My rib cage was already starting to throb painfully.

"Gee, what a surprise," Simon said. He did not sound surprised. "Are you sure of your sources?"

"Pretty sure. You knew."

"I most certainly did not." He was lying. I knew it. But from roughly nine thousand miles away there was nothing I could do. "Do you think I would have sent you into the middle of a war zone without a warning?"

Yes.

"What do you want me to do?" I asked. Every time I took a breath my chest hurt.

There was a pause. I could hear Simon sitting up in his bed, probably going to the window to see if anyone was out there on the street spying on him in the dead of a Washington night.

"Kill Blackford, Sally. Close the deal." I heard a faint buzzing coming down the line indicating that Simon Still had hung up on me.

And sitting there on the floor of my room, I felt very bad about the choices in my life that had led me to this place.

12

I follow Maria to the laundry room but stay back about ten feet in the hopes that she won't notice I'm there lurking in the shadows. She hums a tune that I can't quite recognize as she opens the dryer, pulling all of the clean clothes into the plastic basket. Suddenly, she gasps.

"Mr. Will do these clothes?" she asks, her back to me, clearly aware of my presence.

Of course Will would not be doing laundry in a washing machine. And he would certainly never turn on a dryer except perhaps if he were held at gunpoint. No, Will would hand wash every item of clothing in a single gallon of cold water using biodegradable soap and, much to the horror of our neighbors, hang everything out on the line to dry. Never mind that the clothes were still covered in chocolate milk stains. It would be energy efficient. I consider letting him take one for the team. But in the end I tell the truth.

"Um, no. It was me."

"Tsk, tsk, Lucy," Maria says, wagging a finger at me. "You need pay attention to colors." To illustrate, she holds up a new pair of Theo's jeans that are now so badly bleached they resemble a 1980s acid-wash disaster.

"White with white. No colors in here. Okay? Okay."

I stare at my feet like I've been reprimanded by the teacher, which in effect I have. In light of the ruined pants, I cannot figure out why exactly I thought I could protect humanity from itself. Honestly, if you can't do a load of laundry you cannot save the world. It really is that simple.

But at the time I didn't know that. So instead of taking Blackford's advice and calling it a day, I did the next best thing, which was to go and visit Sovann directly. I was sure that if I could convince Sovann not to sell his wares to Blackford, no matter what the silver-tongued ex-spy had promised him, I could stop the chaos on the horizon.

Sovann lived in a huge house, protected by a twenty-five-foot security fence, topped with tightly coiled razor wire. Dogs and armed guards patrolled along the inside perimeter of the fence. From the outside, the place resembled a federal prison. And with good reason. If you wanted something done in Siem Reap, or anywhere in Cambodia really, Sovann was the guy to see. He specialized in illegal weapons, but was only too happy to engage in human trafficking, drugs, and stolen antiquities if given the opportunity. Rangsey cut the bike and we both sat there looking at the compound.

"Big," Rangsey commented.

"Looks secure," I added.

"Lots of guards. Carrying guns."

"Dogs."

"High-voltage fencing. I think I'll wait here."

"Who said you were invited anyway?"

Rangsey laughed. "I'll stay right here for you."

I climbed off the back of the bike.

"Don't wait for me," I said. "Go home. I could be a while."

Rangsey shook his head before I'd even finished the sentence. "I'll be right here when you come out."

"If I come out," I said, suddenly tired.

"Of course you'll come out. Karma owes you one."

"How do you figure?" I asked.

Rangsey grinned in the darkness. "You saved me and Ary. Spiritually, that is pretty high up there."

I thanked him for his positive energy and began my long slog to the fortified gate in the distance. A deafening din rose from the jungle insects, beginning to assemble for the night.

There are a lot of ways to get into someone's house. You can dress all in black, paint your face like a soldier, climb a tree, jump over the fence, and elude the guards and the snarling Dobermans waiting to rip you to pieces on the other side. Then you can shimmy up an outside wall of the house like you're free climbing El Capitan, wiggle through an open window, and fall, if you're lucky, into an empty room. And there you are. Broken and entered.

Or you can crash the gate with your Kevlar reinforced SUV, shoot the guards, and break down the front door. Then you can take hostages and demand information. Less subtle certainly, but in the end no less effective.

Or you can knock and hope the occupant invites you in, which was my choice on this sticky, hot night. I figured Sovann would find it so strange that I'd come right up to his door that he'd let me in simply to satisfy his curiosity.

The guards, of course, held me at gunpoint while they asked Mr. Sovann if he was expecting me. He wasn't but that didn't stop him from opening the gate. One of the guards drove me to the mansion's front door in a golf cart while holding his AK-47 across his lap, barrel casually pointed at my stomach.

Once I was inside, the maid led me to the library. Surrounded by rich cherry paneling and antique oriental rugs, among bookcases holding a multitude of unopened classics with oiled leather covers, sat tiny Sovann. He was dressed up like an English gentleman, relaxing at the country estate the night before the annual foxhunt. Satin smoking jacket, silk ascot, slippers with a Chinese dragon motif. I smiled. I couldn't help it.

"Welcome, Miss Sally Sin!" he said with exaggerated enthusiasm. "I've been expecting you. Please sit down. Make yourself at home. My home is your home." He puffed deliberately on a cigarette held in a long ivory holder, spinning it ever so slightly between his delicate fingers.

I did as I was told although I wasn't convinced by the "my home is your home" bit.

"I am assuming you are here to see the temples, to take some special time among our beautiful wonders of the world. Perhaps a chance to rekindle your spirit after a trying year?" Sovann's English was formal, the result, I found out later, of a long affair with his private tutor who learned English from old *Masterpiece Theatre* reruns such as *Upstairs, Downstairs*. She obviously enjoyed the upstairs part the best.

"Who doesn't want to see the temples?" I asked. "Why would I come all this way and not see the temples?" Sovann smiled. It was not a warm and fuzzy smile.

"If that were true, I'd be happy to offer you tea and let you be on your way. But . . ."

"But?"

"I fear that you are not telling me the truth. There is no honor in deception, Sally Sin. I suggest you head back home. The jungle is no place for a nice girl like you."

Boy, people were really anxious to get me to go home, although I did appreciate that he thought I was nice.

"Who are you selling to?" I asked, starting to sweat a little in the heat of the room.

"See? There you go again. Are you not paying attention?"

"I never was very good at following the rules."

"Yes, that's what I've been told." Sovann looked thoughtful, as if trying to figure out how to dispose of me without messing up the carpet. Behind him, mounted above his massive mahogany desk, was a row of surveillance monitors. One of the eyes kept a steady gaze on two armed guards standing outside of what looked like the hulking shadow of a warehouse. Was this where he kept what he was preparing to sell to the Blind Monk? Was I that close?

"Listen," I said, peeling my eyes from the monitor, "you made a deal with the Blind Monk. If you back out of it, he will kill you. And it won't be pretty or fast. I don't know what Blackford has told you, but none of it is true. He can't protect you from the Blind Monk. He wants what you have stockpiled out there and will say anything to get it. You can't listen to him."

"Are you giving me career advice?" Sovann asked, breaking into a wormy smile. "How kind."

Suddenly, I heard a scream. There are many kinds of screams. Those of surprise or shock or terror or hysteria. Or those of pain, excruciating or otherwise. This was one of the latter. The doors of the library flew open and two men entered, dragging a third man between them. The two men standing were Cambodian. The man on the floor was none other than Roger, the scientist who had been out looking for pretty purple flowers.

"Oh shit," I said. Roger was bloody, although not so much so that he was in danger of anything beyond passing out. His face was bruised, but cautiously. These men had knocked him around but not in any serious life-threatening way. They dropped Roger at my feet. He moaned pathetically. Sovann, still in his chair, examined the both of us.

"It's my day for Europeans, I suppose," he said.

"I'm not European," I said.

"What's the difference? You all look alike to me."

Sovann pointed at the crumpled Roger with his cigarette holder. "This fat man was caught snooping in places he ought not to have been. He's lucky he's still in one piece, being as he won't tell us who he is. Perhaps you can tell me? Is he one of yours?"

"No. He's not mine. He's a scientist."

With that, Sovann squealed with laughter. "This fat man? A scientist? In the jungle? And pigs will walk!"

"Pigs will fly," I corrected.

"What about pigs? Oh, never mind. Who cares who he is? My inclination is to kill you both and be done with it. I have things to do other than deal with intruders all day long."

I didn't think reminding him that he had invited me in would improve things much.

Meanwhile, Roger had pulled himself up to sitting, wiping his forehead with the back of his hand, eyes wide at the sight of blood and sweat that appeared there. He leaned heavily on my legs, almost knocking me over backward.

"Hey, down there," I whispered, "take it easy."

Finally, Roger looked up, a surprised expression replacing the one of abject fear.

"You? From the train?"

"Yup."

"I'm confused. You were sightseeing. Temples. Nirvana. That sort of thing."

"Um, not really."

"Where am I? Who are these people?"

"Now is not a good time," I said, gesturing at our grim hosts.

"Right. Of course," Roger said.

"So before I dispose of the two of you," Sovann interrupted, "I want you to understand something, Sally. I'm not afraid of the Blind Monk. I'm not afraid of Ian Blackford. This is my country. I own it and I'll do what I want."

Roger stared at me, eyes huge, lips quivering. I could feel him shaking against my legs.

"These men are not your friends. If you agree to turn yourself over to me, my organization can protect you."

Sovann snorted at the audacity of my suggestion, accidentally getting smoke up his nose, causing him to lapse into a coughing fit. He turned so red I thought he might actually pass out, which would have improved our situation immensely. But no.

"Why would I ever do that?" Sovann sputtered.

"I don't know," I shrugged. "But I had to mention it." My gaze floated up to the ceiling. Constellations, painted in the finest detail, brought the night sky into Sovann's library.

"Must have cost a fortune," I said quietly. "Beautiful work."

"Yes, an Italian artist. Enjoys Cambodian boys and working on my ceiling."

"You didn't need to tell me that," I said. "Why would you tell me that? Now you've gone and ruined the ceiling for me."

"Are you stalling, Sally Sin, trying to think of a plan to save yourself and your scientist? Don't think you can use any spy tricks on me, dearie. I'm better than that."

Before he could properly finish putting me in my place, I heard a loud pop. A split second later, the huge picture window behind Sovann's throne exploded. I threw myself over Roger, hiding my face and closing my eyes. Sovann shrieked. It sounded like a small animal caught in a trap. The glass rained down on us. I felt a shard slice my exposed arm, the warm blood running down toward my wrist. Sovann continued to scream. His soldiers, still huddled near the floor, hands protecting their heads, made no move to save the general.

I shook the glass off me like a wet dog after a swim. Pulling Roger to his feet, I made sure he had on shoes and I shoved him forward, toward the broken window.

"Go! Now."

"What? What's happening?" Roger was confused, shocked, but did what I said. The glass crunched under our feet.

"Stop them!" Sovann howled.

I heard another pop.

"Down!" I shouted. Roger fell to the floor, covering his head and face as best he could. The second picture window exploded. More screaming from Sovann.

"Shit!" No time to wait. We were going to resemble colanders by the time we made it out of here.

"Up. Now." I shoved Roger toward the gaping holes, ragged as shark's teeth. And before he could consider alternatives, I pushed him out of the second-story window. I knew there was a lush tropical garden bed under there. Maybe our luck would change and we'd land on it. I heard Roger hit the ground with a sickening thud. Or maybe not. I jumped. I figured we had about ten seconds before the guards would come bursting out of the house, spraying bullets like water from a fire hose.

The landing was not soft. My skin was slick with sweat and blood. Roger lay still among the sweet-smelling frangipani. But I could hear him breathing, so all was not lost. About fifty feet to our left, beyond Sovann's exquisitely manicured gardens and lawns, was the jungle. Like at the temples, it was simply biding its time until it could once again consume all these pathetic attempts at civilization. Now, the jungle at night was about as appealing as an evening swim from Gansbaai Beach with one of your legs cut off, but it wasn't as if we had much choice.

"Get up. Time to go," I said. "Or die here in a bed of lovely tropical flowers."

A small voice came up from the heap that was Roger. "I'm considering all options."

"Well, your demise won't be nearly as poetic as it sounds." I hauled him to his feet and pushed his great mass toward the dark edge of the jungle.

It's not easy to move through a dense jungle in the best of circumstances, which these certainly were not. A short distance in, we huddled down and tried to be as still as possible. The guards spread out across the lawn, weaving through the gardens, shouting commands, and trading insults. A squad of six headed down the driveway, the most obvious escape route because even they wouldn't believe we'd be stupid enough to go into the jungle at night.

"Don't even blink," I whispered to Roger.

Flashlight beams swept right in front of where we sat. But this jungle was so thick that unless the guards were actually upon us, we would remain invisible. Ten long minutes passed and they gave up. I could hear them berating each other for losing us, working up the nerve to go back inside and tell one very angry Sovann that not only were we gone, but there was no sign of whoever had shot out the windows. We stayed completely still for another five minutes, and right around the time when I thought we might be able to wait them out and kind of creep down the driveway undetected, I heard a most unpleasant noise, the snorting, snarling growl of a guard dog.

"We need to go now," I said, turning to head deeper into the thicket.

"That way?"

"Yes. Why? You have a better idea?"

"No, not really."

"Fabulous, get moving."

We plunged, unwilling but desperate, deeper into the tangle. Behind me, I could hear Roger wheezing with exertion. But I suspected he would rather die of an asthma attack than let me get too far ahead.

"This is dangerous," he managed between gasps. "A jungle like this, well, something very bad could happen to us."

"Other than being shot at, you mean?"

"You are not the easiest person to talk to," Roger said. He hunched over, hands on his knees, trying to catch his breath. His bald spot was shiny with sweat and glowed in the darkness.

"I get that sometimes."

"Who *are* you? And what are you doing here? Because this has turned out to be a very unusual day. If you don't tell me, I swear I will dedicate the rest of my life to finding out."

"Here's hoping that will be longer than ten minutes. Now please shut up, will you?" All around us was silence. The guards had retreated. The dogs had retreated. Better to lose one's prey than to follow it into the jungle in the dead of night. Great.

"Let's take a moment and assess our situation, shall we?" I suggested.

I spun around in a slow circle, trying to find anything to orient myself in a darkness challenged only by a silvery sliver of moon. Roger sat down on the thick jungle floor.

"We are in the jungle," I began.

"No shit, Sherlock," Roger muttered from his position at my feet.

"Hey! Enough of that. You are not allowed to be snippy unless you have a better plan and I think we already agreed that you don't."

"I might come up with one if I had more time and perhaps a piece of paper and a pencil," he sniffed. I ignored him.

"It's night," I said. "We have no supplies. There is practically no moon and I can't remember how I'm supposed to use it to navigate anyway, so that's a complete loss. But the jungle. We have the jungle. All this jungle. So much jungle." I sat down next to Roger.

"I hate the jungle," I said.

"What have you got against the jungle?"

"Where does one begin?" I asked. "Hot, wet, bugs, spiders, snakes, land mines, angry man-eating vines that grow six inches a minute, unexploded ordnance from a war that never happened. And oftentimes, if I'm really lucky, like now for example, men with guns trying to kill me."

"That was a rhetorical question, but the way you describe it sounds lovely, especially the land mines part."

"Yes, that's certainly a highlight," I said. "Now let's go. Get up."

"Which way?"

"I have no fucking idea," I said. "How about that way?"

"We're going to die," Roger moaned.

"Maybe. It's always a possibility. Up. Time to move."

We began a slow, arduous trek through the nighttime jungle in a direction I hoped would run parallel to Sovann's long driveway, eventually dumping us out on the dirt road I came in on.

"Can you please explain to me what made you think you could go poking around Sovann's place without getting caught? Do you know who he is? Whatever you are searching for, it cannot be important enough," I said, trying to stomp down a particularly dense section of vine.

"Your name is not Camilla, is it?" I could hear Roger close behind me, swatting at the plate-size mosquitoes that had finally discovered our hot, sweaty bodies. If we were truly blessed, we'd both leave this jungle with a whopping case of malaria.

"No, it's not. What were you thinking?"

"Well, I didn't mean to end up there," Roger said, grunting as one of the vines whipped him in the face. "I was given some information and paid rather well to follow up on it. "

I took a minute to digest that.

"Who do you work for?" Roger asked, waiting for me to clear the way. "What is the Agency? What was Sovann talking about back there?"

"I think a better question is who do *you* work for?"

"Oh, I can't tell you that. I signed confidentiality papers."

"Well, in that case, maybe I'll leave you here."

"No! Wait. Being as we're probably going to die anyway, I suppose it can't do any harm. I was hired anonymously to see if I could find the mythical Blue Wing Lily. My source was supposed to have found new evidence of its existence. I rarely go into the field anymore, but how could I say no to all that money?"

"Did your source tell you why he was looking for this particular flower?"

"Well, everyone knows about the Blue Wing Lily and its ability to alter consciousness."

"In a good way?"

"No. Definitely not in a good way."

I didn't think so.

"And it's supposed to be here, in the middle of nowhere?"

Roger shrugged. "So they say."

"I hope it's a really pretty flower, Roger."

"Yes. I agree. Do you really think we are going to get out of here?"

"Alive? Of course," I said, grabbing onto a thick vine and pulling. This one came off with surprising ease. I threw it back over my shoulder. Roger screamed, the snake, my easy vine, now awake and dangling around his neck, hissing and spitting.

"Get it off me!" I couldn't see well enough to determine if the snake was poisonous, so I said a quick prayer that it wasn't and snatched it behind its head, tossing it to the ground. There it sat, coiled and ready to strike.

"Don't move," I whispered. We stared at the snake and it stared at us. Finally, it decided we weren't worth it and slithered off into the jungle. Our first break.

"Damn," Roger said, swatting furiously at the accumulating bugs, the sweat pouring down his face. "This is crazy."

"I'll say. But look on the bright side. At this moment I'm not frantically trying to suck snake venom out of your neck."

"Are you a blind optimist or just completely insane?" Roger asked. It didn't seem like a question worth answering. We trudged on. I figured it was about one ridiculously long mile from Sovann's house to the dirt road.

"I heard something when they were holding me back there," Roger said after a while. I paused for a moment in my bushwhacking and wiped my dripping forehead with the back of my arm, which served only to spread the blood from my various wounds all over my face. Couldn't win for trying around here.

"What did you hear?"

"The guards in the room where they were holding me. They were talking about the coming wave of blood. Something along those lines."

"You speak Cambodian?"

"No, but I can understand some of it."

"Did they say anything else?"

"They were afraid, thinking about not sticking around."

"And that was it? No more details?"

"That was it. What do you suppose a wave of blood means?"

I took a deep breath, gearing up to continue my battle with the jungle.

"I don't know exactly. But I think it's a safe bet to say it's not good." I crushed a huge bug on the inside of my thigh, the wet guts stuck like glue to my fingers. I didn't want to think about the leeches clinging to my ankles contentedly guzzling down my blood like it was happy hour, and I thought it wise not to mention them to Roger yet either. We kept going, slowly pushing forward. I prayed we weren't walking in circles.

We both smelled the flowers at the same moment. It was a silky scent, floral and light and somehow damp, too. It was soft but all-encompassing, wrapping us completely in its warmth. We stopped abruptly and took a few deep breaths.

"What is that?" Roger asked.

"I don't know. Isn't this your area of expertise?"

The scent grew more potent the longer we stood there, intoxicating, sickly sweet. "They told me to expect this but wow . . . it's . . . magical," Roger said.

"Did your source tell you?"

"What?"

"You just said you were told to expect this. Who told you?"

"What?" he said again, sounding stoned. And I gave up, the fragrance somehow making it okay for me to not give a shit. Our dire situation suddenly seemed irrelevant and silly.

"It's wonderful," I agreed.

"I'd like to eat it," Roger cooed, as if he was talking to a baby. I giggled and my face felt like Jell-O.

We looked around to see if we could identify the plants, but the darkness and the jungle did not cooperate. I wanted to stop and roll around in the scent like a cat in a bed of catnip until someone thought to rescue us. Which would probably be never at the soonest, but I didn't care.

But there was the voice in the back of my head, sounding suspiciously like Simon Still, telling me to get the fuck up.

"Okay, okay," I said, when it appeared the voice would not be shoving off any time soon. "Roger, we need to keep going."

"Poppies, poppies," Roger murmured, staggering around like a drunk.

"Don't sit down!" I shouted, sure I could never get him back up without the assistance of a crane. "You are not Dorothy and that is not the Emerald City over there. That is more impenetrable Cambodian jungle and it is the middle of the night, do you hear me? Now stand up!" I pushed him forward.

"Wait!" He got down on his hands and knees and started crawling around on the ground. "A sample," he said. "I need a sample if we are going to grow it."

Grow it, I wanted to ask, and do what with it? But any questions would have to wait. I grabbed Roger by the back of his sweaty shirt and, with my remaining strength, pulled him back up on his feet, steering us as far away as possible from the mind-bending scent of those flowers.

With the first rays of light, I saw the cut of the road in the jungle. We'd been bushwhacking with nothing but our hands, my hands, for what felt like an eternity. My tongue was dry and swollen in my mouth. My fingers were raw and burning. Roger was barely upright. I sat him down and popped out onto the road to see if Sovann and his men were waiting to mow us down for our effort. But there was no one, only the low hum of Rangsey's motorbike approaching.

"Here is our ride," I said, trying to get Roger upright.

"Mr. Ford and I thank you for saving my life, Camilla or whoever you are," Roger whispered. "God knows you didn't have to."

I dropped him to the ground.

"Mr. Ford?" I asked, my dehydrated stomach clenching in a tight knot. "Does your Mr. Ford happen to have blue eyes, really blue eyes?"

"Funny you should ask that," Roger said, his head bobbing around oddly on his neck. "Yes, he does. A lovely color, like a Centaurea cyanus. The cornflower." And with that he passed out. No, no, no. I shook him hard.

"Wake up!"

"Sally, are you trying to kill him?" Rangsey asked, pulling up beside me.

"I'm considering it," I said. I mean a personal botanist? What kind of person has a personal botanist? Now I could understand an accountant, a secretary, a lawyer, a hairstylist even. But a botanist? Not so much. I got down on the ground and put my lips right up against Roger's ear.

"Did he shoot out those windows?" I shouted. "Did he set me up to save you? Is he everywhere?" Roger did not even stir.

"Hey, Sal?"

"What?" Rangsey was staring at my legs.

"That's a lot of leeches, Sally."

I looked down and almost swooned. My legs were thick with the bulging bloodsuckers. I was definitely being punished. Slowly I began to pluck them off, fat and soft between my fingers. The blood flowed freely from the little holes they left behind, like a red rivulet down my ankles and onto the dusty road. Maybe this was what the guards meant when they were talking about the coming wave of blood? But somehow I didn't think so.

13

The night that Theo was born, deep in the winter rainy season, the wind was howling so intensely I thought the heavens might actually split at the seams. Will and I were watching TV. I was alternatively standing, sitting, lying on the floor, bending over the couch, and complaining.

"Should we start counting?" Will asked, tension spread across his normally calm and serene visage.

"Counting what?" I snapped. "Sheep?"

Will picked up the day's *Wall Street Journal* and held it between us like a wall.

"The paper is upside down," I said. He flipped it but continued to use it as a shield. He was patient. He would wait for me to answer his question about counting the contractions if he ended up having to deliver the baby himself, which was not something I saw myself enjoying.

"The doctor said a pain moving from back to front in waves," I said. "This is not a pain moving back to front in waves. It is a pain from my head to my toes and not taking the time to do the wave thing. So I don't think it's it."

"Are you sure?"

Just as he asked, I felt a huge gush of warm water cascading down my legs.

"No," I said meekly. "Definitely not sure."

"Shit!" Will jumped up from the couch, ran down the hallway, ran back, did a lap around the couch, and stopped short in front of me, still standing in my puddle.

"What are you doing?" I asked.

Will started to laugh. "I don't know," he said.

"You need to calm down now, okay?"

"Okay, okay." He nodded, regaining his composure. "I'll get your bag. Let's go."

At the hospital, the nurse yelled at me. "Why did you wait so long? What were you doing?"

I shrugged. "I didn't think this was it."

"Not it? This baby is almost ready for college!" With that she took off down the hall, barking orders at everyone she passed.

Will stroked my hair and looked adoringly into my eyes. "I think it's too late for the epidural," he said.

I thought about that for a moment. As every spy I knew, I'd taken the occasional beating on behalf of my country. But I'd never been broken, never gave up anything that I wasn't supposed to. As the searing pain in my abdomen gathered force, I hoped that would count for something.

"Try breathing," Will suggested.

"I am breathing," I growled. "If I wasn't I'd turn blue and die. Got it?"

Will closed his eyes and gathered his resources. "You are a strong person, Lucy, stronger than anyone I know. You can do this."

To prove it, I gripped his hand so hard he winced. But I held on as the tidal waves of pain washed over me.

"Why didn't he kill me in Madrid?" I gasped, my vision blurry from exertion.

"Who, baby?" Will asked.

"Blackford," I snarled. "And how dare he go and get himself dead before he could explain?"

Will gave me a funny look. Right at that moment, the nurse returned with the doctor on call.

"How are we doing?" the doctor asked.

"She's babbling incoherently," Will said.

"Oh, that can happen. Don't pay any attention to it."

Twelve minutes later, Theo burst on the scene. And Will never asked me about Ian Blackford and why exactly he didn't kill me in Madrid.

. . .

Back at home, carrying around my wrinkled and red bundle of joy, I slipped into a fog of contentment. Yes, I was exhausted, up every two hours, wrestling with diapers and tiny little pajamas, and freaking out that my baby would die of SIDS if I didn't check his breathing every ten minutes. I was hopped-up on a cocktail of anxiety and exhaustion that reminded me of life in the field and yet I felt oddly at peace.

I knew it was weird because I'd never felt it before. It was as if the slate was suddenly wiped clean and I could start again. The person I was before was gone. I was now Theo's mom and my job was to help him grow and learn and keep him safe. That was it. Simple.

Will was impressed with my multitasking mothering skills, with my ability to talk on the phone, change the baby, feed the cat, and put away the dishes all on twenty minutes of sleep and about a hundred cups of coffee. He said I had two pairs of eyes. Which was true. When I started my Agency training, Simon told me rule number one was to grow eyes in the back of my head. So I did. They came in handy being a mother. I can't tell you how many times I've grabbed Theo as he was about to fall down a set of stairs or trip on an uneven stretch of sidewalk. Even if he's behind me, my hand flies on its own, grasping onto his collar at the last second, stopping him from tumbling into oblivion. So maybe being a spy is good training for being a mom? Maybe.

It is 8 P.M. when my husband rolls through the door into our very clean house. Theo has been fed and bathed and has been sleeping soundly for thirty minutes already. Instead of collapsing on the couch with a magazine, as I usually do, I've been pacing around trying to banish Simon Still, Ian Blackford, and the Blind Monk from my consciousness, sloshing red wine out of my very full glass with every agitated step. Short of banging my head against the actual wall, I'm at a complete loss as to how to shut off the noise in there.

Will looks at the red spots all over the floor, a small trickle of wine running down my wrist.

"Rough day?" he asks.

"No, it was fine."

"Are you sure?"

"Yes. Terrific day. Really. Here. Have some wine." I shove my dripping glass into his hand.

"I have to go to yoga in about three minutes. Can you wait for dinner until I come back? If you're starved there's food in the oven." I wonder if he can sense the nervous tension rising from me like an off-color aura.

"No, I can wait. I have a few work odds and ends to catch up on."

"Of course you do. Why wouldn't you?" I say.

"Are you sure nothing happened today? You sound a little angry."

"Nope. Perfectly fine. Not my fault you're a workaholic. Theo is asleep but you should go in and see him. If you can spare the time," I say, grabbing my yoga mat and bag and heading toward the door.

"I hope the yoga makes you feel better," Will shouts after me. "If not, you can beat me up when you get home."

As I jump in my car, I can't help but smile. I should run back in and kiss him and tell him I'm sorry for being so nasty. None of this is his fault. But I don't.

Since my meeting with Simon, I feel like I'm suffering a relapse. I'm looking around too much. I'm expecting to see something out of place. I'm waiting for someone to come at me from the shadows. It feels a bit like putting on an old but beloved leather jacket and discovering it doesn't fit exactly like it used to. Your body is different, changed in some small but fundamental way.

Avery has saved me a space on the floor between her and Sam. Sam is the only man in the class, the only grandfather, and by far the most flexible human being I've ever met. When I asked him how he got that way, he said he used to be a trapeze artist with a traveling circus. I still don't know if he was kidding.

"Sorry I'm late," I whisper, assuming my downward dog. It hurts. I can feel the pull in my ass in a way I never would have ten years ago. There is nothing like running for your life on a regular basis to keep you fit. Now I have incredibly strong arms from toting around my son, but the rest of me has gone to hell. I grimace.

"Redistribute your weight," Sam whispers. "More on your heels." I do as he says and the pressure disappears. The instructor glares at us. He would like us never to come to his class again, but cannot figure out a nice way to ask. I try to concentrate on my practice, but all I can see is Simon sitting in the Java Luv, waiting to ruin my life.

"Of course he's not dead. No one ever saw the body. You *always* see the body."

"Who's dead?" Avery asks, under her breath.

"Did I say that out loud?"

"You said something."

"Blithering," I say, tapping my head. "Mommy brain." We have moved on to sun salutations, which are far more painful than being kidnapped by a turncoat. The room is quiet, everyone trying very hard to block out the day, the frantic energy that keeps us all going from early morning until late at night.

I remember the last time I saw Ian Blackford, the last time he snuck up on me in a dark alley and, within seconds, had me over his shoulder, hauling me off to some hotel room where he would lock me in the bathroom for a while. Such a cliché to be abducted in a dark alley. I didn't even bother to scream.

"What is it this time?" I asked from my somewhat uncomfortable position dangling upside down, watching the street pass below my head.

"Time for a conference," Blackford said.

"Can you please let me walk? I'm not going to run away," I said.

"And why is that, Sally Sin? Why is it you don't run away? Do you enjoy the slightly illicit quality of our meetings?"

"What are you suggesting?"

"Exactly what I said. I think you might be disappointed if I stopped carrying you off every once in a while."

"That's ridiculous," I said with a little too much bravado, considering my situation. "Every time I see you, you threaten to kill me. It's not very nice."

"Then why don't you run?"

The real answer was because I had a sneaking suspicion that my running would do nothing more than make the game more enjoyable for Blackford. And I still had my pride. What was left of it anyway.

"No smart answer for that one?"

"I could shoot you," I said.

"Yes, but that would require you to carry your gun. Where is your gun, Sally?"

A fine question. In my desk drawer. In my office. About eight thousand miles away. But I couldn't very well tell him that.

"Fuck off, Blackford," I said instead. And that just made him laugh.

In about ten minutes, Blackford put me down. We were outside a small bar on a tight Hanoi street crowded with street vendors, scooters, chickens, and people.

"I thought I'd buy you a drink," Blackford said.

"Do you promise not to put anything in it that's likely to have me wake up thinking I'm the reincarnation of Anne Boleyn?"

"Yes, I promise."

"Does that mean anything coming from you?" I said.

He fixed those eyes on me and smiled slowly. "Yes," he said, "in fact, it does." Caught in his gaze, I almost believed him. He swung open the door to the tiny bar and we went in.

We talked about the beaches in southern Vietnam. We talked about the Guatemalan jungle and how awful a Mexican prison can be if you can't find anyone to bribe. We talked about how thin the air is at nineteen thousand feet when you are running for your life and what it feels like to watch your guy get away. In the end, there was no point to any of it. He simply said he thought we should have a drink together. He seemed a little sad, although I would never have asked him why. After an hour, I said I had to go, work to do the next morning and that sort of thing. He was the enemy after all, although I was having a hard time keeping it straight.

"It was nice to see you, Sally," he said, as we stepped out into the night. "You be good." He started to walk away.

"Wait!" I shouted. He turned back toward me, the rush of people streaming by him on both sides. He could barely hold his place on the makeshift sidewalk. "Where does this all end?" It was not a question I'd intended to ask, nor did I know exactly what I meant by it. "When I'm dead, Sally. But don't worry. It's on the horizon. I can almost see it." Then the crowd swept him away. For a few minutes, I stood there in the bar entryway, unable to shake the feeling that I would never see Ian Blackford again.

I am deep in this thought when our yoga instructor, Conrad, makes the mistake of trying to adjust my triangle pose. His job, after all, is to make my triangle the best triangle it can be. But as I said, my old habits make for unpredictable behavior. Conrad simply lays his slim, pale hand on the small of my back, attempting to shift my weight a slight bit forward. And without thinking, in one swift move, I grab his arm and pull his entire body up and through the air, bringing him down hard on his back on my not-so-soft yoga mat. The next move in this series would have my knee on his throat and my gun to his head. Fortunately, I don't have a gun and stop my knee about two inches from its destination. Suddenly, everyone in the class is bolt upright, eyes wide, staring at me and at Conrad, laid out like a rug on the studio floor.

"Oh no," I mumble, "I am so sorry." I pull Conrad up to his feet. "Are you okay?"

It takes him a second to answer. "I think so," he says.

"I'm taking this self-defense course," I start. "Maybe I'm thinking about it too much? God, I'm really sorry."

"Of course you are," he says, glaring at me. "Okay, class. Back to triangle pose, please." As he walks slowly back to the front of the class, I can see his hands are shaking. I try to regain my triangle pose but it's not looking so good.

"Holy shit," Avery whispers. "What the hell was that?"

"Nice move," Sam adds. "Where did you learn it? Because I'm not believing for a second it's from a self-defense for ladies class."

"People," Conrad shrieks. "People, please, we are here for yoga. Get centered. Now everyone assume triangle pose. Calmness, please."

He sounds like a man on the edge, and I am half sure he is going to cry. What I did was inexcusable, a classic overreaction. I blame Simon. The remaining twenty minutes of the session are disjointed. People keep looking at me, and I keep trying to ignore them. This is bad. On a lot of levels. The class ends.

"I'm really sorry, Conrad," I say.

"You *attacked* me," he says, as if he just realized it. "I'd prefer it if you practiced with another instructor from now on." With that, he turns his back on me. I could have killed you, I want to say. So maybe consider this a good day.

Out on the street, the fog has swallowed everything. As we walk through the soup, Avery and Sam beg for an explanation.

"I did some martial arts in college," I say.

"That was so fast. I mean, he flew through the air. Can you teach me that move?" Sam asks.

"No," I say, a little too loudly.

"Okay, fine. See you ladies later," Sam says, sliding behind the wheel of his BMW.

"Really, Lucy, what was that about?" Avery asks. "You scared the hell out of that guy."

"He never really liked us anyway," I say.

"True, but that doesn't mean you had to beat him up."

"That was really awful, wasn't it?" But Avery has started to laugh.

"Did you see his face? Oh my, it was hilarious. Poor thing."

Now we are both laughing and I've avoided having to explain how it came to pass that I dropped our yoga instructor to the floor with the intent of crushing his throat.

I would like to turn off these impulses forever. But that does not appear to be possible. They still lurk below the surface, and when I'm not paying attention, that's when they bubble up and shock me. I leave Avery and head toward my car, badly parked two streets over. I can beat up yoga instructors with ease, but parallel parking is still not my strong suit. Leaning against the hood, a half-smoked cigarette dangling from his lips, is Simon Still.

"I thought you quit," I say.

"I did," he says, "most of the time anyway. This city makes me want to smoke. All the fog or something."

"Did you follow me?"

"I've been freezing my ass off out here for the past hour and a half. What exactly is it you do in there anyway?"

"You should have worn another layer. And I'm not going to change my mind. Whatever you want me to do, I'm not doing it."

"You don't have a choice, Sally. I wish you did but you don't. Blackford is going to find you. How are you going to explain that to your yoga friends?"

On a logical level, I know he's right. There is no way to rewind and stop the inevitable. I just hate being used.

"I wish you hadn't done it this way, Simon," I say. "I wish you'd left me out of it."

Simon doesn't say anything. Instead, he takes deep drags on his cigarette. Blackford is Simon's white whale, and forgetting that makes me think Simon can be rational about things. And that is simply not true.

"Tell me how you found out Blackford was still alive and I'm going home. You can fill me in on whatever diabolical plan you have later."

"He sent me a letter, about a year ago, after being off the radar for the better part of six years," Simon begins. It turns out Blackford was looking to kidnap me again and thought it was odd that, for all intents and purposes, I'd vanished. He was worried I was dead. So he thought he'd go ahead and ask Simon directly. I want to laugh, but am fairly confident Simon will knock me unconscious if I do. Blackford certainly knows how to push the right buttons.

"Did he happen to mention why he wanted to see me?" I ask.

"Old times' sake. Said he missed talking to you."

"And what did you tell him?"

"Nothing. What do you think? I wrote him back? That we're pen pals now? The word was already out that you were dead, but I guess he ignored that part."

"And this professor?"

"I thought you said you wanted to wait until tomorrow?"

"Shut up, Simon. What about this mysterious professor?"

"We think Blackford is working with Professor Malcolm on a new biological weapon, something devastating. We assume this project is the reason he faked his death and went underground. He wanted to make progress on this new weapon without all the bothers that come with being alive. Our fear is that it is almost ready for delivery to Blackford's pals—North Korea, Iran, the usual suspects."

"Are you kidding? An actual mad scientist?" I say. "What is going on, Simon? Are you out playing golf all day? Is anyone minding the shop?"

"Calm down, Sal," Simon says. At which point I grab him by his coat collar and lift him two inches off the ground. Simon is a few inches taller and at least thirty pounds heavier than I am. He is surprised to be two inches off the ground. His hand swings automatically to the .357 magnum, about the size of my right arm, tucked in his shoulder holster. But he doesn't pull it out.

"You are making a big fucking mess of my life," I say, "and I want you to know I don't appreciate it."

"Put me down, Sally." Which I do. "And don't do that again." Which I won't. Simon smooths out his coat. I really should go home. This night is getting ridiculous. Who knows what I'm likely to do next?

Simon holds open his box of cigarettes, offering me one.

"No," I say, swatting his hand away like a three-year-old.

"Gee, Sal, you're not much fun anymore," Simon says.

"I never was, remember?" I say, slipping into the front seat of my car. Simon doesn't move, still leaning against my hood. I roll down my window.

"I'm leaving," I say. "And I will run you over if you don't move."

"When I call," he says, "I suggest you answer." And with that he flicks his cigarette butt over my roof and walks away into the fog.

I sit there for a minute, trying to focus all of my hate on Simon, thinking maybe I can use my mental energy to cause him to spontaneously combust or something. Alas, nothing happens and he disappears down the street.

When I get home, Will is in his office pounding away on his laptop. I put myself between him and the machine.

"How was your class?" he asks, trying to peer around me to his computer screen. "Are you still mad?"

"No," I answer. "I'm feeling very centered now." I do not tell him about how I assaulted my instructor. I do not tell him I was considering strangling my old boss.

"I'm getting the sense you don't want me to finish up here," Will says.

I slide my hands under his T-shirt, his skin warm beneath my fingers. "What gives you that idea?"

"Oh, you know, it's a thought," he says.

"You are very wise." I take a small nibble of his ear. It's salty from his afternoon workout. He pushes his laptop aside, picks me up, and puts me on the edge of his desk.

"Did all that yoga make you flexible?" he asks, burying his face in my neck. "Can I do obscene things with your legs?"

"Sky's the limit," I say.

14

Preschool days are chaos. You'd think with my background getting a small child fed, dressed, out the door, and into the car wouldn't be a big deal. Right.

"What would you like for breakfast, pumpkin?" I ask, as Theo races his Hot Wheels cars around my feet. "Waffles, pancakes, French toast, oatmeal?" I've been told never to give too many choices to children under eighteen. Clearly I haven't learned my lesson.

"French toast and waffles." He shoots one of his cars up my pants. "Whoa! Look at that go!" He stuffs his small arm up there too, in hot pursuit of the car.

"How about French toast?"

"How about spaghetti?"

"Spaghetti isn't a great choice for breakfast."

"Why?"

I have no idea. But it's not on the list.

"Because," I say. Theo makes a face that says I'm not trying hard enough.

"Meatballs?" he counters.

"How about waffles?" He shrugs.

"But no gross brown spots." It's always nice to have a child innocently point out your flaws, like my inability to make a waffle without burning it a little bit.

I pull out the waffle mix and get to work, trying to avoid the so-called gross brown spots lest I start a breakfast-related hunger strike before school. Theo eats the waffles on the kitchen floor, surrounded by his cars. School runs from 9 a.m. until noon, twice a week, the longest, most anxious hours of my life. The school is small and well protected, with one way in and one way out, all things

I looked for in a place. While everyone else was obsessing over the quality of the teaching staff, the ratio of teachers to students and how well the kids tracked to the good elementary schools, I was looking for a place from which it would be difficult to abduct my child. I leave all the breakfast dishes and pull clean clothes out of the dryer for Theo. He barely acknowledges me as I yank off his pajamas and bend him into his daytime clothes.

"Okay, time to get moving," I say, grabbing my bag from the cluttered kitchen table.

"No. Not ready yet."

"Yes, you are. We're out the door."

"No. Not ready yet."

I try not to get irritated. I really do. I mean, he's only three. It's not like he's purposely trying to drive me insane. Or is he? I reach down and scoop him up under an armpit. He howls in protest.

"I'm not finished!" he wails, still clutching at least one of his cars.

"Yes, you are. The race is over. That guy won." I point to the car in his hand.

"Nooooo. That guy never wins."

"Maybe today was his lucky day?" My suggestion is met with a pout, after which Theo folds himself into a ball and refuses to move. I pick up the whole of him and, after a struggle, get him strapped into his car seat and ready to go.

By the time we arrive at school, he is sunny and bright and can't wait to get out of the car and start his day. All in two miles. Remarkable.

After I drop him off, I walk one half block down to the Java Luv. Leonard, the tattooed barista, automatically hands me an espresso shot.

"Morning, Lucy. How's things?"

Oh, what a question! You don't want to know.

"Fine," I say. "Thanks for this." I toss back the espresso and leave the cup on the counter. In about thirty minutes, I'll order a latte and a cinnamon bun and make them both last until Theo is dismissed at lunchtime.

For now I sit at my table, eyes focused on the front door of the preschool. And I don't move.

What I should have done after my nice little stroll in the jungle was to follow everyone's advice, board the next flight out, and head home to my safe empty apartment, nice warm shower, and soft fluffy towels. I should have taken my broken body, tucked it into a comfy first-class seat, charged to Simon's personal account of course, and called it a day. But I didn't. No, that would have made too much sense.

Slipped under my door while I tried to recover from my night in the jungle with Roger was an engraved invitation to the opening gala for the Grand Event Hotel. Perfect. It was comforting to know that money could still be used to buy my way into things to which I was not actually invited, at least here. I looked at my knapsack, half open on the still-made bed. One clean white T-shirt, one pair of khaki pants, flip-flops, toothbrush. These items screamed tourist, not gala, which was kind of a problem.

The seamstress was Rangsey's cousin's wife's daughter-in-law. Or something along those lines. She was startled at my rather bedraggled appearance.

"We need much fabric to cover all this," she said, kindly pointing out the cuts, scrapes, and bruises that now comprised most of my skin. "Long sleeves, very tight, red."

"Not red. Black. And not too tight."

But at least we agreed on the need for long sleeves. I stood before her, hoping she wouldn't swallow any of the pins in her mouth as she rattled on about how this fabric was very forgiving and wouldn't cause me additional pain. Only I would end up using "potential to cause pain" as a criterion for selecting a dress. Every time this tiny woman touched me I wanted to scream. But I bit my lip and let her work her magic. The vague pattern of a dress way too sexy for me began to take shape.

"Can I wear that?" I asked her, in all seriousness. She gave me an incredulous look.

"I make, you wear," she said with authority, and that pretty much settled that. Within minutes, I fell asleep on the tattered sofa in the main room of the shop and stayed like that until, a few hours later, the seamstress shook me awake.

"Done." She held in front of her a sleek black dress with long bell sleeves and no back. The fabric draped to the floor in an elegant puddle. Not exactly the subtle I'd intended, but how could I argue when I was sleeping? I wiggled into it with some assistance and appraised the result in the full-length mirror.

"Wow. Nice work."

"Look good. You go to Grand Event?"

"Yes. Tonight."

"You stop show." Uh-oh. I peeled the dress off and pulled my own clothes back on, thanking her for her speedy work.

Rangsey met me outside. When I showed him the dress he made a strange face. "Sally in a dress. Interesting."

"Jeez. You'd think I never, you know, wore anything but this," I said, gesturing at my dull clothing.

"You don't," Rangsey pointed out.

"You're right. But I could if I wanted to."

He shrugged. "Okay."

"You're no help at all."

"Okay."

"I need some black hair dye if I have any chance of getting away with this."

"Okay. But, Sally, where are you going to keep your gun in a dress like that?"

"I don't know. I think I lost it in the jungle anyway."

"Oh, Sally," he said, sounding not unlike a disappointed parent. "Should I get you another?"

"No! Guns are dangerous." Rangsey rolled his eyes. Cambodians are fond of their guns.

. . .

The Grand Event Hotel was indeed grand, even for this outpost of civilization. Several fountains lined the long, curved driveway of the new hotel. Lights twinkled in the pools, like a reflection of the night sky. Inside, the entry hall was all gold leaf and marble and towering columns and rich upholstered furniture that promised to swallow you whole. Tuxedoed men passed trays of champagne and food that looked like it had been imported from New York. The guests, too, looked like they were mostly imported. I could feel the eyes on me the moment I walked through the door and I wondered why I'd let Rangsey's aunt's cousin's mother-in-law talk me into the three-inch stilettos. I was now taller than almost everyone else in the room. So much for blending in and being inconspicuous. I spotted Sovann right away, surrounded by his crew. He looked right at me, my first test. And nothing. No recognition. All it took was a fancy dress and jet-black hair and I was unrecognizable. I really had to do something about my wardrobe.

I was here with a vague notion of a plan, something about a last-ditch attempt to convince Sovann not to betray the Blind Monk and start a war that none of us had any hope of controlling. In my book, the controlled and orderly flow of illegal weapons was preferable to the complete chaos that a Blackford main event would bring. I was banking on Sovann being surprised enough by my being alive and here at the Grand Event that he'd have no choice but to listen to me. The trick was not to let the Blind Monk see me first.

I swept past them and began to make my way through the crowd, waiting for the right moment to get Sovann alone. I saw the Blind Monk, in a small group, looking bored. He sipped champagne and feigned interest in whatever the people around him were going on about, but his head was somewhere else. He slowly rolled his glass between his thumb and forefinger, biding his time until he could escape to something more interesting. His eyes drifted over me like I was just another vulture here for the free champagne and crab cakes. Maybe I would get away with it after all. I grabbed a glass of champagne and threw it back like I was at a football tailgate. Before the waiter could disappear, I snatched another glass. People were dancing now and I started back around the dance floor toward Sovann. My body felt battered from the long night in the jungle and the champagne only served to make me dizzy, but at least it was distracting.

"Shall we dance?" In an instant, I was spinning out on the dance floor, being led by Ian Blackford in a dark suit and pale blue tie. He looked clean and crisp, as if he'd walked in through a wall of fairy dust rather than out of this hot, steamy night.

"Didn't the invitation say black tie?" I croaked, unable to maintain anything resembling my cool.

"I don't know. I didn't get an invitation." He spun me through a waltz as if we'd been born dancing together. I tried not to think about how good he smelled. "You didn't take my advice."

"I have to try once more to convince Sovann not to sell to you," I said, with as much conviction as I could muster. My comment didn't seem to register. I started to pray that the music would stop, but it kept us turning around and around the dance floor.

"You look decidedly unlike yourself tonight, Sally," Blackford said.

"Anything for a good cause."

"Yes. I guess sometimes you have to jump off the rock, don't you think?" I shook my head. I wasn't following him.

"Never mind. Here is something you may find interesting. The Blind Monk is going to take out Sovann tonight. Here. He's always gone in for the dramatic, that one. It's going to be ugly, so don't be surprised if you end up running in that crazy dress you're wearing."

"You don't like the dress?"

"Quite the contrary, Sally. Quite the contrary."

"But why kill Sovann? The deal isn't done yet. Wait a minute. Is the Blind Monk planning on killing Sovann and stealing his stash? That seems unprofessional even for you criminal types. Besides, Sovann's got a small army out there guarding the place. I know. I saw them recently."

"The warehouse is empty, Sally," Blackford whispered in my ear. I suddenly felt sick to my stomach.

"No, it's not. I saw it on the security cameras. Last night. The warehouse was full of . . ."

Blackford smiled, enjoying my confusion. I was too late.

"Best there ever was, right?" he said. With that, we spun in a graceful circle and Blackford released me ever so gently into the crowd of guests.

When I regained my footing and frantically scanned the crowd for him, he was gone. I grabbed a glass of champagne and drank the whole thing in one gulp. Before I could wrangle yet another and get to work on getting seriously drunk, a scream erupted on the other side of the ballroom. Guests started to run, charging the exits in a panic. I pushed, like a salmon swimming upstream, toward the source of the screaming.

Blackford was right. Sovann was very dead, his throat slit in such a way that most of his blood was already spread around him in a shiny puddle. Two of his guards were also in the same condition, lifeless eyes staring up at the freshly painted cathedral ceiling. I searched the massive ballroom for the Blind Monk. He was walking, very slowly, toward the kitchen. He was not in a hurry. He even stopped to take a cold glass of champagne off of an abandoned serving tray before turning to survey the madness behind him. I was standing over Sovann and his dead friends when our eyes connected over the emptying hotel. The Blind Monk, grinning like a Cheshire cat, raised his gun and aimed it right at my chest. I froze, unable to save myself, unable to run. He casually pulled the trigger as if I were nothing more than an injured dog on the street. I felt the impact, the searing hot bullet ripping through my flesh, crashing destructively into bone, tearing and shredding my insides. I hunched over, placing my hands on the blood gushing from the wound.

But to my surprise there was none. No blood, no hole, no torn-up guts. The Blind Monk looked as confused as I was, shaking the gun and opening the barrel. The sounds of police sirens drew closer.

That was all I needed to hear to snap me back to reality. No need to hang around while the Blind Monk reloaded. I was swept up in the last wave of fleeing guests and found myself out on the dusty street in the middle of the night running for my life in a too-tight black dress and uncomfortable shoes.

15

Simon is waiting on my front porch, sunglasses on and a hat pulled down low over his eyes, when Theo and I return from preschool.

"You'd look less obvious," I say, "without the hat and glasses."

"It's the man who won't play trucks," chimes Theo. "Does he want chocolate milk too?"

"I don't know," I say, staring at Simon, "but my guess is probably yes."

I unlock the front door and the three of us pile into the foyer. Simon does a quick appraisal.

"Nice place," he says. "You chose wisely with old William, Sal. Keeps you in the style to which you had become accustomed."

"Theo, can you go and play with your toys?"

"Yes, Mommy," he says, like the Dr. Jekyll to this morning's Mr. Hyde, and skips off to the playroom. Simon follows me in the other direction toward the kitchen. My heart is beating too fast and I can't slow it down.

"Okay, so tell me," I say without preamble.

"The plan is very basic. You will go about your business, live your normal life, and Blackford will find you. When he shows himself, we'll pick him up. Easy."

And it sounds easy. Except in my experience, easy never works. Easy always ends up being complicated. Remember me dangling over the Chao Phraya in Bangkok?

"That's not a plan, Simon. That's just a hope."

"Well, Sal," he says, a little exasperated, "you go to war with the army you have, not the one you wish you had."

"That might be the stupidest thing I've heard all day. And it doesn't even make sense in this situation."

Simon continues. "We are going to install an agent as your nanny to give Blackford a chance at you when you are alone."

"No," I say, automatically, "that's not going to happen."

"Do you want your kid in harm's way?"

"Oh, stop acting like you care, Simon. You're the one who put him in this situation in the first place."

"I'm sorry, Sal. But this is the way it has to be. It will be over soon. I promise."

A promise from Simon Still is not worth much, but I don't point that out to him. I pick up the Matryoshka dolls from the kitchen floor. I methodically begin taking them apart. When I reach the littlest doll, I shake it. The rhythm is soothing. I put the dolls back together and place them on the counter. Simon watches me silently.

"I'll send her over for you to meet in the morning," he says, finally. "And all the old rules apply. No one needs to know what is going on." With that, Simon gets up, puts his coat on, and heads toward the front door.

"Good luck, Sal," he tosses over his shoulder.

"Lucy," I yell after him. "My name is Lucy."

"No, it's not. But I won't tell anyone." And he is gone, but the idea of him lingers in my kitchen like the smell of bacon three hours after you are done cooking it.

I find Theo curled up on his bedroom rug, clutching his favorite blanket in one hand and a toy train in the other. I sit down on the floor next to him and watch him sleep. I run my fingertips over his cheek and he twitches at my touch. As I slide both hands under his little body and lift him into his bed, the train falls from his hand, but he keeps a tight grip on the blanket. Once in bed, he rolls onto his belly, buries his hands under his chest, and pops his backside straight up in the air. I stroke his hair and silently promise him I will not let these particular monsters out of the closet.

. . .

Even before Simon Still showed back up in my life, I would be the first to admit some cracks were starting to show. Not so many that I couldn't manage them, but some cracks nonetheless.

Like the incident in East Palo Alto, for example, a part of town the residents would really like to see go away. Or, at the very least, have the decency to change its name to something like, say, Nothing to Do with Palo Alto. I was taking a shortcut back to the freeway when my very new car suddenly got a very flat tire. And looking at the road littered with nails and glass, I thought of the Ivory Coast and had the sneaking suspicion it was all a setup meant to conclude with the jacking of my fuel-efficient hybrid. Theo continued to nap in his car seat as I climbed out with a sigh.

"Inconvenient," I muttered, stepping back and appraising the situation. Did fuel-efficient hybrids have spare tires or was that considered a luxury? I pulled out my cell phone and called roadside assistance, or at least my version of it.

"Does this thing have a spare?" I asked the second Will picked up. "I mean, is it included, full of real air and all that, or is it a do-it-yourself kind of thing where I need to blow it up?"

"Lucy, there is a spare right in the trunk where spares usually reside. Would you like me to call Triple A for you?"

No, I just want my old car back.

"No," I said. "I can manage. Theo is asleep anyway."

"Where are you?"

"Palo Alto." Sort of.

"Okay, call me back if you need help and I'll send someone. Call me back anyway."

"Fine," I said, still a little huffy at his having stolen my car and replaced it with this fuel-efficient go-cart. Secretly, the thing was growing on me, but I'd never tell Will. He'd give me that "I told you so" look and I'd be bitter all over again.

This particular neighborhood is crowded with bungalows in disrepair, shutters falling off, paint peeling, fences tipped over and broken. Sadly, a few miles down the road, these same houses would sell for millions. I surveyed the street and saw no one hiding in the bedraggled shrubs waiting to leap out and rob me. Maybe I was wrong, guilty of always thinking the worst.

I headed to the trunk to get the jack and the spare. Opening the trunk, I knew two things: 1) There were more stuffed animals jammed into it than seemed possible for the space, and 2) they were behind me, probably seven or eight of them. Young, I could tell from the sounds of their nervous shuffling feet. Okay, so if pressed, I'd probably describe them more like thugs than anything else, complete with do-rags, jeans down to their ankles, newly minted gang tattoos, and bad attitudes. I had to smile at the scene. Gangsta wannabes land Prius with woman and very small sleeping child. It was too easy. How could they resist? I almost couldn't blame them.

They approached with that walk that I can't stand and don't get, sort of sliding along, holding their pants up with one hand. It's hard to look cool with your pants falling off, but I guessed no one had mentioned that to them. It's also hard to run away with your pants bunched up around your feet. But we'll get to that.

For a moment, I thought they might offer to help, but that was only for a moment. The leader stood over me. I held a two-foot-tall, striped orange Tigger in my right hand. How it ended up in my trunk is anybody's guess.

"You shouldn't be here," the boy said, eyeing the stuffed tiger with a hint of confusion.

"Well, I don't plan on staying," I said. "I'm changing a tire."

"There's a penalty for that," he said. He couldn't stop looking at Tigger.

"No," I said, shaking the tiger at him, "there isn't."

"You dissin' me, suburban lady?" His eyes darted side to side, surveying the reaction from his buddies. He was a newcomer to this gang leadership thing and suffered from a touch of performance anxiety.

"No," I answered, getting irritated. "I'm changing my tire and you're distracting me."

He turned to his boys. "You hear this? She says I'm distracting her." His posse, on cue, started hooting and hollering and pumping up this teenager who had nothing in his life but the hooting and hollering of these wayward children.

"Listen," I said, "you seem like a smart kid. Probably could do something more interesting with your life than this. So why don't you turn around and head on back the way you came. You can even have the tiger, if that will help."

His eyes widened in response, equally shocked that I wasn't afraid of him and that I was offering him life advice, not to mention a giant stuffed animal. He hitched up his pants, first on one side and then the other. They immediately started to slide back down his skinny hips, pulled by gravity and a huge studded belt.

"And what is with the pants?" I asked, sitting Tigger on the bumper.

All the boys looked at their pants.

"What's wrong with our pants?" someone asked from the back. The leader gave him a dirty look for speaking out of turn, but the boy shrugged, as if to say he really did want to know what was wrong with his pants.

"Your intention is to jack my car, right?"

The group nodded in unison, looking all of a sudden innocent and very young.

"But you are not all going to fit. It's a Prius, if you haven't noticed. You know, gets great gas mileage, doesn't require a key in the ignition to start, and even if you have perfect hearing it stands a pretty good chance of running you over, it's that quiet. But this particular car has a seating capacity of five and that's if you squish yourselves into the backseat. Are you following me?"

All the heads bobbed up and down, except for the leader, who was starting to look frantic.

"So let's do the math here. Five seats, eight criminals. What does that leave us?"

"Three criminals with no seats!" the youngest boy, hidden in the back, shouted out.

"Very good. So three of you are going to have to run because you won't fit in the car. And running very fast in those pants, well, we all know how that goes."

Silence. "You're fucking with us," the leader said. "Now get out of the way so we can take the car."

He stepped forward, sliding his fingers under the handle of the rear passenger door, behind which my baby continued to sleep peacefully.

"Get your hands off my car," I said quietly. He laughed, a cynical, sad laugh.

"Or what?" he said. I took a step forward, eye to eye with this boy.

"Step away from the car and we'll call it good." But even as the words left my lips I knew this was going to end badly for this kid. He couldn't back off now, not in front of his boys. If he did, he would lose their respect and be relegated back to the rank and file, which I knew he'd worked hard to rise above. I almost felt bad for him. Almost.

"Please," I said, tossing him a last chance, "take the tiger and head on out."

"No one tells me what to do in my 'hood," he replied with his most intimidating snarl.

The moves came with ease, sort of like riding a bike. The tire iron connected with the soft flesh of his throat with such force that he immediately dropped to the ground, gasping for air. To help him out, I grabbed his hair and pulled his head back, straightening out his windpipe and letting him take a breath. One of the boys in the group had, by now, pulled out his gun and, although his hand was trembling, he aimed it at me the best he could.

"Put that thing away," I said, pointing at him with the tire iron. That seemed to be enough. The ringleader was still sucking wind at my feet. "Take your friend here to a hospital. He needs treatment."

The boy with the gun nodded.

"Yeah, hospital," he repeated.

"Now," I said. "And give me that Glock. You're going to hurt someone." The boy, still shaking, handed me the gun. I dropped the clip and ejected the remaining bullet from the chamber. As it fell, I caught it in the air and simultaneously pushed the button to the side of the safety that released the slide from the body of the gun. With that, the entire thing fell into ten pieces on the ground. I kicked them to the curb for emphasis.

The boys stood watching, dumbfounded.

"Your friend here doesn't feel so well," I reminded them, pointing to the ringleader now flat on his face in the dust. "Hospital. Now."

I went back to the trunk to take out my spare tire. The boys gathered up their friend. But they found it hard to hold up their pants and hold up their friend at the same time. There was some internal discussion about how to manage this situation and still look cool. Two of the boys rolled the tops of their pants over a few times so now they almost fit correctly. Finally they scooped up their leader, whose skin grew more ashen by the second.

"What do we tell them at the hospital?" one of the junior thugs asked, looking a little sheepish. "They always ask, you know, when there is blood and stuff."

"Well, what do you usually tell them?"

The boy shrugged. "Gang stuff."

"Why don't you try telling them the truth?"

The boy's eyes opened wide. "I don't know about that."

"Well then why are you asking me? I'm busy here. Have to change the tire that you boys ruined. Now go."

They nodded their heads and started toting their wheezing leader down the street to an old Honda Accord, probably stolen right here, arguing amongst themselves about what to tell the hospital.

I finished changing my tire and went home, ready to tuck the incident away in the catacombs of my memory.

Two days later, there is a tiny mention of it in the paper, something about a woman with a flat tire and beating up a local gang member and how police were looking to question her. Will didn't say anything, but he did cut the piece out and leave it on the kitchen table, under the salt shaker. Did he mean it as a cautionary tale, an indication that I should probably stick to the main routes nowadays?

Did he think it was me the police were looking for? Either way, I crumpled it up and tossed it into the recycle bin, hoping that would be the end of it.

But would I have told him the truth if he asked me directly? And why didn't he ask? There is a part of me that believes Will doesn't want to know the truth, whatever it is. Because then he and I and this whole world we've created comes crashing down around us and all the king's horses and all the king's men would not be able to put it back together again.

16

When I married Will, I was more concerned about when I would have another opportunity to rip his clothes off and less about what normal married life actually looks like. I could not conceive a life with a house, a car, a couple of kids, roast beef on Sundays, and the like. I didn't think there was any way a girl like me could live like that.

And Will hadn't exactly planned on a girl like me either. There were times when I would catch him staring at me and I swear I could read his mind. It went something like this: "Maybe I have taken this rebellion against my parents one step too far. Maybe I didn't actually have to go for the gold and ask her to marry me."

Soon after I moved into Will's condo, his ex-girlfriend Laura paid me a visit. As it turned out, I wasn't that busy, having no friends to meet, no job to go to, and no belongings to unpack. She didn't knock or ring the bell; instead, using her old key, she barged right in and found me sitting on the floor reading magazines. At first, I thought she was there to kill me, for thinking I could retire from the Agency or something crazy like that. But after a second I recognized her from the photos Will had discreetly hidden away when I first arrived.

"So you're it," she sneered. I can't be sure, but I'd put money on her having had a few martinis for breakfast. She looked around the place with distaste.

"This place looks like shit," she continued.

"I'm Lucy," I said, standing up.

"I know that," she hissed. "Everyone knows that. But I had to see the competition in person."

Competition? This was getting scary.

"I will get him back," she slurred. "No, that's not exactly right. He will come crawling back. You'll see. I mean, look at you, what are you really? Who are you? You're nobody. William would not be so stupid as to marry someone who isn't really anyone."

How right you are, I wanted to say. But instead I stood there, quietly, waiting for her to finish.

Her tirade was obviously exhausting because before I knew it she was passed out on the couch. I called Will at the office.

"Your ex-girlfriend is passed out on the couch," I said.

"You're kidding?"

"Do I sound like I'm kidding? Here, you can listen to her snoring." I held the phone up to Laura's slightly sagging mouth. "See? I'm not kidding. Is there a protocol I should follow for this situation?"

"Oh, for God's sake. Okay. I'm on my way."

I almost volunteered to take care of Laura myself, but I got the feeling that Will's definition of taking care of someone and mine were vastly different. He arrived home thirty minutes later, but Laura still hadn't moved an inch.

"This is ridiculous," he said, standing over her. "I thought we could deal with this as adults, but obviously I was wrong. What is she doing here? Did she say?"

"She came over to check out the competition or something like that. Basically, I think she wanted to see who took her place in your bed. Morbid fascination maybe?"

"I'm so sorry," Will said, rubbing his temples as if the whole episode was giving him a splitting headache.

"This isn't going to work," I said suddenly.

"No, she obviously can't stay here, but we have to wait for her to wake up."

"No," I said, "I mean this, you and I, this isn't going to work. I have no business being here. This is her house, her life. I don't belong here."

Will rubbed more vigorously at his temples. All that rubbing made the hair on the sides of his head stick straight out.

"God, Laura, you always were good at making things complicated," he said.

"And you," he continued, taking me firmly by the shoulders, "I
love you. I look forward to waking up now because I know the first
thing I'll see will be your face. I think about you all the time, every
moment of the day, every second. Everything in my life is brighter,
better, and that is because you are in it. Does that make sense? You
belong here. With me. There is no question in my mind that we met
on that dive boat in Hawaii because we were supposed to. We are
meant to be together. That's a fact." Then he put those lips to mine
and I thought maybe I could believe him, that maybe the doubt I
sometimes saw in his eyes was all in my head.

The next day the condo was on the market and Will put a bid on
the place that I now call home. I still run into Laura on occasion.
We both pretend not to notice one another, and life goes on without
incident.

Will and I make a good pair. He is calm, efficient, logical, and
yet hopelessly romantic. He never lets the practical get in the way of
the desirable. The truth is my experience with men before him was
limited mostly to those I met while masquerading as someone else.
In the occasional honest throes of physical passion, I had to work
hard to remember what language I was supposed to be speaking.
These relationships were doomed from the start. You cannot build
a lasting foundation with someone if you cannot tell him your
address.

But on the flip side, this small fact made these relationships,
if you can even call them that, very straightforward. There were
no romantic entanglements to distract me, no obligations that I
could not possibly meet. These men came in and out of my life,
leaving nothing but the vague sense of having lost some time and
the knowledge that on some level this was not the way it was meant
to be.

The first time I saw Will, his slow smile and the outline of his
eyes hidden behind dark sunglasses, I felt something in me give. It
started small like a ripple on a pond and grew, within the course of

our morning dive, into a tidal wave. It was desire but not just the primal kind. It was the desire to read a magazine in my own bath-tub with my own towels in my own house, and climb into my own bed with my own sheets, and pull my own comforter up to my ears, and sleep without the fear of waking up dead. It was a deep and suddenly painful longing for normal, even if I had no idea what that looked like. And for reasons beyond my understanding, it all cen-tered on the man standing next to me, his wetsuit unzipped to the waist. I knew I was sunk.

But I know what you're thinking. That while Will knows my address, he does not know my name. How good or real can a rela-tionship be if you are not telling the truth, if you are leaving out significant pieces of information about your past? This is a very good question and one for which I have no answer. With every day that passes it becomes less likely that I can tell Will about Sally Sin. It becomes more likely that telling him would destroy us, taking down Theo, who has done nothing more than be born to one very nice parent and one complete idiot.

So I go around and around and get no closer to figuring out how to fix what isn't right. Would Will believe me if I suddenly blurted out that I was a spy in my former life? He might find it easier to digest if I had Playboy Bunny on my resume. At least that is some-thing that people actually do. No one is actually a spy.

And now this. I have put my family in danger by being me. Even if everything turns out fine, which it never does, I will never forgive myself for bringing us so close to the line.

What I want now that I'm in this mess is to do something. Ac-tion has always been my drug of choice. During my first five years with the Agency, I was on the road twice as much as the next guy. I couldn't sit still. I wanted only to keep going, keep up the momen-tum. Simon said that either I suffered from an obsessive-compulsive travel disorder or I was the most dedicated patriot he had met, on account of what I was willing to do for my country. Truth be told, it had nothing to do with my country. I liked it well enough. With the exception of a secluded beach in Thailand, I hadn't been to any other places I actually wanted to live, but that wasn't what drove me. I was running hard and fast. Away from whom, I couldn't say, and toward what, I had no idea. But the Agency provided the perfect way for me to barrel down the highway, bypassing the exits to introspection and self-evaluation.

On September 11, 2001, I was drinking coffee at a sidewalk café in Rome, watching a young priest take his coffee several tables away. What I knew that no one else drinking coffee on this fine afternoon did was that the priest literally had state secrets up his voluminous sleeve. I was at that moment enjoying my coffee and contemplating how I was going to relieve him of those secrets. I had not come up with anything even remotely worthy of a plan when the whole square suddenly started to buzz. Information turns us into systems, and this system existed to funnel bits and scraps of the strangest things to my ears. Towers, planes, fire, falling, smoke, collapse. Everyone started rushing around going nowhere, and before I could stop him, my priest disappeared into the crowd. But I didn't care. I could find him again later. After all, I knew where he lived. What I really needed to know was what the hell was going on. I stepped inside the café and inquired of the owner, who pointed to the television in time for me to watch the second tower collapse to the ground in a deadly rage of smoke and dust. I actually gasped out loud, a very English "Oh my God," slipping from my lips. The café owner shot me a surprised look.

"American?" he asked, curious and confused.

"No," I said and slipped out of the café without further conversation. On the street, the crowds were growing, people unsure of what to do taking solace in the fact that nobody else seemed to know what to do either. Starting to panic, I pulled out my phone and called Simon.

"This is not a good development," he said without preamble. And I felt my heart sink, heavy and fast.

"Simon, how did no one see this coming?"

"Well, that's a fine question, Sal, and one we will all be called upon to answer, that I can assure you. What is going on there?"

"Nothing," I said, glancing around the crowded square. "Everyone is sort of mulling around looking freaked out. I lost the priest in the chaos. Where are you?"

"New York," he said, "Ground Zero actually. I left the building about twenty minutes before the planes hit." Another wave of dread washed over me.

"Simon," I whispered, "what were you doing there?"

"Nothing in particular, Sally. Sightseeing."

I could hear shouting and noise in the background, yet Simon sounded cool as ever. Three thousand miles away, I shivered in the fading afternoon sun.

"We're going to war over this. Are you ready to go to the desert, Sal?" I held the phone away from my ear, not wanting to hear what came next, and let the sounds of the square wash over me. I wish I were someone else, I chanted slowly to myself, like Dorothy in her ruby red slippers. Except I didn't want to go home. Instead, I wanted to vanish forever into the body and life of any other person. Suddenly, I glimpsed my priest moving along the outer edge of the square, heading toward an alley.

"Have to go, Simon. See you when I get back," I said, flipping the phone shut and starting out after the priest.

As I followed him down the quiet back alley, I wondered how it was we could have suffered such a breach in security. I wondered about Simon's involvement. I wasn't paying attention, moving along in a fog and thinking about the mess that was sure to be coming, when the priest stepped out from a recessed doorway and grabbed my arm. I wasn't all that surprised. It seemed fitting that today, of all days, I'd fuck everything up royally.

"Why are you following me?" he asked in broken Italian.

"I think you know why," I replied in Portuguese, which I took to be his native language. He almost smiled.

"It would be better for you and everyone involved if you didn't, you understand?"

"Yes, I do understand. But unfortunately, I can't stop. You've been up to some nasty tricks for a man of God."

The priest snorted at that one. "Man of God, please. It is all hypocrisy. Me saying I speak for God. You passing moral judgment on my actions. The whole world is falling apart."

He had a point, but that did not make him any less of a thief.

"I don't care why you are the way you are," I said. "Maybe your mother neglected you as a child. Maybe you were born this way. All I want is what you have stashed under those robes. I think you know what I'm talking about."

"Why do you care what I do with these documents?"

"Because innocent people always end up dead when these sorts of documents are passed around like Life Savers."

"Life Savers? I don't understand you."

"Forget it," I said. "Candy. Passed around like candy."

"Innocent people die anyway. Look around you. It is the way of the world."

"Forgive me, Father, but I don't think you are in any position to be telling me about the ways of the world. You lost that right when you stole from your leader."

I am not a religious person. I don't identify with any of the world's major religions, or minor ones for that matter. In fact, I don't understand religion at all and as far as I can see the only thing it does is hasten the slaughter of people who generally seem to be minding their own business. But I had to admit, standing in that alley with this very naughty priest, I felt bad for the Pope. If he can't hire reliable people, well, who can, really?

"Who do you work for?" the priest asked, still gripping my arm a little too tightly.

"I can't tell you that. That's not how this works."

"How does it work?"

"You tell me who you are working for. I like that better."

"I think you are being smart."

"How smart can I be when I just got jumped by a priest in a dark alley?" I ask.

"Not very. Now how do we proceed?"

"You give me the papers you stole, I will take them, and we will both go our separate ways. I will, of course, have to inform your people about your extracurricular activities, but you probably already knew that."

"And why would I let that happen?" he asked, his eyes black as coal, his mouth twisted into a strange smile.

"Because," I said, reaching around to the back of my pants, "I have a gun and you don't. Or at least I don't think you do." He released my arm and we stood staring at each other. I let the gun dangle down at my thigh. There is something unsettling about aiming a gun at a priest, even if he is not a very good one.

"Yes, I see that you do," he said.

"Now, slowly open your robes and hand over the papers."

"What difference does it make? I've already committed the information to memory. What is to stop me from telling my employers what I know?"

"Why are we having this conversation? Okay, there is nothing to stop you really because even though I would be totally justified in leaving you here in a bloody heap, I don't think I can actually do it. So the only thing that will stop you would be your conscience. If you still have one of those. Sometimes getting caught is a good first step toward redemption."

He thought about what I said for a few moments. "Perhaps you are right."

"Listen, Father. You're clearly new to this espionage thing, and you're not very good at it, so why not go back to fathering or whatever. Leave the bad behavior to those with more of an inclination for it, like the politicians."

He gave me a little laugh, reached up his sleeve, and handed me an envelope.

"I will pray on this event," he said.

"Oh, please," I said. "And what is that worth?" But he was already gone. I thought about informing the Vatican that they had a traitor living among them, but in the end I didn't. My revenge against Christianity? Maybe. Or maybe on that day I just wanted to believe in second chances. And I'm hoping, when this is all over, that Will feels the same.

17

Agent Nanny shows up at my house the next morning at 9 A.M. sharp. Mary Poppins she is not, dressed stiffly in khakis, a white button-down shirt, and a blue blazer.

"This is not the FBI," I say by way of greeting. She looks hurt.

"I don't have kids myself," she says meekly.

"Of course you don't." Not compatible with the professional responsibilities of a USAWMD Agent. I give myself a mental kick in the ass. This is not her fault. I extend my hand.

"Lucy Hamilton," I say. "It's nice to meet you." I can tell from her eyes she knows Sally Sin and she is intimidated and, at the same time, surprised to find that Sally Sin is barefoot and wearing dirty jeans with her hair pulled up in a messy ponytail. It never occurred to me I should do anything to protect my reputation as a superspy, being as I didn't know I had a reputation to protect.

"Can I get you some coffee?" I offer, trying to make amends.

"Yes, please," she says, looking a little more relaxed.

"Sit," I command, and she quickly pulls out a kitchen chair and plants herself in it. "Tell me about yourself." She pauses. I can tell she doesn't know if she should tell me the real story or the fake one, whatever it is they cooked up for this assignment. I help her out.

"The actual one, please, not some Agency bullshit authored by Simon." I swear she almost smiles.

"This is my second assignment. I did some work in Canada last winter but that's been it. I'm grateful for the chance to help out in this situation and, of course, to meet you."

"Sure you are."

"No, I really am. We hear stories about Sally Sin," she says and catches herself. "Sorry. Simon told me I was not to call you that under any circumstances."

Simon, I think, you still get off on scaring the kids, you sick old man.

"Don't worry about it," I assure her. "Now, to be clear, this is the most important assignment of your life. Don't let me catch you treating it otherwise." In the back of my mind, I am already formulating a plan on how to test this new agent. Does Simon think he can send me someone still wet behind the ears and that will be it? He's slipping.

Theo picks this moment to come parading into the kitchen dragging his favorite mangled teddy bear. He climbs up on my lap and settles Teddy on the table before demanding juice. Agent Nanny jumps into action. "The apple juice is in the fridge," I instruct her. "Pour it into that sippy cup."

"Who is she?" Theo asks.

"This is . . ." I pause, realizing I have no idea what Agent Nanny's name is.

"Pauline," she supplies. "I'm Pauline." I know that's not her real name. She still has a problem saying it.

"Pauline is going to play with you for a few days while Mommy does some . . . work. How does that sound?"

Theo shrugs, noncommittal. "Will she play trucks?" he asks.

"I'm sure she will play trucks, if you ask her nicely and show her how," I say, seeing the fear in Agent Nanny Pauline's eyes. This assignment may drive her into early retirement.

"Why don't you go and get a few to show her?" I suggest. Theo slides to the floor, clutching his juice, and wanders off to find some trucks.

"Now, it's very easy," I say to a terrified Pauline. "All you have to do is play with him. You will do all your playing here in the house or in the backyard until I say differently. Don't let him out of your sight even for a second. I've made a list of his schedule, what to feed him, etc. Follow his lead and you will be fine."

Pauline is pale. She sees her whole career going down the toilet because of a bratty three-year-old and an inability to understand the concept of playing trucks. I search for something reassuring.

"This should all be wrapped up in a few days," I say, sounding far more confident than I am. "After which you can go back to things that are really scary."

She smiles halfheartedly, turning toward the noise that is Theo dragging a half dozen toy trucks down the hallway. He dumps them with enthusiasm on the kitchen floor, squats down, and gets busy with the playing. After a few seconds, he glances up at Agent Nanny Pauline and says, "Well, come on. Play trucks." Agents are good at taking orders, and Pauline does as she's told, assuming a cross-legged position on the floor next to my darling and bossy boy.

"I'm going to be upstairs in the office," I say, refilling my coffee cup. "Don't forget to remind him to pee every once in a while. Let me know if you need anything."

"Okay," they say in unison. I shake my head at the weirdness of the blazer-wearing Pauline on the floor playing trucks and go upstairs.

My first order of business is to orient myself. I don't know who this professor is or why everyone seems so interested in him all of a sudden. I don't know what he does. I don't know how he knows Ian Blackford. It seems I don't know anything anymore except how to make banana bread with whole wheat flour and raisins that Will insists reminds him of a brick. And speaking of Will, there is the little issue of telling him why Agent Nanny is down in my kitchen at this very moment. I could tell the truth but that won't work. I could say I'm doing a bit of freelancing, but having not mentioned work in any real capacity throughout our relationship, the timing seems bad. After careful consideration, I decide to deal with it when Theo announces to his daddy that he had fun with his new friend today and his daddy turns to me for explanation and I don't have one. Sounds like a plan.

. . .

Once upon a time in a jungle I can still not bring myself to mention by name, Simon Still, delirious from malaria, was ranting about the government of Pakistan. Because it was not good for our life expectancies to have the supposed Frenchman howling in English about extremists hidden in the mountains, plotting our downfall, I lay down next to him on his grass mat and tried to soothe him. I stroked his sweaty hair back from his forehead and sang verse after verse of "Oh My Darling Clementine" in French, which he seemed to like very much. After a while, he felt cool and limp in my arms. But as I tried to slide my arm out from under his shoulders and escape back to my own scratchy mat, he reached up and grabbed me, panicked.

"Stay," he whispered, his eyes clouded with an unknown terror.

"Okay," I said. "Fine. I'll sing. Calm down. Go to sleep."

"No, Sally," he said, squeezing me tighter. "The passwords are secure. They are. I just add another number on to the sequence every month. Is that good enough? You must tell me."

I am not normally an opportunist, but this seemed like due compensation for having to stay up all night singing.

"What's the sequence, Simon?" I asked. "I'll keep it safe."

"The day it all began," he said, as if I should have known. "The day I signed my life over to them. I like to remind myself of the time that has passed."

Why he wanted to torture himself like that I would never know, because before I could ask he passed out cold. I wriggled out from under him and crawled back to my own mat. As I dug through the layers of mosquito netting to find the opening, I repeated Simon's password to myself a few times. Not that I was at any risk of forgetting it.

In my head, I count off the number of months I have been gone from the Agency. I add those to 415288, the month and day that Simon began service to his country followed by the number of months he'd been at it when I left, and I'm in. It shouldn't be so easy. If I liked Simon better right now, I might even point that out to him.

I remind myself that accessing the network is a small victory. The USAWMD was not known for its commitment to an electronic universe. The most important information, the things that would make the average American cringe with distaste and perhaps be moved to rail against our methods of democracy, those things were loosely bound together by rubber bands, stashed in cryptically labeled boxes, and stored in the belly of an undisclosed mountain. They were also written in a code so irritatingly complex that I used to make things up to see if anyone bothered to really read them. My conclusion was no.

But background information, dossiers on individuals of interest to the Agency, sometimes showed up on the network. And today I just got lucky.

Professor Albert Malcolm is sixty-eight years old, unmarried, no children. He lives alone in a small house near the University. The attached photos indicate that the house has a perfectly manicured front lawn with a row of rosebushes along one side. Professor Malcolm has owned the same car for thirty years, a white Volkswagen Beetle. Hailing originally from Minnesota, Malcolm is considered a genius in his field of analytical chemistry. And because he is considered a genius, his obvious insanity is dismissed as eccentricity. Isn't it cute that he wears the same clothes for twenty days in a row, not coming out of the lab except to use the toilet? Can someone please go in there and clear out the pizza boxes before we lose a student? Yes, we would, except no one knows the code for entry and the nutty professor is not about to answer a knock at the door. After a while, he would emerge but refuse to say what he was doing in the lab. His logs would be blank and his eyes would be spinning like saucers in his head.

His students hate him, at least those who have had the honor of actually having met the guy. Professor Malcolm believes teaching is for idiots. And I'm not drawing conclusions here. According to the writer, he actually said as much. "Teaching," he pronounced in an academic journal, "is for idiots with nothing better to do with their time. If the university wanted a teacher, they should perhaps hire one of these idiots I'm speaking of and be done with it."

Shortly thereafter, the university issued an apology to teachers everywhere on behalf of the professor. Of course, he was not involved with the apology; no one expected he would be. So Professor

Malcolm's teaching assistants conduct his classes while he hides out in the lab. And the university looks the other way, thinking that it's probably safer for everyone involved if he stays away from the fresh young minds of the students.

Which is not to say that Malcolm doesn't have his followers. There is a group of students who appear to worship at his lab door. He is deeply critical and insulting of these particular students, which only fuels their desire to please him. Impressionable youth. I smile. It will make it far easier for me to scare the shit out of them and get some actual, usable information.

I lean back in the desk chair as far as I can without falling over. What I really want to know is how Blackford met Professor Malcolm. I want to know about the very first time they laid eyes on one another. Did Malcolm find Blackford or the other way around? How long have they been working on this little project together and, most importantly, when is it going to be done? But I somehow doubt the answers to any of these questions are going to show up in Albert Malcolm's file. And that can mean only one thing: I have to go on a field trip.

Downstairs, Agent Nanny Pauline has shed her blazer, rolled up her sleeves, and kicked off her shoes. Theo is busy showing her the proper way to set up the Thomas the Train tracks so there is a jump for the train to sail off. Pauline has obviously accepted her beta role and is nodding her head agreeably. She looks almost happy.

"Hi, kids," I say. They both startle.

"Hi, Mommy," Theo says. "Pauline is helping build jumps for Thomas."

"Yes," I say, "I can see that. Do you mind if Mommy goes out for a little while and you stay here and play with Pauline?"

"Nope, I'll stay here and play with Pauline," he says, as if struck by a brilliant idea. "When you come back, we go to the park."

"Deal," I say. "I'll be gone two hours at the most. Don't be scared." But that does little to chase away the look of fear on Pauline's face. "You'll be fine. My cell number is on the table. Call me if you need anything or if anything happens. Okay? Okay. Good. I'll be back."

I grab my bag off the table and realize it is not actually necessary to lug twenty pounds of wipes, toys, sippy cups, crackers, and other kid paraphernalia with me on my student-stalking mission. Feeling oddly liberated, I pull out my wallet, stick my cell phone in my pocket, and head out the door.

Now, a normal person living a normal life would secure the necessary references from a new babysitter and call each and every one. A normal person would ask a series of carefully crafted questions designed to uncover relevant information, such as whether the babysitter in question was a practicing ax murderer in her spare time. A normal person living in my city probably would go the extra mile and have a proper professional background check conducted as well. But no. Not me. I have my own approach.

Instead of hopping in my car and heading across the bridge for a rendezvous with Professor Malcolm, I creep around the house and slip into the kitchen through the back door. Nanny Pauline appears ten seconds later, a toy train in her hand, ready to cudgel me to death with it.

I tap my watch. "Ten seconds. Too long. What if I had a gun? You have Thomas the Train. Not really an equal fight."

Nanny Pauline looks crestfallen. "I was told not to carry my weapon on the assignment."

"And that is as it should be. But pick up something heavier." I gesture to the cast-iron frying pan, still dirty, on the stove. "Like that."

Pauline nods. "Yes. That would be better." In comes Theo.

"Mommy? I thought you were leaving."

"I am, sweetheart. Right now. See you soon." I kiss his blond head. Then I look at Pauline and again tap the face of my watch. "Too long."

She trudges out of the kitchen after Theo, looking like a puppy who has just been scolded for peeing on the floor.

This time, as I actually get in my car and drive toward the bridge, I try very hard to think about Professor Malcolm. But it's not easy. My heart is beating too fast, the rushing blood echoing in my ears. My hands grip the steering wheel so tightly my fingers are white. I can feel the wheel growing slick with sweat. Theo is out of my sight. I try counting backward from one hundred, but that does nothing to alleviate my panic attack. Finally, I dial Simon.

"Listen," I bark into the phone. "She better be the very, very, very best thing the Agency has produced in a decade because if anything happens to Theo it's your head. And I mean the part about the head."

"Calm down there, Sally. It's not as if I sent you someone fresh out of school. She's done some things. I have great hopes for her."

"You're full of shit," I say.

"Am I?"

"I meant the thing about the head."

"I know. I heard you the first time. Where are you going?"

"Nowhere."

"But you are in the car."

"So what? Information is on a need-to-know basis," I say and hang up on him. He dials me back several times, but I've tossed the phone into the backseat, where I won't be tempted to answer it. I practice my deep yoga breathing for a few minutes. After what seems like forever, my pulse begins to slow and steady. This will be fine. It has to be. I will accept no alternative.

And now, back to Albert Malcolm. He publishes when he must, but mostly he hides out in his lab like a mad scientist. People give him the benefit of the doubt because he has been labeled a genius. But why do we assume that because someone is a genius they are up to something lifesaving or revolutionary, such as inventing a cure for cancer? Why don't we assume that the reason the professor keeps his door locked is because behind it he is messing with unspeakable evil?

The campus is beautiful, landscaped, and blooming. It looks exactly like it does in the brochure. I think about the cold gray of my own college experience and wonder why it never occurred to me to transfer somewhere warm with beaches and palm trees. I mean, chemistry 101 is still chemistry 101 even if it is 75 degrees outside with blue skies and sunshine, right?

I park my car in a visitor lot and head toward a campus café known as a science major hangout. How do I know this? I thank my anonymous USAWMD writer for giving me at least one useful tidbit of information. The place is mobbed with students chugging double lattes and scarfing trans fat in the guise of donuts and pastries. Caffeine and sugar. Who needs drugs? I work my way up to the counter and order a single decaf, much to the shock and horror of my barista.

"Are you sure?" he asks. "Decaf?"

"Yes," I say, "and hurry. I'm feeling light-headed." Coffee in hand, I find an empty seat and watch the college kids move in and out. I try to decide who is who. Who are the cool kids? The geeks? Who is most likely to be in Professor Malcolm's inner circle? Being as I don't actually know the professor, this is harder than it might appear. Using my master sleuthing techniques, honed over years of hard-won experience, I turn to the guy next to me and say, "Do you happen to know anyone who studies with Professor Malcolm?" The kid, no older than twenty, lifts his head from his textbook for a mere second and points to a table in the corner of the café. "The Disciples," he says, "they usually sit over there." He returns his head to the book.

"Thank you," I say, but he has already forgotten I exist.

The table in the corner has eight seats pulled up around it and they are all full. The students range in age from maybe twenty to at least twenty-five or -six. The Disciples appear to be grad students. They are not a particularly noteworthy bunch. One boy has on white socks and black shoes. The two girls look hipper, although one of them is so thin a strong gust of wind might carry her away. She reminds me of a whippet. Nervous and jumpy. She is my student of choice. I sit and wait for her to leave or to be left alone.

About a half hour later, she gets up, gives a kiss to one of the older guys at the table, collects her bag, and heads out of the café.

I keep an even five paces behind her, and right before she enters the library, I pounce. Catching her by the arm, I spin her toward me with no effort at all. She is so tiny and frail, I worry my light grip will leave a bruise.

"Hey," I say. She looks surprised to find a strange woman holding her arm.

"Hi," she says. I let go. "Do I know you?"

"No, but can you tell me where I can find Professor Malcolm? I have an appointment with him and I'm lost." I shrug. "Don't like to keep the man waiting."

"Yeah," she says, "he hates that. So rigid when it comes to his own schedule and nice and loose when it comes to other people's." She rolls her eyes. Perfect. This woman is in the Malcolm circle because the guy she likes is in the Malcolm circle, not because of any personal loyalty to the man.

"I know," I say, lying to keep the conversation going. "I was here to interview him once before and he didn't even show up."

"Are you a reporter?"

"Freelance."

She nods as if that explains it all. "I wish I understood everyone's fascination with the old guy. Barry, my boyfriend, is obsessed with him, says he's on the verge of being able to program us all to act like zombies or something, which he thinks is totally cool. Not that I'm supposed to mention it. He'd kill me if he knew." More eye rolling.

"You don't study with Professor Malcolm?"

"Me? Are you kidding? No way. I'm premed. Not even close to being smart enough to hang with the professor. He only lets a couple of people into his lab and if he suddenly decides he doesn't like you anymore, well, then you're out on your ass. Barry is one of his boys. Listen, I have to go. Is there anything else I can help you with?"

"Where is the Professor's office?"

"Jade Hall, second floor," she says. "I'm Chloe, by the way. Good luck with your article. I hope he shows up." With that she turns and heads into the library.

I find Jade Hall at the end of a tulip-lined flagstone path. It is an old building, planted oddly in front of a new state-of-the art research building named for the rich alumnae who made it all possible. I wonder why they bothered keeping the old building at all? Sentimentality? I check the directory for Malcolm and find him, indeed, on the second floor. There is a secretary guarding the entrance to five different offices. She informs me that Professor Malcolm is in the lab for the duration of the day and she doesn't expect to be seeing him tomorrow either.

"He rarely comes here," she says. "Not even to get his mail." I thank her for her time and head toward the new building. It is all under lock and key as I suspected it would be. I begrudgingly accept the fact that I will have to come back at night. However, sneaking out at night is not as easy as it once was.

As I stand outside the research fortress, I note the manufacturer of the security system. On television, when the good guy wants to break into the bad guy's lair and it is protected by some impenetrable security system, the good guy whips out a little zipper case of tiny tools and gets to work rewiring the entry panel so that it obeys his every command. All in about three minutes. And he doesn't get caught. Ever. But that is not really me.

And so I set out in search of Barry the Boyfriend and his magnetic entry cards. Barry doesn't know it but he's about to be mugged.

Barry is not quite good-looking enough for Chloe. Right now, he has his pointy-headed geek chic thing going for him, which will keep her interested until she finds a guy who changes his underwear more than once a week and drives a 1967 convertible Porsche. Then it's bye-bye Barry.

Barry walks with a slight stoop, something that might belong to a man in his eighties. His dark hair is already wispy and thinning at the top. Clearly, he belongs to the school of obsessive academics too engrossed in his work to actually feed himself; his slightly dirty jeans hang low on his hips, revealing a heart-patterned pair of boxer shorts that I can only imagine came from Chloe. He is chattering away intensely on his cell phone, head down, brows furrowed. The stress follows behind him like a trail of dust. On his heavily loaded backpack is a carabiner. On the carabiner are keys and entry cards.

It's easy to take something from someone who isn't expecting it. They're going along, thinking that the world is one way, when really it isn't that way at all. As Barry passes me, I stick out my foot and trip him. He goes down hard on his face. His cell phone flies out of his hand and hits the sidewalk. The battery lands somewhere in the grass. The overstuffed backpack crashes to the ground, its contents scatter into the flower beds.

"Oh my God, I'm so sorry," I gush. "Here, let me help you. I'm such a klutz."

"Yes," Barry says, trying to regain his composure. "I'd say you are." He's focused on reassembling his cell phone. I slip the carabiner off its loop and into my pocket. I stuff his books and papers and laptop back into his bag, all the while apologizing all over myself.

"I'm really so sorry. Are you okay?"

"I'm fine. Pay more attention to where you are going next time."

I nod my head solemnly, fingering the collection of keys filling my pocket. Barry heads off in one direction. I head back to my car.

I am back home in a little under two hours. Theo and Pauline are enjoying peanut butter sandwiches at the kitchen table.

"I had no idea how good these were," she says, holding up a half-eaten sandwich with a gob of strawberry jam slipping out the side. "So good."

Theo is singing to his sandwich, something about a castle. He barely looks up when I walk in. And there I was thinking I was indispensable.

"Everything was fine here," Pauline says, washing down the peanut butter with a splash of milk. "Theo is a doll."

What happened to Pauline? I think. Did my blond-haired, blue-eyed baby steal her heart in a mere three hours? I look at him singing away and think it's probably true. I walk Pauline to the door.

"Tomorrow same time?" she asks. I nod. This is getting complicated. I have to explain to my husband why I suddenly have a nanny for Theo who isn't charging me twenty bucks an hour and demanding her own Mercedes SUV. I have to sneak out of my house in the dead of night to break into the lab of a rogue scientist and somehow avoid Ian Blackford until I have enough information to be on even ground with him. My landline rings, interrupting my reverie.

"Is this a secure line?" Simon asks.

"Probably." I look out the kitchen window. "There's no one in my backyard either if that makes you feel better."

"What exactly do you think you were doing today, Sal?" Simon asks. He doesn't sound happy.

"Being bait," I say, innocently.

"By checking in with Malcolm?"

"Just being friendly."

"Listen, this is not a joke. What I meant by being bait was to go have coffee, wander around Union Square, get your nails done. Whatever the fuck you want. I did not mean turning up on the doorstep of one of the players in this scenario like it's no big deal."

"What's the problem?" I ask. "Afraid I might actually stumble upon something useful and make you look bad?"

There is silence down the line. Simon Still is doing his version of deep breathing, willing himself not to say anything he can't take back. For some reason, this makes me feel good.

"I do not need to explain things to you, Sally. You are not authorized to do anything except exactly what I tell you to do. Should I say it in Swahili too to make sure you understand?"

"Your Swahili sucks, Simon. And yes, I understand, but no, I'm not agreeing to it. You're out of your mind if you think I'm going to sit back and wait for you to catch Blackford, all the while hoping you don't get me and my family killed in the process. And I think you know better than to ask." It's quiet. Either he is speechless or I'm exhausting him.

"You always were a pain in the ass, Sally Sin," he says finally.

"Stop calling me that, will you?"

"I can't help it. Calling you Lucy isn't working for me. I'm sorry. Why did you go to Malcolm's office?"

"I want to know what he's working on in there, what exactly about Malcolm caught Blackford's eye. He's particular about who he works with and what he agrees to sell. To get involved with a newcomer like Malcolm is risky. There has to be a huge upside to make it worth Blackford's while. I want to know what that upside is. If you would tell me what you found in the lab, I wouldn't have to go busting in there on my own."

There is a pause. Simon is thinking. He pauses and thinks only when he is trying to figure out the best way to deliver news that you don't want to hear.

"Well, we haven't actually been able to get into the lab yet," he says finally.

I am sure I have not heard him correctly. "Tell me you're kidding."

"I wish I was."

"Come on, Simon, what sort of outfit are you running these days?" His embarrassment is palpable over the airwaves.

"We had a few problems with their electronic security system and scheduling and things."

"Well, in that case, I'll be sure to give you an update when I get done over there," I say. "If your schedule allows, of course." I hang up. Simon rings me back, but I don't answer. I want to finish lunch with my son.

18

Now I don't want you to go off thinking that Ian Blackford was really some deeply misunderstood soul. At the end of the day, he was a criminal. Yes, he was kind enough to decide not to kill me on several occasions, but that is not enough to excuse him from notoriety.

After the mess at The Grand Event in Cambodia, things got much worse. The only bright spot, according to Simon Still, was that the Blind Monk didn't manage to put a bullet in me. Because after what happened, Simon Still wanted that privilege all to himself. Or so he said.

As punishment, I was forced to sit at my desk. I tried to keep my chin up and not complain. After all, I'd had the largest stockpile of nuclear components we'd ever encountered in one place stolen right out from under me, so I didn't really have a leg to stand on. And within days of Sovann's murder, that stuff started showing up everywhere. It wasn't good. Remember that incident in Beijing and the one in Frankfurt? Well, Agents 1 through 25, or however many, were scrambling, barely able to keep up with how efficiently Blackford moved those materials out of Cambodia and all around the world.

The Blind Monk was apoplectic. Rumor had it, he'd had Blackford's cat assassinated. But that was only a rumor. And Blackford didn't care anyway. He just kept at it, kept moving the merchandise. It was masterful really. And boy did it make Simon mad. I started to think he was torturing me with desk duty to make himself feel better. But at least I had the sense to stop short of asking him if that was indeed the case.

So I'm sitting there down in the daisy at my desk, taking my punishment, staring at my computer, toggling back and forth between

People magazine and the *New York Times,* when suddenly Simon Still and three other USAWMD agents burst in from the elevator bank.

"Get your stuff, Sal," Simon shouted, rushing into his office. I couldn't see what he was doing, but it looked like he was putting together his field knapsack. I shut my laptop slowly.

"Where are we going?" I asked, not sure I really wanted an answer. Mentally, I was already preparing a list of hot, unpleasant places with large biting insects and angry dictators to which I might be headed. I tested the waters. "Myanmar? North Korea?"

Simon stopped, turned toward me, his face paler than usual. "As a matter of fact, New York City," he said. That got my attention.

"Here? Who would dare?" Simon heaved a heavy aluminum suitcase filled with surveillance gear right at my chest. The impact almost knocked me on my ass.

"Who do you think?" And for a second he looked at me as if I was the enemy, as if this whole situation was my fault.

"Blackford," I said.

"Your guy seems to think he can get away with anything. He seems to think that we'll all look the other way as he peddles his Easy-Bake nuclear bombs up and down Fifth Avenue. Well, let me tell you, I have had about enough of him." Simon's face flushed with anger.

"He's not my guy," I said quietly.

"He's a dead man," Simon responded, marching out the door. The four of us obediently followed after.

As we sped toward the airport in black sedans, red and blue lights flashing and sirens wailing, I tried to understand what Blackford was doing. There was an unwritten rule in the underground world of illegal arms dealing that transactions didn't take place on U.S. soil. The idea was that we, as a country, had a lot of fire power to throw at the problem, and if we ever wanted to get really serious about it, we could more or less shut down the whole industry, and who wanted that to happen? In truth, as you can probably guess, we could do no such thing, but the illusion that we could kept the hard stuff thousands of miles from our borders. And that was worth something in this ugly business.

But now Blackford was blatantly flaunting the rule. This could make things very complicated for us at the Agency because if Blackford could do it, why not everyone else? And there goes the neighborhood. Once in the air, Simon Still told us what he knew, which wasn't much.

"Blackford apparently brought the fully assembled weapon into the United States by boat right into New Jersey in a cargo container marked with some Chinese characters. We do not know the whereabouts of the container at present, but are making headway on that front now. The buyer is also a bit of an unknown. Two streams of information. One indicates that the buyer is from Dubai and not associated with any active terrorist organization. Number two indicates that the buyer is Chinese and associated with a homegrown Chinese terrorist organization. Neither option is any good, as you can see. From all our intelligence," he waved a single sheet of paper in the air, "we believe Blackford is meeting his buyer at four o'clock this afternoon." He checked his watch. "We have a team at the docks in Jersey trying to track the weapon. I want you four to find Blackford. Find Blackford and put a bullet in his head. And I don't care who sees you do it."

I wanted to point out that New York City was kind of a big place and the chances of one of the four of us bumping into Blackford were rather unlikely. But Simon was fuming, and I thought he might take my comment the wrong way. He handed the other three agents lead sheets containing lists of places Blackford might be. Simon was asking the impossible. There was no way we could cover that much ground in four hours.

"Start at the top and move fast," he said to the other three agents.

"You," he said, turning to me. "Follow your nose. Or maybe just stand there and let him find you." I felt an angry heat rise on my cheeks. Blackford was not my creation. I was simply along for the ride.

We landed abruptly and dispersed. Simon didn't mention what he himself was going to be doing while the rest of us combed the tristate area for bombs and bad guys, but he went stomping off the tarmac with purpose so none of us asked.

New York was never my favorite city. It's crowded, cold, and slushy in the winter, and hot and smelly in the summer. But I admired the people for their tenacity; it took a certain hubris to believe you could make it here. Blackford fit right in. He believed he could do anything and do it right under our noses. Whatever was happening, it couldn't be about a bomb. It had to be Blackford's coming-out party. After his triumph in Cambodia, this was his way of announcing to his underworld buddies that he was the king now and anyone who got in his way be damned.

I stood on the street, watching the people pass, chatting on their cell phones, carrying containers of coffee. There was no way we could find Blackford here. To try and do so was almost embarrassing. Resigned to being useless, I began to hike uptown. On one of the bus stops was an advertisement for the Top of the Rock, a chance to see New York City from the top floor of Rockefeller Center.

And it hit me. Of course. The last time I had seen Blackford at The Grand Event, he had said something about jumping off a rock. Hadn't he? Or maybe it was about crawling under one? Not exactly the same, but no matter. It was the only lead I had and I was going to use it. I started to run.

Only here could a relatively normal-looking woman run at a breakneck pace through the city streets without calling attention to herself. The sweat started to roll down my face, but I didn't stop to remove my jacket. It was a long way from the heliport on Thirtieth and the Hudson River to Rockefeller Center. If I had any chance of making it, I couldn't stop, not even for red lights.

By the time I reached the ticket booth for the Top of the Rock tour, I was soaked in sweat and breathing hard.

"You okay, lady?" the woman in the booth asked.

"Yes," I gasped. "Fine. Late to meet a friend."

"You say so." She slid my ticket toward me. I grabbed it and ran around to the entrance. There, standing in line with everyone else, waiting to go through security, I pulled the gun out of my pants and quickly dropped it into a garbage can. I didn't have the time to negotiate it through the guards. And if I ended up being right, this would not be the first time I faced Blackford with little more than my dazzling wit and good looks.

I passed through the security checkpoint and made my way to a line for the elevator. Sweat streamed down my face. People gave me a wide berth. Finally, the elevator spat us out on the top floor. I made a quick pass around the roof. No Blackford. What a waste of time. I sat down on one of the benches and cleaned the sweat spots from my sunglasses, although it only seemed to make them worse.

As I sat meditating on my failure, I noticed a small stairway leading up to another deck above the main viewing area. How had I missed it? Slowly, I climbed the stairs. I had no idea what I would do if it turned out he was actually there on the roof.

About halfway around the deck, there he was, admiring the view. In his left hand, Blackford held a small aluminum briefcase. Then, almost as if he could smell me in the breeze, he turned. And smiled.

"Sally Sin," he said, "you remembered. I wasn't sure if you would."

Seeing him standing there, relaxed, taking in the sights, made me so mad I almost couldn't speak.

"Do you know how many people died in Beijing?" I asked. "They were regular people, minding their own business. Going to work. Going to school. How do you sleep at night?"

"Fine. Thanks for asking. Don't take it so personally, Sally. I don't."

How badly I wanted to push him off the edge of the building was written all over my face. He laughed.

"I know what you are thinking. But it won't work. Why don't you shoot me?" He moved closer so that we stood a mere foot apart.

"The building is surrounded," I said. "You'll never get out alive." This really seemed to crack him up.

"Sally, you're good at a lot of things, but lying to me isn't one of them. The USAWMD never surrounds anything. And they never ever ask another agency for help in surrounding anything. So the chances of this place being surrounded and me being, well, shit out of luck, are pretty slim. Not that I was planning on the elevator anyway. So go on, do it. Shoot me. Imagine what a hero you would be if you came back with my head on a stick. What a triumph." Suddenly I wanted nothing more than to run away, but there was nowhere to go but down.

"Tell me where the cargo container is and I'll let you go."

"Don't negotiate, Sally. Stand your ground. Don't be intimidated. Pull out your gun and fire." Both of my hands were jammed in my pockets. I wondered if I could get away with strangling him. "Oh, wait a minute. You don't have a gun, do you? Dumped it to get up here. Oh well. Lost opportunity."

"Goddamn you, Blackford," I hissed. "Why do you do this? People die, people who are just living their pathetic happy lives. Why do you make everything such a big fucking mess? The world doesn't need more chaos. It needed you to help. Why did you give up?" I hoped to see regret in Blackford's crazy eyes. But there was nothing.

"Saving the world gets tedious once you realize you can't win."

I wanted to stomp my foot like a child and demand a real answer, but that wasn't going to happen. While I stood alongside him, helpless to do anything, he hoisted a backpack over his shoulders and fastened a series of buckles.

"There is no cargo container, Sally. That was a diversion, something to keep you folks busy. And clearly it worked beyond my wildest expectations if we are both standing here right now." Blackford kept at the buckles, pulling, adjusting, shrugging his shoulders to get everything right, comfortable.

"A diversion from what?"

"Business of another sort altogether. I was visiting with an old friend in California. We had a lot to talk about, big plans for the future, and I wanted to make sure none of you government types got in my way." He pulled out a pair of goggles. "And this part," he gestures to the harness, "this part is about having fun. You should try it some time."

"What are you talking about? Hey, what are you doing? You are not . . . you can't . . . you are not jumping off of this building, are you? You owe me some answers!"

"I don't owe you a thing," he laughed, holding up the briefcase. "I believe it is you who owes me."

"What the hell is in that briefcase?" I shouted, but it was too late.

In a flash he was over the side. I ran to the ledge in time to see him pull the rip cord on his parachute. A security guard ran up next to me.

"Did he just . . . ?"

"Yes! He jumped." The guard started shouting into his radio. I pushed my way into a departing elevator and headed down. The lobby was buzzing with the news that someone had jumped off the Top of the Rock. How did he get through the barriers? How did he get up there with a parachute? How could this happen? Easy, I wanted to shout. He's Ian Blackford and the world appears to bend to his whim.

Out on the street, a small crowd had gathered. Several uniformed police officers chattered into their handsets. I scanned the sky, but there was nothing. The whine of cruiser sirens drew closer. Wherever Blackford had intended to land, it wasn't nearby. The wind blew from the west to the east. He had taken off in the direction of the Empire State Building. I took a deep breath and started running toward the East River. Traffic chugged slowly along beside me. A man in a cab looked at me curiously as we moved forward at about the same pace. I pulled off my jacket and let it fall to the ground. I kept looking for a purple and yellow parachute, but there were only blue skies.

Seconds from collapsing, I found myself at the edge of the FDR Drive. The traffic was at a standstill even though it was the middle of the afternoon.

"God, I love New York," I said, my lungs on fire, wheezing. I ducked under the congested highway and kept running toward the ferry terminal. The only practical way out of this city was by water or by air. Boats were heading in and out with purpose; nothing looked out of place. About fifty yards from shore, there was a small private yacht, remarkable only for how it gleamed white in the sun. On the deck, standing beside the captain, was Blackford. I doubled over, so out of breath I thought I might pass out and topple into the river, never to be heard from again.

"Nice try, Sally!" Blackford yelled, as the boat pulled out into the river. "You must really want this." I looked up in time to see him hurl the aluminum briefcase in my direction. It landed a few yards shy of shore. The last thing I saw Blackford do was shrug as if to say, *Sorry, I tried.* Without giving it a second thought, I dove in. The water was cold and brown, and the current was moving faster than I expected. The ferry passengers started to get excited. I didn't have much time. I grabbed the case and hauled it and myself back to shore, clawing my way out on an old concrete piling, all that remained of a dock lost long ago. The minute I was upright, I opened the briefcase. Inside was a foam inset designed to carry five four-inch vials of something liquid, something delicate, something precious. But the vials were gone. In their place were five bullets, clean and unexploded. *I believe the Blind Monk meant these for you,* the note said. I could almost hear him laughing.

"Goddamn it!" I put my head down and almost cried, exhausted and wet, stranded on a hunk of concrete in the East River.

Simon wasn't happy about the bullets in the briefcase and the nonexistent cargo container.

"What was he doing in California?" he asked, during the lengthy debriefing where I began to feel like a criminal myself.

"I don't know. He didn't tell me that part. He said he was out on the coast. Visiting wine country maybe?"

"Sally," Simon said through clenched teeth. "They found traces of some plant life on the foam in that briefcase. Is he changing professions? Opening a flower shop in the East Village?"

"I don't know." But I was thinking about Cambodia, the jungle, those lilies. "Maybe it has something to do with the botanist?"

"Shut up, Sally. Do not mention Cambodia to me right now or I might actually kill you. I need facts, not theories."

"I don't know," I said again.

"Don't know? Or don't want to tell us?"

I was about to remind him that he wanted facts, not theories, but I remembered that he was going to kill me and decided to keep quiet.

"Blackford has done a lot of things since leaving the Agency. He's done unspeakable things. But this . . . this is different. This is plain rude. So somebody better figure out what the hell he was up to out there today or heads are going to roll. And I don't mean that in a nice way. Got it?"

I nodded. Add it to the list of disasters.

I saw him once more in Hanoi. Two months after that, word came that Blackford was dead.

19

An hour after I return from mugging Barry the grad student, Theo and I are ensconced at the playground with Avery and Sam and a host of others. I still have Barry's keys in my pocket. Their weight is somehow comforting.

"I still wish you'd teach me to knock out yoga instructors with such finesse," Sam says with a smile. "I'm a quick study."

I can see Claire the ex-investment banker's ears perk up. "Who knocked out a yoga instructor? Wouldn't that lead to, like, one hundred years of bad karma?"

Just what I need.

"Forget it," I say. "Forget the whole incident."

"What incident?" Belinda asks, licking the leftover applesauce off her sleeve and dusting the sand off her flowery skirt.

"Apparently Lucy beat up her yoga instructor last night," Claire offers.

Belinda's eyes open a little too wide for my liking.

"Why? Did he hurt you? We can sue him for professional misconduct, you know. Just because someone claims to be spiritual doesn't mean he's a nice guy."

"No, nothing like that. He was trying to adjust her triangle pose and . . . BAM . . . he was flat on the floor," Sam explains.

"Kind of like this," adds Avery, using Sam to simulate my brutal attack on poor Conrad.

"Then I was worried that yoga man put a hit out on you on account of the weird guy in the hat hanging around your car that night," Sam continues, "but at least I'm pretty sure you can take care of yourself."

Simon, you idiot, I think. I play dumb.

"Really? Probably someone thinking about stealing it. Lots of car theft going on lately."

"Especially your kind of car," Sam says.

We lock eyes, Sam and I, and in his expression I read disbelief. There are too many weird little pieces for him, and he wants to put them together. He wants to make sense out of all this random information. I cast my eyes down toward my feet. He knows I am lying, but as much as I'd like to tell him the whole sordid tale, I cannot. Fortunately, my crew here spends so much time with two- and three-year-olds that they are very easily distracted. Suddenly, Belinda brings up the annual sale at our local children's clothing store. I join in with great enthusiasm and force Sam back into his role as lone male voice screaming in a gale of hyped-up women with nothing better to do than shop.

Speaking of being easily distracted, it is possible to become obsessed with one's nemesis to the point of distraction, and that is what happened to me. After Blackford kidnapped me the second time, I felt compelled to understand him and how he became the way he was. Simon reminded me that my job wasn't to explore the troubled childhood and resulting psychosis of Ian Blackford, but rather "to catch the bastard or, at the very least, kill him." Neither option was all that appealing, and when I told Simon that, he also reminded me that finding my assignments appealing was completely irrelevant and I should stop thinking like a girl. If I wanted appealing, he said, I could go and work for the State Department. I didn't really understand why working at the State Department would be better, but the look on his face did not encourage further discussion. I dropped the subject with Simon, but made a point of bringing it up with the Old Timers.

The Old Timers were an invaluable resource to the Agency— men who'd been there since its inception, who acted as the Greek chorus, the living archive, the moral compass for those of us running around in the field. There were three of them. There used to be four, but nobody was willing to say what happened to the fourth one. The Old Timers were indistinguishable from one another, and they spent their days camped out in the cafeteria, drinking bad coffee and talking about baseball. It was understood that an active agent could pick their collective brain regarding Agency history and they would be forthcoming. It was why they were still on the payroll. Well, that and the fact that they had the ear of the Director. Word was that they had all worked together in the past. They were tight. Like family.

I had never talked to them before, being a relative newbie with the Agency, but they knew all about me.

"Sally Sin!" the fat one bellowed as I approached their table.

"Scored higher than anyone in the history of the Agency on that silly test," the bald one added.

"And has a truly unique gift for languages," the short one with wiry eyebrows continued. "Better than our Simon even."

I didn't know that I'd done better than anyone on that test, but I kept my face neutral. No need for them to know I was clueless.

"Sally has never come to the table and we are now wondering what deep, probing questions she intends to ask," Fatty, clearly the ringleader, barked. He pulled out an empty chair and pointed to it. I sat down.

"Sally has achieved fame for being snatched multiple times by none other than our own black sheep ex–Agent Blackford," Baldy said. They sounded like sports broadcasters, and it was all I could do not to flat-out hate them. Shorty poured me a cup of black sludge from the carafe on the table.

"Drink," he said, pushing the mug toward me. The coffee was the consistency of motor oil, barely moving in the cup as I raised it to my lips. An initiation of sorts. They watched me intently.

"Sally Sin is going to do it black, straight up, down the hatch, no sugar, no cream," Shorty whispered. I took a sip of the black goo. It required all of my resources not to spit it back out on the table. I swallowed, kept my face steady, and placed the mug back down on the table.

"You know," I said, "that coffee is not very good."

"No," the three men chimed in unison, "it's bloody awful! We save it for you new kids." With that, they burst out laughing.

"Now, what can we do for you, missy?" Fatty asked. "Because we're pretty sure you didn't come down here for the coffee." Another round of hysterical laughter.

Oh, God, I thought, watching them convulse, is this going to be me? Am I going to be sitting here with Simon Still in thirty years, wallowing in the glory days that never really existed? I started to sweat. Somehow, that troubled me more than being known as the girl who kept getting kidnapped.

"Ian Blackford," I said, trying to get the conversation back on track. "I'd like to know why you think he flipped."

"Oh, well," Baldy said, "that's a pretty big question, one that we've been pondering for quite some time now. Might help to have a pastry or two to get us focused."

I trudged dutifully to the cafeteria counter, picked out several pastries that looked more like hockey pucks than food, and returned to the table.

"Ah, the apple fritter goes a long way toward loosening the lips. Okay, Ian Blackford."

"Bad seed."

"Rotten apple."

"A real Darth Vader, if you get my meaning. Couldn't resist the lure of the money, the power, the high life."

"Wanted the glory, couldn't stand being anonymous, wanted everyone to know he was a hero."

"He was from nowhere. No roots. No connections. Moving through this universe untethered."

Something about those words, the idea that a person could really be from nowhere, made me squirm. I was sure all three men noticed my discomfort.

"Simon found him," Baldy said. "He was teaching karate to kids in Ohio or North Dakota or something."

"What's the difference? Ohio or North Dakota? Who cares?" The laughter started again. It sounded like nails on a chalkboard, but I forced myself to smile right along with them.

"But really, we all know what it was about," Fatty said, "the reason he flipped."

Baldy nodded aggressively in agreement. "Yes. It's always about the girl, isn't it?"

"The girl?" I asked.

"Of course. Love lost. The most motivating emotion to be encountered by man."

"Or woman," Fatty tossed out with a wink. Jokester.

"The Czech girl. Or Bulgarian girl. Who can remember? Anyway, he loved her and she was dead. The Blind Monk did it. At least that was the word put out on the street."

"Put out on the street? So the Blind Monk didn't do it?" They were losing me.

"Well, you never can tell in this business."

"And it didn't really matter because Blackford thought it was the Blind Monk. That was what was important."

"But it was already too late. He was gone." They sat in silence for a few moments.

"So he is out there trying to avenge his lost love?" I had never considered, even for a moment, an emotional component.

"Hard to say. Maybe he just likes being bad." They laughed again.

"Well, thank you, gentlemen," I said. As I pushed away from the table, Fatty suddenly took both of my hands in his. His grip was strong. I slowly sank back into my seat.

"You should know," he said, eyes boring into me, "that Blackford is a psychopath. Regardless of what turned him, remember he has no capacity for love, no ability to feel empathy. He is, at the end of the day, a very dangerous man. Go carefully, Sally Sin, go very carefully in the direction of Ian Blackford."

And I saw a glimpse, at that moment, of the agent this man used to be. A small shiver shot down my spine.

I found out from an illegal pilfering of personnel records that Ian Blackford had no family, had grown up in a series of foster homes, some of which had been particularly ugly. He was a gifted athlete with a keen interest in the martial arts. He was the only Agent on record that did not finish college. There was a note in his file that this made him insecure. He compensated by embracing the physical parts of sleuthing. When it came to things like hand-to-hand combat, guns, blowing things up, breaking into buildings, setting traps, or generally causing mayhem, no one was better than Blackford.

There was no mention of a girl, dead or alive.

He was an odd choice for the USAWMD, an agency that tended to favor people who preferred to fly under the radar. Blackford was flamboyant, too loud, calling attention to himself more often than not. But he always delivered the goods, so his behavior was tolerated at the highest level. When he flipped, those same higher-ups looked around for someone to blame, but there was no one. They knew it was ultimately their own fault. After his defection, the Agency tightened up. By the time I came on board, the place could only be described as gray.

"What are you doing tonight, Lucy?" Avery asks. "Do you and your boys want to come over for dinner? Jonathan is out of town and we could use some company."

I come reeling back to the present. Tonight my plans include getting my husband very drunk, sneaking out of the house, and breaking into the lab of one Professor Albert Malcolm. But I can't exactly say that.

"Can we take a raincheck? Will's got some thing going on."

"Sure."

After an hour or so, Theo is tired and we head home. I keep checking my rearview mirror for Ian Blackford, sure that one of these times he's going to be there. I almost expect to find him sitting at my kitchen table waiting for me.

As soon as we are in the house, Will calls and tells me he has to jump on a plane for Washington this afternoon.

"They want me to give testimony at a hearing on alternative energy. An honest dialogue at the highest levels of government. Isn't that great?"

"Fabulous," I say. I don't have the heart to tell him that he should never use the word "honest" and "government" in the same sentence. It will only hurt his feelings. As he hangs up, I hear him yelling to his assistant to go out and buy him a clean shirt and a tie and see if his suit is still at the cleaners. I wonder if he remembers how to tie a tie? Oh well, I'm sure some lobbyist will be more than happy to help if he doesn't. They like to have their hands around your neck.

I miss Will when he's gone, even for a night. I miss the warmth of his body. After so many years of sleeping alone, I have grown accustomed to the comfort of another person in my bed. However, tonight this will work perfectly. I call Agent Nanny Pauline.

"I need you here tonight around ten P.M. Don't be late," I say and hang up. Tonight I will figure out what the professor is up to and maybe that will help me understand what all this fuss is about.

For dinner, Theo demands macaroni and cheese, not from a box but conjured from the mystery that is my refrigerator. We grate a pile of cheese, melt it with the macaroni, and call it good. Theo could not be happier. He digs in, insisting on feeding me every other bite.

"Mommy," he asks, cheese smeared across his cheek and in his hair, "what's your job?"

Of all possible dinner conversation topics, I will admit this is not one I was expecting.

"Taking care of you," I say.

"That's not a real job."

I wipe some cheese from his eyebrow. He pushes me away as he always does when I try to touch his face with a napkin.

"It feels like a real job to me." Some days more than others. Where is this coming from? "Why don't you think it's a real job?"

He shrugs. "Dunno. Harry's mom drives an airplane."

That may be true, but has she ever jumped out of one into a war zone at night in the rain? I add some more pasta to his bowl, suddenly hostile toward Harry's mom, who is nothing short of lovely. All my playground friends have answers to these types of questions. They can fall back on doctor or lawyer or investment banker or marketing executive or whatever. And sitting here, elbow deep in fake macaroni and cheese, I'm equally jealous of their normalcy and bothered that Theo will go through life thinking that in my heyday I was nothing more than a government analyst sitting in the dark, pondering the end of the world.

20

This is the one about the girl.

She was from somewhere in Eastern Europe. A gypsy. Perhaps Romanian or Hungarian, although which I can't say for sure. She was beautiful. Tall and lithe, with long dark hair and violet eyes. She seemed almost incandescent, somehow lit from within, and she was said to have long, delicate fingers that fluttered around when she was nervous. She would sit on the street in Prague or Sofia, near nice hotels and restaurants, offering to read the fortunes of the passing tourists. She could not have been more than twenty-two years old but seemed to have wisdom beyond her years. For some Eastern Europeans, the fall of the Soviets came like a spring rain, refreshing their hope in life. For others, it began only another phase of hardship. She was destined for the latter, but desperately wanted to believe life could improve. When Blackford saw her, sitting behind her little table, a deck of tarot cards laid out before her, it's said he was so taken with her beauty, he could not restrain himself. He offered her a pile of money for a private reading, and she returned to his hotel with him. This was not the first time she had provided such a private reading.

But Blackford was half in love with her by the time they arrived at his room and could no sooner take advantage of her offered services than he could shoot himself in the foot. They sat up all night on the balcony of his shabby communist hotel, looking out over the city lights, talking about the future, mostly hers. He told her he was an entrepreneur and could maybe use her help in gathering information. He could pay her a small salary, enough to keep her off the streets. He said he would visit her from time to time, and she seemed pleased by that prospect.

As the sun rose and the wine ran dry, he leaned in close and gently kissed her full, red lips. She pressed her hips to his and wrapped her long arms around his neck. She could feel his heart pounding in his chest and the dampness of his palms as they slid under her shirt.

Did he fall in love with her because she was beautiful or desperate or delicate? Did he want to save her? To save something real? I can only imagine.

Some say they made love that morning, with the balcony door open, on the squeaky old bed, and afterward watched the sun rise high in the cloudless blue sky. Others say it was raining, and that with the dawn of a gray morning, Blackford did nothing more than kiss her and promise her the world, or at least as much of it as he could deliver.

They also say the girl was a spy for the other side, sent to kill Blackford. But there seems to be no consensus on this point.

Blackford used her as an errand girl, to deliver packages and messages to the middlemen of the cartel he was trying to infiltrate. These middlemen, fat and lazy, came to anticipate with excitement visits from Blackford's girl.

The details on how they spent the intervening months is anybody's guess. Some say Blackford would take her on picnics in the country. He'd take her boating out on the river, to museums, to cocktail parties, shopping. He even got her a passport and took her to Paris. I can see them together, bodies intertwined, looking down on the city from the Eiffel Tower. I can see them holding hands, stopping to share a kiss in the Tuileries. I imagine they must have laughed, too, in that way new lovers do, as if no one else in the world exists. But I can't actually get that mental image to come up. I've tried, but it won't stick. Blackford never laughed. At least not really.

Someone once told me that they suspected he might have even been happy during that time. And maybe he was.

But happiness at the Agency was not an asset. It just gave you something else to lose.

They'd been together for about a year when she turned up dead, strangled, in the apartment they shared. She'd been there for a few days when Blackford finally found her. It was summer, and some say the heat had not been especially kind.

Simon Still pulled him from the case, replacing him with a new agent whose name I can't remember. And Blackford came home. No one asked about what happened. Quietly and carefully, as if they were walking on eggshells, everyone went back to work. A few weeks later, Blackford was shipped out to South Africa. Although Blackford's behavior never betrayed any distress, Simon said a few months in the nice weather might be good for him.

And it was hard not to notice his eyes. Once lively, they were now dead, like a shark's eyes.

After Blackford started kidnapping me, there were whispers, conversations that would stop awkwardly when I came around the corner. Finally, annoyed, I announced that yes, I had been abducted against my will by the notorious Ian Blackford, but was quite certain it wouldn't happen again. And I thought that put an end to it.

Our holiday parties at the Agency were always sad little affairs. Whoever was home and not celebrating in some cave in Pakistan would gather at a local watering hole and get falling-down drunk. The agent seated next to me was old by Agency standards. He would be forced out soon, only to discover most of his life was over and he had nothing to show for it, but for now he was enjoying himself. Toward the end of our mediocre Italian meal, he leaned in close, the alcohol strong on his breath.

"It wasn't the kidnapping, Sally," he slurred. "We've all had our little humiliations. Keeps us humble."

"Thanks for that," I said, mock-toasting him. "It makes me feel much better."

He gripped my wrist and pulled me toward him.

"No, it's that you remind us of her," he slurred. "The dead girl. The spy."

"Who killed her?" I whispered, thinking this drunk old guy might be out of it enough to give me the goods.

"We thought he might be the coldest person in the world," the old agent said, looking right at Simon Still. "Then we realized someone had to give the order."

21

After dinner, Theo and I sit together on the couch and watch an episode of *Sesame Street*. There is joy here, huddled with my son, so warm and soft. I try not to move. If I disturb the moment, if I don't respect it, it will disappear and I will never get it back. Theo plays with the ties on my sweatshirt and eventually settles in to chewing them vigorously while keeping at least one eye glued to the TV.

"Who's that?" he asks, spitting out a soggy sweatshirt tie.

"Grover."

"No it's not."

"Yes it is. I swear that is Grover."

"No it is not," he insists.

"Fine, it's not Grover," I say. I'm not really paying attention, thinking more about how I'm going to get into Malcolm's lab than which furry blue monster is doing what on the television.

"Yes it is Grover. He's the blue one," Theo says, exasperated.

"That's what I told you."

"No you didn't. I know everything."

How do I argue with that? I go back to thinking about getting caught breaking and entering. I'm not sure exactly how I would explain this particular set of circumstances to my friends and relations. Will would be especially ticked off if he had to fly home to bail me out of jail. And getting rescued by Simon Still is plain out of the question. I'm slowly coming to the conclusion that this whole thing is stupid, that maybe I should sit back and follow Simon's dim-witted plan about drawing Blackford out.

There is a little secret among the covert agencies of the United States and that little secret is that we rarely know what we are doing. Half of our success can be attributed to good luck and the other half to timing. Our plans and strategies are far less elaborate than the ones that spies come up with in the movies. We are usually making it up as we go along. Anyone who tells you differently is lying.

Theo is fast asleep when Pauline shows up, dressed exactly as she was earlier.

"How do you keep your shirts looking so pressed?" I ask.

"I changed into a new one," she answers. Of course she did.

"Theo is asleep. Will is in D.C. I should be back in a few hours."

"Where are you going?" she blurts out. I am wearing black pants, a black T-shirt, and a black jacket. For a second, I consider telling her.

"Bar hopping," I say finally and head out the door.

This time, when I sneak back around and into the kitchen, Pauline is standing there, wielding the cast-iron frying pan.

"Nice," I say. "You're getting it."

"Are you going to do this every time you leave?"

"I haven't decided yet. But your reaction time is improving. You should be proud."

She gives me a look that can only be described as hostile.

"Okay. I'll see you in a couple of hours."

She doesn't move or put down the frying pan or say anything. She just waits for me to leave.

I sit in the university parking lot with my lights off, trying to remember how to do this. I feel ridiculous, like an imposter, a fraud. I don't remember ever feeling this way before.

"You used to be good at this," I remind myself. The car remains silent. "Well, sitting here hyperventilating is not going to get you into Malcolm's lab anytime soon." I kick open the door and step into the crisp night air. There is no fog tonight. I almost wish there were so I could hide in its mist and disappear. I walk toward the lab deliberately, like I have a reason to be here. Simon falls into step beside me.

"Out for a stroll, Sal?"

"Are you stalking me?"

"Yes. I'm stalking you and your nanny. Have to cover all the bases," he says. "Actually, Pauline is under orders to report her activities directly to me, and I made the logical leap that in the middle of the night this might be your destination."

"You're a genius. What is her real name?"

"You know I can't tell you that."

"Yes, you can. But you won't."

"Same thing."

"Not at all."

"What are you planning on doing here, Sally?"

"Your work for you, it looks like."

"Resources are limited these days, Sal. I can't throw everything I've got at this."

"Is that why I'm involved? I'm the cheapest solution to the problem?"

Simon doesn't answer. He pops a piece of Nicorette gum into his mouth and starts chomping.

"You sound like a cow," I say.

"Your support for me while I attempt to improve my health is overwhelming," he says. "I'm touched."

"You know, Simon, my resources are somewhat restricted too, but even if they weren't, I'd still find it strange that Blackford comes back to life and suddenly strikes up a relationship with a guy you've never heard of who is concocting who knows what in his hermetically sealed laboratory."

Simon glares at me. "You need to save me from myself, Sal," he says, mocking, "like before."

"Oh, forget it."

We walk on in silence. After a few minutes, he asks me if I remember anything about breaking and entering.

"Not much. You?"

Simon shakes his head. "I've not been out in the field lately, at least not doing anything interesting." We stand in front of the lab building.

"Of course," I say, pulling the security cards out of my pocket, "these might help."

Simon grins. "You know stealing is illegal."

"I've always been better at theft than straight out breaking and entering. It's good to know your strengths. I think you told me that."

The lab is quiet, but all the lights are still on. It smells faintly like Theo's pediatrician's office, clean and sterile. I try to put Theo out of my head. I have to remember how to concentrate. We head to the second floor, third anonymous door to the left. The security card gives us the green light, and we swing open the massive door.

"I hope he cleaned up whatever nastiness he's been cooking in here," Simon says with a shudder. "I'd hate to have my eyeballs melt out of my head."

"You really have lost your edge," I say, looking around the lab. It gleams white and silver, everything tightly organized. "You think maybe the good professor is available for housecleaning?"

Automatically, Simon heads right and I head left. We will cover every inch of this lab as fast as possible, meeting in the center on the other side.

In the second drawer of a huge filing cabinet, I find lab notebooks, completely full of notations in pencil. I pull out the most recent, flip to the last page with writing, and start trying to translate, which is almost impossible, Chemistry 101 being the pinnacle of my training. At this rate, I will be here all night. I take a tiny camera out of my pocket and snap pictures of the last twenty pages or so of the notebook.

"You kept that camera?" Simon asks.

"Of course," I say, "it never failed me."

"Old technology, Sal. You should see the stuff we have now."

"So show me," I challenge.

"Well, I didn't bring any of it with me," Simon says.

"Then don't gloat about your cool spy gear."

"Fine."

"Good." We both go back to our respective sides of the lab. In the drawers and cabinets, I find an assortment of microscopes, lenses, petri dishes, labels, droppers, syringes, chewed-up pencil nubs, a pack of gum, a pack of cigarettes, and several Chinese take-out containers. A single pizza box is stuffed in the garbage.

"There is nothing here, Sal," Simon says after an hour of searching. "I told you there was nothing here."

"Simon, something is here. We just can't see it." I touch the camera in my pocket. There is definitely something here. There has to be. A final sweep of the room assures us that nothing is out of order, and we head out of the lab, running smack into a security guard on regular patrol.

"Good evening, officer," Simon says. "Nice night out?"

"Yes," the man says. "Enjoy it, Professor."

"I certainly will." Simon takes my arm and we walk confidently down the hall. I've seen him do this before, take a situation that looks wrong all over and make it seem completely normal. The security guard did not even think to question what this strange man was doing in this restricted-access building in the middle of the night. If Simon had remained silent, it would have registered for the guard that something was off. But Simon acts like he belongs and almost commands others to believe the same. I was never as good a liar as Simon Still.

Back in the parking lot, Simon pulls out another piece of Nicorette.

"That's almost as bad as smoking," I say.

"I might keep doing it just to annoy you," he says. "Now that you're done with your little exploration, can we get back to the original plan? You hang around and draw out Blackford, and we drop the net."

I give up. "Sure. Tomorrow we will do it your way and see what happens."

"Thank you for humoring me."

"What makes you think he's not hiding in the bushes right now, watching our every move?"

"Nothing. It might, in fact, be true. That's why I thought I should accompany you on your obviously pointless fishing expedition."

"Well, thanks for chaperoning but I have to go home now." I get in my car and without saying good-bye head back toward the bridge.

When I get home, Nanny Pauline is asleep on the couch, sitting up straight. I don't know how people can sleep that way. I give her shoulder a little shake, and her eyes fly open.

"It's okay," I say quietly. "I'm back."

"I'm sorry I didn't tell you about Simon," she says, rubbing her eyes like Theo after a nap.

"You work for him," I say, shrugging my shoulders. "What are you supposed to do?"

Pauline casts her eyes toward her shoes. She has too much morality. She will die one day because she pauses too long to consider the consequences of her actions.

"You can sleep in the spare room, if you want," I offer. "It's late." Pauline looks at her wrinkled shirt.

"No, I'd better go. I'll see you tomorrow." As I let her out, I see a light go off in my neighbor Tom's living room. He's been watching the comings and goings at my house, but I'm pretty sure he won't say anything. It's a hard thing to admit you've been spying.

22

The next day, I go about the difficult business of being a stay-at-home mom, with no job and a nanny. I make an appointment to get a haircut, a facial, lunch with Avery. My first stop is the nail salon. When I show the lady my nails, she frowns.

"You bite," she says harshly. "No biting." I look at my ragged cuticles and cannot think of a witty retort. I started chewing on my cuticles the first day I went into the field for the USAWMD and I have never stopped. I take immense satisfaction in gnawing them down to a bloody pulp. And I'm the first to admit it is a horrifying sight.

I smile apologetically and don't bother with any excuses. "You need come here more," she continues in disgust. "Nails very bad."

How do women do this? How do they go out and get insulted in the pursuit of beauty and perfection day in and day out? I want to draw my hands back from this woman and hide them in my pockets. As she gets busy, she starts in on me in Vietnamese. Why can't a woman like me take care of myself? What am I doing all day? Her coworker nods her head and comes back with a question about how come we always dress like slobs. Jeans, tennis shoes, never heels, never anything nice. So much money and so little taste, she says.

"Why wear nice clothes," I ask in rusty Vietnamese, "if some kid is inevitably going to wipe his greasy hands on your cashmere?" My manicurist's face turns red.

"This only happens on TV, right?" I continue. "Where the client actually knows what you are saying about her in a language most Americans have no hope of understanding. I'm right, aren't I?"

One of the women starts laughing. "Where did you learn Vietnamese?" she asks.

"In Vietnam, of course."

"You speak very well. You are the first white person to come in here and speak it. I've been here for ten years."

My manicurist apologizes for insulting me. I dismiss it. "You're probably right," I say. "I wear the same thing every day. Except when I'm breaking and entering. For that, I wear black." They both laugh, although it is clear they have no idea what I'm talking about. The Vietnamese feels funny on my tongue and in my mouth. It has been a very long time. By the time I'm ready to leave, my nails look better than they ever have and my toes are positively gorgeous, which is some sort of miracle. I am advised to come back again soon and visit with my new Vietnamese friends. I promise I will, thinking it will probably take Theo's graduation from high school or some event like that to get me to go back. I have an hour to kill before I meet Avery for lunch, so I sit outside a coffee shop with a double espresso loaded with sugar. I close my eyes and think of Rome.

I was there because a United Nations official was using the World Food Program to transport weapons to rebels in Africa. It was a brilliant strategy. Bury the guns under the rice and no one was the wiser. However, he was making certain people very angry and we were asked to stop him. And I did, borrowing a page from Blackford's playbook. I lured the gentleman in question back to my very lovely hotel room and handcuffed him to a chair. When I told him the handcuffs were actually meant to restrain him until EU officials arrived rather than for deviant sexual acts, he was very disappointed and called me all sorts of names. After he left with his escorts, I filled the giant bathtub and submerged myself up to my chin. I thought it might help me relax, which was, of course, a ridiculous idea. I never relaxed. I was not even sure how it was done. I closed my eyes and tried to quiet the ringing in my ears.

Ian Blackford chose that moment to appear in my bathroom doorway. He was dressed in dark jeans and a black sweater, and he eyed me like prey.

"What are you doing here?" I screamed, practically levitating out of the tub. I grabbed one of the huge fluffy towels from the rack and covered myself as best I could while still in the water. "Get out," I demanded. "Now!"

"You have fantastic breasts," he said.

"That is so cliché," I sputtered, furious. "It's like James Bond and those fucking martinis."

"Are you suggesting I resemble Mr. Bond?" He took a long look at himself in the mirror, turning side to side.

"Sean Connery?" he said.

"Oh, please, don't flatter yourself."

"Pierce?"

"What are you doing in my bathroom?" He stared at me, silent.

"Okay," I said finally, "maybe Pierce, but only the parts where he looks like shit. Now can you please get out of my bathroom?" The last part came out a little bit squeaky for my taste.

Blackford continued to admire himself in the mirror. "Sally, you and I both know that Pierce never looks like shit."

"Please leave."

Blackford ignored my request and took a seat on the closed toilet, one hand dipped casually in my tub, perilously close to my foot. Don't touch me, I thought. Please dear God, do not let this man touch me. I don't know what I'll do if he touches me. Die, most likely.

"Sal, you did a bad thing tonight. Bruce was my friend and now he's useless. I wish you'd told me."

"Well, checking in with you is not really high on my priority list," I said, although it's hard to be indignant with any authority while sitting in a bathtub partially covered in a wet towel.

"Sal, Sal, Sal," he said, shaking his head, "but we have this history together. Doesn't that count for anything?"

"What history? The fact that you keep turning up rather unexpectedly in places like my bathroom? That is not history. That is crime."

He laughed. "Is your moral compass so true that you cannot appreciate the finer points of this relationship?"

"We have no relationship," I shouted, standing up in a cascade of bath water and putting my hands on my naked hips for emphasis. "Now, please get out of here so I can get dressed."

Ian Blackford's icy blue eyes started at my knees and slowly made their way up my body. As they moved, I could feel the heat radiating off my skin. I reached for a dry towel, my shaking hands giving me away.

"Don't," he said in a voice I'd never heard before. "Let me finish." And for some reason my hand stopped short of the towel and hung there in midair, hovering like a butterfly, as Blackford completed his survey of my body. Die for sure.

"Thank you," he said when he was done. Standing to his full height, he gave me a last glance and left the bathroom. When I was dry and dressed, I went out into the room, expecting to see him lying on my bed, helping himself to my uncorked bottle of cabernet. But he was gone. I can admit all these years later that I felt something akin to disappointment. It took several days before the thought of his eyes drinking me in did not cause a thin sheen of sweat to blossom across my forehead. Even now, sitting here in the sun, downing my double espresso, I shudder at the thought of him.

I scan the sidewalks, my eyes sweeping back and forth as if I have front row seats at the U.S. Open. And of course, I see him everywhere. Standing at the ATM, in line at the bagel shop, passing in a car or on the bus, in the middle of the crosswalk, talking on a cell phone, eating a sandwich two tables down. I could never sense when Blackford would show up. There were times, dark ones, boring ones, when I found myself praying for him to appear, and he never would. It was always when I wasn't thinking about him, when he'd drifted into the dark recesses of my mind, that he would show up, almost as if he knew I was forgetting.

But now he is nowhere. I wonder if he really knows I'm here. I wonder if Simon Still is telling the truth or manipulating me for some other purpose of which I am unaware. It is a habit of ex-spies to see conspiracy everywhere. I can sit here and tie myself up in paranoid knots or I can try and enjoy the last sip of my espresso.

Avery admires my nails as we wait for a table at a very hip restaurant I've never heard of.

"Where is Theo?" she asks.

"Oh, Will's sister is in town and she's looking after him," I say.

"I thought Will was an only child?" Avery asks. Damn. Yes. This is true. Now why didn't I think of that?

"It's actually his cousin but he calls her a sister because they were very close growing up," I say, which sounds like bullshit even to me. Avery nods her head. There is a reason why I've asked her to lunch, and while I very much enjoy her company that is not it. Avery's husband is a chemistry professor at the other big-name university in the Bay Area, and I desperately need him to translate Malcolm's notes. However, I still don't have a plan for how to ask her without making it seem totally weird and out of the ordinary. Gee, Avery, I broke into this famous professor's lab last night and stole his notes and I'd really like Jonathan to help me translate them into a language I can understand. Do you mind passing these on to him? Somehow I don't think that will fly.

"Have you ever been to Mexico?" Avery asks. "We're thinking of a house rental on the beach there sometime in the next few months."

Yes, but not to anyplace you'd like to visit.

"I hear Cabo San Lucas is nice," I say. "Feels kind of remote." Once I ended up walking a twenty-mile stretch of very empty Cabo desert without so much as an ounce of liquid in sight. I'd chased a gun smuggler into the endless sandy brush. He had extra gas on board his vehicle. I did not. I lost that round, but I made him pay later.

"Really remote." I swallow down a huge gulp of water; the thought of the Baja Peninsula is enough to make my throat dry. "It's a nice vacation spot."

"My Spanish is lousy," Avery admits. "How did you get by? Do you speak at all?"

"A little," I say. "I can manage."

Our salads come, mine drowning in goat cheese and oil, hers cheese- and oil-free. Avery stares at my plate.

"How do you do it?" she asks.

"What?" I shovel in a huge mouthful of salad. Criminal activity in the middle of the night leaves one with a serious appetite.

"Eat like that and look like you do," she says.

What do I look like other than the brown hair and blue eyes? Well, it's a good question. I'm five feet seven inches with pale skin. I've never had a problem with weight, mostly because I tend toward the hyperactive side. I'm meticulous about avoiding the sun, which is good considering I spent a lot of years in a hat and sunglasses. Overall, the word that best describes me is ordinary. There are certain men and women who find that very thing attractive and others who would not notice me if they tripped over me on the sidewalk. Which very nicely served to keep me alive on a number of occasions.

I look at Avery over another heaping forkful of salad. She is, by anyone's definition, the perfect woman. Perfect height, shape, hair color, eye color, face symmetry, voice tone. And yet she does not see it.

"It's lettuce," I say, holding up some greens. "For exercise, I beat up yoga instructors." Avery shakes her head.

"You are a strange one, Lucy Hamilton, and someday I'm going to figure you out."

I hope not. You might not like me as much if you did.

"Can I ask you a favor?" I ask.

"Sure. Anything."

"I'm working on an article," I begin, "for a chemistry monthly, and I have some notes that need translating, some stuff beyond my level of expertise. Do you think Jon would take a look for me?"

"Of course he would. I didn't know you were a writer."

"I used to do some stuff on the side. This is a favor for an editor friend of mine." I'm just making this up as I go along and hoping for the best.

"Jon's around. Just stop by and I'm sure he'll have no problem taking a look."

Now, I think, how does now work for you? Blackford is going to pop up at any moment, like one of those whack-a-mole carnival games, and I have nothing to bargain with.

"Maybe over the weekend?" Avery nods her head in response and is back to Mexico and other vacation possibilities.

After lunch, I wander in and out of a few expensive clothing boutiques that have absolutely no relevance to my life. I walk slowly among the racks, touching the soft fabrics, but buy nothing. I stop for another espresso even though my hands are literally twitching from too much caffeine. I keep looking for Blackford. I keep seeing him everywhere. By late afternoon, I'm out of useless time-killing activities and I announce to no one in particular that I'm going home. Wherever Simon is, even he can't argue that I didn't follow my orders.

23

I am in the kitchen trying to make salsa, which is kind of comical, when Will walks through the front door. I hear his key, his hello, the thud of his suitcase as he drops it in the hallway. Theo leaps up from the kitchen floor where he is filling a pasta pot with wooden blocks and tears down the hallway, launching himself into Will's arms.

"Whoa there, cowboy," I hear Will say.

"Daddy, Daddy, Daddy," Theo howls. Ten seconds later, the two of them, now tangled up with one another, enter the kitchen.

"Hello, love," my gorgeous husband says and kisses me. I feel a little bolt of electricity travel from my lips to my toes. Nice.

"Hello," I murmur into his neck, "welcome home." I always find myself breathing a sigh of relief when Will returns from wherever he has been. It's almost as if when he's gone, I can't quite believe he exists. When he is here, I know he's real. I can touch him for proof.

"How was your night?" he asks, trying to settle our very excited child back on the floor with limited success.

"Fine," I say, "nothing much happened."

"Pauline came," Theo chimes in from at my feet. "She played cars. I like her."

Will raises his eyebrow at me. "Who is Pauline?"

"Oh, no one," I say, panicking. "A friend who was here."

"Mommy went out." Suddenly I find myself wishing for the days when my little boy didn't possess a vocabulary beyond "gimme" and "no."

"She watched him. I had an appointment. Um, you know, dentist, teeth cleaning. Do you want a glass of wine?" I say, hoping to redirect this conversation to any other topic.

He nods and gets down on the floor with Theo. I watch them there, two blond heads bent together over the business at hand. I wonder what, if anything, my DNA had to do with the making of this child. He resembles his father in every way, and the older he gets, the more of Will's personality starts to show through. I want to get down on the floor and squeeze them both to me and shut out the ridiculousness of Ian Blackford and Simon Still. But I don't. Instead, I turn back to the massacre that is my salsa and try to steady myself.

After Theo is in bed, Will and I sit on the couch drinking wine and eating chips and salsa. He really must love me because he does not make one negative comment about the soupy red mixture I have placed in front of him. It is also a point in his favor that he finds the occasional dinner of chips and salsa perfectly acceptable. In fact, we are in agreement that the simple pleasure of a wonderfully greasy chip and a bite of tongue-burning salsa can sometimes be better than dinner at Chez Panisse. Okay, maybe not. But it will do in a pinch. We start in on a bottle of red, totally inappropriate, but pretty good anyway, and within a few minutes we start to relax.

"I love Washington," Will says. "Don't you miss it?"

"Well, let me think about that. No. Not at all."

Summers in Washington did terrible things to my hair, not to mention the rest of me.

"I thought we got a lot on the record. It was hopeful."

"You might be the only person I've ever met who has used 'hopeful' to describe Washington."

He throws a chip at my head. I eat it.

"Small steps, Lucy. If we all keep taking small steps, we'll get there."

"You should put that on a poster."

Our bare feet are layered like bricks. I examine his toes, which are the only toes I can remember seeing that aren't hideous. Mine are hideous. Even with the killer pedicure, they are still cringe-worthy.

"Nice toes."

"Thanks. My reward for surviving the dentist," I lie.

"Good. You should treat yourself to things. You are too selfless."

I stifle a horrified laugh and blurt out, "What if someone you thought was one way suddenly turned out to be entirely different?"

Will sits up a little straighter. My feet fall away from his.

"Are you talking specifics or hypothetically?" he asks slowly.

"Hypothetically," I say, swallowing hard. "Something someone asked me at the playground the other day."

He thinks about this for a minute.

"You know all of my secrets, and someday I hope to know all of yours," he says. "Because I'm pretty sure I don't yet. But that's one of the reasons I married you. I want to take the rest of my life to find out."

It's a pretty good answer. And as much as I'd like to believe him, I have yet to encounter a happily ever after without strings attached.

The next day is Saturday and I sleep in. Will gets up with Theo, and I hear them muddling around in the kitchen, Theo making unreasonable demands and his dad trying desperately to figure out if this is normal. Does he really get to eat chocolate bunnies for breakfast? Or chocolate milk, for that matter? I lie in bed with the covers pulled up to my nose, reveling in the amazing softness of the sheets, how cool they are on my skin, kind of like Theo's hands when he is exploring my face, touching my nose and eyelids and mouth. I love these moments. The weekend holds such promise, a chance to undo the drudgery of the week, shed the weight of obligation and routine, and do only what you feel like doing. Exercise free will.

I had no idea weekends could be so great until I actually had a few. Agents with the USAWMD don't have weekends. I mean, technically they have them when they are not on a mission, but I don't recall ever realizing I was having one. I worked every waking hour of every day. If I didn't, inevitably I got to thinking about what a train wreck my life was and that was downright depressing.

But now the weekends are cherished, a time for the three of us to wander through the empty and unscheduled days together. When I eventually make it downstairs, Will has a mug of sweet, milky coffee waiting for me. Theo is under the table, playing with his mini yellow Corvette. There are tinfoil chocolate bunny wrappers on the floor.

"I see he found the chocolate," I say.

"Hardly seemed like a battle worth fighting," Will responds. "I didn't see myself winning."

"No," I agree, "there was very little chance of that happening. He's relentless."

"And we've already been through the sugar high, so you timed your entrance wisely."

"Excellent." I take a long slug of coffee. "What should we do today?"

"I have that kite-surfing lesson down at Crissy Field. Do you guys want to come and watch me get run over by a tanker or two?"

I smile, thinking about Will in a wetsuit. I fully expect that by the end of the lesson he will be able to give the instructor a few pointers. One of his friends tells a story of how, after two weeks of surfing in Australia, no one, not even the hard-core surfer dudes, could tell he was an amateur. It was assumed Will had been born with a surfboard attached to his feet. He is a gifted athlete. On one of our first dates, he beat me senseless in a tennis game, after which I couldn't walk for a week, my body not used to the side-to-side motion. Me, I'm good at running away, which is not all that helpful on the tennis court.

"We would love to come and watch you, although I have a hard time imagining why you would want to get into that water. It's cold. Really cold."

"Thank you for your concern."

"Daddy, are we going swimming?" Theo calls from under the table.

"Only me, sweet pea. You are going to play on the beach with Mommy."

Theo considers this. "Okay. We'll go swimming next time with the trains."

"I promise," Will says, raising his eyebrows at me as if to ask for an explanation. I shrug. Even I can't interpret all of Theo's thoughts.

Crissy Field is one of the joys of living in San Francisco. Meticulously restored to its natural state, this long stretch of coast is the perfect playground for adults and children alike. With a view of Alcatraz, Angel Island, and Tiburon across the bay, it is as good a place as any to waste a weekend afternoon. In the parking lot, we help Will wrestle into his wetsuit. I stand back to admire the result.

"You look kind of hot," I say.

"I am hot," he says. "I'm boiling actually."

"No. That's not what I meant."

"Oh." He smiles. "Thanks. I think you're crazy. I look like a sausage."

"Good luck, sausage," I say, kissing him. "Don't drown." We leave him standing in the parking lot, pulling on booties and a hood. Did I mention that the water here is cold, as in really, really cold? It would take a lot more than curiosity about some new sport to get me to jump in. It's true. I'm the first to admit that I've gone soft.

Theo and I camp out on a silky stretch of white sand. There are dogs everywhere, tearing into the surf, racing up and down the beach. Theo runs immediately to the water's edge to fill his yellow bucket. When he returns and dumps it over my bare feet, I gasp.

"Your father is crazy," I say.

"I'll get more!" Theo volunteers.

And suddenly there he is, standing at the other end of the beach, far enough away that I can't clearly see the features of his face, but I know he is watching me. He is perfectly still, dressed in jeans and a T-shirt, a Giants baseball hat, and Ray-Bans from the 1980s. He gives me a small salute and walks in the opposite direction.

For a minute, time stretches and everything slows down. Ian Blackford has found me again.

When I reach for Theo, I am shaking. He holds tightly to his bucket full of freezing water.

"Mommy?" he asks. I try on a neutral expression.

"What, baby?"

"Too tight. It hurts," he says, peeling my fingers from his arm. They have left red marks on his delicate skin.

"Oh, sweetheart, I'm sorry. I didn't mean to squeeze you so hard." I give him a hug. "Do you need more water?"

But my voice is unsteady and I have to sit on my hands to settle them. I am, it seems, still terrified of Blackford. I sweep my eyes up and down the beach, out onto the water where white sails float on the bay like seagulls. He is gone.

I dig my toes into the sand. Maybe it wasn't him. Maybe I am really seeing things now. Maybe I'm actually finally losing my mind. But then he sits down on the sand next to me.

"Hello, Sally Sin," he says, brushing a finger across my cheek. I recoil at his touch. When I try to speak, nothing comes out.

"Hi," Theo pipes up from his newly excavated sand hole. "Who are you?"

"An old friend of your mother's," he says with a smile. "He is yours, isn't he? Cute kid."

I am still without my voice, my whole body shaking now as if the temperature suddenly dropped forty degrees.

"Relax, Sal," Blackford says, "I'm not going to do anything to you. Just thought I'd stop by and say hello. It's been a long time."

"Relax?" I manage after what seems like forever. "You're supposed to be dead and I'm supposed to relax?"

"Well, the dead thing worked well enough for a while, and now I've been reborn. Aren't you pleased to see me?"

"No," I say with a little too much force. Theo stops digging and looks at me. I smile to reassure him and he goes back to his shovel. "No, I'm not happy to see any of you, frankly. You, Simon, the nanny."

"I agree with you on Still. He's a pain in the ass, always has been. Don't know much about the nanny so I can't comment on that one. But come on," he says, giving me a quick punch in the arm, "you didn't miss me at all?"

I turn to fully look at him for the first time. He is the same, the blue eyes, the black hair, the perfect skin that shows no sign of age or wear or distance. And I shudder.

"Cold?"

"I'm fine," I say, inching away from him.

"So your man is out on the water? Brave soul. It's cold out there."

"What do you want?" I ask.

"Oh, I don't know, see old friends, reminisce about the glory days."

"I have no idea what you are talking about."

"I don't appreciate you working with Still to set a trap for me. Don't you know me well enough to know I don't fall into traps?"

I immediately begin to flail around for an excuse, but Blackford holds up his hand.

"Nothing you could do. I get that. Simon's about five minutes from here, so I'm going to go. Don't want to make things too hard on you and your little family."

He stands, brushing the sand off his pants. "I'll see you around," he says. "You look good, Sally, better than ever. This life suits you. On some level, I find that surprising."

With that, he walks off down the beach. I want to chase after him and ask him what he could want from me after all these years. But that is not a possibility.

Theo and I continue to dig his hole until his father returns, wet and exhilarated, from racing around on the bay attached to a giant kite.

"That was amazing," he says. "Nice hole. Are you okay? You look a little pale."

"I'm fine. Great, really. Fine. Do you need help getting out of that thing?"

"Sure," Will says. I peel the wetsuit off of him like a banana. Underneath, his skin is white, with a slight blue tinge, and cold to the touch. I rest my hand on his chest, making a warm spot. My voice catches in my throat and for a minute I think I might cry.

"Hey," Will says, tilting my chin up, "are you sure you're okay?"

"I'm fine," I say, "really."

But I'm not. The adrenaline rush from Ian Blackford is still surging through my veins. I feel like a coiled spring, the tension almost too much to bear. I try to steady my breathing. Now is not the time to fall apart. In the parking lot, I see Simon behind the wheel of a Mercedes convertible. He nods at me and I ignore him, holding tightly to my husband's hand, hoping against all hell that he can keep me from disappearing down the rabbit hole.

24

'm awake on Sunday morning before the sun is up. Will sleeps beside me, an arm tossed over my hip. I can feel his heat and want nothing more than to slip back into a foggy delirium alongside of him. But that is not going to happen. Even before my eyes opened, my brain was at full throttle, desperately trying to put the pieces together. There is something here that I'm missing, something important, but it remains out of focus. I throw off the down comforter and slide my feet into a pair of fuzzy pink slippers. I pull Will's discarded sweater, on the floor from the night before, over my head. It smells like him. I tuck the covers back around his body and head down the hall to Theo's room. It's about 5 A.M., and Theo will sleep for another hour and a half before he starts to bellow for Daddy to come and get him. I stroke back his matted hair, watching his eyelids twitch and flutter with the activity of some unknown dream.

Down in the kitchen, I fire up the coffeemaker, taking a seat at the table. Is it possible that the critical thinking part of my brain has atrophied from lack of use? I want to reach in through my ear and scoop out the cobwebs that must be clogging up the works in there. Instead, I pour a huge mug of strong coffee and hope for the best.

The players are the same: Simon Still, Ian Blackford, the Blind Monk, and Malcolm, playing the roll of the new guy doing some new thing that is making everyone else behave badly. The game is the same: Blackford and the Blind Monk both want what the new guy is selling, and Simon Still wants two things. First, he wants to rid the world of weapons of mass destruction. Second, he wants to put Blackford in a body bag. Not necessarily in that order. The big difference, I realize now, is me. I am not the same. I used to jump into this with both feet. Following the Blind Monk or Blackford was second nature. It was what I did, it was what I thought about. And there was nothing else in my life, nothing so critical that it would crowd them out of my head and out of my life. My purpose was important. At times, the security of the world depended on what we at the Agency might be able to pull off. But through it all, I remained not altogether serious about my work. It was like playing a global game of chess, and that is exactly how I treated it. If I died, who would miss me? If I succeeded, who would know?

But now everything is different. The thought makes my head ache. I refill my coffee mug, knowing that there is not enough caffeine in the world to help me through this. There is nothing but me.

I hear Theo stirring in his bed, shouting out something about a taxicab and settling back in for a little more sleep. How nice it would be to go upstairs and crawl into his crib with him and dream about bright yellow taxis.

Today is a big day, a family outing to get Theo a brand-new, big-boy bed. He is thrilled at the idea, if not completely sure of the practice. It won't be fair to Will or Theo if in my head I'm floating around in the deep mysterious past rather than paying attention to the present.

I always believed that I was good at my job, not a superhero but good enough. Whenever I asked Simon for feedback about my performance, his annoyance was palpable.

"You're alive, aren't you?" he'd say. "Now take Jacob. Jacob is not good at his job."

"Jacob is dead, sir."

"See what I'm getting at?"

But what if I wasn't any good? I think about the note on my Agency file, the one wondering if I should be referred to Simon as a potential hire at all. I think about the question mark. And that leads me to Director Gray.

When I asked Simon Still why it was I'd never met Director Gray, the head of the Agency to which I had sworn allegiance until death do us part and so on, he frowned at me in a deeply unnerving way. Simon didn't experience regular emotions. At best, I'd hoped for a snarky reply and a belittling dismissal. At worst, I thought he might totally ignore me, pretending I wasn't standing twelve inches from his nose, tapping my foot impatiently. But I asked and he frowned, which could only mean he had no good, prepackaged, well-rehearsed line to throw back in my face, ultimately intended to make me shut up and go away. Troubling. So rather than count my blessings and hit the road on back to my own little bat cave, I had to keep at it.

"I've been here for two and a half years. Do I embarrass you? Has he met anyone else new? *Is* there anyone else new?" I asked, plopping myself down on one of Simon's cruel metal folding chairs, intending to stay in his office until he answered me. He sighed.

"Sally, sometimes you remind me of a mosquito. And I don't mean that kindly. Don't you have work to do?" He rubbed the bridge of his nose, hard, calling up a nasty red mark. Also not a good sign. I put my feet up on his desk, expecting him to toss me into the hallway without even a "have a nice day." But he didn't. He sat down. I moved my feet.

"Oddly enough," he began, "the Director has requested to meet with you as of this morning." I brightened up.

"Really? What did I do? Congressional Medal of Honor?"

"Yes. And I'm going to the Moon on the next flight out. Listen, Sally, when Gray wants to see you, well, it's never a good thing."

"But I didn't do anything wrong," I said, frantically going back over my last few missions in my mind. At least, nothing that stood out. What did he know? Simon read my mind.

"Gray knows everything. Don't even try to come up with a good story to cover your tracks."

I followed him up out of the subbasement back into the land of light. We walked for miles, down corridors and through hallways, entryways, and thruways. We went in doors and out, left and right and right again, and finally we arrived at the Director's office.

Simon nodded at the well-dressed secretary. She gestured for him to sit. No words were exchanged.

"Wow. I guess if you're the boss, you get real furniture, huh?"

Simon stood back up. "You stay here. I'll see you when he's done with you. If you haven't been reassigned." He disappeared back the way we'd come, leaving me with nothing more than the secretary for reassurance. Her face was blank, without the slightest hint of compassion for my predicament.

"Great. I'm fucked," I muttered.

"He'll see you now," she said, almost in response.

I marched into the Director's office with as much swagger as I could muster, which, let me tell you, was not a whole lot. The Director sat with his back to me facing a wall of huge, clean windows. He got to look outside. We, down in hell, got to look at puke-colored cement walls or, worse, each other. He was talking on the phone. I stood in front of his desk, silent, waiting, my heart pounding in my chest.

After a minute, he finished his conversation and spun toward me.

"Sally Sin," he said, as if the name left a bad taste in his mouth.

"Yes, sir," I said. I couldn't help but stare. There was something so familiar about him, something so close but still out of focus. I knew this man, I would swear to it, yet we had never met until this exact moment.

"Well, Agent Sin, if I may call you that. Tell me about Blackford."

"Ian Blackford, sir? I'm not sure I can . . ."

"Can and will," he said, pushing back from his desk.

"I'm not sure what I can tell you that hasn't already been in my reports."

"Why don't you start at the beginning? Tell me everything. Don't leave out any details. Make me understand why Blackford picked you."

I'll admit, this last part made me feel a little bit bad, but no matter. I began to tell the not quite fairy tale starring little old clueless me and big, bad, superspy traitor Blackford. When I got to the part about his request that I tell Gray he could get to me anytime, anyplace, I could see the old man's face tighten, but he said nothing. He kept his eyes closed and listened.

"I know how he can be," he said when I was finished. His smile was like an arctic wind blowing through the room. "Sweeps you right off your feet, doesn't he? Makes you think you are important." The last word came out like a hiss.

"Don't be fooled, Agent Sin. He will tell you things, fantastic things. None of it is true. It's all make-believe. Is that clear?"

I nodded, although I had no idea what he was talking about. Blackford never told me anything. He just played with me like a cat with a three-legged mouse.

"Well, even if you do believe him," he said, leaning toward me, "it can't change the circumstances. It can't change what has been done."

I sat so still I might have been dead.

Director Gray stared intently in my direction, but it was as if he were seeing through me to some other time, some other place. Abruptly, his eyes flashed, and he was back in the present.

"Go," he said. He spun in his chair, leaving me to ponder the back of his head. "This conversation is over."

"Thank you, sir," I said, the flush rushing to my cheeks. I backed out of the office like he was the Queen of England. And that was the first time I met Director Gray.

25

Avery's house is on a hill with a panoramic view of San Francisco. From her bathtub, you can actually see the Golden Gate Bridge. We are good friends but not so good that I could ask to borrow her bathtub and not have her look at me funny. The house is catalog perfect, a designer's dream, and yet it manages to feel homey and lived-in at the same time. I'm not afraid to walk on her carpet or sit on her sofa.

Jonathan is in the kitchen, bifocals low on his nose, the Sunday *New York Times* unfurled on the table. It is 9 A.M. At home, Will and Theo are working through their scrambled eggs. My husband will try to read the paper, and Theo will not allow it.

"Daddy, let's play cars. Daddy, what are you reading? Daddy, what are you doing? Daddy, is that coffee in there? Can I have some?" And on and on until Will relents, gets down on the floor, and gives Theo his full attention.

Thirty minutes earlier, I promised to be back in plenty of time to go shopping for Theo's new bed and slipped out the door. In my bag, Malcolm's photographed notes are rubbing elbows with left-over apple slices and a leaky bottle of water.

Jonathan is older than Avery by a decade. With silver hair and a crooked smile, he looks every bit the professor, the kind the girls can't help but flirt with. Avery gets me coffee, which may push me over the line into a state of hyperactivity from which I cannot return. She has an odd look on her face, a tight smile that might fracture into a million pieces with the slightest provocation. She avoids eye contact with Jonathan, focused entirely on delivering me my drink. From my bag, I pull the notes, only slightly damp. I slide them in front of Jonathan.

"Sorry they are a little wet." Jonathan picks up the limp notes between his thumb and forefinger as if they might give him a bad case of cooties.

"Just water," I assure him. He nods and gives me a weak smile. Jonathan, from what I understand, is not a hands-on dad. He doesn't enjoy poopy diapers, snot, sand, spit, drool, barf, sticky fingers, or mushed-up food in his hair. He is a scientist, a professor, and he has a reputation to maintain even within his own home.

"I need a little help understanding these," I say, "for an article I'm writing."

"Sure," he says, running his eyes over the pages. "I didn't know you were a writer." After a minute, his brow furrows, and I wonder how smart bringing another person into this mess really is. But in the end I have no choice.

"Where did you get these?" he asks.

"I stole them out of Albert Malcolm's lab," I say before I can stop myself. Avery laughs and Jonathan smiles.

"I almost believe you," he says. "These are lab notes with some very complex formulas. They are not complete so I can't tell you exactly what they say, but it looks like someone is messing around with the idea of the Death Lily."

"The what?"

"The Death Lily. Not a flower you'd want to have in your table-top arrangement exactly. Have you ever heard the story?"

I shake my head.

"Well, you probably have never been to Cambodia, so why would you know?"

Nope. Never been to Cambodia.

"In any case, the writings on one of the temples in Siem Reap describe in great detail a lily so powerful that it can basically turn a human being into an automaton, making him susceptible to external influences. The Khmer drew a series of scenes in which they used the lilies to turn whole armies back on their masters. It's pretty powerful stuff. But no one ever found the lily, so it remains what it is—a story."

He holds the notes gingerly. "Whoever is working on this is trying to mimic the components of the Death Lily in the lab. However, that's hard to do if you don't have a sample. The possible combinations become infinite.

"Really, where did you get these?" he asks again. "Because I know you didn't steal them."

Right, I think. It's more like I borrowed them.

"From one of his students," I say, which is, technically speaking, true, even if said student doesn't know it.

"I'm surprised a student would be willing to give up something like this. It's fascinating. I didn't know Malcolm worked in this area, but he never publishes anything and never speaks, so it's hard to know what the hell he's up to."

"No good," I say, only half joking.

"Hmmm. Interesting. There is a notation here that indicates he was close to success, but something went wrong. It might mean that there is a component involved that cannot be easily synthesized."

I look at him blankly.

"Some element from nature that cannot be created in a lab and have the same effect. He would need a bit of the actual lily in order to proceed."

"Why would anyone want to undertake this?" I ask, sure I'm not going to like the answer.

"Well, there is the academic challenge, of course. But think about it," he says. "Think about what was described on those temple walls. There would be no need for weapons of mass destruction, right? Whoever controls this substance controls the world. You simply turn the armies back on their masters." We both sit in silence for a few moments, contemplating such a world.

"Mind control," I say.

"Total mind control," Jonathan says. "But don't worry. This sort of nonsense exists only in movies, not in real life. Malcolm is wasting his time. I always thought he was a bit of a kook."

If only what he said were true.

"Well, I'm sorry to interrupt your Sunday morning, but I greatly appreciate your help."

"Of course," he says, already back to his newspaper. "Good luck with the article."

Avery stands at the kitchen door, arms folded across her chest.

"I'll walk you out," she says, grabbing a fleece jacket from the coat closet.

"What's up?" I ask as soon as the front door slams shut behind us.

"I think," Avery says carefully, "that my dear husband is having an affair." The tight smile is back, like armor. My instinct is to comfort her, to tell her that's ridiculous, that Jonathan would never cheat on her, he loves her and the kids and so on and so forth. But I get the sense that is not what she wants to hear.

"Evidence?" I ask.

"He smells like someone else. He sleeps in his office. On Thursday night, he didn't actually get home until three in the morning. And when he is home, it's like I'm invisible. I'm thinking about hiring a private investigator."

Uh-oh. "Have you tried asking him if something is wrong?"

"Talk to him, you mean? Yeah, we haven't really done that since we were dating." The perfect world that I have always associated with Avery starts to fragment. It's bumming me out, frankly.

"Do you think you are going to want to hear what a private investigator has to say? Once the cat is out of the bag . . . well, he doesn't ever get back in willingly."

Avery looks at her feet, kicks a small twig in my direction. "You seem different, Lucy, like if this happened to you, you'd know what to do, that you'd have a plan all laid out and ready to go. Me, I'm paralyzed and I'm not sure how to unfreeze myself."

These friends in my new life, these people with whom I spend an inordinate amount of time chatting about nothing of consequence, what do I owe them? They are my first experience with adult friends, real ones that is, and I feel oddly protective of them. However, I stop short of offering to go in and kick Jonathan in the head on her behalf. Avery wipes her eyes and tries to pull herself together.

"Do you know what's strange?" she asks.

"What?"

"I almost want there to be another woman. At least that is something solid, something tangible. If there isn't, we are broken. And I'm not sure there's a way back from that."

I give my friend a hug. "You be strong, okay?" I say. She nods, tears filling her eyes again. "You are going to be fine. I promise." And I think for a minute she might believe me.

The fog is back, blowing softly down the street as I walk to where my car is parked. It is wet and cold and cancels out all the ambient noise so you feel like you're walking through cotton candy. I expect to see Simon or Blackford waiting for me. But for now, there is no one around.

In case you were thinking otherwise, let me tell you, life at the Agency was not always exciting. It was not all car chases and danger and exotic locales teeming with bad guys. There were times, when I was home in Washington, when Agency work was downright dull. Just because we were not supposed to exist didn't mean you escaped filling out yards of post-mission reports that no one would ever read. I was not as good at the paperwork as Simon would have liked, and he'd ride me hard, threatening never to send me out into the field again unless I finished, leaving me to rot in the home office forever. I tried to create relationships with some of my coworkers, but it never really got off the ground. We'd occasionally find ourselves out for dinner and very drunk, at which point we'd start comparing war wounds, mental and physical, much to the horror of the neighboring tables.

During one particularly long stint at home, I met a relatively harmless guy at the Laundromat. After spending two Saturday afternoons in a row folding our underwear in front of each other, he asked me out for coffee. I gladly accepted, desperate for something to kill the hours before I'd be on a plane again. Joshua Cole had dark hair and brown eyes. He had big hands and a hearty laugh. He was divorced, currently living alone in a tiny apartment among his unpacked boxes, trying to figure out what to do with his life now that it had basically fallen apart. I wanted to warn him against me, but I also wanted his company, however temporary.

It didn't take long to move from the coffee shop to his bed, both of us dropping our laundry baskets on the floor in the cramped hallway of his place.

The sex was frantic, sweaty, but also highly satisfying, especially as I couldn't remember the last time I'd had someone even want to hold my hand let alone my other parts. Afterward, Joshua got a faraway look in his eyes, kind of a sad longing which I attributed to an ex-wife out there somewhere who no longer loved him.

I started leaving the office at 5 P.M. sharp rather than at 8 or 9 as had become my custom when at home having nothing else to do. I'd meet Josh for dinner, which we'd eat as fast as we could before rushing back to his apartment and ripping each other's clothes off. This went on, very pleasantly, for about two weeks.

It was a Tuesday and I was sitting at my desk filling out yet more forms about how I'd nabbed an exotic dancer who worked as a mule for the Blind Monk. She'd been aboard a yacht off the coast of Tahiti. I got on the boat. I grabbed her. I threw her overboard and jumped in after her. End of story. Simon Still told me my snotty reports were going to get me in trouble. He even alluded to that life behind a desk I mentioned earlier. And that was so horrible I felt compelled to sit there and think up longer and more complex sentences to satisfy the bureaucrats upstairs. It was not pleasurable work.

Suddenly, as if to save me from myself, an instant message popped up on my computer screen. The name was unfamiliar, Anon 15. The message went something like this: He's working for the other side. Not a good idea to be sleeping with the enemy, even if it is fun.

It was signed with the initials IB. No, no, no. I looked around, sure I'd find him sitting right behind me, down here in the daisy.

Blackford? I typed and quickly hit send, as if my keyboard were suddenly very hot.

Of course, he shot back. I could almost hear his impatience.

What enemy? I asked.

Your current lover, he wrote.

In a second, the room was swimming before my eyes. How did Blackford know?

Where are you? I pecked with one finger.

Meet me at the Vietnam Memorial in twenty minutes. Don't be late.

And the screen went blank. I was sweating, holding on to the arms of my chair until my fingers were white and throbbing. Not possible. Not Josh. He was harmless, a sad divorced guy. I put my head down on my desk, hoping to regain some equilibrium, when Simon Still showed up in my office.

"Sal, what the hell is wrong with you? Done with those A580 forms yet? It's been long enough, even for you."

There was something about the way Simon smelled, the combination of cigarette smoke, hand soap, and laundry detergent that made my stomach turn. I pushed him aside and ran for the bathroom. Simon, of course, followed me right inside.

"Did you contract malaria in the jungle last visit?" He laughed at his own joke. "Go home, will you? You're an unnatural color."

What I should have done was tell him that Ian Blackford would be at the Vietnam War Memorial in exactly fifteen minutes, that in one quarter of an hour he could finally really truly get his man. But I didn't. Because saying so would force me to admit I'd been screwing the enemy three times a night for two weeks, and I wasn't sure I could deal with the overall embarrassment. Instead, I splashed some water on my face, avoiding Simon's intense gaze.

"Thank you, Simon. I think I will go home. I am definitely not feeling well." I darted past him, grabbed my bag, and ran for the door. I checked my time. Thirteen minutes. I could make it if I got lucky.

I was a minute late in arriving at the Vietnam wall and I hoped Blackford wouldn't punish my tardiness by having already left. But no, there he was, coming around the south end of the wall, collar turned up against the wind. And as usual, I let him talk, finding myself terrified and tongue-tied in his presence.

"The guy," he said, taking my arm and forcing me to walk with him, "the one you are fucking, is no good. I know you're having fun in the sack and all," he continued as I blushed a furious and uncontrollable red, "but he works for the Blind Monk, who is, apparently, really mad about what you did to his hula girl."

"She wasn't a hula girl. She was a prostitute who had information we needed."

Blackford raised his sunglasses so I wouldn't miss his look of disbelief. "Details, Sally. Don't get bogged down in the details. Whore or hula, who cares? You threw her overboard, and now he is taking the show directly to you."

I kept pace with him, trying to digest the information without falling on my face. A cold sweat started to run down my back, soaking into the waist of my pants.

"So let me get this straight," I began, my voice unsteady despite my best efforts to control it. "Josh is working for the Blind Monk and he's here to . . . do what exactly? Kill me? Why hasn't he done it already and gone back home?"

"He's not here only to kill you, at least not yet. They want you to tell him where I am. After which he'll kill you. Two birds with one stone. That kind of thing."

"Fabulous." I took a deep breath. "So what do I do?"

"What do you think you do, Sally?"

"Great."

"Well, the next time you need a roll in the hay, try doing it with someone who has honest intentions."

"Yeah, I guess," I said, stopping. Blackford was still attached to my arm, so my abrupt stop brought him to a standstill as well.

"Why are you here?" I asked. Slowly, quietly. "Why not let him do it?" Blackford turned in my direction, but kept his sunglasses in place. I could not even see the outline of his eyes.

"Because if anyone is going to kill you, Sally, it's going to be me, not some two-bit criminal climber whose only asset is that he speaks a decent Tibetan."

"I guess that makes sense. In a totally fucked-up way."

"Of course it does."

With no further explanation, he peeled off into the crowd of tourists, leaving me alone and a little nauseous.

While I believed what Blackford had told me, I also wanted some proof that he wasn't simply setting me up to bump off an annoying competitor. Or worse, a completely innocent man, because it might amuse him for a few minutes.

That night, before dinner, I made Manhattans, adding a little something extra to Josh's glass.

"You make a mean cocktail, Maggie," he said.

"I do," I replied. "I learned a lot about what is good to drink and what isn't while traveling. Have you done any traveling, Josh?"

His eyes twitched, ever so slightly, from my face to the floor and back again.

"No, I'm mostly a homebody. Or I used to be, when I had a home." He laughed.

I refreshed his drink.

"Was the divorce bad?" I asked, with all the sincerity I could summon under the circumstances.

"She was having an affair with one of my old friends. And I found out about it when I got her cell phone bill and saw that she'd been talking to this guy every day for hours. It couldn't be anything else. When I confronted her, she caved immediately. They got married not that long ago, so I guess it was the real thing." He held his glass up to toast me. "To love," he added.

"It's not always easy to know what someone is up to, is it? They can be right in front of you and yet you have no idea what they are thinking, let alone doing." The Tibetan came easily off my tongue, woven into our conversation with deliberate intent. When Josh answered me, something about deception, his accent was flawless, as natural as if he'd been born to it. It took him a few seconds to realize what he'd done.

Slowly he put down his glass. "How did you know?" he asked, still in Tibetan, his tone completely flat now. I could feel the air getting sucked right out of the room.

"Anonymous tip," I replied. My gun was in my bedside table, not great planning on my part. I wondered if Josh would excuse me to the bathroom if I asked politely. Probably not.

"Well, Sally, this has definitely been fun. But I guess the fun is over." He moved like a panther across the space that separated us. His warm hands closed around my throat. I gasped for air, crushed under him. We rolled off the couch and crashed to the floor, upsetting the glass coffee table. What remained of his drink splashed in my face. For a moment I was sure I was drowning. He held fast to my throat, a quiet peaceful look on his face.

"Don't you even want to know where Blackford is?" I managed to squeak out.

He relaxed his grip.

"Right. I'm supposed to ask you where Blackford is. So, where is he?"

"The last time I saw him he was by the Vietnam Memorial. But I don't think he's there anymore."

"Wrong answer. Which is fine by me. I've been looking forward to killing you since the moment we met in the Laundromat."

How romantic. He got back to strangling me. This was not going well.

Finally, I managed to free one leg, bringing my knee up, hard and quick, into his stomach. He grunted and for a second lost his death grip on my throat. But it was enough. I rolled away from him, scrambled around the coffee table, and ran to the bedroom, with a groaning Josh right on my heels. Just as I was about to reach into the bedside table, he grabbed my ankle, pulling my legs out from under me. I went down hard, the wind knocked from my lungs.

"Why struggle?" he said through clenched teeth. "I'm going to kill you." His matter-of-fact tone was insulting.

"Not if I kill you first." With all my strength I pulled my knees into a bent position and, holding the bottom of my bed for leverage, I kicked him in the face. He recoiled. I rolled on top of him, pulling his arm back and up high over his shoulder blades. When I met some resistance from his stretched tendons, I pulled harder. Josh didn't scream. As I went past the point of no return, he let out a respectable yelp.

"Bitch," he moaned.

"I learned that trick from your boss," I said, snapping a pair of handcuffs on his wrists.

When my guys came to get him, Simon was in tow.

"How did you know he was with the Blind Monk?" Simon asked, standing over my drugged ex-lover.

"He talks in his sleep," I said after a moment. Simon raised a curious eyebrow in my direction, indicating he knew I was full of shit, but was not going to press it.

However, I remain grateful to Joshua to this day. Although he was not very enthusiastic about the idea of interrogation, he eventually provided enough useful information to put me back on the trail of the Blind Monk, getting me as far away from Washington as a girl could get.

I sit in my car, parked precariously in our steep driveway, trying to put the pieces together. I remember Simon Still reminding me that the government wasn't paying me to psychoanalyze the psycho, but I can't help it. The key is in front of me, the path out of this mess, but I still can't quite get a hold of it.

My boys are sitting at the table, waiting for my return so we can commence with our shopping expedition. I stand in the doorway watching them. Suddenly I'm up to my eyeballs in adrenaline. It's a familiar rush, like getting off the Tilt-A-Whirl at the town carnival after one too many turns. I will get my man. I always do. Okay, maybe not always, but at least some of the time.

26

"I hate to do this to you," Will says. But my guess is, from his tone, he's going to do it anyway. "I got a call from the office. There is a potential investor in town who wants to talk about methane. Did you know that there are eight hundred sixty-four landfills in the state of New Jersey alone? That's a lot of gas, Lucy. Anyway, he can only do it this morning. Can you two manage the IKEA trip without me?"

"You know that stinks," I say, kind of proud of my terrible joke. But I look at Theo and he thinks this exchange is anything but funny. His lower lip starts to quiver.

"Daddy is coming," he insists.

"Sorry, baby. It looks like Daddy has to go and play in his own sandbox for a while. But we'll have fun together. Meatballs. Ice cream cones. New bed. Fun, right?" I glare at Will over Theo's head.

"Daddy?" Theo is about to cry. Will is not looking much better.

"I'm sorry, Theo, but Daddy has some stuff to do. I promise we'll play whatever you want when you get home."

"I don't want to play later. I want to play now!" He throws the toy car in his hand across the room. Will looks surprised.

"Okay," I say, "that's enough. Let's go." I pick him up. Or try to. It's a little like trying to hold on to an angry, greasy badger. He flails, pounding me with his little fists. I turn him away from me and hold him like a straitjacket. This only serves to intensify his attempts to pound me into oblivion. Will sits frozen at the table.

"It would be helpful if you could open the front door for me," I say. I'm starting to sweat with the strain of holding on to this furious thirty-five-pound child. He jumps up.

"Sure. Yes. I'm really sorry. I didn't think he'd care that much."

"You're kidding, right?"

"No. I mean, what difference does a few hours make, really?"

If I had to sum up what all of my parenting experience has taught me so far, it would be this: Never try to logic a preschooler. They will only try to hit you. I want to put down my bundle of illogical fury, grab Will by the collar, and throw him against the wall.

"All the difference in the world," I say. I kick the door shut behind me. Will opens it immediately.

"Lucy, I'm really sorry. Shit, now I feel terrible."

"You said that already."

"Shit," says Theo. A sneaky smile replaces the look of pure anger on his face. "Shit."

"Oh for God's sake, did you have to?" The same small smile that is gracing Theo's face now creeps across Will's. "Don't you laugh," I order. "You won't like what happens to you if you do."

"I'm not laughing." But Theo is at full grin now, and it is hard for Will to control himself. I open the car door and shove Theo into his car seat. He continues to chant a healthy chorus of obscenities.

"Where does he learn this stuff, Lucy?" Will asks. "Where is it exactly that you two hang out during the day?"

"Go inside," I say, without turning around. "Really. Go. Now." I climb into the driver's seat and start the car. I think about lecturing Theo on why using curse words is not okay. Instead, I turn up the music so I can't hear him.

We manage a smooth ride through town and over the Bay Bridge. Theo points out the enormous cranes flanking the west side of the bridge, part of the new bridge construction project that has been going on for approximately four hundred years. The sky is clear and the sun is bright. To the west, we can see the Golden Gate Bridge. The water sparkles as if embedded with a million tiny jewels. I take all this beauty to mean that our luck is changing and that Theo and I might pull off a pleasant and productive afternoon after all. Of course, that's usually when everything starts to go to hell.

The parking lot is jammed, but we find a space in the garage. Theo is already badgering me for meatballs.

"After we pick out a bed, I promise we can have meatballs." He doesn't like my answer.

"Meatballs first," he whines. It's like nails on a chalkboard, making all the little hairs on my arms stand up at attention. I grip his hand and haul him toward the store.

Once inside, he is off like a shot. There is nothing better than IKEA for a little kid. Running, food, everything on the floor, nothing you can't touch. Wonderful. I manage to direct him toward the children's section, but not without some effort. Finally, we circle the whole joint and end up right where I want to be.

The toddler beds are pushed up against a wall. I squat down to touch the mattresses, the wood, the sheets. So cozy, these tiny beds with their miniature blankets and pillows. I try to picture a sleeping Theo in each bed. "How about this one?" I ask, pointing to a bed with cute animal cutouts on the headboard.

"Blah, yuck. That one," Theo says. He points to the row of bunk beds.

"Too big for you still, honey."

"No. I'm big. I want that one."

"You have to choose from one of these on the floor here, okay?" He pushes his lower lip out in a pout and tilts his head to the left. Then he stamps his foot.

"No. Never. I'm never sleeping in one of those. I hate those." He stamps the other foot for emphasis. I sense that my day is actually going to get worse.

"Why don't you sit on one and tell me if you like it."

"No. I want meatballs."

"Please?" I beg. "Here, try this one." I try to maneuver him onto one of the beds, but he is having none of it. Before I know it, he collapses in a boneless heap at my feet and starts shrieking as if I just dunked him in a pot of boiling oil. I pretend he's not mine, but nobody is buying that.

"Okay," I say, bending to scoop up this mush of a child, "that's enough. Get up."

"Nooooo," he wails. Magically, he slips out of my grasp and back onto the floor. Someone is standing too close to me, probably a person wanting a better view of what a lousy parent looks like up close. I turn toward the person, ready to dispatch them with some searing sarcasm. But instead, I find myself looking up into the clear eyes of the Blind Monk.

"It's been such a long time, Sally," he says. And my heart feels like it has actually stopped beating. I can hear the hollow reverberations of the last beat followed by nothing. I put my hand on my chest. Nope. Nothing. I must be dead and yet I'm still standing up. Strange. Theo's screaming intensifies, breaking through my shock at no longer having a beating heart.

The Blind Monk looks the same. Somehow he hasn't aged a minute. Why is that these terrorist types seem to have such good skin while the rest of us are covered in wrinkles?

"You have got to be kidding me," I say. "Now is not a good time, as you can probably see. But if you intend to kill me, please do it immediately so I don't have to listen to any more of this noise." I shove the Blind Monk out of my personal space and bend down to get Theo again. Once I have him, I hold him tightly to my chest. He twists violently, trying to escape. I hold him tighter, turning his face toward mine.

"Stop it right now."

"I haven't done anything yet," the Blind Monk replies.

"I wasn't talking to you. Theo, stop it."

"Mommmmmmmyyyyyyyy. Down. Put me down!"

"Forget it," I say to my child. "What do you want?" I say to the Blind Monk.

"There are people in my organization," he says, "who are not able to see how toxic you are. But I know. And it is my duty to dispatch you."

"You tried that a few times already, remember?"

His face darkens. Maybe now is not such a good time to remind him that I killed his friend in the Chao Phraya river, or about the gun with no bullets.

"If you had permitted your karma to go at the river, as it was meant to, we would not be in this situation," he says.

"You are not allowed to talk about murder and karma in the same sentence. That is just wrong on so many levels."

"Down!" Theo screams again. In his rage, he kicks the Blind Monk, who for a moment looks surprised and confused by how this is unfolding.

"Nice one," I say.

"You always seem so sure of yourself, Sally," he says. "It will be your downfall."

I start to laugh. Me? Sure of myself? He clearly doesn't know me as well as he thinks he does. The Blind Monk backs me into a corner. There are all these people around, all these shoppers. I want to scream that there is a terrorist in their midst, a real one, but I know better. Screaming for the police would only make things more complicated. I back up slowly, still holding tightly to Theo.

"Who's that?" Theo asks suddenly, pointing to the Blind Monk. "He looks funny."

"How about those meatballs, Theo?"

"Yeah! Meatballs!" My back is against the wall. The Blind Monk is too close. I catch a glimpse of the Heckler & Koch machine gun hidden discreetly under his black overcoat.

"You have to go, Sally. You are too much of a distraction."

"I'm not with the Agency anymore. I am completely uninteresting. Trust me, you are wasting your time. Now if you'll excuse me, I'm going to get back to my shopping." The Blind Monk grabs my arm. His grip is like a tourniquet.

"Let me go," I say quietly. With Theo in my arms, I can't do anything. I am pushed against the wall and a bunk bed.

"I will savor this moment for many reasons," he says, making me feel a little like a lamb chop.

"Let me go," I say again.

"I don't think so."

"You know, I'm trying to have a nice shopping experience here, buy a new bed for my kid. And you are really starting to piss me off."

The room is crowded, the space around me and the Blind Monk tight. I am still holding Theo, with no room to maneuver. So he doesn't expect it when I lift Theo onto the top bunk of the bed next to us. I take my free arm and, using his grip on me as leverage, flip him over so he lands with his full weight over the rail of one of the toddler beds. The bed immediately collapses under the force of one falling Blind Monk. Okay, so that bed is out, I think. He lays at my feet, on his back, the splinters of wood fanned out around him. A small bit of blood appears where his head hit the concrete floor. But he breathes regularly. Unfortunately for me, it appears there is no permanent damage and IKEA is really not the proper place for me to finish the job. By now, about a hundred shoppers are staring at me with disbelief. No one will ever believe that someone like me could do what I just did to the Blind Monk. I'm counting on it sounding ridiculous.

"This man collapsed!" I shout. "Call an ambulance right away. Stay with him. I'm going to call store security." I grab Theo, wide-eyed, off the top bunk and slip through the gathering crowd.

"I didn't like any of those beds. Did you?" I ask Theo as we head for the exit. He shakes his head solemnly. I want to pretend he didn't see me drop the Blind Monk to the floor, that instead he was gazing at the butterflies strung from the ceiling, floating on a climate-controlled breeze. A girl can dream.

"Let's go to Discovery Lane and buy you that Thomas the Train bed that you liked. What do you think? And maybe pizza afterwards?"

"Oh, yes, Mommy. I like that one! " My child is happy once again. But I feel sick to my stomach.

27

On Monday morning, Nanny Pauline is getting into it. I can see the wheels turning in her head. She won't last at the Agency. In a few years, she'll start to panic about not having any children and throw herself off the Agency bus. If she lives that long.

Today, she shows up in jeans, a worn black hoodie, running shoes, and white socks.

"I hope it's okay that I dressed down," she says, following me to the kitchen.

"I was wondering when you were going to ditch the white shirts. White and children, not compatible."

Nanny Pauline smiles, a real smile. She suddenly looks very young.

"I'll be gone a few hours. You can take Theo to the playground. Directions on the table."

"Where are you headed?" Pauline asks. The red floods her cheeks. She is embarrassed that she is supposed to spy on me. And not very good at hiding it.

"Simon is following me anyway," I say. "No need to report to him what you uncover while in my house."

Pauline examines her feet. "No. Of course not," she says.

"Don't apologize. But don't keep doing it."

"Right." At that moment, Theo comes bursting into the room with his human-size stuffed Elmo. He's shrieking something about Elmo and Big Bird and how they are coming down the hallway. I see Pauline's hand go unconsciously to where her gun should be.

"Relax," I say quietly. "Elmo and Big Bird are the least of our problems."

Pauline sits down, a shocked look on her face. The Agency excels at convincing you that behind every smiling face is a potential nuclear holocaust. It's not easy to admit you've been drinking the Kool-Aid.

As I'm about to leave, Pauline shouts after me, "Are you coming back again? Should I get the frying pan?"

I poke my head back into the room. "No," I say. "I trust you."

This time I use my neighbors' fancy new deck, a bit uphill from us, as a launching pad onto my roof. I almost don't make it. How embarrassing it would be to fall off my own roof and have to explain why I was trying to break into my own house to the nice doctors in the emergency room. I climb up to the top of the roof and make my way across to a crawl space window that is slightly open. I wedge myself in through the tiny window and feel carefully along the floor for the drop-down ladder. Slowly, I lower it and unfurl the ladder. I climb down as quietly as I can. The house seems oddly silent. I begin to creep toward the staircase. As I pass Theo's bedroom I hear, "I brought a rolling pin this time. Thought it might work better than a frying pan. You know, easier to manage."

I turn around slowly, unable to stop myself from smiling.

"Nice work," I say.

"Not really. You've established a pattern. Simon says that anyone who establishes a pattern is easy prey."

"Ah, that Simon is wise, don't you think?" Before she can answer, Theo comes out of the bathroom, still hitching up his pants.

"Mommy? I thought you were leaving." I kiss him on the head.

"I am, sweetheart. Just forgot something." I give Pauline a wink, dash down the stairs and out the door.

At the university, I pull into what is now my usual parking place. Talk about establishing a pattern. If my information is correct, Professor Malcolm should be coming down the path toward the labs building in about five minutes. I drink what's left of my coffee and check my mirrors for Simon. Two minutes. Time to go.

"Excuse me, Professor," I say. With my body, I block the path of the gray-haired and stooped Albert Malcolm. He mutters something

about being late, never looking up from his feet. This is the evil genius? I'm a little disappointed.

"I know, sir, but this will only take a second," I say. I wrap my
fingers around his frail forearm and squeeze enough to make a
point. My touch startles him and he finally looks at me, a combination of anger and fear sweeping across his face.

"Well, what is it?" he says, pulling himself up straighter.

But for a second I can't say anything. His eyes, piercing blue
lost in a sea of wrinkled flesh, glare at me. I fumble for words,
completely forgetting my rehearsed monologue from seconds before.

"I'm working on an article," I start, "for a magazine."

"Why do you people insist on bothering me? I don't talk to your
kind. And now you are making me late." He begins to walk around
me. I grab him again.

"It's about your flower project," I say. This seems to stop Professor Malcolm dead in his tracks.

"I don't work on flowers. I'm not a botanist. Your information is
wrong." But I've regained my composure.

"No," I say, "my information is not wrong. It comes from the
source." I hand him one of the pages of notes from his own lab
books. Albert Malcolm turns white as a sheet.

"Where did you get these?" he asks. His voice is hushed, steely.
"Did Barry give these to you? Stinking traitor."

"You are going to end up dead, Professor. Guys like Blackford,
they make you feel really special. Powerful, even. But don't be deluded. It won't end well for you."

The professor stands completely still for a moment, the page of
ill-gotten notes clutched in his hand. Finally, he looks right at me.
"I don't recall asking for advice. Do you?"

"No. But it's free. You should take it." This was getting away
from me again.

"Who are you?"

"Doesn't matter. You'll find out eventually. Do yourself a favor
and remember what I said."

I've had better closing lines, but unable to come up with something more memorable, I leave the professor standing on the sidewalk outside his lab, trying to piece it all together.

Simon Still is parked next to me.

"You're always a little late to the party," I say. "Do you do that on purpose?"

Simon smiles, but I see fatigue in his eyes. His whole body sags.

"You are making things worse, Sally. Why can't you be good and do as I ask?"

"And what is that? Sit around waiting to get my head blown off? Forget it. Your plan is lousy. My plan is better." Or it will be when I get around to coming up with one.

Simon gets out of his car, lights up, paces.

"What happened to the gum?" I ask. "And your life of good health and all that shit?"

"Shut up, Sally. If I want to smoke myself to death, that is my business. And don't you even start in on secondary smoke or I will shoot you right here in this parking lot."

I give him a small salute. Touchy.

"So?" he says finally.

"So the professor denies that he knows anything, but he's lying. He's working on the Death Lily. You ever hear of the Death Lily?"

Simon looks at me like I'm an imbecile. "Of course," he says. "Everyone knows about the Death Lily."

"Well, I didn't."

"You," he says with great relish, "are retired. Besides, it's a myth. It doesn't exist."

"Boy, you seem awfully sure of yourself in light of the circumstances. You don't have any intel on this guy?"

Simon shakes his head. "We've been busy with other things, Sal. Haven't you noticed the whole world is a big fucking mess these days?"

"Yes," I say, "I have noticed that. But still, nothing?"

Simon shakes his head again.

"Okay," I say, "so let's think about what we do know. Blackford is here." Simon interrupts me before I can continue my summation of our dire situation.

"Did you see him? When? Where?"

"If I have to tell you that, you ought to consider a second career as a congressman or something. I hear they have great benefits and a private dining room."

"Now is not the time, Sally."

"I'd say it's really the time. Blackford walked out on the beach, said hello to me and Theo, and disappeared. Where were you? I don't remember it being like this."

"It's always been like this," Simon says. He looks a little depressed.

"So Blackford is here. The Blind Monk is here."

"No. Not possible. The Blind Monk is not here. Last we heard, his newest syndicate had cut him loose."

Sure. And Ian Blackford is dead. And I'm not a liar. And life is just one big fat bowl of ruby red cherries.

"The Blind Monk may in fact have been cut off from whomever was most recently bankrolling him. I can't claim to know the details as you apparently do. But he is most certainly here. He was even considering offing me in IKEA yesterday. I imagine the only thing that saved me is my superior karma."

Simon looks suddenly pale. He closes his eyes, but his eyelids twitch.

"What else do you know?" he asks.

"Well, I know that the last time we all spent quality time together was in Cambodia, and that was more or less a disaster."

Simon shudders at the memory.

"Something is about to happen," I say. But at this point all I know for sure is that I'm starting to get hungry. Simon's cell phone chirps in his pocket. He pulls it out, examines the number.

"Damn, Sally," he says, "I have to go. We'll talk later."

With that, he jumps in his car and peels out, leaving me in a cloud of exhaust. I don't even have time to yell at him about calling me

Sally. Nice. I get back in my car. On the radio, there is a report about a major terrorist cell in Pakistan that has been infiltrated and disbanded by members of a U.S. intelligence agency. The reporter does not offer any specifics, but she doesn't need to. I know who they are talking about. It just goes on and on.

28

Nanny Pauline and Theo are both asleep on the couch when I finally get home from the university. There are toys and trucks and trains in every corner and on every surface. The refrigerator door is slightly ajar and the kitchen counters are covered in cheese sticks and empty cups and popcorn, not to mention peanut butter on rice cakes face down on the floor.

I leave the mess and the sleeping Pauline and Theo and go upstairs to the spare bedroom that serves as Will's home office. Out of the goodness of his heart, he gave me a filing cabinet that is all my own. I dig through a number of randomly named files until I find a folder with the initials IB scrawled across the front in my handwriting. Inside is yet another folder, although this one is stamped with CLASSIFIED LEVEL 7 in big, unmistakable red letters.

For all the money in the world, I cannot tell you what inspired me not only to steal Ian Blackford's Agency personnel file but to hang on to it all these years. Maybe I knew that someday I'd need it. Or maybe I figured that he was dead so where was the harm?

I sit down at Will's desk and open the file. The pages inside are yellowing, and some of the typed words are faded. I start at the beginning, scanning his test scores, his psychological evaluation, his background check, his self-supplied history. And it is here that I pause.

Minnesota. A small town. Abandoned by a single father, made a ward of the state at age four when no other relatives could be found. Nobody knew if the boy and his father came from Minnesota or if they simply ended up there at some point. From all accounts, the father, an assistant professor at a rinky-dink college in town, seemed like an okay guy. Not going to win any parenting awards, but stable enough. One hot summer day, the neighbors find the boy, half starved, sitting on the steps of their rental house. He was dirty, confused, tired. They called the police, but the boy's father was gone. And it appeared that he left with intent, taking all of his textbooks with him but somehow forgetting his kid. He never came back, and Ian Blackford became another poor soul lost in the chaos of state-run foster care.

I pull up Albert Malcolm's file on the USAWMD database and confirm. Minnesota. I Google Malcolm and find a picture. I zoom in on his face. I stare. Those familiar blue eyes that threw me for such a loop this afternoon stare back at me. I know that short of a DNA test I can't be 100 percent sure, but I'd bet my life—something I really try not to do anymore—that Albert Malcolm is Ian Blackford's father.

By the time Blackford got around to kidnapping me in Paris, I was no longer surprised. I started to have that woozy feeling about halfway through my house red wine, before my meal even arrived.

"Goddamn it," I muttered, forgetting for a brief second how to curse properly in French. "Where are you?" I didn't have to wait long. He was already striding through the front door, through the smoke, as if he owned the place. I held on to my seat, sure I would slide to the floor in a heap if I let go. He pulled out the chair opposite me and sat down, unable to stop himself from smiling.

"Couldn't you at least wait until I got my food?" I asked.

"Why would I do that?"

"Common courtesy?" I suggested.

"If I exercised common courtesy, as you call it, nothing would ever get done. I'd spend all of my time trying to get you on the phone."

"Hey, what an idea. The phone! Brilliant. Next time, how about you call and let me know you'd like to meet?" And that was the last thing I remember saying before my world went completely black.

When I came to, I was not locked in a bathroom or handcuffed to the desk or tied up or bound or restrained in any way. I was lying on a nicely made bed with beautiful orange silk pillows. I sat up slowly, still feeling dizzy. Outside the gauzy curtains was a stunning vista of Paris at night, with the Eiffel Tower as its centerpiece twinkling like a star with blue and white lights. I made my way to the window and gazed out, my head not clear enough to do much else.

"It's my favorite view in the world," came a voice through the dark. I turned slowly, afraid I might fall down. Blackford stood in the doorway watching me. I could barely make out the outline of his body, the neck of his white T-shirt under what could only be a cashmere sweater, and the shine of his dark leather jacket.

"Where am I?" I said. My throat was dry and my voice cracked.

"My house," he replied. The words hung in the air between us. Blackford had a house? He actually lived somewhere? I sat down on the edge of the bed.

"Is this the end?" I asked.

"Come on now, Sally. We're almost friends, you and I." I couldn't tell if he was joking.

I started vigorously rubbing my temples, trying to drive away the foggy, out-of-focus feeling. "Okay," I said, "let's get on with it. What am I doing here? What do you want?"

Blackford was quiet. He moved across the room, quiet as a cat, and looked out the window.

"Have you ever gone looking for something, Sally, believing that without it you could never be whole, only to realize what a fool you'd been? A sentimental fool?" I nodded, unsure where this was going, but too afraid to ask. Blackford continued.

"Well, then you know what I've been up to. For some reason, I couldn't let it lie, accept the fact of my life as it is." He pulled the curtain aside, stared out. I shifted slightly toward him so he'd still be aware that I was listening. "The old guy denied that I ever existed, however, and that is something I simply cannot accept. He will pay, Sally. I will make him pay. And I will make it hurt."

Somewhere in the distance I could hear the blaring of car horns, the casual conversation of people passing beneath the window.

"Twice I have allowed myself to indulge in the fantasies of a normal life. Twice I have failed. I won't do it again. Do you understand?"

I could think only of the girl, the Hungarian, the Bulgarian, whatever, dead in Blackford's arms. I had no idea what the other thing was. I didn't want to know.

"You can go, Sally. I shouldn't have brought you here. I trust you will forgot where it is I live."

"Of course," I said, quickly. I pulled myself up and, using the wall for support, made my getaway. The house, I observed in my foggy state, was beautiful, a work of art, everything in perfect order. I still swear there was a Modigliani at the end of the hallway, although my experts assured me that particular painting was back at the Guggenheim in New York. I fumbled with the front door lock and tripped down the stairs onto the empty sidewalk. There I tried to get my bearings. When I looked up at the bedroom window, I saw Blackford watching me. I gave a little wave, not sure if that was the right thing to do. He turned away from the window without waving back. Was I the closest thing Blackford had to a friend? It was a terrifying thought, kind of like Henry VIII asking you to marry him.

I called Simon as soon as I got back to my hotel.

"He took me to his house," I said. "I know where he lives." Simon was on the next plane to Paris. When we arrived at Blackford's house, all the blinds were drawn. Simon was the first one in, something I had never seen happen before. But it didn't matter. The inside of the house was completely empty. Nothing left but a few dust bunnies rolling around on the polished wooden floors. After that, Simon sent me above the Arctic Circle for two months. He said the cold would be good for improving my obviously faulty memory.

It's 2 P.M. and my cell phone rings. It's Avery, wanting to meet at the park. I agree to head over when Theo wakes up. I leave out the part about him right now sleeping on the couch with a USAWMD agent masquerading as a nanny. I continue to stare at Albert Malcolm's face. Does he have any idea? Is it possible you could be in a room with your own child and not know it? It seems ridiculous to even consider.

I hear noise downstairs, a plaintive wail for Mommy from Theo. I close the computer, re-stash the stolen files, and hurry downstairs. Theo is confused and hops into my open arms gratefully. He buries his head in my hair and sighs. Nanny Pauline looks sheepish.

"I can't believe I fell asleep. It won't happen again, ma'am, I promise."

"Playing with a toddler can be exhausting. And don't call me ma'am."

"I'm sorry. I don't know what to say."

I sit down next to Pauline. "Listen," I say, "they picked you because you have some special talent. Maybe you're fast on your feet. Or maybe you can tell a convincing lie and not feel bad about it. Maybe you speak ten languages. Or maybe you like being totally disconnected from the world. The thing to remember is that it, whatever it is, does not make you infallible. Believing that you are something greater will only serve to get you hurt in the end."

"But how will I ever know if I'm any good?" For a second I think Pauline might burst into tears.

"You won't," I answer honestly. "Not even when it's over. If feedback is something you crave, I suggest you consider a career change to banking. Or the law."

I stand up.

"Okay, Theo and I have a playdate. You are welcome to stay here because I'm sure they have you in a crappy hotel somewhere out by the airport, right?"

She smiles, wiping invisible tears from under her eyes.

"Cheap bastards," I say. "Some things never change. Well, no rush. Hang out if you want to."

With that, I leave her on the couch and start organizing our going-to-the-playground stuff. I pile everything and Theo into the car and head out. I keep my fingers crossed that she'll clean the kitchen while we're gone and not spend the whole time digging through my underwear drawer looking for secrets.

Avery is sitting where she usually sits. Sam is next to her. On an adjacent bench sit Claire and Belinda. They wave us over. Theo takes off in the direction of the kids, and I plunk myself down next to Sam.

"You look tired," Belinda comments.

"Do any of you remember a time when we weren't all tired?"

They all shake their heads to the negative. "So what's going on?" I ask, wanting to talk about anything but me.

"Oh the usual. Avery is ranting about life versus fiction, about how TV presents this idea that women can do everything—work, family, house, etc., all the while being fit and beautiful and clever," Claire informs me.

"That's not exactly what I was saying," Avery interrupts. "I was saying that life tends not to be as exciting as a story. I mean, it's not like we all have secret lives that involve fast cars and beautiful men, or women, and espionage and things."

I look down at my feet in the sand. I wiggle my toes. I scratch my elbow. When I look up, Sam is staring at me. I look back at my feet. Avery continues.

"I am only saying that sometimes life is boring and that's okay. Life is not always imitating art. Sometimes art is flashier. Does that make any sense?"

Belinda and Claire nod in agreement. Sam continues to look at me. I continue to look at my feet. Suddenly, the kids appear. Belinda, Claire, and Avery gather theirs and head to the bathrooms. Theo and Carter demand snacks. Sam and I set to pulling out cheese and apple juice and crackers.

"You know," Sam begins, adjusting the top on a sippy cup, "I used to work for the CIA."

I briefly pause in my task of peeling back the wrapper from a cheese stick.

"So is the traveling circus trapeze artist a cover story?" I ask.

"Now, when I mention the CIA thing to most people, the usual response is 'Wow, were you undercover? Did you ever have to kill anyone?'" He stops long enough to give me a chance to be impressed. I look at him over my cheese stick.

"But I'm guessing the reason you are telling me this is because you don't think I'm going to fall all over myself wanting to know about your life with the CIA, right?" I ask.

"I wasn't anything covert," he says, "just an analyst dealing with the Soviets. But, you know, you hang around that sort of paranoid environment for long enough, you develop a sixth sense for when things are not quite as they seem. Wouldn't you agree?"

I respond with something between a nod and an involuntarily twitch of my head. The snack is out now. When Carter and Theo are happily munching away, we sit back down on the benches. I have to say something, anything. If I don't, the friendship that Sam and I share will die on the vine.

"Everyone has baggage," I offer. I don't look at him. I scan the streets around the playground. "Some baggage is heavier than others."

"Well," Sam says, "if you ever feel inclined to put it down, I'd be happy to help."

"Thank you," I say, meaning it. "Someday it will be time. But not today."

"Understood," he replies. "And the circus story might be true. You never know, do you?"

I have to laugh. My new friends, these moms and dads and grandparents, they want to know me, and for the first time that idea is something I'm willing to entertain. But it is not without its discomforts.

Avery, Claire, and Belinda return from the bathroom. We go back to talking about inconsequential things, such as the front coming through promising to dump actual rain on us for the first time in many months. I keep scanning the playground perimeter, but see no signs of anyone who is not meant to be there.

29

Whenever I arrived somewhere new, a new country, a new city, I had the same routine. I'd drop my well-worn knapsack in some flea-bag guesthouse and start to walk. I wouldn't take a map, preferring to use my senses to orient myself. I'd spend hours wandering in circles, stretching my legs and my tongue, getting it ready to pretend to be something it wasn't for as long as it took. I'd stop for food, asking the street vendor about the coming monsoon or the shop owner about his daughter's wedding. I'd find out where to go for a good drink or a good meal, ferreting out the highlights of the place as clues to its culture. It was like dating. The city would show me all her beauty and sparkle and I'd sit back and enjoy it. Eventually, I'd force her to show me her dirty underbelly, the places where bad and ugly things happened. But in the beginning, she was nothing but beautiful.

The long walks also served to clear my mind, to get me focused on the task at hand, whatever it was. I'd fully absorb all the intelligence I'd been force-fed before leaving Washington and the last few bits I'd tried to digest on the plane. I'd let it all swish around in my body and finally come together in some meaningful way. At some point during these walks, I'd find myself suddenly at a complete standstill. And that was the moment when I got it, when everything made sense and I had a plan to accomplish the thing I'd been sent to do.

This morning, Theo safely tucked away with Nanny Pauline, I find myself in Golden Gate Park, walking fast along a winding path toward the ocean. The air is cold and foggy and shows no signs of warming. I keep my hands deep in the pockets of my down vest. And this is the way I imagine it played out.

. . .

An Agent of the USAWMD, or the CIA or the FBI or the NSA, or any of
those initial-laden government groups for that matter, would have
access to a host of resources needed to find someone intent on being
lost. Blackford calls in a few favors, maybe visits with the Old Timers. After drinking the sludge and buying them doughnuts, he asks
for their help.

"He left me when I was quite young," Blackford would say. The
Old Timers would nod in unison. They already knew all this. They
knew about his abandonment, the sad fact that his father took his
books, his shirts, and his pots and pans, but left his child behind.
They knew everything.

"I was always sure there was some sort of mistake, some misun-
derstanding, don't you think? I mean people do terrible things, that
much we all know, but abandoning your own child in an empty
house . . . well, even to me, that seems . . ." Blackford would be at a
loss for words. The Old Timers would wait.

"It's wrong," he'd say finally. "I want to find this man. I want to
understand what happened. What really happened. Not only what
I've already read in court documents."

"We think," Fatty would answer, "that you seek closure. Under-
standable."

"However," Baldy would add, "not always wise. Sometimes it is
a good idea to leave well enough alone."

Blackford would examine his coffee cup, swirling the thick coffee grounds around on the bottom.

"You know," he would say, "I have considered that. But in this
case, I can't let it go."

The Old Timers would bend their heads together, muttering
fiercely, while Blackford would await their judgment.

"We agree to help you locate your father," Baldy would announce.
"Give us a little time. We'll contact you when we have something
useful." And with that, a younger, less jaded Ian Blackford would be
dismissed from the Old Timers' table of knowledge.

He waits patiently for several months. Eventually the Old Timers return, telling him they have come up blank. In truth, they have not. But to save Blackford from himself is their first responsibility. They believe, falsely, that he will let it go.

After defecting to the other side, Blackford begins to throw enormous sums of money at the mystery of who is his father. He hires lawyers and private investigators, and fans them out across the country. Eighteen months later, he hits pay dirt. A PI named Dewey faxes him a single sheet of information. On it is a name and a picture. Professor Albert Malcolm is a professor of Analytical Chemistry and lives on Walnut Street. Blackford makes the mistake of feeling joy at the revelation. He believes he will go to California, meet his father, and somehow the black hole in his chest will magically be plugged. He forgets that this man staring out at him is the same one who deserted him in a house with an empty refrigerator.

But Blackford is nothing if not a good spy. He knows not to give anything away for free. He checks out Malcolm and when he's satisfied that the information Dewey has given him is accurate, he makes a phone call. He asks Malcolm if he ever had a child. Malcolm vehemently denies this and grows hostile with the continued questioning. Finally, Blackford clicks the hang-up button on his phone. His ears are red and his eyes burn.

He's ashamed of himself for caring, oddly paralyzed by his need for this stranger to love him. After a few minutes, his heart slows and he stops sweating, comforted by his decision to ruin Albert Malcolm if it is the last thing he ever does. He wants a clear view of the old man's face when he realizes what is about to happen. He thinks it might heal him.

I'm stopped now, having made it all the way to the beach. The gray and violent ocean rolls in and out. The wind is icy. My nose runs.

"All this because your father didn't love you?" I ask. I know he is close enough now to hear.

"It was more than that." Ian Blackford steps forward so we are now shoulder-to-shoulder, staring out at the raging ocean. "Big storm out there somewhere."

"Just because your father left you doesn't make you a bad person," I say. I don't add that, according to most, he really is a bad person anyway, fatherlessness aside. Blackford laughs.

"Do you know a thing or two about being left behind, Sally?" he asks. His voice is not kind. I can't answer.

"Anyway, nice psychoanalysis, but bad is something I perfected all on my own."

"Was revenge the point all along?"

"Revenge can feed you when you've lost your appetite," he says. "You have something of mine. I need it back."

What?

"You'll take me back to your house, get it for me, and this will be over."

He watches me for a reaction.

There is a move I learned from a man in China. It's complicated, and if you don't execute it fast enough, the person you intend to kill will have a fine opportunity to kill you first. I want to be fast enough. I want to be as good as I once was.

"Don't do it, Sally," Blackford whispers.

But I can't help it. I've had enough. I step into the move at the exact moment Blackford does. But he is better. He has always been better. In about a second, I expect to hear my neck snap.

Instead, I see them out of the corner of my eye. Simon Still is not wearing his hat. Two agents dressed in dark jackets and gloves flank him. I find myself wondering what numbers they are. Forty-five? Twenty-seven? They are on us faster than I expect.

"Well, this is inconvenient," Blackford says. He spins me around so my back is pressed to his chest. I feel the muzzle of his gun against my temple. I can't swallow; my tongue feels thick and dry in my mouth.

"You aren't going to kill her," Simon shouts. "Sally is the last person in the world you would kill. Some say she is your only friend." Simon and his crew take a few steps closer. Blackford and I take a few steps backward toward the ocean. A wave breaks, and the water sloshes around our ankles. It's like stepping into a bucket of melting ice cubes.

"You know me, Simon. What was your conclusion? Sociopathic tendencies? A lack of empathy or some such nonsense? So what would stop me from pulling Sally out into the water and drowning us both?"

Simon is thinking. One gun to my head, four guns on Blackford. What are the odds? The water hits my thighs as Blackford backs us deeper into the ocean.

I see Theo at that moment. I see him sleeping, his little blond head on a blue pillow, clutching his fuzzy blanket in both hands, hanging on for dear life. I can feel my lips on his cool forehead and see his tiny chest rise and fall in his striped tiger pajamas.

I start to struggle as if my life depends on it. But Blackford doesn't care. He simply tightens his grip.

"Don't," he says in that voice. In the past, that voice would have caused me temporary paralysis due to pure terror. But I'm not that person anymore. Simon inches forward. Blackford is holding me so tightly now I'm losing circulation in my arms.

"There's nothing you can do, Simon. Like always, you are too late," Blackford shouts above the wind. I see Simon nod ever so slightly to one of the agents. It's the signal, the one that means *take him out now, collateral damage be damned*. Except I am the collateral damage in this case. The men move quickly, but they are no match for Ian Blackford. He drags us both into the freezing ocean. It is up to my chest now. The salt water stings my eyes and skin. I can no longer feel my legs.

The waves crash overhead. I struggle for any air I can get, the water so cold I can't expand my lungs. Blackford still holds me tightly by the back of my vest as I try to bend my arms and wiggle out of it. But wet down is kind of like wearing bricks, and the vest acts like a sea anchor, dragging me toward the ocean floor.

A huge wave breaks over our heads, pushing us straight toward the sandy bottom. We are in the swirl of the wave's whitewater now, not sure which way is up. Suddenly, Blackford pulls me to the surface and we burst through at the same time, desperate for air, gasping, spitting. And because things can always get worse, suddenly I feel a riptide nipping at my legs, threatening to whip me into a frozen oblivion.

"Oh, God," I whisper. "Don't do this."

The rip snatches us both, greedy. I grab onto Blackford's jacket, wanting to use him as leverage to push myself out of the riptide's evil grip. But he has different ideas.

As if he is standing on solid ground, Blackford lifts me waist high out of the water and throws me forward, clear of the riptide's path.

"Go!" he shouts. "Swim, Sally!" The riptide takes him, and in an instant, he is gone, no longer visible in the thrashing gray ocean. I start to swim as hard as I've ever done anything. I strip off the vest, kick off my shoes, and haul my body toward the shore. The waves crash again and again over my head. Each one sends me on a death-defying spiral toward the bottom of the sea. I come up sputtering and gain a few more yards toward the beach.

I can see Simon Still standing on shore. The two agents are in the water up to their knees. Simon is shouting at them, but I can't hear his words. I pull closer. Another series of waves, and I feel solid ground beneath my feet. I try to stand up, but I'm too weak and cold. Instead, I fall to my knees and drag myself forward with the remaining strength in my arms. I'm out of the water. I collapse on the sand, my breath coming in spasms.

Simon runs down the beach toward me. I can't get up. I stay with my face in the sand. Simon tries to lift me by the arms, to pull me beyond the ocean water that is still lapping at my feet. I am dead weight. One of the agents steps in to help him.

"Get off me," I gasp. "Let me go."

"Come on, Sally. You are hypothermic. If we don't warm you up, you are going to feel really bad in a few minutes." They lift me up. I dangle over the shoulder of the biggest guy like a sack of potatoes. I have no idea how long it takes, but soon I'm in the backseat of a minivan, under a heavy blanket, with Simon trying to force me to drink hot coffee.

"Take me home," I say.

"We have to talk about this. I need to know what he said to you."

"Listen, I did what you asked. I drew him out. And what do I get in return? You were going to shoot me! Now take me home before I strangle you right here in this shitty car."

"Come on, Sally. You know it's business, nothing personal." I stare into my coffee cup and refuse to speak another word to Simon Still. After a while, the van pulls up in front of my house. The windows glow with warm light. There is still no sign of the sun. I stumble out of the van, barely able to support my own weight. The van pulls away from the curb. I look up at my house and, for the first time that I can remember, I want to cry. But there are no tears running down my cheeks. They stay dry as a bone.

30

The end of my childhood as I knew it was more complicated than it may have sounded at first. I didn't have any siblings, so I was the little princess of the family, with my parents doting on my every action, no matter how mundane or downright stupid it was. It was an isolated existence, Luke from the next farm basically my only friend. I had to get up before the sun to go to school and the bus ride was well over an hour. I had a posse of girlfriends at school with names like Gwen and Patty and Tracy, but I never saw them outside of the red brick building. My mother was not the kind to arrange a sleepover and tell us ghost stories while we snuggled into thin sleeping bags on the living room floor and ate popcorn.

My parents kept to themselves. They were perfectly friendly, but in a way that did not invite a closer look. The only person I remember them ever inviting into our house was the man in the blue overcoat. And after our first meeting, when, much to my mother's horror, I answered his knock at the door, he always arrived in the dead of night, long after I had gone to bed, as if to avoid any further contact with me. But there was something about his voice, its depth and cadence, that would float up the stairs to my room and yank me from sleep, no matter the time. I would fold back my blankets and creep a little closer to the conversation. My parents and the stranger, huddled around the wood stove, would whisper in hushed tones. The conversation I remember most vividly went something like this.

"We are concerned about reports coming in over the wires," the man said.

My parents looked at each other. Even from upstairs I could see stress on my mother's face. "How concerned?" they asked together.

"I'm afraid this might be real, that you've been compromised. The Group is considering a move."

My father rubbed his eyes, and my mother leaned back in her chair, weary from a long day and this news.

"What about her?" my father asked, casting his eyes in my direction. I shrunk back against the wall, hoping he wouldn't catch the bright red of my flannel pajamas.

"The Group is considering a move," he said again. "For her own safety, she will have to be relocated. We cannot protect her otherwise. We have a family waiting to receive her in Vermont. She will be cared for."

My mother buried her face in her hands, a quick sob sneaking out. My father patted her gently on the back.

"We always knew it could come to this," he said softly. She nodded her head, but kept her face hidden behind her rough hands. "We didn't expect to get this much time with her. Every minute has been a blessing."

With that, my mother stood up. "I will never forgive you for this," she said to the man. "Never." Then she stomped up the stairs, causing me to flee back to the warmth of my bed.

At the time, I thought they must have been talking about one of the farm animals. Maybe Pepper, the horse that everyone was always trying to buy, or the fat pig that would soon be sent off for slaughter.

The man and my father talked deep into the night. When I woke up to pee, hours later, they were still at it, heads close, whispering. I heard a few words like *Mexico, New York City, accident.* But I was sleepy and less interested in what was going on down there than I'd been earlier in the night.

When the crash happened and the state police came to tell me that my parents were dead, I didn't think once about the man who only visited in winter. I was too devastated. The aunt and uncle who took me in were no more my relations than the frogs in the stream I used to play in. But it never occurred to me to question what was happening. Life suddenly seemed like something to be endured rather than enjoyed.

The teachers and the counselors and my new relatives tried to help me. They wanted me to grieve and move on. But how could I move on if I could never get myself to cry? Try as I might, the tears wouldn't come. And before too long, it all began to recede into the background like a bad dream.

Other than going to see the truck driver that one time, I only made one other enquiry into what had really happened. I visited the Old Timers.

"Do I have to drink the coffee this time?" I asked, desperate to avoid the sludge. "I'll buy you extra doughnuts."

"Ha," said Baldy. "Miss Sin thinks she can tap the oracle without drinking the magic brew. Forget it."

"No one gets past the coffee," Fatty said. "It shows us you are sincere."

I took a deep breath and threw it back, trying not to gag on the thick grounds swirling around in my mouth.

The Old Timers clapped at my performance. "Well done! Now we will take those doughnuts that you promised us."

I went dutifully to the doughnut display in the cafeteria and selected six of the least offensive-looking ones. Once the doughnuts were on the table, I was given permission to ask my question. The whole thing was starting to remind me of the Magic 8-Ball I used to consult when I was a child.

"Okay. Have you ever heard of something called The Group? If I had to guess, I'd say they operated in the 1970s, probably in Soviet Bloc countries."

Baldy sighed. Fatty cleared his throat. Shorty examined his pastry.

"We had hoped to avoid this day," Baldy said finally.

"We never get that lucky," Fatty added.

"The sprinkles on this doughnut resemble a Madonna and child, don't you think?" Shorty asked. The other two glared at him.

"The Group?" I prompted, hoping to bring them back to the topic at hand.

"There is no Group, Sally," Shorty said. He bit off the Madonna's head with relish. "There is only the Agency. There was nothing that came before it and nothing that will come after."

"How can you know that?" I asked. "I mean, the after part?"

"Ignore him," Baldy said. "We know nothing of any organization called The Group. Even if we did, we would not be able to provide you with any details."

"Does that mean you know something?"

"That means that if we did know something, we could not tell you. The Agency would not permit it."

"The way you talk about this place, sounds kind of like it's alive. You know what I mean?"

"We do that sometimes. It is not our intention. We still cannot tell you anything of The Group."

"Can't or won't?"

"Is there a difference?"

"You aren't going to help me, are you?"

"No," they said. "We are not going to help you. It's for your own good. Trust us on this one."

"Shit."

"There is work to do, Sally. Move forward."

So I did. Not because the old guys refused to help me, but because finding out if The Group even existed was not going to change my past. That was over. And the Old Timers were right. I had work to do.

There is one last thing to confess. When I was a child, still on the farm, I would dream with the dark intensity of an overactive imagination. There were many nights I'd wake up screaming in terror, the strong arms of my mother no match for the dream's grip. She'd rock me slowly, whispering, singing, stroking my hair until my trembling subsided and I could go back to sleep. What I never told her, what I never told anyone, was that those dreams were different from my regular ones in more than the obvious way. Those dreams spun their tales in a language at once strange yet completely familiar to me. When I entered my teens, the dreams disappeared, and I did not think about them again until my first mission to Moscow. As I exited the plane into the crowded airport, I suddenly understood something.

Those dreams, those terrifying nightmares, had unfolded in perfect Russian.

31

Bath time is a backbreaking experience. On my knees tubside, trying to soap up a small person who is more intent on pouring cupfuls of water onto the bathroom floor, I feel the nine years of relatively hard living I did at the Agency. My knees ache, my lower back is tight, my neck is knotted like a rope. I'm a wreck. But maybe it's not so much the tub as the partial drowning I experienced earlier. All I really want to do is lie down and sleep, but motherhood doesn't give evenings off for near-death experiences.

Theo, on the other hand, is happy as a clam. I am barely paying attention to him as I try to organize the day in my head. But like the rest of me, it hurts. I'm having trouble keeping all the balls up in the air. Theo yanks on my sleeve with a wet hand.

"Is Daddy back with dinner yet?" he asks.

"I don't think so, baby. Probably ten more minutes. Are you starved?"

"No. I hear the door."

His words make me freeze. The door.

"Okay, honey. Probably time to come out now."

"I'm still playing," he whines. But my ears are tuned elsewhere. I don't hear footsteps on the stairs. Maybe Will forgot his wallet? I pull Theo out of the tub despite the increasingly loud protests. I wrap him in a towel and carry the whole damp bundle down the hallway to his bedroom. Still no unusual sounds.

"Mommy, who is that man?"

I'd be lying if I told you I react calmly to this question. I don't. Not really. Standing next to Theo's crib is Ian Blackford, none the worse for wear. He has both hands deep in the pockets of his overcoat, which hides a navy pinstripe suit. It's strange. The suit, I mean. Yes, it is also strange that Blackford is in my house in Theo's room, but it is the suit that strikes me.

"If you try anything, I swear you will regret it," I say, clutching Theo to my chest, hoping he didn't hear me. "And what's with the suit?"

He looks down as if he's forgotten he is wearing it.

"Oh. Right. Work thing."

"That's weird. This whole thing is weird. Get out of my house."

"I can't do that."

"Then go downstairs and wait for me." He nods his head and disappears down the stairs. I'm breathing hard. Blackford appears to have nine lives.

"Mommy, I'm cold," Theo says. He seems unfazed by the stranger hanging out in his bedroom in the dark of night. Pretty secure kid. I dry him off and pull him into his dinosaur pajamas. I tuck him in front of the TV and he goes into that trance-like state of a child who doesn't get to watch very much. In my closet, behind the box of old maternity clothes, is a locked metal safe. In the safe is a shoebox. In the shoebox is my gun. It's dusty and I have just three bullets, but that's enough. I only need one. I load it, tuck it into the back of my pants, and go downstairs to see what the hell Blackford wants, because for the life of me, I can't figure it out.

He sits in my kitchen, munching on an open bag of pretzels, and drinking my leftover cold coffee.

"Make yourself at home."

"Thanks. Mind if I put this in the microwave?" he asks, holding up the coffee mug.

"Would it matter if I said yes?" I ask. I lean back against the counter, watching him.

"Aren't you going to ask me how I am?" he says. And suddenly I'm mad, really mad, maybe the maddest I've ever been. I must be, because when Blackford turns back from the microwave with his coffee, I punch him square in the nose. The coffee goes flying, splashing dark brown stains on the cabinets and ceiling. Blackford feels his nose, the little trickle of blood. And he starts to laugh.

"Sally! You didn't think I was really going to drown you out there, did you?"

I am shaking with fury. "How dare you?" I hiss. "This is my life. How dare you show up here? I don't know what you want or why, but I will kill you if you force my hand."

Blackford looks contemplative for a moment. "Okay, I'm getting that," he says. "So why don't I state my case and go?" He wipes the blood from his face on one of my cloth napkins. "I need the dolls."

"The what?" My adrenaline levels drop and I suddenly feel like one of Theo's stuffed animals, all weak and disjointed. I pull out a chair and sit down.

"The dolls. The ones I sent to Theo when he was born."

Somewhere from the deep recesses of my mind comes the image of a delivery box, brown paper, lots of tape, a postage stamp from New York, but no return address, no note, no nothing.

"The nesting dolls?" I say confused. "They were from you? How did you know?"

"I remember telling you once, a long time ago, that the reason I am better than everyone else is because I know everything. That remains the truth."

The idea that Blackford has been keeping tabs on me all along feels not unlike someone dumping a bucket of ice water on my head.

"The dolls?" Blackford asks.

"What's in the dolls?" I ask. "Theo plays with those dolls."

"He plays with them?" For the first time, maybe ever, Blackford looks surprised. "Sally, that set is an antique. Quite valuable, in fact. And you let him play with them? They are meant to be admired. From a distance."

"Well, maybe you shouldn't have given them as a baby present. Maybe you should have sent me some monogrammed washcloths or a hat or something." Maybe you should have stayed dead.

"Do you still have them?" A flash of doubt in his eyes.

"I've taken those dolls to the playground, on picnics, to the zoo. Theo liked to chew on the middle one when he was a baby. You do know that babies eat things? Wood, plastic, keys, cell phones, sand, basically anything not nailed to the floor." Blackford looks horrified when I say sand. He cannot fathom a baby in any context. "What is in the dolls?" I ask again.

"Doesn't matter. Do you still have them?" He is growing impatient.

"I don't have them anymore," I say. At the same time, we hear Will's key in the front door, home with the takeout.

"Be expecting me back," Blackford says and slips out the backdoor as my husband comes through the front one. I grab a dishtowel and start cleaning up the coffee.

"Hi, babe," he says, "what happened?"

"Oh, nothing. Knocked over a cup of coffee."

"Good shot," he says, dropping the take-out bags on the counter. "It's on the ceiling."

Great.

Later that night, as the house sleeps, I sneak out of bed and find the dolls, worn and sandy. With a gentle tap from a hammer, the smallest doll splits open to reveal a hard substance, the shape of a sugar cube and density of resin. I hold it up to the light, turn it. It has no marks, no distinguishing characteristics. It's simply a brownish-green cube of something that Blackford seems to want back. Badly.

I smell it. Jungle. Darkness. Decay. Sweat. Blackford's botanist. They say that the sense of smell is intricately tied to memory and I don't think they are kidding. I sit down, dizzy, at the dining room table. I remember as if it were yesterday, the intoxicating effect of the flowers we couldn't even see for the darkness. What they are doing in resin form in my son's doll is another question entirely.

I throw the cube into an old sugar bowl and put it up on a shelf. I add a few grains of rice to the broken doll and carefully glue it together. I go back to bed, visions of the jungle dancing in my head.

32

The cube is still in the sugar bowl when I get up to make Theo breakfast. Now, you may wonder why I don't call Simon Still and tell him that I have something that Blackford wants. Simon could have the cube sent back to the lab in Washington and we'd know what we were dealing with and we could proceed in an orderly manner. Right. As if we ever proceeded in an orderly manner. Just yesterday, Simon had indicated how expendable he believed me to be. He had no compunction at all about shooting me in the head if it helped him get Blackford. For now, he was no better than the enemy. I was on my own.

I take the cube out of the sugar bowl and turn it over and over in my hands. It doesn't look like much, but clearly if Blackford wants it, so must everyone else. And if there is anything about which I am sure these days it is that they will all be coming for it soon. I dial Nanny Pauline. She sounds like she has been up for hours. Probably has a spin class and a nutritious breakfast under her belt already.

"Come now," I say and hang up without further explanation.

I'm not happy about what I'm going to do. In fact, it's making me a little queasy, but I don't see the alternative. I have to know if this cube is what I think it is. I sit in my car and wait. He comes out, briefcase in one hand, travel coffee mug in the other, completely unaware that he is being watched. As he sets off toward the freeway, I follow, a few cars behind. We head south in stop-and-go traffic. I listen to the radio and roll the cube over and over and over in my pocket. It's starting to get mushy and soft inside the plastic bag. I consider rolling down the window and tossing it out onto the freeway. What would happen then?

Finally, we arrive. I pull into a spot next to his car and get out. I'm about to cross the line.

Jonathan looks surprised to see me, which is a totally appropriate response, all things considered.

"Lucy? What are you doing here?"

"Hi, Jonathan. Looking for you actually. I need a favor." I hold up the cube. "I need to know what this is."

Jonathan looks a little concerned, glances at his watch. "I'd love to help you, but I have a class in about twenty minutes. Maybe if you left it, I could get to it later this week?" Jonathan is already starting to walk away, toward his normal day in his normal life.

"I hate to do this," I say, falling in next to him, "but it's critical." I take his arm.

"Lucy?"

"I know that you're having an affair, Jonathan. I know the person. If you want me to keep this information to myself, you will take me to your lab right now and tell me what this is. Okay?"

Jonathan looks pale. "How dare you accuse me of such a . . . a . . ." he stammers.

"Shh," I say. "Don't waste your time denying it. In fact, don't say anything. Let's go." He nods, face flaming red, and we head toward his lab.

I sit on a stool and watch Jonathan work. He says nothing, every once in a while throwing me a hateful look. I want to remind him that I'm not the one having the affair. I don't actually know who he's sleeping with and don't much care, but that's not important right now. As long as he thinks I know, we're going to do fine.

"You're not writing an article, are you?" he says finally, eyes fixed on a computer screen that is streaming row after row of numbers.

"I could be," I say.

"This has to do with those notes you brought me." I don't confirm or deny. More silence. Finally, Jonathan sits down next to me.

"This thing," he says, holding up my cube, "is a plant." His eyes suddenly light up with a dreadful realization. "The Death Lily? It can't be. Not possible. How did you . . ."

I snatch the cube from his hand and put it back in my pocket.

"Thank you for your help," I say. "It would be best if you didn't discuss this with anyone."

"Does she know?" he asks as I'm halfway out the door. I turn back.

"She suspects." A look of true sadness settles in on his face. His shoulders sag.

"He's so wonderful," he says, mostly to himself. "How do I give him up?"

I have no answer to that question, so I leave him to mull over the strange turn his morning has taken.

I drive too fast up the 101. There is, blissfully, no traffic so I push my green automobile into the red. It's not pleased, whining in protest. This car is so light, at this speed I feel like I might actually take flight. But time is important. Ending up in jail for going 100 miles an hour on the freeway would be a major inconvenience, but it's a risk I'm willing to take. I fly across the Bay Bridge and right into my familiar parking place near Albert Malcolm's lab building. I do a quick survey. No Blackford. No Simon Still. No Blind Monk. It could be that I am totally undetected in my activities, but I doubt it. I head straight for the student union. Barry is in place at the corner table, surrounded by the other slightly greasy disciples of Professor Malcolm.

When you need someone's help, there are myriad factors to consider in selecting the method by which you will attain it. If you have time, you can push a person gently toward a desirable goal, all the while having him think it was his brilliant idea in the first place. But if you don't have time, well, then all bets are off. Before Barry has any idea what is happening, I have him under his arm and am hauling him out of the student union. There is enough activity that we don't stand out, but his friends look confused, concerned. I bank on these men having a lengthy conversation about what is happening, but not actually making a move to intervene. I walk with Barry, holding his arm tightly. He struggles.

"What do you think you are doing?" he protests. "Let me go."

"Not a chance. Bring me to Malcolm."

"Are you crazy? I'm going to call the police."

I nudge him slightly with the butt of my gun, hidden in my jacket pocket.

"I wouldn't do that if I were you."

"You don't think I'm going to fall for that trick, do you? I watch TV. I wasn't born yesterday." I pull the Colt out of my pocket and show it to him.

"Oh, shit. That's a real gun. What do you want? Please don't kill me. I'm not done with my dissertation yet!"

"I need to talk to Malcolm and I need to do it now. Make that happen and you won't get hurt."

He nods, little beads of sweat popping out on his fuzzy upper lip. "He should be in the lab."

We walk arm in arm down the path to the lab building. I notice Barry's new entry cards and smile. People so rarely pay attention to what is going on around them, it's a wonder we survive at all. He has no memory of my having mugged him in broad daylight in this exact spot. It is often easier to use human weakness as a means to your end rather than coming up with a complicated plan that involves electronics.

We enter the main hallway, pass by the security guard, and enter the lab. Professor Malcolm is sitting at a small steel table in the corner, poring over notes, scribbling madly with the nub of a pencil. He doesn't even bother to look up.

"Barry, this formula. It's a disaster," he says. "Start over." Barry clears his throat.

"Excuse me, Professor. I've brought someone to see you." With this, Albert Malcolm looks up and sees me, and he's not at all pleased.

"How could you bring this . . . this . . . infidel into my laboratory?" he growls. Barry drops his head. He sees his future slipping away.

"Oh, don't blame Barry," I say, waving my gun around. "He didn't have a choice. And don't hit the security button, Professor. That would be bad. Besides, I have something you need."

I pull the resin out of my pocket, turning it in my fingers. The professor exhales, like a tire with a slow leak.

"The lily. Ian said you had it. He said you would give it to him."

"He said that?" For some reason it annoys me that Blackford thinks I'm so easy.

"I'm not here to give it you, Professor," I say. "Quite the contrary."

"But you must!"

"If you and Blackford both want it so badly, well, that can't be a good thing. I don't exactly trust either of you, if you know what I mean."

The professor, almost twice my age, lunges at me. And he's fast. I slide a rolling instrument tray in his way and he crashes into it, going down. I put my knee gently on the back of his neck.

"Never surprise a person with a gun," I say. "It's a really good way to get shot." He squirms. I lean harder. He stops. Meanwhile, Barry is frozen like a statue in the corner. It's possible he is enjoying watching his mentor get a little bit beat up. I bend down, close to Malcolm's ear. He groans under the pressure from my knee.

"In case you missed it," I whisper, "Ian Blackford is the little boy you left all those years ago. You remember the one? When you decided to take your books and the cat and your socks and underwear but leave your son, well, that's the sort of thing that can come back to haunt you. Blackford's only purpose in life right now is to humiliate you. And after you've been disgraced in front of the world, he might take pity on you and waltz into whatever prison you're rotting in and kill you. But then again, he might not."

I roll my knee off his neck. The professor gulps in a few deep breaths but doesn't sit up. I toss the fake cube, half of a set of dice from one of Theo's board games, on the floor. The professor's hand darts out and snatches it. I step over him.

"Thanks for your help, Barry," I say, patting him on the back as I head out the door. He continues to stand there, motionless. As soon as the lab door swings shut, I pull out my cell phone and call Nanny Pauline.

"How are things there?" I ask. There is a pause, a second too long.

"Fine," she says.

"And Theo? What is he doing?"

"Oh, I fed him some grapes for lunch. Yes, sir. He enjoyed those grapes, I'll say."

My heart starts to race. It's the code.

"I'm coming. Has anyone touched Theo?"

"Nope. A-OK on that front. Not much interest in that, I don't think."

A furious mama rhinoceros once chased me through a Nepalese jungle. Compared to how fast I am now running to my car, I'd be tempted to question her commitment.

33

Picture this. My nanny, not really a nanny but a secret agent, and my nemesis, a handsome rogue named Ian Blackford, sitting together at my kitchen table while my son plays happily among their feet with his Lincoln Logs. Nanny Pauline gazes at Blackford like a heartsick schoolgirl. I want to give her rosy checks a quick slap.

"Can I get anyone coffee?" I ask, setting my bag and car keys down on the table. "Or maybe I can smash your heads together and we can call it good?"

"Sally," Blackford practically purrs, "where is it?" On the table are the Russian nesting dolls. Several of the dolls are smashed, the colorful shards of wood scattered across the table.

"Where is what?"

"Don't fuck around now, Sally. All bets are off here. I am not on your side. I never was."

"Wow," I say. "And there I was thinking we were all in the service of God, country, and the American way. Or something."

"Where is it?"

"I don't have what you want."

"Yes, you do." He picks up a splinter of broken doll. "Yes. You do."

"Do you think I'm such an idiot that I would keep my only bargaining chip here in this house?"

"Yes," says Blackford with conviction. He clearly doesn't think that much of me.

"What you want is somewhere safe and most definitely not in this house," I say.

"It's the last known sample of the Blue Wing Lily found only in a jungle you once walked through in the middle of the night," Blackford says.

"I wouldn't say walked. I'd say it was more like we clawed our way through that jungle."

"However you like."

"So why all this madness? You knew where Roger and I were that night. You shot those windows out, right? So why not go back and get more?" He looks at me like I'm crazy.

"I tore that jungle apart, Sally. They could have paved the whole place and put up a Wal-Mart when I was done. But there were no lilies. Whatever you and Roger stumbled upon, it was all gone."

"A pity."

"Yes. You killed it. These plants are apparently . . . very fragile. They rarely survive contact with humans."

"That's ridiculous."

"Life is full of mystery."

"And if I don't give it to you?"

Blackford leans back in my lovely kitchen chair and closes his eyes. He's troubled. I wait.

"I know where you live, Sally. I know the secrets you are keeping. Isn't the lily worth holding on to this life you've created?"

After all this time, he's blackmailing me. How demeaning. It's not fair, but blackmail seldom is. And I don't think Blackford cares.

"I don't have the flower," I say. "It's in a safe place. Meet me at the Point Bonita Lighthouse tomorrow, three P.M., and I'll give it to you."

"Sally, as much as I'd like to indulge in a scenic-wonders-of-California tour, now is not the time. I need the flower. Hand it over now and I will disappear into the night. And I promise you will never see me again."

"You're supposed to be dead," I remind him. "Your promises are not worth very much to me, to be honest. And like I said, I don't have it here."

"You have not learned to be a better liar in the intervening years."

"In that case, why don't you kill us all, tear apart my house, and find it, if you are so certain?"

As he steps closer to me, I hold my position, but not without effort.

"Because then again, with you, I'm never quite sure." He rolls back on his heels. I exhale.

"Tomorrow. Three P.M. At the lighthouse," he says. "And Sally?"

"Yes?"

"Don't turn this into another one of your disasters or you will regret it."

"Sure," I say. "Like always. Now please get out of my house and understand that it's nothing personal, but if I find you in here again, I will not hesitate to kill you."

Blackford smiles at me as if we are quarreling lovers. "Understood."

As soon as he is gone, Nanny Pauline starts to overflow.

"He appeared out of nowhere, at the table. I was getting Theo a snack and all of a sudden he was sitting there, exactly where you found him. I didn't hear a door open, nothing. I have no idea how he did it. I mean, was that really Ian Blackford, the actual man? I had no idea he was so . . . so . . ."

"Gorgeous?" I offer.

"God, yes." She almost swoons but catches herself when she realizes I am less than pleased.

"From now on, you and Theo come with me," I say.

"I'm so sorry," Nanny Pauline stammers. "I really screwed up. Are you going to tell Simon?"

Simon? Probably not. I'm still mad at him for authorizing his men to fire at Blackford while he was using me as a human shield. It seems that's the sort of grudge you can safely hold for a day or two without anyone accusing you of being overly sensitive.

"No," I say. "When Blackford wants something, there is not much you can do to stop him. You should be glad he didn't drug you and lock you in the bathroom."

"What?" Nanny Pauline looks confused.

"Never mind," I say. But she is not done.

"In these situations, Simon always says to stick to public places, preferably with a full bar. The lighthouse seems so random."

Seems random, I want to scream. How about *is* completely random, the first place that popped into my head. There is no logic here, no well-thought-out plan. There is just me, flying once again by the seat of my pants.

What a mess.

34

Nanny Pauline starts to pick up the toys scattered liberally around the kitchen floor. It is hard to take a step without crushing a maraca or a Thomas the Tank Engine. And let me tell you, there is nothing like stepping on Thomas the Tank Engine with a bare foot to put things in perspective.

I am sitting at the kitchen table, sipping my coffee, running over exactly how I am supposed to proceed. Do I give the lily to Blackford and play the odds that whatever they are cooking up will fail? Do I refuse and hope he's in a good enough mood not to toss me headfirst into the Bay? By the time I get to the bottom of my cup, I'm convinced I don't actually have any choice. I have to give Blackford the flower. It is the only way I can be sure of protecting Theo and Will. I will make the trade.

Pauline sits down at the table next to me. "Is he as bad as they say he is?" she asks, still reeling from her brush with greatness.

"Worse," I say. "Do yourself a flavor. Trust no one. I know it's cliché, but in this case, it's absolutely appropriate."

I scoop up Theo from under the table and carry him into the living room. We read *Olivia, Flotsam, Clifford the Big Red Dog*, and *Winnie-the-Pooh*, the one where he inexplicably learns about gravity. Weird.

"Mommy, who was that?" Theo asks.

"Nobody. An old friend of Mommy's. Why do you ask?"

"He was scary."

"Did he say anything to you?"

"No. But he wanted my dolls. The rattling one. But I don't want him to have it."

"I know, baby. We won't give it to him."

"Okay, you have it now? It's itchy."

What? "Theo, where is the rattle doll?"

With that he starts to wiggle and squirm. Reaching down into his Superman underwear, he pulls up the smallest doll of the set and hands it to me.

"I hided it," he says, full of pride.

A chip off the old block.

35

The next morning, after dropping Theo at school, I sit in the Java Luv and mentally write my obituary. Here lies Sally Sin, it will say, or whoever the hell she was. She was an okay mother and a lousy cook and clearly suffered from caffeine addiction. Pathetic.

"You don't look like your usual perky self today, Lucy," Leonard says, laughing at his joke. "Get it? You? Perky? That's a pretty good one." With a damp rag, he wipes the same circle on the counter over and over.

"Do you know," I say, "that I used to be a spy? I once got thrown off a boat in a hurricane."

He does not consider even for a second that I might be telling him the truth.

"Bullshit. Nobody is really a spy. Will you call me if anyone comes in? Need a smoke to take the edge off."

Off of what? I am the only customer in the place and, if need be, I could go around behind the counter and make my own coffee.

"Good God, Leonard," I shout after him. "If you can't take it, what is going to happen to me?" The only sign of him is a sweet drift of smoke floating out from the back room.

I stare absently out the window. The cherry trees are losing their leaves, which blow softly in the breeze. The cars at the intersection idle, waiting patiently for their turn to cross. A young couple, one in a wool hat and down vest, the other in shorts and flip-flops, are intertwined, hoping for a number 32 bus any minute now. I feel a sense of relief in the familiarity of this place. I've never stayed anywhere as long as I've stayed here, and it feels good. Maybe, just maybe, I'll get lucky and it will all work out.

And then I see him. The thing I've been waiting for, the person who is not supposed to be there, closing in on Theo's preschool door.

I leap up, upsetting the bistro table. The ceramic cups and my water glass crash to the floor. I grab my bag.

"Hey," says Leonard, running in, coughing, "are you okay?"

"Sorry about the mess," I say, already halfway out the door. "I have to go."

Behind me I hear "Jesus, you really are crazy." I speed through the intersection; cars kindly swerve to avoid running me over. The drivers are screaming, cursing through rolled-down windows. I dash up onto the sidewalk and race toward the Blind Monk, approaching Theo's preschool. He turns toward me as I launch myself into the air and tackle him. We go down hard on the sidewalk, but we don't stop there. The mass of our combined weights, mostly his, gives us momentum, and we tumble over the edge of the sidewalk barrier and down a steep embankment. The sticks and rocks and debris stab as we roll over each other on the way down. The Blind Monk smells like incense and mothballs and, despite all that is happening, I want to sneeze. We come to a sudden stop at the bottom of the incline, with me on top. I reach around for my Colt but it has fallen out on the ride down. The Blind Monk takes advantage of the momentary distraction and, as if I am light as a feather, tosses me off him. His forearm comes down with punishing force on my throat. I gag. He leans. I see stars and rainbows and fireworks. Just as I think I'm going to black out, my fingers brush a fist-sized rock. I grab it and, with all the force I can muster, I smash it into the back of the Blind Monk's head.

He slumps over on top of me. Using both hands, I heave him off to the side.

"Did you really think you could get to me through my kid?" I snarl into his unconscious face. I want to continue to smash him with the rock, but I don't because if I arrive at pickup covered in blood, someone is bound to notice. Instead, I give him a good hard kick in the kidneys. Something for later.

I climb down the ravine and tumble out onto someone's driveway and onto another sidewalk. Quickly, I make my way back up to the preschool.

I have a few minutes until dismissal so I sit on the steps outside of Theo's school, trying to catch my breath and picking twigs out of my hair. Some of the other moms show up, and we talk about the storm the other day, the upcoming class trip to the baseball stadium, and the best way to get a child to eat broccoli. Not one of them asks why I have dirt stains on my elbows and knees and plant matter in my hair. They're nice that way.

At exactly noon, the kids spill out of the school. Theo jumps into my arms and takes a deep breath of my hair.

"Mommy," he says, "we painted flowers with glitter glue today." His face is sparkling with tiny bits of red and green and silver.

"I can see that," I said. "Should we go inside and get your coat and things from your cubby?" Theo nods and leads me by the hand back into the school.

Teacher Wendy is standing at the center of a swarm of preschoolers, with a serene look on her face. I don't know how she does it. She gives me a big warm smile, like I'm four years old.

"Hi, Lucy. How are you today?"

Honestly? You don't want to know.

"Fine," I reply. "How was Theo's day?"

"Wonderful. Today Theo really demonstrated what a good team player he is becoming. We're learning that when you work together, things get done faster and better." Sounding like she is reciting the script to a PBS kids' show, Teacher Wendy leans toward me to pick some dried leaves out of my hair.

"Were you gardening?" she asks innocently.

"Not exactly," I say.

"Mommy, I'm a good team player," Theo pipes up, tugging on my pants.

"Of course you are, sweetie. You're fabulous. Let's get your things."

We bend down together to excavate the contents of Theo's cubby. Out comes his jacket, several toy cars, the glitter glue picture, some spin art, and something unidentifiable made out of clay.

"These are beautiful, baby. Can I hang them up when we get home?"

"Yes. Me and Max worked together doing teamwork and made the lion," he says, pointing to the lump of gray clay. "We're best friends. We do the same stuff."

The same stuff. The same goals. Teamwork. Together. One taking the high road and one doing the dirty work. Squatting in front of Theo's cubby, zipping up his yellow Windbreaker, I realize that Ian Blackford and the Blind Monk are now playing on the same team and maybe have been for some time. The Blind Monk is not here to take his revenge on Blackford. No, he is here to do Blackford's bidding, which appears to involve getting rid of me. And while Blackford may have a problem killing me, I never remember him promising he wouldn't hire someone to do it for him.

36

Theo sits in the backseat, playing with a contraband Elmo See 'N Say, taken out from under the bed only when Daddy is at work. Elmo's squeaky voice keeps yelping out random words like "sea" and "truck." I can feel my right eyelid start to twitch with every new turn of the dial. Nanny Pauline sits next to me, spine perfectly aligned, hands folded neatly in her lap like a recent graduate from the Miss Manners School of Etiquette. She stares straight ahead. She is still smarting from her interlude with Blackford. Ten minutes with the guy can take weeks to wear off. This I know from experience.

"So when we get there, you are going to drop me off and drive into Sausalito. Stay in public places. Buy Theo an ice-cream cone and don't come back until I call you."

"And if you don't call?"

"I will call. Not calling is not an option."

"Okay. Sausalito. Ice cream. Easy. This is going to be bad, isn't it?"

"What gives you that idea?" I ask.

"Well, you know, that whole thing with the hotel and things," she says, suddenly sheepish.

"The Grand Event?" I ask, surprised. "What do you know about the Grand Event?"

"Oh, there was stuff. Stories, mostly, about you and Blackford and the Blind Monk. And a really great dress."

What the hell?

"Jesus, Pauline. You've been holding out on me."

"No, I haven't. I figured you knew all the stories. I mean, you were there!"

"All the stories? There is more than one?"

"Yeah, about how that Cambodian was murdered by the Blind Monk right in front of everyone, and you tried to save him, but Blackford ended up having to save you. And you were wearing some crazy dress that made you look like Wonder Woman or something."

"Wonder Woman didn't wear a dress," I point out. "She ran around in a strapless bathing suit with high-heeled boots and magic bracelets. And Blackford never saved me." At least not that I can confirm beyond a shadow of a doubt.

Pauline shrugs. It's all the same to her.

"It was nothing like you are thinking. And remember what happened next? Big explosion. Lots of smoke? Dead people? So keep in mind that is the sort of horror Ian Blackford willingly creates. Don't go falling in love with him. He is not a romantic hero. He's a lunatic and he will not think twice about dispatching you to your maker if you inconvenience him." I hear in my words an echo of the Old Timers. They'd appreciate that I've taken their lessons to heart. "This is not a game. At the end of the day, it is about survival."

As the words pass my lips, I suddenly understand my evolution. For all those years, it *was* a game. I was Agent 26 of the United States Agency for Weapons of Mass Destruction, and my job was to win the game. But now, right here in the front seat of my environmentally friendly car with my fake nanny and my son, I am just a mom. And that is far more important than anything else I've done before.

"It's all about survival," I say again. Pauline nods solemnly. She is already rehearsing the stories she will bring back to the Agency if she lives through this.

We cross the Golden Gate Bridge. The sun dances on the blue-green water. Curls of fog are starting to form out on the horizon. A steady wind pushes and shoves the car as we cruise off the bridge into Marin. The sharp hills that comprise the Marin Headlands are covered in a dense scrub that, if you get close, smells like soapy water drying on hot pavement. The beauty of these hills is not their lushness, but rather in the starkness of the land as it meets the sea. The water, having traveled thousands of miles, finally crashes into a barrier that won't yield. Frustrated, it keeps coming, pounding the coastline day after day, somehow knowing its relentlessness will eventually pay off.

A few minutes later, we are snaking up the back of the Headlands. There are no other cars as the fog begins to push in earnest over the land. I pull over to the side at the bottom of a steep hill.

"Okay, Sausalito, ice cream, do not come back until I call. Understood?"

"Yes," says Pauline.

"If anyone suspicious comes along, if Theo is threatened in any way," I say quietly, "don't miss."

Pauline swallows. I can almost feel the dryness in her throat. "I won't," she says.

I hand the keys to Pauline. I give Theo a big kiss.

"Mommy will see you in a little while, baby. Pauline is going to buy you an ice-cream cone and you can get something in the toy store too. Okay?"

For the first time, Theo looks like he might not be down with this plan.

"I want to go with you," he says, pursing his lips.

"How about you get a sundae with whipped cream and extra cherries?"

"Oh. Okay," he says, his face relaxing. I kiss him again and slam the door.

"Go," I say. Pauline pulls away. My hands are shaking. I have nothing more than my gun with three bullets tucked into the back of my pants and Blackford's precious piece of lily hidden in my shirt. I find the beginning of the footpath that will lead me over this hill and right to a spot where I can look down on my ultimate destination, the lighthouse.

"What on earth were you thinking, Sally?" I ask myself. "Another great plan. It would be less isolated if you were dropped out of an airplane in the middle of the Pacific Ocean. At least there you'd have the whales to keep you company. Wait a minute. Did I just call myself Sally? Okay, now I'm really mad."

There is a cold wind being pushed in front of the fog and I shiver. Beyond the next set of hills is the ocean; the salty air feels good in my lungs. I take a few deep breaths and start hiking up the trail toward the Point Bonita Lighthouse and my date with destiny. If you believe in that sort of thing, of course.

37

By the time I reach the top of the hill, the fog is coming strong and steady. Its cold fingers reach out and run through my hair, around my face, making me wish for a thick fleece jacket and a hat. I start down the hill, the dry red clay slipping under my feet like ball bearings. When I finally reach the bottom, the parking lot for the lighthouse is empty.

I walk around the gate blocking entry to the trail and begin making my way down the steep concrete path. I duck through a tunnel blasted out of the rock and finally step onto the suspension bridge leading to the actual lighthouse. The bridge is old and wooden. It sways precariously in the wind. There is enough space between the railing slats for a small child to slip through. Probably not a great destination for Theo, I think, although he'd think it was cool. I give myself a mental slap on the face. Focus.

The foghorn wails and goes silent, wails and goes silent. The light atop the lighthouse flashes, warning sailors to steer clear. Not a bad idea, all things being equal. Seventy-five feet below, I can barely see the waves crashing on the rocky coast.

When I look up, I see Simon Still, standing on the far side of the swaying bridge. He has the Magnum in his hand, but it is pointed, for the moment, at the ground. He walks toward me slowly, trying to maintain his balance on the wobbly bridge.

"I need whatever it is he wants, Sally," Simon says. "It's a matter of national security, as I'm sure you know. You are obligated to hand it over to me. As a citizen of this great country of ours."

"Did she tell you?" I have to ask even if I know the answer.

"Of course she did. She's Agency first, Sally, like you used to be."

For whatever irrational reason, I feel disappointed that Nanny Pauline gave me up yet again. Will I never learn?

"Hand it over," Simon says.

"Oh, enough with the bullshit, Simon. I'm still mad about the beach. You were going to shoot me."

Simon shrugs. "Roberts is good. He would have missed you."

"That's not the point," I say.

"I need it," Simon says again. "Don't make me do anything uncomfortable, Sally."

"Do you even know what it is? No. I didn't think so. It's the Death Lily, Simon. The one you were so sure didn't exist. And you know what makes it even funnier? I'm actually responsible for it being here in the first place. If I had taken your advice, I would never have bothered to save Roger in that goddamn jungle and then we could have all stayed home today and watched the World Series or something."

Simon looks confused. "The Death Lily?"

"Yes," I shout. "How many times do I have to say it? The. Death. Lily."

"Well, I guess I'm going to need the Death Lily, Sally. Hand it over."

Suddenly, we hear the chirping of crickets. For a split second, I think we are actually going to experience a plague of locusts on top of all our other miseries. But no, it's my cell phone. Will's number flashes across the screen. And of course I answer it because wouldn't you do the same if you were in my shoes?

"Hi, baby," I say.

"Where are you? Sounds loud."

Hell. I'm in hell. Send me a postcard, will you?

"Walking to Twenty-fourth Street. You know how the wind is out here."

"Are you okay?"

"Great. Sure. Why do you ask?"

"You sound a little strange."

"It's the wind."

Simon is making "cut if off" signals with his hands. I turn my back to him, holding on to the bridge railing to keep steady.

"Anyway, can you pick up my suit at the cleaners? That black one? I need it for tomorrow and I don't think I'm going to get home before they close."

"Yup, sure, you got it, not a problem. Okay? Great. Gotta go. Love you. Talk later."

I hang up in time to see Blackford emerge from the fog on the other side of the bridge. Suddenly, I'm not so keen on the symbolism of being on a bridge trapped on one end by Simon Still and on the other by Ian Blackford.

"There's a sign over there that says only two people on this bridge at one time," I say. "Somebody better get off." They both ignore me, focused only on each other.

"Simon, old pal, I've missed you," Blackford says. He grins like a lion eyeing his prey.

"And I you," Simon says. Simon's gun is aimed at Blackford. Blackford's gun is aimed at Simon. I feel left out.

"Well, this is nice, don't you think? The three of us again. Kind of like old times," Blackford says.

"Great. I'm freezing," I mutter, sinking down to a sitting position on the bridge. "Why don't you two hurry up and shoot each other so I can go home already?"

They appear to be considering all options.

"The lily, Sally," Blackford says, edging closer to me. "Remember what we talked about. Now reach in your pocket slowly and take it out."

"If you reach in your pocket for that flower, Sally, I will shoot you in the head," Simon says quietly from right behind me.

So here I am, stuck between a rock and a hard place. What do girls like me do in situations like these? Good question. I used to sing lullabies to Theo when he seemed intent on staying up all night screaming, and it always soothed his inner beast. But right now, the only song I can think of is "Baby Beluga" and that seems oddly inappropriate.

"The lily, Sally," Blackford repeats.

"For God's sake, can't we all at least agree that we'll call me Lucy? That is my name now. There is no more Sally Sin."

"I don't want to shoot you, but I will." I turn to Simon, right behind me.

"I heard you the first time," I say. "That is not really something you need to repeat."

There was a day not too long ago, an ordinary Saturday evening, when Will and I sat at the kitchen table watching Theo race his cars around the kitchen with wild abandon. We weren't talking to each other, we were simply watching the little blond head bob and weave around the chairs and under the table. On Will's face was a look of peace, a serenity that I immediately understood and felt myself. This was all there was. This was all there need ever be. When I exhaled, thirtysomething years of frantic living disappeared and were replaced with only the here and now.

With that ordinary Saturday evening in my mind, I shake my sleeve. Simon and Blackford watch me intently. I wiggle my arm and rotate my shoulder and, finally, the little cube of poison lily slides down my arm and into my hand. I hold it up between my fingers.

"That night in the jungle, it was so dark I couldn't even tell you what color the flowers were," I say, "but I remember the smell. Never would forget that smell." Blackford takes a step toward me. He eyes the cube, the anticipation burning in his eyes. He holds out his hand. Simon cocks the Magnum. The barrel is inches from my head. Both men are focused on the resin, like dogs on a single bone. I think at any moment, they might start barking. This thought makes me laugh.

"What's wrong with you, Lucy?" Simon asks. Now I'm laughing so hard I'm crying.

"Just *look* at us," I say. "What a mess we make of everything." As the laughter fades, I plant my feet on the rickety slates of the bridge and I throw the last remnant of the Death Lily up into the sky, out toward the ocean. I see it in slow motion, sailing higher and higher into the foggy air. Simon and Blackford lunge forward over the edge of the bridge, hands extended like receivers after a Hail Mary pass.

I duck down and dodge around Blackford. The bridge trembles and weaves as I race off it and on to freedom.

Now, my plan would have worked. I would have hoofed it off that bridge and back to my nice, kind of normal life, if the world wasn't a totally fucked up place, which it is, as I'm sure you've figured out by now. Instead of escaping, I trip over an uneven slat of bridge and land flat on my face. The Colt falls out of my jacket pocket and over the side. I grab for it, but it is too late. It disappears into the fog. Gone. Before I can get back on my feet, I hear the cock of two separate guns close to my head. I guess no one caught the lily.

"You'd better tell me that was a fake," Blackford whispers, his voice a little unsteady. He cannot believe I would have the nerve.

"You'd better, Lucy," Simon adds.

"Wow. Are you two agreeing on something?"

"Mommy?" Again the slow motion, the distinct sensation that time has stopped moving. We all turn to stare as Theo comes through the fog and onto the bridge.

Nanny Pauline stands behind him with her hands clasped behind her head. The Blind Monk stands behind her, his machine gun aimed at her back. I feel a sudden wave of nausea as I try to stand up.

There are so many guns. This is not good. I lock eyes with Theo, who looks confused and frightened. If I live a thousand years, I will never forgive myself for that look of fear.

"Theo, look at me, look only at me." He nods his head. "It's going to be fine. I promise." He nods again, clutching his dirty stuffed lamb.

I look at Simon. Despite losing the lily, he is smiling—grinning, actually. For him, this is better than Christmas morning.

Blackford doesn't look quite as happy. "I told you to wait for my signal," he growls at the Blind Monk.

"You have lost your way, my friend. You have lost your vision. I can save you."

"You work for me, remember? And I'm not paying you to save my soul."

"She is toxic," the Blind Monk says, pointing at me. "Worse than the Death Lily for you. Clouds your mind. We get rid of them all today and we finish our business as we planned."

Blackford refocuses his attention on me. There is nothing but fury in his eyes. Maybe the Blind Monk's plan sounds pretty good all of a sudden?

And rather than shooting them both and calling it a day, Simon Still stands there as if he has grown roots. He appears to be enjoying the dialogue.

Now what?

"That was the real lily," I say, in case they think I have the actual one in a safe-deposit box down on California Street. "It's probably in the belly of some really stoned sea lion already." The crickets are chirping again in my pocket. I don't answer, the outside world seeming suddenly surreal.

Of all the people in the world on whom to take a leap of faith, Blackford is pretty low down on my list, especially now that he is really mad at me. But at this moment, I bet my only child's life on the sole reason Blackford never killed me, something I've never admitted even to myself. And that is, despite his best efforts to feel otherwise, Ian Blackford is in love with me.

Since being shot in Budapest, Simon's lungs aren't what they once were. As I'm yelling about sea lions, I grab Simon's shoulders and fire my knee into his right lung as hard as I can. He gasps. I grab the Magnum, heavy in my hand, as he starts to double over. In a split second, I bring it up on Blackford, right in his face. Then I move it to the Blind Monk and back again to Blackford with quick jerky movements. Simon collapses at my feet. I dig the heel of my shoe into his back. He grunts.

"Nice move," Blackford says. "Budapest?"

I nod. "You?" I ask.

"Yes. You messed it up as usual," he says.

"I'm good at that."

I turn to the Blind Monk, who now has Theo in front of him, his oversize gun casually pointed at my child's chest. Theo's eyes are wide, brimming with tears.

Enough is enough. My blood is racing, hot. I start to sing "Baby Beluga" while I calculate the shots in my head. One, two. One, two. One, two. Can I do it? Am I still good enough? It doesn't matter if I am. They have Theo. And that isn't working for me.

Suddenly, there is a loud pop. I swear I can feel wind from the bullet as it passes by my left ear. In my mind, I see my hand darting out and snatching it in midair, interrupting its intended flight path toward my child. But even I am not that fast. I force my eyes to stay open, to watch what terrible thing is going to happen next.

On the other side of the bridge, ten steps in front of me, the Blind Monk collapses, an explosion of red from his chest. He starts to take Theo down with him but Pauline grabs Theo and, with my flailing son in her arms, starts to run back toward the tunnel. Theo screams but she doesn't stop. Good girl.

I look at the Magnum. Did I fire the shot? I look at Blackford.

"Turns out everyone was right, Sally," he says. "You are my only liability." He reaches his free hand around my waist and pulls me toward him, closing whatever space was between us. "And I do so wish it wasn't the case."

A second later, he shoves me away as if I am as toxic as the Blind Monk suggested. I stumble, regain my footing, and run for land. Time is speeding up again, and I'm running flat-out toward Pauline. I grab Theo from her arms and clutch him to me. I bury my face in his hair.

"Mommy, Mommy," he says over and over, clinging to my neck. I hear sirens in the distance. Time to go. I stuff Theo into his car seat and fire up the Prius. I don't want to be anywhere near this place when the police arrive. There will be too many questions I don't want to answer.

38

"**Y**ou're bleeding," Pauline points out as we pass two CHP cruisers hauling ass in the opposite direction. I wipe my nose, and my hand comes away smeared with red.

"Shit." My face hurts, my body hurts. My heart aches. Pauline passes me an old spare diaper stashed in the glove box. I wipe my face and hand it back to her. I can see Theo in the rearview mirror.

"Are you okay, baby?" I ask as brightly as I can manage. He nods, thoughtfully.

"Yes, Mama. It was the man who won't play trucks."

"It was. Yes."

"I don't like them. I like my friends."

"I like your friends too."

"Okay," Theo agrees and looks out the window. I don't like to think about what I have done to my child in the course of a single day. I make a deal with myself to confront the guilt later, after I've had a shower and maybe a cocktail or seven.

Pauline sits quietly next to me, folding and unfolding the bloody diaper. I know what she is thinking.

"Was he dead?" she whispers finally. I assume she's talking about Simon, but who knows?

"No. It would take a lot more than that to knock off Simon Still."

"Doesn't matter. I left him down. I'm done."

I pat her on the thigh. "Don't worry," I say. "You did the right thing. And sometimes it works out in the end." I see a long cold Russian winter in her future, but I don't tell her that.

I also don't tell her that Simon will be in the back of some mini-van with tinted windows right now on the way to San Francisco International Airport. There, he will enter a secure waiting area and will be tended to by a doctor who will not even ask his name. After he's patched up, he will board a private plane to Washington, D.C. Once back in the office, it will be business as usual. No one will ever ask him to explain what happened out here. He will simply keep chasing.

"And Blackford? Will they catch him?" Pauline sounds worried.

"He was wearing a climbing harness," I point out. "The police will find a rope attached to the bridge and not much more. Blackford is probably halfway to Japan by now." But I'm lying. He has unfinished business. And I will not be able to stop him.

"Your nose is bleeding again," Pauline says, handing me back the diaper. We ride the rest of the way home in silence.

39

Theo is sound asleep when I pull into the garage. I pry him out of his seat, and he snuggles into my shoulder, squirming and mumbling. Pauline follows me up the stairs and unlocks the door. Standing in the middle of the foyer is none other than my husband, looking pale. Which is a little unexpected.

"The last time I asked you to pick up something at the dry cleaners," Will says, "you told me to fuck off. You said that you would raise my child, cook my meals, do my laundry, and make my bed, but you were never going to pick up my dry cleaning come hell or nuclear holocaust. Those were your exact words. Believe me, I remember. So why don't you tell me what is going on?" I open my mouth to say something, but nothing comes out. I squeeze Theo a little tighter. Pauline is behind me, completely still. I feel a small trickle of blood run from my nose.

"My God, Lucy. You're bleeding. What the hell is going on?" Will clenches his fists. The muscles along his arms ripple under his shirt.

From here, it could go like this.

I could stand up as tall as possible, fill my lungs like I'm in a yoga class, and on the exhale tell Will that I was a spy for the United States Agency for Weapons of Mass Destruction for nine years. I could tell him my real name, the one I have not heard since I walked through the doors of the USAWMD underground. I could tell him other things, too, things like how it feels to run for your life or to kill someone. I could tell him that the only two people worth living for are right here in this room, and I would do anything to protect them. And I do mean anything.

My confession would most likely be followed by a dark silence.

A small, strange smile would flicker across Will's face, one that I have seen before. His eyes would dance and jump, unable to meet mine.

In that pause, that silence, my life would slip away. There would be nothing left but the wreckage.

But it doesn't go like that. Not today anyway. Instead, it goes something like this.

"We went to the playground after I talked to you," I say finally, wiping the blood on my sleeve. "I took one of those metal swings right on the bridge of my nose. Pauline here was kind enough to drive us home. I was a little dizzy." Pauline nods vigorously in agreement.

Will looks at me and I force myself to meet his gaze. It's not easy. He knows I am lying, but I don't avert my eyes. Neither of us move. The only sound comes from Theo's muffled snores.

"Well, then," Will says, dropping his eyes, surrendering the round, "why don't you give me the boy and get some ice for your nose? Pauline, it was nice meeting you."

Will takes Theo from my arms and sweeps by both of us toward the stairs. I can feel the chill trailing him as he moves away.

Pauline puts her arm on my shoulder. I shrug it off. I don't need sympathy. These have all been my choices.

"It will never end," I whisper, not necessarily to Pauline.

"What?"

"Never mind."

"I'll get you an ice pack."

Maybe the icy fist closing around my heart is enough.

40

have been sitting on the steps since midnight, wearing the same clothes I almost died in earlier, the blood on my sleeve now brown like dirt. It's a dark night but clear, and I can see the stars twinkling overhead. I pull my down jacket tighter around me and I wait.

A black Mercedes sedan the size of a city block pulls up to the curb. A liveried driver slides from behind the wheel and opens the rear passenger door. Like royalty, Blackford steps out.

"You're waiting," he says.

"I thought you might decide to double-check whether or not it was the real lily," I say. "It was. " We both understand the magnitude of what happened on the bridge. The muscles in his face tighten almost imperceptibly. The lily is gone.

"I'm glad you got out of the spy thing, Sally," he says finally, giving me a cynical smile. "You still have so much hope for humanity."

And the way he says it, it's like a slap in the face.

"The professor?" I ask.

"His job was to synthesize the lily in the lab," Blackford says, his voice flat. "He failed. I no longer needed him."

I close my eyes. Malcolm is dead. I will spend the next week combing the papers for the story, but there will be nothing more than a single line in the missing persons section.

"Before I go, a parting gift," Blackford says, reaching into his jacket pocket and producing a white envelope, unsealed, which he hands to me. I don't want to take it, but in the end I can't help myself. I pull it open, enough to see a single faded Polaroid and a sheet of paper. There are three people in the photo. Two men and a woman, arms wrapped around each other, laughing at some unknown joke. It is summertime and they are wearing shorts and T-shirts and tennis shoes with no socks. The photograph is yellowed and worn but they still seem to glow with the power of possibility, of an unwritten future.

It is easy to pick out my parents, although I cannot remember ever seeing them so carefree. They are frozen in time, their shine not yet tarnished by the hard work of living.

The third person stoops down beside them, his bony knees bent to ensure his head isn't chopped off in the picture. Without his heavy overcoat covered in new snow, I barely recognize the man at the door, the one I was not supposed to talk to. But as he comes into focus, the pieces start to fall around me like hail. How could I have been so blind? The tall man is Director Gray.

And suddenly I understand that Blackford is not here to kill me because this, what he has just done, is so much more fun.

"Maybe we are not so different after all," he says, watching my face, waiting to see what it will reveal. But I give him nothing. He will get no satisfaction from my shock.

"Good-bye," Blackford says. "For now." As he disappears into the darkness of the car, he murmurs my real name, the one I was born with, over and over like a prayer. I want to shout after him. I want to understand him, but in the end he is simply shades of gray.

And, anyway, it is time for me to go back inside.

Acknowledgments

There are so many people who contribute to the creation of a book, directly and indirectly, that it seems an impossible task to thank them all. But I'm going to try anyway.

First, thank you to my agent, Leigh Feldman, for reading this manuscript instead of watching the Super Bowl, and agreeing to take it on. Everything flows from that.

A profound thank you to my editor, Barbara Jones, at Hyperion, for her carefully considered ideas and suggestions, all of which made this book infinitely better. I'm indebted to the team at Hyperion for their enthusiasm, experience, and overall brilliance. They have made this process a pleasure on so many levels.

This book never would have seen the light of day without the four degrees of separation of Sheri Belafsky and Emily Birenbaum, and for that I am eternally grateful. I also owe a big thank you to my first readers, Debbie Anderson, Sheri Belafsky, and Peter Belafsky, for being kind and not telling me to go out and get a real job.

Thank you to my parents, Henry and Eva Von Ancken, for a love of storytelling in all its forms, and to my brother, David Von Ancken, for always going first and making the scenes of mayhem far more realistic.

I also have to acknowledge the folks at Peet's Coffee for letting me stay longer than I should and never looking at me like I was crazy for swatting at the flies with my flip-flop.

And of course, thank you to Max and Katie for keeping my feet on the ground and reminding me that a book deal, while very cool, does not excuse me from making lunch and playing Legos. And to Mike, without whom there would be no book and no point. Let's just keep walking through this world and see what happens.

Finally, to my readers out there, I have had so much fun living in this world. I hope you have fun here, too, because in the end that is what it is all about.

TO SIN AGAIN

AGAIN

A Sally Sin Adventure

Beth McMullen

To my parents,

Henry and Eva Von Ancken

Prologue

The memory is framed in the fog of dreams, as if it has no true beginning and no end. I want to reach out and grab her, the little girl with the long hair, snarled and knotted, and the bright blue eyes. I want to make her safe but I can't close the distance. For now, I can do nothing but watch.

She wears a hand-me-down parka that was probably red in its prime but has turned the color of dishwater. It is many sizes too big and her three-year-old body almost disappears in the folds of fabric. In her lap she holds a brown paper sack containing the most important of her worldly possessions.

"She can take only what fits in that bag," the tall man said, casting a quick glance around the single room that was her home. "Everything else stays behind."

In the sack, there is a yellow teddy bear with a limp purple bow around his neck, an illegal translation of *The Cat in the Hat*, worn at the spine and water stained, and a pink hairbrush that at one time had rhinestones imbedded in the handle. But like so many things in her short life, the rhinestones are by now lost to history. She clutches this sack with such ferocity that others on the train notice her white knuckles and wonder what might be hidden inside it.

Sitting next to her, on this overnight train from Norilsk, is the tall man. He wears a dark wool overcoat that smells faintly of wet dog. It is January and they waited for the train in a heavy but ordinary snow. She thought he might pick her up, lift her out of the wet Russian snow, but he was no better than a statue standing beside her while her little shoes soaked through. It will be days before she can feel her toes again.

When he arrived at the tiny house to get her the day before, he looked her up and down as if he were considering a purchase. Then, without a word, he sat down at the scarred wooden table and accepted a chilled glass of vodka from the men who had come before him.

The girl noticed his hands shook as he lifted the glass to his cold lips. She wanted to cry but knew her mother would be disappointed if she did, so instead she simply sat in the corner, holding on to the bag for dear life. It was all she had left.

They ride on through the night. She sleeps fitfully, sometimes waking up with her cheek pressed up against the man's coat. It is scratchy against her young skin. Once when she opens her eyes, the man is staring at her. He immediately looks away, but she sees something in his eyes—something her young mind can't place. She has the sense that he doesn't quite know what to do with her. He ignores her when they are awake, but in the night he takes off his overcoat and wraps it snugly around her. He whispers her name over and over while she's asleep. It sounds wrong falling from his lips, tainted by his unusual accent. When her mother says her name, it is a song.

In the morning, the guards come through demanding papers. As the man hands them two blue passports, she catches a glimpse of a photograph of a little girl. It could be her but it is not. She stays very still and quiet until the guards return the documents and continue down the train aisle.

Sometimes, as they slice through the empty countryside,

the man passes her dry crackers and cups of water. She is not hungry but eats the crackers and drinks the water because after she does, the man looks satisfied. It is better than the other look he has which is vacant, as if someone reached into his chest and yanked out his heart and he can't understand why his body is still going on.

After a while, they depart the train and climb into an old waiting Jeep. The rugged terrain rattles the girl around in the backseat. She is aware that over the past few days she has become nothing more than a bag of loosely tied bones. She is hollow, the space in between the words.

Once, during the ride, she reaches into her coat pocket and pulls out a photograph of a ballerina standing at the barre in pointe shoes and a pale pink tutu. Her long swanlike neck tilted slightly to the right to reveal muscles most people don't have, she does not smile. The girl holds the photograph close to her face on the off chance that she might somehow absorb the woman right into herself that way. After a few seconds, she hides it back in her pocket.

They park in front of a farmhouse. It is winter but two horses are out in the pasture, looking forlorn in ankle-deep snow. A young woman wrapped in a heavy coat waves from the front porch. Her husband joins her. They are smiling. The woman runs to the Jeep, sweeps the girl out of the backseat and into arms that are strong and warm. She smells of vanilla.

"She's yours now," the man says to the woman. "For as long as we can."

The woman locks eyes with the man as he ducks back into the Jeep. As it pulls away, the girl remembers the paper sack, still in the backseat. She feels a scream crawling up her throat, the tears threatening to spill. But she pushes them back down. Her mother told her not to cry, never to cry, and she won't. Maybe not ever again.

I wake in a puddle of sweat, my hand clamped over my mouth to keep the scream from escaping. Beside me, Will sleeps peacefully. I hear Theo's soft snores coming from his room down the hall. He is perfect, safe, but I need to see him with my own eyes, just to be sure. As I stumble down the dark hallway, remnants of the memory cling to me as if I walked through the sticky web of a black widow. The threat of the scream lingers in my throat. The dream used to show up once in a while, infrequently enough that I could write it off as an aberration. But now she comes all the time, the lost little girl in her red parka who will spend her life wondering who she really is and where she came from.

And I know this, because she is me.

1

stand in the middle of my postage stamp–sized backyard and spin in a slow circle. If you didn't know better, you might think I was reliving the glory days of a Grateful Dead concert, strains of "Touch of Grey" playing in my head, eyes closed in a semi-hypnotic state.

But things are not always as they appear. I am really quite busy. As I turn, I examine the perimeter of the fence, the roofline, the little space under the stairs that is always infested with spiders. I inventory the flowers and trees and shrubs. I study the plastic baseball bat tossed haphazardly on the grass, the small wooden play structure, the empty water table. I continue to spin.

After a minute, I have to admit there is nothing amiss. It's simply another lovely San Francisco morning, the sun is shining, the fog is rolling back toward the ocean, and everything appears to be perfectly fine.

But don't get me wrong. Just because I don't see anyone in my backyard does not mean they aren't there watching. They are always watching. I used to think I was paranoid but as it turned out I wasn't crazy, just right.

Five-year-old Theo appears in the open back door.

"Mom, I'm hungry. When's breakfast?" At the top of the

stairs, he stands with his hands on his hips, looking down at me with disapproval.

"You didn't squish our castle, did you?" he says. "Me and Zach worked on it yesterday for, like, one hundred years."

I look down to discover I'm standing in the middle of the sandbox, among a series of sliding sand ramparts decorated with twig and leaf flags, and manned by Lego guys with tiny plastic guns. In one hand, I hold a bag of garbage intended for the trash bin, the reason I came out here in the first place, and in the other, a blue sand pail, uncovered in the grass on my way to the bins. Throwing out the trash turned into tidying up the toys, which led to looking for suspicious characters lurking around in my backyard, and ended with me in the sandbox, spinning like a stoned and aging Deadhead.

"The castle is okay," I say, hoping Theo is too far away to see the damage. "How about we get started on breakfast for you?"

Inside the house, stuck to the refrigerator with a Golden Gate Bridge magnet, is a list of Theo's morning responsibilities. Theo's preschool teacher told me that using the word "responsibilities" rather than "chores" to describe these tasks was better. I have no idea why and was afraid to ask for fear that any further conversation would reveal me to be hopelessly out of step with today's underlying educational theories.

Theo has three responsibilities. Number one—put on your clothes. Number two—brush your teeth. Number three—feed the cat. If he does all three, at the end of the week he gets two dollars. I think the list is reasonable, but Theo acts as if he is Sisyphus destined to push that damn rock up the hill every morning, just to be rewarded with it rolling back over his toes every afternoon. When I remind him of how many dollars he needs to save in order to buy that LEGO *Star Wars* set, the one with two Luke Skywalkers, he becomes much more focused.

By the time I reach the kitchen, Theo is hard at work on task number three. He very diligently measures out scoop after scoop after scoop of cat food and adds it to the dish until there is a mini Everest of kibble starting to avalanche every which way.

"I think that's probably enough cat food," I say to the back of his blond head. He shakes me off, a cocky rookie pitcher to his veteran catcher.

"No," he says. "I need to fill up the other bowl, too." He is deliberate, on task. If he weren't making such a mess, I would commend him on his effort.

"But that bowl is for the cat's water," I point out. "All living things need water to survive." He turns, looking at me as if I am a complete idiot.

"I know that," he says. "We learned that at the science table. But I'm making soup because Sprinkles likes soup. How do you spell soup?"

I could argue but there's no good way to win an argument with a five-year-old without someone ending up in tears, usually me. I spell "soup."

"S-O-U-P."

"S-O-U-P," he parrots back to me.

"And you're responsible for cleaning up when you're done doing whatever it is that you're doing."

"No I'm not," he says with total confidence, "because Sprinkles is going to eat it all up."

After which Sprinkles is going to build a rocket out of household appliances and fly to Mars. I mean, what are the chances? Outside the kitchen window, trees sway in the breeze.

Theo continues to make a soggy brown concoction in Sprinkles' water bowl. Sprinkles sits nearby, looking depressed.

A brisk knock at the front door draws my attention. Out on the porch stands a UPS man, his face obscured by his trademark brown cap. As I open the door, I realize that while his cap is indeed the right color, it lacks a logo of any kind. A bolt of electricity shoots the length of my body as if I stuck a metal fork in the toaster.

"Can I help you?" I ask. Giving me a flat smile, the faux UPS man takes in the scene: average-looking woman with messy hair, slightly grungy jeans, and flannel slippers with a hole in the toe. Ultimately, he decides I'm no threat. It's not the first time I've been dismissed in this way.

"Special delivery," he says, handing me a small box wrapped in brown paper. My name, with no address, is scrawled across the front in black Sharpie. Seeing the wide, loopy handwriting has roughly the same impact on me as falling through thin ice might. My lips move but no sound escapes, my arms move around with no apparent purpose. I lean against the doorjamb for support.

The man's flat smile widens. I remind myself that fainting like Vivien Leigh in *Gone with the Wind* is no guarantee that the package will go away. If it were, believe me, I would already be in a heap on the floor, hoping for a rescue and some iced tea.

"What if I don't want a special delivery?" I say finally, still propped up against the door.

"It's kind of an offer you can't refuse," he says.

"I've heard that before," I say. He passes me the package and I take it.

"Thanks," I say. "I guess."

"Good luck," he says with a smirk. Down on the street, a black government-issue sedan awaits his return.

"That face isn't necessary," I say. "I was having a nice morning and now I'm not. Why don't you go before I do something I can't take back?" He gives me a small salute, jumps down all five front steps in one leap, and vanishes into the car. Theo appears at my elbow.

"Who was that?" he asks. "Hey, a package? Can I open it? Is it for me?"

"I'm pretty sure it's for me. And no, you can't open it."

"You never let me do anything."

"I know," I say. "I'm an awful mother."

Standing in the hallway, I peel back the paper from the package. Theo watches with great anticipation because, after all, a package is a package. Underneath the paper is a plain white box; inside the box is a black cell phone, with no screen and only a single button, nestled in a bed of crumpled up *Washington Post.* A note in the same loopy handwriting reads "Call me. Let's have coffee." I can almost hear him laughing.

I start to sweat.

"That's not very cool, whatever it is," Theo says, peering into the box.

"I don't think it's meant to be cool, Theo," I say.

In fact, it is meant for one purpose and one purpose only, and that is to connect me directly and securely to the mother ship. Now, if I were James Bond, this boring plastic phone would do much more, like simultaneously wash my sports car, fix me a nice cold martini (shaken, not stirred, of course), and bloodlessly dispatch the bad guy. But in real life, spy gear tends to be much more practical. And I should know. I used to be one.

A spy, that is.

2

On the surface, I look like your average stay-at-home mom. My jeans always bear some evidence of what we had for breakfast and I could certainly benefit from more frequent showering. But I wasn't always like this. I used to carry a small handbag with room only for a fake passport, a ChapStick, and a small stack of foreign currency.

Now I carry an oversized shoulder bag stuffed full of antibacterial wipes, water bottles, crackers, a bulging wallet with VIP cards for every supermarket in a twenty-mile radius, and that same ChapStick, except I really have no hope of finding it once it sinks to the bottom of the bag. My doctor has recommended physical therapy for the damage the bag has wrought upon my innocent right shoulder. Some days it is hard to distinguish me from Quasimodo.

My name is Lucy Parks Hamilton, mother to Theo and wife to William Wilton Hamilton III. Right around the time we met, my husband started a green-energy investment fund that has done surprisingly well in the robust environment of guilt in which we live. Will is known for speaking with a hushed reverence about geothermal energy, solar cells, and a variety of recycling methods. Lately, it seems his commitment to saving the world is rubbing off on our child.

"Mom!" Theo will wail. "You put the newspaper in the garbage again. The planet loves you. You have to love it back!"

With that he will dramatically collapse on the floor, exhausted from having to manage my inability to properly recycle with his five-year-old vocabulary. My pleas for leniency fall on deaf ears. I'm trying to do better, to remember that today's garbage might be tomorrow's egg carton, but Theo does not give points for effort.

We live in a carbon-neutral household. My husband claims it's a matter of credibility.

"I cannot preach the green gospel," he says, "if I do not practice it."

We have planted approximately five thousand trees in an effort to offset the carbon footprint of Will's air travel. And I do my part by forgetting to wash the sheets for weeks at a time. When Will caught wind of it being polar bear week at Theo's preschool, he sat Theo down and gave him a lecture on why polar bears were soon going to be extinct and why it was our fault, after which Theo cried hysterically for a solid hour. Will is very committed. Sometimes to a fault.

I run the continuous stay-at-home mom loop that includes the following stops: breakfast, playground, soccer, preschool, lunch, grocery store, snacks, laundry, dinner, more snacks, more laundry, books, complex LEGO towers and so on. The stops don't necessarily occur in that order or, in fact, any order at all.

In the background, a soundtrack of low-level parent anxiety plays. Where should I send Theo for kindergarten? Is he eating enough vegetables? Will he be an early reader? Am I pushing him enough? Is he being tormented on the playground? Is he tormenting others on the playground? Are those gummy vitamins going to rot his teeth? How mad is he going to be that I didn't wash his favorite *Star Wars* T-shirt so he can wear it for the fifth time this week, and how much do I care?

As you might expect, there are occasional seasonal variations to the soundtrack but the idea remains reliably constant.

I can speak extensively on a variety of useless mom topics, such as whether the lining of your soup can is going to kill you or how much Omega-3 fatty acid exists in the average cage-free egg. I search out wild-caught Alaskan salmon and organic blueberries and have been known to drive all over town looking for humanely raised free-range pork chops. It's not entirely lost upon me that the humanely raised pig is still cut into little pieces and wrapped in plastic.

I'm proud to say I'm no longer intimidated by the prospect of having three or four of Theo's friends in my house all at the same time. Had you suggested to me eight years ago that I'd be baking chocolate cupcakes with a bunch of sticky five-year-old hands in the batter, I'm not sure what would have shocked me more, the kids or the cupcakes. But then, I'm a long way from where I used to be.

Which was Nepal, Hong Kong, Morocco, Romania, Pakistan, a number of places that seemed to be comprised entirely of sand, Uzbekistan, Kazakhstan, Turkmenistan and several other members of the Stan family, and even the South Pole. Although the South Pole thing was more about punishment, specifically mine. Even now, ice cubes clinking merrily in a glass make me shudder and not in a good way. Once in a while, I went to exotic locations like tiny secluded islands in the South Pacific or in the Caribbean. But usually once I arrived, there was shooting and that took the fun out of it.

As it turns out, people shoot at you when you're a spy. Maybe if I'd known I would have gone in for something a little less painful, like being a Walmart greeter perhaps—but it's not as if they tell you about the shooting part up front. By the time I figured it out, it was too late. And for nine years, there I was, Agent 26, aka Sally Sin, a covert agent for the United States Agency for Weapons of Mass Destruction.

As you probably already know if you watch the news, read the papers, or Google "the end of the world," the USAWMD is comprised of a bunch of white-shirted, loafer-wearing analysts sitting around trying to figure out who has the biggest ill-gotten nuclear arsenal and when they plan on using it. Or selling it. It's not an easy job. Terrorists are fickle, changing their minds as often as a teenage girl changes her clothes.

What they aren't telling you in the news is that buried under all those conservatively dressed analysts is a small group of covert agents who, if you ask anyone directly, don't exist. These are the people trained to ferret out elusive information, the name you need to bring down the house of cards. Their work is not always pretty. Sometimes it's just a big fucking disaster.

However, the important thing to remember is the covert agents of the USAWMD are always out there trying to stop our global march toward annihilation. When it works, no one knows. When it doesn't, it's always very loud.

I was recruited out of college because I have a unique gift for languages. Give me two weeks and a couple of Berlitz books and I can basically master any language you throw my way. When I was five years old, a young Brazilian man worked for a summer painting our house and barn. He loved to tell jokes while up on his ladder and by August, I could speak Portuguese as well as I could speak English. My parents' discovery of this was followed by many whispered conversations after I was thought to be in bed. Eventually, we all agreed it would be better if I kept this gift to myself.

Or *they* agreed. I just kept soaking up the words. While the other kids were reading books overflowing with preteen angst, I would be under the covers with a flashlight and the Swahili-English dictionary. To this day, I have yet to meet an esoteric dialect I could not decode. The words are water and I am the tap.

Simon Still was my boss at the Agency and his main goal in life, after trying to save the world, seemed to be sending me into situations where I was sure to come home in a body bag. It was the sort of thing that made it hard for us to build a lasting friendship. Simon was peculiar in a number of ways. Although he was perfectly at home in a room full of lunatics with twitchy trigger fingers, at the sight of blood he would turn so pale you might confuse him with the undead.

"Sally, you're bleeding," he said to me once on a dark, deserted street in Sofia.

"I know, Simon," I said, squeezing my arm tightly through my jacket, the warm blood running down the inside of my sleeve. "That's because there's a bullet in my arm. Remember?"

"I know. It's dreadful," he said, turning his back so I could bleed to death in private. No one ever accused Simon of possessing a good bedside manner.

I've seen Simon in the jungle where it's onc hundred degrees and humid, looking as if he just walked off a photo shoot for Icelandic Airlines. I'm not sure how he does it. Actually, I'm not sure about anything when it comes to Simon. Because although we spent long stretches of time together over many years, I still know next to nothing about him. Except that he will do anything in the name of his country and he does not send me presents unless he wants something. And it usually isn't coffee.

Nobody knows about Sally Sin, including my husband, child, and closest friends. That was part of the deal I made when I joined up. Of course, at the ripe old age of twenty-two, a secret identity seemed kind of cool and not that big of a deal. I'm sure somewhere in the fine print it mentioned that my commitment was, technically, forever in nature, but who reads the fine print? There are too many other fun things to do than bother with the details.

Also nestled in the fine print was the Agency's right to call me back into service whenever they felt it necessary. The last time they activated me was two years ago and I made such a mess of things I secretly hoped they wouldn't dare try it again. Maintaining a secret identity in real life is hard and I'm not sure the secret part of it would survive another activation. But the Agency doesn't care about that. They just want me to be quiet and do as I'm told, like I said I would. So I do. I have no interest in finding out what happens if I don't.

There are other reasons for keeping quiet too. Being a spy is not like being a surgeon or an airline pilot, professions you might brag about while waiting around for preschool pick-up.

"Lucy, did you ever kill anyone?" the other moms would ask in that hushed tone usually reserved for inquiring if the disease is terminal.

"Yes," I'd answer, "but only because they tried to kill me first." At this point, my friends would resemble those drivers who rubberneck the fatal traffic accident, horrified but unable to turn away.

My job now, in what I've come to accept is a chaotic world, is to keep Theo safe, to help him grow and learn, and eventually break the news to him that the *Star Wars* saga is all made up. And call me crazy but I have a sneaking suspicion that pressing the single button on the black plastic cell phone is not going to improve my ability to do any of those things.

And yet, I'm about to do just that.

3

let Theo push the single button on the phone. If Theo ever becomes president, they might consider changing that notorious button we always hear so much about to a switch or a lever or there is sure to be a nuclear war. Theo has never met a button he did not want to push.

"Just once," I say. He does it and looks at me with anticipation.

"Now what?" he says.

"Nothing," I say. "Maybe go and play a little."

"That was not very fun," he says, but he takes the box the phone came in and begins to fill it with LEGO guys. "This will be their ship!" So maybe not all is lost.

I hold the phone up to my ear. There is never any proper ringing with these phones. They click and buzz and whine and in the dead silence that follows you can assume you are connected.

"You guys are getting pretty fancy with your gadgets these days," I say into the phone.

"It's a difficult time," a voice responds. "In case you haven't noticed, the world has become a bit untidy." The voice is the same one I hear in my own head, berating me when I've done something incredibly stupid, like run out of gas or spilled bleach on my favorite black sweater. It is the voice of Simon Still.

"If the world is really that much of a mess," I say, "you might try baby wipes. Unscented, of course."

There's a silence during which I can see him shaking his head in dismay. What on earth happened to Sally Sin?

"Constant vigilance might prove more effective," Simon says finally. "How did Agent 34 do with his delivery?"

I've always wondered if the Agency recycled numbers or if, once an agent died or went off the reservation, their number was retired, like in sports. Is there another Agent 26 running around out there right now getting shot at? If there is, I'm not sure how I feel about it.

"Agent 34 was dreadful," I say. "You're lucky I didn't break his neck just for being annoying."

"He's actually quite talented," Simon says.

"I don't care," I say. "What do you want?"

"Mom!" Theo shouts from the living room. "How do you spell 'LEGO Guys'?"

"L-E-G-O G-U-Y-S," I shout back. "And it's two words."

"Excuse me?" says Simon.

"Nothing," I say.

"Are you speaking in code?"

"If I were, I would never tell you," I say. With my back against the refrigerator, I slide slowly to the floor. "Criss-cross-applesauce" dances inappropriately through my head as I fold my legs over one another.

"You cannot still be upset about the bridge," Simon asks, "can you?"

"You tried to kill me," I remind him. "Twice."

"It was two years ago," he says, "and, besides, it's bad for your health to hold a grudge."

"Your concern for my well-being is touching. Now tell me what's going on," I say, "or I'm throwing this thing in the toilet."

"I don't think you mean that," Simon says. His absolute confidence makes me want to scream but there is no denying he's right. If I didn't call, Simon would simply have shown up at my front door, uninvited and about as welcome as the Ghost of Christmas Future. He's just that kind of guy.

"I might mean it," I say, with enough bravado to save face.

"It's waterproof," he says, "and more importantly, we have a situation."

"Mom, how do you spell 'Luke Skywalker'?" Theo shouts.

"Oh, wow," I say. "That's a long one. L-U-K-E S-K-Y-W-A-L-K-E-R."

"Why do you keep doing that?" Simon asks. "Are you listening to me? We have a situation. S-I-T-U-A-T-I-O-N."

I take a deep, calming yoga breath that does little to actually calm me. Whenever Simon Still says we have a situation, it's never because something good has happened, like you won the lottery or a lifetime subscription to *Reader's Digest*. By definition, his situations are always bad.

"I'm retired," I say. "Remember?"

"Retirement is something you do after a lengthy and full career," he says. "You didn't retire. You quit. There's a difference."

A harsh red flush rises on my cheeks. Simon remains mad at me for a number of reasons. Primary among them, I suspect, is the fact that I had the nerve to quit the Agency at all.

Nobody quits the Agency. You die or they kick you out, but you never quit. My departure is an asterisk on my record, a scarlet letter. Wherever he is, Simon clears his throat, indicating he's about to tell me why my morning has gone off the rails before breakfast.

"It appears that Righteous Liberty has kidnapped Director Gray," he says. "And, oddly enough, they insist they will negotiate his release only with you."

My heart jumps in my chest, as if it is playing a vigorous game of leapfrog with my stomach. Charles Gray was the director of the USAWMD before I joined and after I left. During the nine years I worked there, I met the man just once, and during that meeting he made it clear how little he thought of me. We were not friends, Gray and I, so the pounding in my chest can come only from the implications of this situation.

Simon makes note of my silence.

"What shocks you more, Sally?" he asks, his voice in neutral. "The fact that someone got to Gray or that they want you, too?"

"It's not possible," I say, immediately aware of how ridiculous I sound. Gray had a small army following him everywhere he went. He wasn't even allowed to take a pee by himself. "How could this happen?"

"The Director is gone."

I feel sick. Whoever these people are, if they can get to Director Gray, they can get to anyone. And they're asking for me. My tongue is dry and thick in my mouth and my heart continues to smash up against my rib cage. Theo wanders back into the kitchen, holding a sword and a light saber.

"Mom, you look weird," he says. "Like a funny color. Can I have some orange juice? How do you spell 'juice'?"

"Mommy's on the phone, Theo. Get it yourself. J-U-I-C-E."

"Is that all you have to say, Sally?" Simon asks.

"S-H-I-T," I say. "Is that better?"

As I'm still sitting on the floor, an unexpected thought pops into my head and that is, I wish they had taken me and not Gray. This particular wish has always been reserved for when Theo is sick or unhappy and I think life would be so much easier if I could just take the pain from him onto myself. But this wish has no place with Director Gray.

"It's the photograph," I say to myself, thinking about the faded Polaroid hidden in my underwear drawer. "Director Gray is in the photograph."

"Sally, can you stop muttering and spelling and being strange, and focus?" Simon says, annoyed.

"Yes," I say, wondering when I lost the ability to have a thought and not say it out loud.

"You will drop Theo off early and meet me at your favorite coffee shop," he says with an authority befitting his station.

"Forget it," I say. "I have a parent-teacher conference at Theo's preschool this morning."

There is a heavy pause. "Your priorities are a bit skewed," Simon says slowly.

I don't expect him to understand how some chitchat with Theo's teacher could take precedence over national security. Simon has never so much as owned a goldfish, let alone a creature of more substantial needs.

"Parenting is not something you do just when you feel like it," I say. I think I read that in a magazine last month and I'm horrified to have repeated it out loud. I want to kick myself. But there's no need because Simon will take care of that for me.

"Neither is saving the world," he says. "A responsible parent might consider that, Sally."

His being right does not help things at all.

"Can you please stop calling me 'Sally'?" I grumble.

"Sally, Lucy, Agent 26," Simon says. "Does it matter?"

Yes. Because my name is not Sally Sin. Sally Sin was a silly joke that, in the long run, turned out to be on me. But my name is not really Lucy Hamilton, either. Of course, I have a real name, the one the second-grade teacher barked at me when I was passing notes or pulling hair. But only a handful of people know this name and it's been so long that if I hear it called out in a crowd, I no longer turn in its direction.

"Things are bad, Sally," Simon says and something in his tone halts any further protests from me. A lump the size of a tennis ball forms in my throat. In another minute, I will choke on it.

"Okay," I say, defeated. In the end, there is no getting around that Theo lives in this world, good, bad, or ugly, and so do I. "I'll meet you."

Having nothing more to add and no use for the niceties of civilized society, Simon hangs up on me without saying good-bye.

4

Happy Times Preschool is a small school with a sunny yellow front door. There are many things to recommend it but the most important is that there's only one way in and one way out and that's through the perky yellow door that I just mentioned. Theo attends four days a week for three hours, during which time I sit at the corner table in the Java Luv coffee shop across the street. I sit and I watch that yellow front door and I make sure no one goes in who is not meant to be there.

When Theo went to preschool only twice a week my door vigil wasn't so bad but now that he is up to four mornings, even I will admit it's getting a little ridiculous. I have tried reading magazines and even knitting but with one eye always glued to the door, the scarves were coming out lopsided. Leonard, the tattooed dreadlocked barista, is convinced I'm flat out crazy and he's now comfortable enough with my presence to voice his opinions on the subject.

"Talk about helicopter parenting," he'll say, cleaning the glass on the front of the pastry display. "You're so obsessed you're going to chop the little guy's head right off his body if you get any closer."

I don't answer. I can't explain to Leonard how it looks when someone has actually had his head chopped off, about how the blood pulses out of the severed arteries and sometimes the eyes still move, searching for some explanation in those final seconds. The people I used to spend all my time with didn't think much about decapitation. Or, for that matter, any of the other unpleasant ways you can kill someone. And that's why I sit at Java Luv every day and watch the yellow door. I know that sometimes the boogeyman does show up. And when that happens, I want to be sure I'm here to kick his teeth in.

I'm thinking about the actual kicking-in of teeth and how you need to be really limber to pull it off with any grace as we climb the steps to school. Claire, who used to be an investment banker and brings the same intensity to parenting, stands to the side of the front door, thumbs flying furiously over her smartphone. My feelings about smartphones are unambiguous. If the phone is so smart, why can't it fold the socks? When I ask this of people, they give me the blank look, the one that says I obviously don't get it. But I do. Don't call something smart unless it is.

Claire is part of the mommy posse, my lady friends with children roughly Theo's age. We met at the playground one dreary afternoon, all of us armed with baby wipes, enormous Starbucks cups, and expressions of dull desperation. By afternoon snack time, the five of us were fast friends.

And Sam, too. I shouldn't forget Sam even though he's not a mom, exactly. He's a grandfather who acts as primary caregiver for his grandson Carter, because his own son and daughter-in-law cannot afford San Francisco living and a nanny. Something had to give and that ended up being Sam. Now he gives every day for ten hours straight, thus earning himself honorary mom status from us and sad pats on the back from his retiree friends.

Claire mutters to herself and doesn't notice me until I'm standing directly in front of her. Then she jumps.

"Oh, Lucy," she says. "I didn't see you there. Why are you here so early?"

Because the federal government told me to hurry up?

Claire is always here early. Her son, Owen, will sit quietly on the steps while Claire diligently stretches her hamstrings in preparation for a spin class that she swears brings her right to the edge of puking. And she says this like it's a good thing. She has invited each of us to join her but I think she needs to work on her marketing campaign if she ever expects any takers. Puking, in my book, is only a good thing if someone has just tried to poison you. If not, it is to be avoided at all costs. As soon as the clock spins to 8:45, Owen is in class and Claire is in the car racing off to her gym.

"We have our kindergarten meeting this morning," I say. Claire jogs in place for a few seconds.

"Aren't you excited to just put this whole kindergarten thing to bed already?" she asks.

Which leads me to a point about these mommy friendships of mine. I went through a lot of years during which time I did not have any friends, mommy or otherwise. Friendships were frowned upon by the USAWMD. In fact, any sort of a life was frowned upon by the USAWMD and if you didn't heed the frown and went off and got yourself all tangled up in a real life, they would be sure to make it go away. And they would not ask your permission to do so.

My current friends exist because we are experiencing the same life. I'm not sure if I met Claire under different circumstances we would have any interest in each other. But having the same schedule generally trumps the fact that both Owen and I find her a little bit scary.

It doesn't surprise me in the least that Claire is excited to sink her teeth into the kindergarten process. As for me, I have been actively dreading it since the day Theo was born. It used to be that you grew up in a particular neighborhood and that is where you went to school. Simple. But in present-day San Francisco, school placement is based on complicated algorithms that only a Ph.D. in computer science could have any hope of understanding. There is nothing natural about algorithms, in my opinion. I'd like to put the whole mess off for another forty years but, at some point, Theo would object.

"I'm sure it will be fine," I say, which is my way of not actually answering Claire's question. She stops jogging in place and lowers her voice to a conspiratorial whisper.

"Did you hear about what happened yesterday?" she asks.

Nothing happened yesterday. I know this because I was watching the school.

"No," I say.

"A student jumped from the play structure to the school roof," she says. "Can you believe it?"

Behind Happy Times Preschool is a small, enclosed playground stocked with the usual play equipment such as slides, swings, climbing structures, and sand pits. From one of the old wooden play structures that Happy Times has been relentlessly fund-raising to replace, a motivated and fearless child could conceivably take a leap of faith and make it to the roof of the school building. But the pitch of the roof is rather extreme so, once there, the child would have to hold on for dear life or risk falling to the ground.

Before I can even express the level of shock Claire expects from her revelation, Teacher Wendy, wearing a gingham shirt under a teddy-bear sweater vest, bursts through the door and beckons us inside for our meeting. Teacher Wendy is tall and blond and she oozes tenderness, warmth, and sincerity from every one of her pores. There are times when I myself want to curl up in her lap and have her read me *Knuffle Bunny* or *Olivia Joins the Circus* while she gently strokes my hair.

"Hi, Theo," she says, immediately dropping down on one knee to his level. "Can you go and play with Teacher Susan while your mommy and I talk? When all the other kids arrive we'll start circle time with a song you pick!"

"I pick 'The Ninjas,'" Theo says immediately.

"I'm not sure I know that one," Teacher Wendy says with a big grin. I brace myself.

"The Ninjas are deadly and silent," Theo sings off key. "They are also unspeakably violent. They speak Japanese; they do whatever they please and sometimes they vacation in Ireland."

Teacher Wendy's eyes open wide.

"Why, Theo," she says, "that is a very interesting song. Now, maybe keep thinking about another one you want for circle time, okay?"

Theo smiles. He does not realize he has just been expertly shut down.

"The Barenaked Ladies," I say, in my defense. "A friend loaned it to us." I have no idea why I say that because it's not true. I bought the album myself when I realized I was at high risk for suicide if I had to hear "Baby Beluga" one more time. Apparently there is no low to which I will not sink to save face in front of the preschool teacher.

"I'm sure it's lovely," Teacher Wendy says. "Now Theo, run along and find Teacher Susan."

Theo nods, his eyes glued to her face. If she asked him to walk on hot coals, he would solemnly get right to it, no questions asked. Frankly, it makes me a little jealous. It can take me the better part of a perfectly good hour to get the kid to put on his shoes.

Teacher Wendy and I park ourselves in tiny purple chairs at a tiny purple table decorated with little green flowers and pink butterflies. I'm of average height and my knees are almost up my nose. It is hard to look dignified in this position but somehow Teacher Wendy appears completely at ease. She pulls out a folder and flips to a page covered with happy teacher handwriting. Under the page of notes are some kid drawings in bold colors.

"There's something I want to talk about before we get to the kindergarten discussion," she says. I shift in my little chair, hoping it doesn't collapse under me. I have a pretty good idea of what is coming.

"We are concerned about Theo's threshold for risk-taking," Teacher Wendy says in a slow voice, the same voice used to reinforce the gravity of a very bad situation with the children. "He seems to believe the laws of gravity do not apply to him."

How does a parent respond to such a statement? "Duh" seems inappropriate.

"Yesterday, Theo convinced Benjamin to launch himself from the play structure to the roof and it's only by the grace of God that Benjamin did not become seriously injured."

"He did what?" I say. "My Theo?" As if there are fourteen other Theos in this preschool. Of course she means my Theo.

I'm not often caught off guard when it comes to my child. Am I reeling from what Theo actually did, or the fact that he managed to keep it from me for close to twenty-four hours? I'm not sure.

"Theo doesn't show much fear," Teacher Wendy continues, "but he also has high empathy and great leadership skills. It's a sophisticated combination for a five-year-old."

She gives me a window in which to respond, to explain the reasons for my child's behavior. There are a few directions I can go. One involves a full confession, but that would require sitting around for eighteen months waiting for a Top Secret security clearance and I doubt even Teacher Wendy has that sort of patience. Another involves a complicated set of lies that run the risk of collapsing under their own weight. And finally, there is the human sacrifice. I, of course, choose the last. I prepare to throw Will under the bus with barely a pause to consider my actions.

"Theo's father was a drama major in college," I say. "He does a lot of role-playing with Theo." Interesting. The human sacrifice doesn't feel so bad. Maybe I'd feel worse about it if Will were the one covered in snot and magic marker all the time. "The stories can be fairly elaborate." I keep eye contact, willing her to overlook the bad kid and the bad parents and buy my story.

And after a moment, she does.

"In that case, I'd ask Mr. Hamilton to tone it down a bit," Teacher Wendy says. "These young minds are so malleable at this stage."

She flips open the folder in front of her, flashing me a bright smile meant to indicate that we have concluded with the serious business and will now move on to something more fun. From the folder she pulls a drawing done in crayon and slides it in front of me.

"I really had to take a second and show you this," she says. "Theo's turning out to be a wonderful artist. His use of color and landscape is exceptional, not to mention his rendering of the human figure. All very advanced. The weapons and bombs and things you see here are age appropriate for boys at this stage so we really try to see beyond them to the ideas I just mentioned."

But I'm no longer listening to her speech because while Theo convincing his friends it's fun to leap tall buildings in a single bound is indeed problematic what I'm now looking at is much more so.

A rudimentary bridge is strung between two uprights. There is a yellow sun and clouds and down below what looks to be a duck bobbing on the blue ocean. On the bridge are several men with guns.

Time begins to do that thing it does sometimes, to slow down to the point of almost stopping completely. Because even as a stick figure, even with an oversized purple head and skinny, oddly proportioned arms and legs, the very sight of Ian Blackford makes me tremble. I try to keep my face as neutral as possible knowing I can't very well tell Teacher Wendy about Blackford. But now is probably a good time to tell you.

5

There are very few things I am afraid of. I'll admit I got a little claustrophobic in those caves in Afghanistan and once I had a panic attack after jumping out of an airplane, when I discovered my parachute was sort of tangled up, but those were isolated incidents. Ian Blackford, international illegal arms dealer and the bane of my existence, inspired real fear in me, the first time I saw him and every time that followed.

It was my privilege to meet a whole slew of demented characters during my nine years serving the USAWMD and very few of them actually scared me. So what made Blackford different? Why was it that the mere mention of him was enough to make my heart race, my armpits sweat, and my skin turn all clammy?

The answer is simple. It was all in the eyes. Those icy blues told you that Blackford played by his own rules and they changed to suit the situation. What you knew to be true yesterday might have no bearing on today. Most criminals are easy to understand. Find their motivation, whether it be financial, ideological, or psychological, and you have the key to bringing them down. But Blackford did not fit neatly into any of those categories. The money was nice but secondary; he was not a religious fanatic or a kook living in a hut, writing anthrax-laced letters to the IRS. Sometimes he played the revenge angle but that was usually reserved for special circumstances, like when he discovered the identity of his father, who had abandoned him as a child. That was complicated for everyone involved, including me.

No. For the most part, Blackford seemed to do it for fun. And that terrified me.

What made Blackford unique in the fraternity of international illegal arms dealers was that he was once a superstar agent of the USAWMD. He was the guy you sent when the situation seemed hopeless or impossible or downright suicidal. No one ever agreed on anything at the Agency but all concurred Blackford was the best. There was nothing he could not do.

Except resist the lure of the dark side, I suppose. One day he went from being with us, the so-called good guys depending on the day of the week and your particular political leanings, to being one of the bad guys.

And just to rub salt in the wound, Blackford specialized in weapons of mass destruction. Cargo containers of AK-47s? Planeloads of grenade-launchers? He left that stuff for the amateurs. The real money was to be found in the very WMDs the rest of us back at the Agency were risking our lives to take out of circulation. Chemical, biological, radiological, or nuclear, if you had a need and a pile of money, Blackford was your guy. Simon Still found this beyond insulting, as you can well imagine. Of course, this was all before I arrived at the Agency, but that didn't seem to matter to Simon.

"Who the hell does Blackford think he is?" Simon would shout from behind his closed door. Immediately, I'd hear three or four other office doors slam shut and lock. These were the seasoned agents. They knew when to hunker down and ride out the storm. It was a lesson I too would learn, eventually.

Ten seconds later, Simon would appear in front of my desk, red-faced, waving a piece of paper containing intelligence on whatever new nasty business Blackford was up to.

"I don't know who he thinks he is, sir," I'd say.

"Why don't you know, Sally?" he'd say. "If you're so smart, why don't you know?"

"I don't know, sir," I'd say again, which was clearly not the right answer.

"Well, goddamn it," he'd shout, "find out!" And with that he'd charge back down the hallway, muttering all sorts of obscenities. Whether they were directed at Blackford or me I couldn't say, but they were not flattering in either case.

Unfortunately for us at the Agency, Blackford was really good at being really bad. Remember those incidents in Beijing and in Rio, the ones that the twenty-four-hour cable news networks couldn't get enough of? Well, the part they didn't tell you was that it was all Blackford, efficiently moving the goods, collecting the money, and not losing any sleep about his wake of Armageddon.

So to say that Simon was put out when Blackford started kidnapping me from time to time would be a bit of an understatement. Actually, to say it was from time to time might also be a bit of an understatement. At my last count, we were up to about twelve kidnappings. I was new to my job, not willing to claim any expertise in anything and certainly not in spying, and it wouldn't have mattered if I did. Blackford was better than anyone. There was no point in resisting. It would only leave you feeling inadequate.

In the beginning, he would usually manage to slip some drug into my cocktail, the result of which would be me collapsed in a heap, at his feet and at his mercy. Eventually, whatever narcotic I'd ingested would wear off and I'd wake up in a drafty apartment or random hotel room with a thoughtful Blackford standing nearby, watching me for signs of life.

I came to think of Blackford as my nemesis, but with a slight variation. He didn't seem all that eager to kill me, as a proper nemesis would, but rather preferred to torture me with unexpected changes of plan.

So you can better understand how these kidnappings usually went down and my resulting professional mortification, let me tell you about the third time I met Ian Blackford.

I was in Budapest, sent on a mission to follow a woman named Katrina Renoir who was suspected of working for a Chinese terrorist organization. My intelligence report indicated she liked to visit the Gellert Baths on a daily basis and soak in the thermal pools. My job was to watch her and see whom she met.

So there I sat, up to my chin in a lovely warm pool of water, trying my best to stay focused. The steam drifted up and around my face, making me a witness to the world through a veil of breezy gauze. On the far end of the pool, I caught sight of Katrina Renoir. She was somewhere in her forties but if there was ever a case for taking the baths in Budapest, she was it. She glided down the stairs, a life-sized Tinker Bell in a tiny bikini, and settled in on one of the underwater benches. With her eyes closed and her head back, she looked thoroughly content, not a care in the world she was helping to blow up.

How come she looked so relaxed and beautiful and I had

the look of yesterday's roadkill? Did the weight of the moral high ground actually cause wrinkles? What a cruel irony.

As I was lost in this deepest of thoughts, I felt a hand grasp my thigh under the water, followed by a sharp prick, as if I had been poked with a pin. A tiny cloud of blood floated toward the surface of the water.

"I suppose I should tell management on the way out about the blood. They may want to drain the pool." And there was Blackford, sitting not ten inches from me, an amused look on his face. "Although you don't look like you are carrying any communicable diseases. Are you?"

"Am I what?" I started to ask but in reality I had already moved on to the question that always popped into my apparently pea-sized brain whenever I saw him, and that was, would this be easier if Blackford didn't look so good? But before I could fall head-first down that bottomless pit, my world went black and I slipped under the water.

When I woke up, I was in a pint-sized studio apartment. The bathing suit I'd been wearing was draped neatly over a windowsill, drying in the sun. In its place, I wore an over-sized button-down shirt and khaki pants that could have fit a whole other person in them. I was on the floor, my neck kinked from the way Blackford had dumped me there. It seemed strange he would take such care to hang up my wet bathing suit to dry but drop me down as if I were nothing more than a pile of dirty laundry.

I sat up slowly, afraid any quick movement would cause my pounding head to explode. Blackford appeared by the open window.

"Dry," he said, tossing the suit at me. Was I supposed to

say thank you? What was the protocol here? Would it be wrong if I just started to scream for help?

"Sorry about the baths," he said, "but Katrina is off-limits to you and your friends. She works for me."

I nodded, giving him a half smile. I could see them together, Tinker Bell and the evil James Bond. They were the perfect fit.

"Are you going to kill me?" I asked. I wondered how he would do it. Quickly with a bullet to the head or would he want to make it last, choosing instead to torture me in new and creative ways?

At least he had the decency to think about my question for a moment. As always, Blackford seemed surrounded by a hazy aura of invincibility. Under his T-shirt, his body rippled with muscles that did not come from a gym. His ice-blue eyes held mine fast.

"Not today," he said finally. "But you tell Simon that if I see him move on Katrina, you'll be the first to go."

"Yes, sir," I said, nodding my head vigorously so he knew I got the message and was in complete agreement with him about this and most everything else, and not considering some wily plan of escape, such as jumping out the window. Speaking of escape, I chided myself, you should be formulating a plan for making one soon. You should be doing *something*. But instead I just kept nodding my head as if my IQ had dropped to somewhere in the low sixties.

"We will stay away from Katrina," I said, agreeing to something totally outside of my jurisdiction. If Simon wanted to kill Katrina, he was certainly not going to ask my permission to do so. As my brain pondered this reality, my mouth took off on its own adventure.

"Did you see me naked?" I blurted. Immediately, I wanted to kick myself. Blackford didn't say a word, just continued to stare at me. Generally speaking, I consider myself a lucky person. I am, after all, still alive. But something about being held tightly in Blackford's cold gaze always made me think my number was just about to come up.

"No," Blackford said in a tone that made it clear he had about as much regard for me as he did for the average flea. "A bunch of mermaids dressed you. You can go now. Don't forget what we talked about."

Stumbling like a toddler in my oversized pants, I fled the room, grateful for the chance to fuck up another day.

Simon didn't like the message and told me I had better watch myself or he was going to transfer me to the State Department, which in his mind was the worst fate that could befall a person. I left out the part about the bathing suit. The humiliation was more than I could reasonably be expected to bear.

It went on like this for a number of years until Blackford turned up dead, killed by angry militiamen in Sudan. And that should have been it, the end of the terrible and tragic saga of Ian Blackford.

But Blackford would never just die. That would be too pedestrian for him. No. Instead, two years ago he was reborn right back into my living room, making a mess of my carefully constructed life and ending us all up on that bridge so brilliantly sketched by Theo, my budding Picasso. But that's a different story that you might want to get to at another time.

I trace the outline of Theo's drawing with my finger. Teacher Wendy continues to smile as if Theo's advanced doodling skills are a product of her own design.

"He does a nice job with the colors," I say, my chair creaking ominously beneath me.

"He has a flair," she says, "so creative." How long would it take for Teacher Wendy to call Child Protective Services if I were to tell her that creativity had very little to do with it?

"Now, should we chat a little about your kindergarten goals before we run out of time?"

No. I don't want to talk about kindergarten or goals or how my kid likes to throw himself onto the roof of the school building or what a genius he is with a green crayon. What I really want to do is go back to bed and wake up when Theo safely graduates from college and enters a nice mundane profession, such as accounting or dentistry, and takes responsibility for his own life, if kids even do that anymore.

But we can't talk about that or anything else right now because right now I have to go and meet Simon Still and I suspect that is going to make me long for Teacher Wendy, evil stick figures, and little purple chairs.

6

Still wondering if running away is feasible, I peer in the window of the Java Luv. Simon Still sits at my usual table with his sunglasses on and his hat pulled down low on his forehead. He fiddles unconsciously with the buttons on his jacket. He looks thinner than he did the last time we saw each other on that bridge in Theo's picture, but otherwise the same, as if David Bowie were tragically lost in the new millennium.

As I pull open the door, the smell of coffee and slow-burning incense hits me hard in the stomach. I bury my nose in the elbow of my jacket, like Theo does when he needs to sneeze, and gulp at the air. Behind the sunglasses, I am acutely aware of Simon watching my every move.

"Buy me something with a lot of sugar," he says as I approach the table. "I'll watch the yellow door." I want to punch him right in his smirking mouth, but people don't do that in regular life. Instead, I go to the counter and order him a mocha with whipped cream. Leonard hands me my usual espresso shot.

"You actually have company today, Lucy?" he says. "Is the world tilted off its axis or what?"

I wonder if Leonard would think less of me if I asked him to add a teaspoon of rat poison from the back storage room to Simon's drink. It wouldn't kill him but it might make him froth at the mouth a little, which I would certainly enjoy watching right about now.

I carry the cups back to the table.

"What's with your pants?" Simon asks, finally removing his sunglasses. His eyes are bloodshot as if he has been up nights with a colicky newborn.

I look down to see two purple magic marker streaks across the right thigh of my jeans and a stain that could be anything. There is also sand in my shoes but Simon doesn't need to know that.

"Marker is better than bodily fluids," I say. Simon makes a face.

"How can you stand this?" he asks. "Aren't you bored?"

Yes! I want to scream. Sometimes I'm so bored I want to scratch my own eyes out. But Theo is why I am here. Theo is the reason I get up in the morning. He is one of two people I would willingly die for. It's a short list. I take it seriously.

"No," I say. "Motherhood is very fulfilling."

"Ha. And we're the good guys."

"Aren't we?" I ask.

"These days," Simon says with a sigh, "it probably depends on who you ask."

I toss back the espresso. It leaves a nice scalding trail down my throat.

"I have to make some decisions about kindergarten," I say. "It's not as easy as you might think. I need to tour eight public schools and two privates. Do you know how much time is involved in touring schools? Plus, Theo is drawing pictures of Ian Blackford during art time."

Simon glares at me over the frothy rim of his coffee. "And your point is?"

Naturally, I don't have one. Simon cannot understand what any of this means. He is tied to no one.

"Tell me what you know," I say. My calm voice belies my frantic need for information of any kind, facts to replace the fantastic scenarios I've been spinning all morning in my head.

But Simon will draw this out, torturing me just a little bit more. He takes a long, leisurely sip of his drink. He sticks a finger in the whipped cream topping and licks it off. I come very close to pulling out my hand sanitizer and forcing him to hold his palms out, face up.

"Two days ago," Simon begins, "Director Gray disappeared from his home in the middle of the night."

"I don't understand," I say. "The man was like a ghost." I sometimes envied his ability to seemingly not exist for months at a time.

"Not everyone got to know his whereabouts," Simon says. "You had to earn a place at the Director's table, Sally."

I consider mounting a defense of the much-maligned kiddie table but immediately think better of it. If I set Simon up to take another shot at me, he will aim at the burgeoning spare tire around my middle and that might be more than I can handle on only a single espresso shot.

"Would you care to hear the rest of the story?" he asks.

I nod.

"Good," Simon says. "Let's move on. Director Gray has never pulled a walkabout before but we all agree he's getting older. Maybe he turned off his cell phone and went wine-tasting in Napa or skipped out to St. Barts for a long weekend. We give him twenty-four hours to materialize."

"But he doesn't," I say.

"Nice to see you are still on top of your game, Sal," Simon

says. "We are almost past the twenty-four-hour mark when the phone call comes."

He sticks his fingers back in the whipped cream.

"Did you wash your hands?" I can't help myself, it seems. "Do you have any idea how many germs can be on your fingers just from opening the door to get in here?"

Simon's hand, the one with the whipped cream on it, lingers in the air, kind of floating there as if it's no longer attached to his arm. Then he wipes the whipped cream on a napkin.

"Is that better?"

"Yes. Go on. The phone call."

"The phone call came to my office. We are Righteous Liberty, they said. We stand for blah, blah, blah. Fill in the latest ideological bullshit and you get the picture. We have Gray and we want to talk to Sally Sin." Just having to say that last part makes his jaw clench in such a way as to foreshadow extensive dental work. "So I told them you were dead and they had better tell me what they wanted. To which they responded we had twenty-four hours to produce you or Gray would die. But the United States government doesn't negotiate with terrorists. Everyone knows that." He glances at his watch. "It's been about fifteen hours since that call."

My insides turn over, the coffee making me suddenly nauseous. I am this close to puking all over the mosaic-tiled bistro table.

"Sally, you look green."

I close my eyes and slowly the feeling passes.

"Who did we outsource it to?" I ask. Because while it is true that the United States government does not negotiate with terrorists, they are more than willing to let private organizations that specialize in complicated human extractions do so when no one is looking. For their efforts, these organizations get heaping piles of money and access to a smorgasbord of government officials and secret information. In return, the government gets to stand by its policy of not negotiating with terrorists and keep its nose clean. But that doesn't mean the whole thing doesn't stink.

"The regulars," Simon says, with a malignant flash in his eyes. It's enough to tell me this is an unsanctioned visit, that whatever Simon is up to, it falls somewhere outside the lines of proper. For a second, I think it might even be personal but then I remind myself that Simon doesn't do personal, so that would be impossible.

"How much did you tell the extraction specialists?" I ask. Leonard, if he's not too stoned and can eavesdrop properly, might assume we're talking about the dentist.

"Enough to get them started," Simon says dismissively. As second in command of the USAWMD, his orders were almost certainly to go about business as usual and make sure this event did not indicate to the outside world that the United States had taken its hands off the wheel. But asking Simon to forget that Righteous Liberty asked specifically to speak to me is akin to asking him to put on a tutu and dance the role of the Sugar Plum Fairy. It's just not going to happen.

"So tell me, what do they want with you, Sally?" he says. "What makes you so special?"

I think about the envelope Blackford handed me two years ago, the one now safely hidden in my underwear drawer. In the envelope is a faded Polaroid of a young Director Gray and my parents, arms draped around one another like good friends, tan skin glistening in the summer sun. The photo was strange for a number of reasons. First, Director Gray was smiling and if you ever met him you would understand smiling was something Gray did not do. Secondly, he never once acknowledged having known my parents. And while coincidence can account for a lot in life, I had the sense it didn't apply here.

As soon as I saw the photo, I knew it was the first step down a path Blackford meant for me to follow to its inevitable end. But I read the original *Grimm's Fairy Tales* as a child and I know better than to wander into the deep, dark woods, following bread crumbs. Consciously or not, I didn't take the bait. Instead I went back to burning the pancakes and driving car pool. Blackford had underestimated my well-honed ability to compartmentalize my past and this made me feel good about myself. I'd show him who was more stubborn.

"Who's behind Righteous Liberty?" I ask.

"We don't know," Simon says flatly.

"But you have a suspicion," I say. "That's why you're here, right? So I can stick my neck out and see who chops off my head and you can go home with your answer?"

Simon smiles. It's an ugly smile, born of too many years blurring the lines between what is good and what is necessary. His duty to his country trumps almost everything except his need to be in control. And I'm willing to bet he doesn't feel all that comfortable with his level of control at the moment. He pulls out a cell phone and lays it on the table between us. It looks like the one he sent me earlier today except this one has more than one button. I'm flattered he feels me worthy of multiple buttons.

"The number they provided isn't traceable," Simon says. "It disappears after stopping in about ten countries. I'm starting to think the Internet might be responsible for the end of civilization as we know it."

The coffee shop is quiet. Leonard sits on a stool at the counter, reading the *San Francisco Chronicle,* muttering about injustice and social inequality.

"You want me to call here?" I say, looking around. "In public?"

"Is there anything more ordinary than a person talking on a cell phone in a coffee shop? It's as close to invisible as you can get these days. Besides, it's a special phone. Dial."

I plug in the number as Simon reads it out to me. There is static, clicking, a few notes from a song that was popular in the 1970s, and finally a voice.

"Hello?"

"This is Sally Sin," I say. I'm a fraud. Sally Sin is gone. Lucy Hamilton with the purple magic marker all over her pants is her replacement. I wonder for a second how well she will do negotiating with madmen.

"Finally," the voice says, disguised with voice-altering software. It could be male or female, young or old. I have no idea. "Looks like we figured out how to get your attention."

"Looks like you did. Now, what do you want exactly because I have all this stuff I should be doing right now but instead I'm talking to you." Simon is plugged into the phone. He fiddles with his headset. It chirps.

"Is there someone on the line with you? My demand was to speak to you alone." I want to tell this person that he or she is hopelessly naïve. There is no alone anymore. "I hope your people are taking this seriously. As I am." And there it is, just the slightest hint of an accent seeping out around the cracks of the voice alteration, as if a steamroller has flattened certain letters. I can't quite place it but it's definitely there. And it's familiar.

"I'm alone," I say. I don't tell him that the "people" I have now are small and really into superheroes. It doesn't seem relevant.

"I'm sitting outside the Notre Dame, watching the pigeons," I continue. "I just finished a delicious fair trade Argentinean espresso and when we hang up I plan on going back and having another. I think I've become a bit of a caffeine addict in the last few years. But it's better than being a meth addict, I suppose. I'm considering flying to Rome for lunch. There's a place that makes a really thin crust pizza that's so good I could eat the whole thing." The funny thing is, I mean it. My head is awash with images of Roman pizza and my mouth starts to water. It's only twelve hours or so on a plane. Might be worth it.

"You can stop talking about yourself now," the voice says. "You Americans, so self-absorbed."

"And you can stop with the character assassination now. You requested this call, so let's get to the part where you tell me what this is all about."

"There's something I want back. Something that belongs to me."

"You need to be a little more specific. Otherwise, you might end up with a Tickle Me Elmo."

"I don't want anyone named Elmo. I want a man named Richard Yoder." Next to me, every muscle in Simon's body goes rigid. Suddenly he looks as if he might benefit from an exorcism. Under his breath, he says something that sounds a lot like "I knew it" but I can't be sure because I'm busy talking to the crazy person.

"We know Yoder is there but he belongs to me," the voice continues. "It's only been a matter of time until we figured out how to get him back."

"Well, I don't know," I say. "Does anyone really belong to anyone else? What is that thing they say? If you love something, set it free and if it doesn't come back to you, that probably means it never liked you in the first place. That's not it exactly but it's the idea that counts. What if your Richard Yoder doesn't want to come back?"

Simon drums angry fingers on the table. Something has changed. A few minutes ago, he was practically bored with this whole situation but now he's furious. And it all turned on the name Richard Yoder.

"He has no choice," the voice says. "He's mine."

"I see problems in this relationship. You're too controlling."

"Stop it right now!" the voice barks. "We're wasting time. The deal is simple. We will trade Gray for Yoder. If you try to bring in any of your agency friends to assist you, he dies."

"I don't have any agency friends but I understand," I say.

"And just to show you we can be reasonable, I'll give you four days. At which point you'll call me back and I will tell you when and where the trade will happen. Is that understood?"

Four days seems overly generous. Do I take it personally that they think I've gotten slow in my retirement or do I let it slide?

"Why me?" I ask.

There is a pause. The question confuses the mechanical voice.

"I thought you knew," it says. "He said you were smart and would have figured it out by now. He said it would be a fait accompli. His words."

"Who said I'd know what?" I press. Again silence. It sounds as if a mini conference is happening on the other end of the line.

"We will proceed as planned," the voice says finally, not answering my question.

"You're in charge," I say. "But just so I'm clear, what happens if I don't call you back in four days?"

"Your man Gray has done a fairly good job holding up under our interrogation methods thus far. But he's not young and who knows how long he'll last? In a final push, we might even get something useful out of him."

"I'll call you back," I say quickly, an image of Gray being water-boarded flashing before my eyes. Oh, wait a minute. Only the good guys do that.

"Wonderful," the voice says, as if I've just agreed to buy an extended warranty on my washing machine. "Thank you for your time, Sally Sin. We will meet again soon."

Again? "Do I know you?" But it is too late. The line is dead. I hang up the phone.

"Who is Richard Yoder?" I ask. Simon rarely exhibits signs of stress. In fact, the only time I remember seeing him do so was when we were about to die in a plane crash and, in that situation, who could blame him really? But here he is tapping his foot so the bistro table jumps, his eyes darting every which way. Before I can push him about Yoder, his other cell phone begins beeping frantically. He glances at the screen.

"You know what happens now," he says to me. "It's the regular drill. Go home and forget this ever happened. Enjoy your weekend."

"Or?"

"Sally, you know the answer to that. Just go back to whatever it is you do now, knowing you've helped your country once again. Be proud. You're a good patriot." It would have

been a nice thing to say if not for the sneer on his face. I grab
him by the arm when he tries to stand up.

"Are you going to get him back?" I ask. I don't understand
why it matters. I'm sure if the roles were reversed, Gray would
not give a second thought to my being tortured to death by a
bunch of indignant terrorists with an agenda hand-delivered
by God. But before Simon vanishes into the Friday morning
sunshine, I have to know the answer to my question is yes.

"Sally," Simon says, peeling my fingers from his jacket,
"he's the director of the United States Agency for Weapons of
Mass Destruction. What do you think?"

Maybe it's the caffeine surging through my veins or his
non-answer but all at once I'm quite sure Simon does not
care if Gray lives or dies. Simon is here because he suspected
a connection between Righteous Liberty and Richard Yoder.
And something about Yoder makes him crazy. Saving Gray
has nothing to do with it.

"Simon, you need to do something," I say, aware of the
odd desperation leaking through. "Those extraction guys,
they're amateurs. They're washed-out soldiers. They always
make things worse."

Simon gives me a funny look. "Really, Sally, why do you
care?" he says. "Gray never liked you anyway."

And with that he walks out of the shop, cackling in a way
that would make the Wicked Witch of the West jealous.

7

Saturday mornings are soccer mornings. At 7 A.M. Theo, already in uniform, is jumping on my bed with his cleats on the wrong feet. The mud from his last game leaves perfect round circles of brown dirt all over my white comforter.

"Theo, no shoes on the bed," I mutter from my position half buried under the blankets. I'm not ready for the day. I can't shake the sound of Simon Still laughing as he left the coffee shop. Every time sleep tried to come waltzing in, that dreadful sound chased it right out again. My eyelids feel heavy and crusty.

"When's the game?" Theo asks, kicking off his shoes and continuing to jump. I'm getting seasick. Would it be wrong to just knock him off the bed? Of course it would be, but I am tempted nonetheless.

"The game isn't until ten o'clock. We have a lot of time. Where's Daddy?"

"He's downstairs."

"Why are you not downstairs with him?"

"He's working," Theo reports. "He says he needs five more minutes."

"Well, go downstairs and tell him Mommy said the five minutes are up and he's not allowed to work on the weekend, okay?"

"But I want to stay up here with you," Theo says, jumping up and coming down on my thigh with his hard little knees. I groan.

"I bet girls don't beat up their mothers," I say.

"Yes, they do."

"No, they don't. Go and find your father right this minute." In response, Theo snuggles up next to me, now all sweetness and warmth. In one hand, he clutches the faded Polaroid. A rush of adrenaline propels me up to sitting.

"Theo, where did you get that from?"

He holds up the photograph. "It's really old," he says solemnly. "I found it when the LEGO guys were in there." He points at my bureau. "The drawer was home base."

It's not unusual for me to find LEGO men stashed in the toilet paper roll, the refrigerator, in my shoes. Why I thought my underwear drawer would be off-limits is beyond me. I'm rusty in more ways than one. Slowly, I remove the photograph from Theo's hand. His fingerprints blur the already fading image.

"This is Mommy's," I say. "Okay?" He shrugs. As I go to slide it between the pages of the novel I've been reading, my eyes drift over the faces and then back to Theo, now attempting to burrow under the blankets like a mole.

I have a fleeting sense of something big, an idea that will change everything, passing me by, like a ghost that has decided not to stay and haunt me after all. My scalp tingles. I want to grab whatever it is before it disappears forever, but I don't have time because Will appears in our bedroom door and the thought is gone. In one hand, he holds a cup of coffee and in the other, his open laptop. A wireless headset is fastened to his ear. To look at him, you'd think my husband would be equally comfortable living the life of a ski bum in Colorado or wearing a ten-thousand-dollar suit to the corner office of his investment bank. His blond hair is always a little too long and his blue eyes seem to dance with amusement at things the rest of us don't even notice. He's very good-looking for a workaholic. It helps.

He chatters into the headset, talking to someone else but looking at me.

"Yes, I know, Dad," he says. "I heard you the first time. He's great. Okay. Gotta run. Yes. Yes. Okay. Good-bye."

There are things that are unusual—being eaten by a shark, for example, or hit by an asteroid. A casual Saturday morning phone call from Will's parents used to be the equivalent of being eaten by a shark while at the same time crushed to death by the asteroid. Which is to say, you could comfortably rely on it never happening.

Will's parents aren't bad people, but they're very different from their son. They live in the Hollywood Hills in a six-bedroom house with a four-car garage, a heated pool, and staff to make them dinner, fold the sheets, and wash the floors. And from the outside, they appear to live this life guilt free, which is really more than their nature-loving, hybrid-car-driving son can handle. If they were to single-handedly replant all the clear-cut acres in the Brazilian Amazon, it still might not be enough to offset their weekly carbon footprint. After they bought their second Cadillac Escalade, Will basically stopped talking to them.

There was also the issue of me. What their well-bred son was doing with a person from nowhere, with no past and no paper trail, was beyond comprehension. If I represented a late-stage rebellion, they thought at least Will would have the good sense to know when to quit. But apparently, he didn't because, much to their shock and horror, he married me. In their world, a person from nowhere was just one step above criminally insane axe-murderer. And it was not a very big step.

When Theo was born, my in-laws made a brief effort to be grandparents but as it turned out they didn't like the sticky, snotty, dirty parts of infancy and, honestly, when you take that away, there's not much left. I overcompensated for Theo's lack of an extended family by creating as rich a life for him as possible and slipping him the occasional plastic toy made in China, probably by slave labor. It was the best I could do. I couldn't conjure loving grandparents out of the ether.

But then one day about a year and a half ago, I was sitting in the Java Luv watching the rain come down and discussing the finer points of a Muni fare hike with Leonard, who was trying his best to convince me that all transportation should be free.

"People need to soar, man," he said, absentmindedly filling sugar dispensers. "You can't keep them down. Their spirits need to fly and be free."

"You sound like a bad seventies song," I said, watching the yellow door with one eye and the growing mountain of sugar on the floor with the other. "Someone has to pay for the soaring spirits."

"A tax on cigarettes," Leonard said with complete conviction.

"Leonard," I said, "I think you might be the only person who still smokes in this city. Honestly. It is practically a crime to light up here. And by the way, you're spilling all the sugar."

"Cool," Leonard said, which was his standard response when he had totally lost the thread of the conversation. He stared at the sugar in his hand and all over his shoes as if he were having an out-of-body experience.

Before I could offer him some useful advice on how to clean up the sugar before the ants invaded and carried us all away, the bell over the door jingled and in walked Will, looking ten years older than when I had last seen him two hours before. He had never come into the Java Luv on a weekday morning. Not once. Someone had to be dead. Or close to it.

Will sat down at my table and stared past me out the window at the rain. He was a man drowning in regrets.

"Dad wanted us to go with them to their place in Maui last year," Will said, before I could ask him what he was doing here, rather than in his office, when the world did not appear to have ended. "I never told you. I just said no. I didn't even consider it."

"Will, what's going on?"

Leonard, sensing drama, pulled a chair up to our table and straddled it. He still held the half-full sugar container in one hand. Will gave him an odd look but Leonard just leaned in closer to make sure he didn't miss something important.

"Leonard," I said.

"What?"

"Go clean up that sugar."

"Why?" he asked, in all sincerity.

"Ants," I said. "Lots of ants. You'll lose your job."

"Oh yeah. Right. The ants." He pushed back from the table.

"Will?"

"My father has pancreatic cancer. The doctors give him three months to live." He looked up at the ceiling as if tilting his head in that way would send the tears back from where they came.

"Okay," I said without pause. "Let's go and pull Theo out of school and head right down there."

I understood action. I understood motion. Sometimes, it was the only choice. Will nodded his head and pressed in closer to me. His eyes closed. I didn't want to tell him it would be fine, that everything would work out, because oftentimes it didn't.

"Thank you," he whispered. The weight of their years-long conflict diminished him. I wanted to take the pain and pull it into myself, free him of the burden. I knew I could handle it. I had survived much worse.

But three months later, William Hamilton II was still very much alive. Better yet, he seemed to be cured, baffling even his doctors.

"A gift," one of them said.

"He has something to live for," another said, looking at Theo clinging to my leg.

And that turned out to be very true indeed. My father-in-law exited his brush with death a changed man and when he looked around at his life, his gaze settled on his only grand-child. Will II and Rose Marie suddenly started showing up at our house about as often as the mailman.

"We were in the neighborhood," he would say, pushing past me toward Theo. Rose Marie would trail behind him, looking angry. *She* had not confronted her mortality and decided her life was lacking and she was clearly bitter Will II had done so without consulting her. Sure, she was glad he was alive, but that didn't mean he wasn't getting on her nerves.

"I would have called," she'd say, not really looking at me, "but William likes the element of surprise now that we're A.C." She often talked about her life in terms of B.C. and A.C. Just thinking about life Before Cancer filled her with such obvious longing that it was almost painful to watch. She did not take solace in a deeper relationship with Theo. He would climb into her lap and get red marker all over her pale green silk suit. He would rest his blond head on her chest and his hair would stick in her carefully applied lipstick. He would slip a half-finished corn muffin laced with spit into her pocket and not tell her. When she discovered it, she'd shriek like it was a dead rat in there, a scenario Theo found hilarious.

But William II was a man with a sweet tooth who had just discovered chocolate. He was insatiable, unable to absorb enough childish energy. His eyes sparkled as he sat on the floor and built block towers or played horsey ride or read story after story until his voice began to fade.

My husband would stand in the doorway, watching his father and son, head to head over some game or puzzle, a confused look on his face.

"I have no memory of him ever playing with me," Will would say. It was almost as if he had caught a fleeting glimpse of what it would have been like to grow up in that alternative universe, the one where his dad sat on the floor and did Thomas the Train puzzles. And he missed the possibility of it.

Will sits on the side of the bed, popping the earpiece out and tossing it across the room onto the bureau.

"It's Saturday," I say, nodding at the computer. Looking appropriately guilty, he offers me the coffee in peace.

"I was almost done when my dad called," he says. "Only a few more e-mails and that's it."

It's never it but I don't want him to reclaim the coffee, so I let it go.

"And then I have that meeting later this morning," he whispers. "Remember, I'm going to miss the S-O-C-C-E-R G-A-M-E this morning."

"Why are you going to miss my game, Daddy?" Theo asks, crawling out from under the covers. "You said you'd come to all of them. You said that."

Will looks to me for guidance but I refuse to help him. He works weekends at his own peril.

"He's a good speller," I say. "We practice a lot."

"How about chocolate chip pancakes for breakfast?" Will says with a wink. Theo takes the bait and leaps onto Will's back from about six feet away. I consider if now is a good time to discuss Teacher Wendy's concerns about Theo's relationship with gravity but decide against it. It's the kind of behavior that might secretly make a dad proud.

As Will and Theo head downstairs, I pull the covers back up to my nose and burrow into my pillow. The pillowcase smells of Theo's new shampoo, light and fragrant and distinctly hibiscus. Normally, the smell of hibiscus makes me giddy in a fruity-cocktail-and-sandy-beach kind of a way. But today my guard is down and it takes me to another place entirely.

8

was still fairly new to the Agency the first time I went to Kathmandu but not so new that I was going to flat-out embarrass myself. No, I'd already passed through Stage One of being a covert operative, the stage known as complete humiliation, and was feeling rather smug about surviving intact. So to a certain extent, I probably deserved what was to come. After all, smugness isn't an attractive quality in anyone and certainly not in a sophomore-level spy.

I was in Kathmandu to gather information about an arms dealer named Claude Chevalier, known affectionately as Chemical Claude. When I asked for the backstory on the nickname, there was much laughter from my fellow agents but no one who would tell. I was the new kid and they weren't done hazing me yet.

In any case, the last time I checked, Chemical Claude had been whiling away his days in Guantánamo, which made it a little surprising to be handed a folder stamped TOP SECRET with his smiling mug clipped to the inside cover.

"We caught this guy," I said. "Isn't he on a forced tropical vacation?"

"Yes, we did," Simon said. "And yes he was."

"So?"

"Well, things change, Sally."

"He got out?" I asked, indignant. "He must be a really good swimmer. It's a long way to Miami."

"People escape," Simon said, a flush of red rising in his cheeks. "It happens."

"It's not supposed to," I reminded him.

"I would rather not talk about this anymore," he said, quietly enough to scare me.

"Yes, sir," I said.

"Your job is to go out and get him back."

"Alive, sir?"

"Yes." Whether the answer was yes because those were Simon's orders or because he wanted to wring Chemical Claude's neck himself, I could not say.

"There's one more thing you should know about him," Simon said. This was the part where Simon usually told me all the things that were too heinous to include in the Top Secret folder. Inevitably, there would be some delightful colorful detail, like perhaps that my new target enjoyed rolling around naked on a bed of rose petals and hundred-dollar bills while being sprinkled with yellowcake uranium or something like that. But what I got was a whole lot stranger.

"It's not in the file," Simon said, "but Chemical Claude is Canadian."

"What?" I said, unable to hide my disbelief. "They only have thirty-five million people in their whole country; statistically, it's barely even enough to produce a decent lunatic. How did this happen?"

Simon shrugged his shoulders. "I have no idea," he said, which was terrifying because Simon always had an idea, even if it was a really bad one. "The world is going completely to shit, Sally."

And for once, I suspected he was right. If you can't trust the Canadians, well, it might be time to just pack it in and go home.

Thirty-five hours later, I got off my plane in Kathmandu with a half-assed plan of trekking toward Mt. Everest and stopping once in a while to ask if anyone had seen Mr. Chemical hanging around acting naughty. My file said Nepal was the last place he'd been seen. Of course, I realized this meant he could be anywhere but I guess I had to start somewhere.

As I pushed open the terminal doors to the outside, the smell of burning garbage and exhaust rushed in. I maneuvered my way around little old ladies carrying chickens in rusty cages and small boys tethered to the family goat by lengths of fraying rope, all milling about on what could have been the airport's front lawn gone to seed. There was a complete lack of the urgency I usually associated with airports. People, chickens, goats—no one seemed to care if they ever actually went anywhere. Off to the side of the terminal, a row of 1970s rusted-out Toyota Corollas lined the dirt road, their drivers waiting patiently for a fare to town. I hopped into the first one and tried to close the door.

"Grab it from the bottom and pull up," my driver advised. "Pull hard." I did as he instructed and the door almost shut.

"Very good," he said. "Don't lean on it. Now, pull your feet up or your shoes will get dusty." I looked down and could plainly see the road beneath me. The car appeared to have no bottom. The man started driving. I held my breath and my feet.

"Where are we going today?" he asked, in lightly accented English.

"Hotel Kathmandu."

"Good choice," he said. "They have toilet seats in most rooms." This made me a little sad. I was getting used to taking it on the chin for the Agency but a girl could still pine for the occasional fully assembled toilet and not be labeled a sissy.

"I'm Min. You need a tour guide while you're in town?" he asked. "Planning a trek to Everest? Annapurna? Want to see the monkey temple? Buddhas? Stupas? I can arrange anything you need. You just let me know."

Min was somewhere between thirty-five and seventy years old. It was hard for me to tell in this part of the world. Crow's feet danced around his bright and lively eyes when he smiled and his dark hair was parted on the right side and perfectly slicked back. He wore a pressed French-blue button-down shirt, khaki pants, and flip-flops. Not only did he have a better sense of style than I did, he was cleaner.

Lining the sides of the road into the city center were mountains of garbage, baking in the hot sun. Naked children frolicked at the edge of a river running an unnatural brown. Plastic bottles floated downstream like little cruise ships headed off to Hepatitis Island.

Eventually we pulled up in front of a ramshackle building missing its third floor. A haphazard sign out front indicated that I had indeed arrived at the Hotel Kathmandu.

"Plenty of room at the Hotel Kathmandu," Min sang softly. "Such a lovely place." The possibility that he was warning me against forces of evil residing inside the hotel never occurred to me. In retrospect, I probably should have paid more attention.

"Ah, Madam, welcome." A small man emerged from a room hidden behind beaded curtains. "I am Kirin. You have reservation?"

I glanced around. It hardly looked as if reservations were necessary.

"No. Are you full?" I asked.

Kirin shrugged. "Let me check the register." On a table buried under a stack of old magazines was a plastic bound notebook with the word "Guests" scrawled across it in uneven letters. Kirin blew the dust from the cover and flipped through the first few pages.

"You are in luck. It seems we have a room for you. Sit please. Ayushi!" he bellowed. From behind the curtains a beautiful little girl appeared. She couldn't have been more than eight years old. A faded flower garland hung around her slender neck.

"Tea," Kirin demanded. Ayushi bent her head in acknowledgment and slipped back into the darkness.

"You don't need to trouble yourself with getting us tea," I said, hoping to cut through the formalities and escape to my room. Kirin looked at me as if I'd grown a second head. And I was so tired I was starting to hallucinate that maybe I did, in fact, have a second head, although it clearly lacked a brain.

"Sit," Kirin barked. Min, also responding to the order, plunked down in the seat next to me. We were now a couple of some strange sort. Then again, maybe Min just liked free tea.

Minutes later, Ayushi came back carrying a tray laden with a teapot and a plate of steamed dumplings. A ceiling fan turned slowly above us, barely circulating the heavy air. The paint on the walls peeled and the patchwork floor of mismatched linoleum tiles was covered in a thin layer of dry dirt. Ayushi picked up a straw broom and began to move the dirt around in figure eights.

"How long will you stay with us?" Kirin asked, handing me a dumpling. His fingers left brown smudges on it, but not wanting to offend him, I popped it into my mouth, said a quick prayer to the gods of immunity, and swallowed.

"Just a night," I said, washing down the sticky dumpling with a gulp of tea. "I need a trekking guide to take me to Namche Bazaar."

"Are you heading to Everest Base Camp?" Min asked.

"No. Not all the way to base camp," I clarified. "Just Namche."

The two men looked at me curiously. "Who goes only as far as Namche?" they asked together. A strange tickling sensation ran the length of my spine. I was blowing this. I cleared my throat and tried again.

"I'm a photographer," I explained. *"National Geographic* wants some shots of the vendors at Namche. And some of the Tibetan market, too." A moment passed and the two men both seemed to relax. Was I in the clear? Was I ever?

"I'll take you," Min said, as if the deal was done. "Now you go and get some sleep." That seemed such a fine idea I didn't bother to mention I preferred to travel alone. "I'll wait outside. I'll be here when you wake up."

Kirin shot a look at Min. "Not necessary. We will take good care of her. You can go and begin gathering supplies for your expedition."

Min sat up straighter and squared his shoulders. "I prefer to wait," he said. Kirin continued to glare at him but seemed unable to come up with a convincing counter-argument. Finally, Kirin bent his head and began to collect the used teacups.

There was something so obviously strange about the exchange even I, clearly in the grips of sleep-deprived dementia, could see it. But I no longer cared if someone tried to kill me as long as they didn't wake me up in the process.

My square room was unfinished, with no glass in the single window. The fatigue clinging to my body as if it were part of my cellular structure was something new. In this line of work, there was no built-in recovery time, no nap after the pressure was off, no restorative long weekend on the beach. It didn't matter if I was awake for seventy-two hours straight. I still had to come off as a person in possession of most of her faculties. Failure to do so would inevitably lead to disaster, followed by professional humiliation.

It wasn't until Theo was born that I began to see the value in it. I was well-trained for the endless sleepless nights, trying to console a crying infant, walking the halls with my little bundle of fury as if I were nothing more than a ghost. In a twisted way, it was comforting. I might not have known a thing about babies but I was a champion at staying awake.

I pulled the crooked shutters closed and tumbled gratefully onto the thin, hard mattress. There, I slept without moving until I smelled a smell just like the one filling my nose right now, the soft scent of the hibiscus flower.

It rose up from Ayushi's starched school uniform in a cloud. She sat cross-legged on my bed, playing with a lock of my greasy travel hair. Sitting next to her on the bed was a single roll of toilet paper and a small bar of bright pink soap I knew would burn my skin if I dared use it. In Nepal, the ritual of toilet paper and soap delivery was taken very seriously. The rules were for the guest to accept the toilet paper and soap gratefully and under no circumstances ask for any more.

"I asked to bring these," she whispered in a sing-song voice, "because I wanted to tell you there is a man downstairs. He is talking to Father and Father is telling him you are sleeping up here in this room and that he is free to come up here to get you at any time. He is paying Father a lot of money. He has a gun." She cocked a finger at me and fired.

The image of that pretend gun is enough to send me leaping out of bed. I take the hibiscus-scented pillow and throw it into the dark recesses of Will's closet. I want that smell as far away from me as possible. I have no interest in this trip down memory lane because I have the disadvantage of knowing how it ends.

Downstairs, I hear noise in the kitchen, pots and pans being moved around, the refrigerator opening and closing, Theo going on and on about whether you can take college classes in Batman. When we met yesterday, Simon was perfectly clear on the point that I was to go home and pretend I knew nothing about Gray's kidnapping. Whatever happens to Director Gray is none of my business. In addition, as Simon was kind enough to point out, Gray didn't even like me, so why should I care what happens to him? Let the experts handle it. That's what they get paid for, after all.

But try as I might, I cannot drown out the voice of my instinct demanding that I do something.

9

"Lucy," Will shouts from downstairs, "get up! I'm leaving."

"Okay," I mutter. "I'm doing it right now." But I don't want to. My body wants to stay right here and sleep until at least after lunch and then maybe squeeze in a little nap before dinner.

I used to take sleep for granted. It was something that happened on a semi-regular basis. Sometimes it was in my nice comfy bed and sometimes it was under a tangle of vines in the jungle, but at least it happened. Now, my sleep is as thin as a wedding veil. If Theo so much as rolls over, I'm awake, fighting the urge to get up and check on him one more time. Just to be sure.

I come downstairs to find Theo in the playroom surrounded by *Star Wars* LEGO people. Their square little bodies are lined up in preparation for what can only be an epic battle. They wear a random assortment of tiny helmets and carry little plastic weapons of moderate destruction. Theo whispers to them. I pause for a second to see if they answer him, but he notices me loitering in the doorway and stops.

"Hi, Mommy," he says. "Daddy went to his meeting. He kissed me good-bye twice. One was for you."

Daddy's phoning it in a little bit more than usual these days.

"That's nice," I say.

Theo spends a minute trying to bring me up to speed on the reasons behind the impending LEGO man war but I ask too many questions about motivation and he soon dismisses me, kindly suggesting I go away.

I wander into the kitchen and make an attempt to clean up after Will's pancake project. I wipe down the countertops, start another pot of coffee, and glance through today's headlines. I even go so far as to check the dryer for clothes in need of folding. But it's empty and I think that must be a sign of something because it has never happened before. I stand at the bottom of the stairs, twirling a strand of hair around my finger. But it's no use. I have the willpower of your average street-corner junkie.

I take the stairs on tiptoe, afraid that if Theo hears me trying to escape, he'll forget he sent me away in the first place and demand I return immediately and create a replica of the Chrysler building out of microscopic LEGO pieces. To scale.

Sitting down at Will's desk, I power up his computer. As I wait, I work on convincing myself I'm here for only one reason and that is the voice that keeps nagging at me to do something. Maybe if I figure out why Righteous Liberty wants me, and only me, to trade Richard Yoder for Director Gray, I can confidently tell the voice to shut up and leave me alone.

So far, the only logical reason I can come up with for their request is that the name Sally Sin is not the kind of name you quickly forget. It sticks to the memory like old chewing gum. Clearly, I would've been better served by being Jane Rogers or something equally bland, but how was I supposed to know it would matter? Had I known, I might have stayed holed up in my dorm room smoking cigarettes rather than trudging out in the snow to volunteer with the psychology grad students and answering a bunch of weird questions that turned out to have nothing to do with a Ph.D. thesis and everything to do with an Agency recruiting exercise. One of the tests asked for a nickname and I gave them one. I even remember being amused by my own wit. All these years later, I'm still embarrassed for my younger self.

Right now, when I really should be downstairs monitoring LEGO World War III instead of sneaking around in Will's office, I'm simply unwilling to accept the possibility of an alternative reason for Righteous Liberty's request. The list of things I'm obligated to be stressed over is long and includes where to send Theo to kindergarten and how to explain to him that telling his friends it's okay to jump from the play structure to the roof at school is, well, not okay. The list doesn't include kidnapping, conspiracy, and possible bodily harm. I'm too busy for that.

Glancing over my shoulder to make sure I'm alone, an old habit I cannot seem to kill, I type in an address consisting of twenty-seven letters and numbers, humming the ABCs tune as I go. As soon as I hit Enter, the computer screen goes black, a single green cursor flashing in the upper left-hand corner. Normally, this would be cause for concern, but now, it's exactly what I want. I enter a password stolen from Simon Still while he suffered from malaria-induced hallucinations in an inhospitable jungle years ago, hit Enter again, and wait.

ACCESS DENIED flashes across the screen in red letters. I half expect a skull and crossbones to appear underneath the words.

"What? You've got to be kidding me," I say, reentering the password.

"ACCESS DENIED—PLEASE CEASE ALL ATTEMPTS TO ENTER HERE OR YOU WILL BE DETAINED FOR QUESTIONING."

This is very inconvenient but calling up tech support and lodging a service complaint will not improve my situation any and might even get me "detained for questioning." I continue to tell myself that the more I know about Yoder, the more evidence I'll have in support of my theory that Righteous Liberty could have asked for any agent, but they just happened to ask for me. And the only place to get information on Yoder is from the USAWMD network.

I need to know what they know. However, when it comes to computers, I'm a realist. While I can perform a mean Google search, anything beyond that requires professional intervention.

"Mom, are you looking at pictures?" Theo stands in the office door, trying to summon up his angry face. I jump as if I just got caught watching porno at the office. "Because you said I could look with you the next time."

One of the problems of not letting my child watch too much television is that whenever he can get in front of a screen of any sort for any reason, he will. He claims his favorite place on the planet is Times Square at night even though the last time he was there it was broad daylight and we were heading to see *Mary Poppins*. He climbs up onto my lap.

"I promise you I'm not looking at pictures," I say.

"Well, then what are you doing?"

Sticking my nose where it doesn't belong. Not following the rules. Not being a very useful engine.

"I'm looking for something," I say.

"This is boring."

"If it's so boring, why don't you go back downstairs and play? I'll be done in a minute." He looks at me as if I have lost my mind.

"No way. I'm staying." Theo is a firm believer in miracles happening. He snuggles down in my lap, ever hopeful that my fingers will accidentally pull up an episode of *Scooby-Doo* or *SpongeBob SquarePants*. I shift him a little bit to the left, trying to reach the keyboard.

"Theo," I say, "I can't move."

"Okay." He pulls himself up on the arm of the chair and balances precariously, a bird on a wire. A large bird.

"What does that say?" he asks, pointing to the flashing message.

"It says 'Go away,' " I explain.

"Where are all the pictures and movies and stuff?" He grabs the mouse and starts racing it around. The cursor looks like a passenger on Mr. Toad's Wild Ride. I pull it from his hand.

"There aren't any," I say. "This is a network for grown-ups. For big people."

"You mean old people?" he asks. "Like you, Mom?"

Gee, honey, thanks for that. "Yes. Kind of like me." He pops up on his knees and starts combing through my hair, doing his best impression of a momma gorilla searching for nits.

"What are you doing?"

"Finding more of those white hairs. I can pull them out like you do."

That's it. Even *I* have my limits. I gather him up and toss him onto the floor.

"Go find something to do," I instruct.

"This is boring anyway," he says, stalking off. I hit Escape and enter "Richard Yoder" into Google. My search generates thousands of hits and none of them seem useful. I search for "Righteous Liberty" and come up with the Statue of Liberty, the Liberty Bell, and life, liberty, and the pursuit of happiness, all of which are lovely but not much help.

In my old world, if I wanted to indulge in a little technological espionage, I would escape the USAWMD Underground, the affectionate name for our subterranean office space, and head up into the daylight. I'd walk out of my building, down the street about two blocks, and into another big brick building that resembled an old-fashioned mental hospital. There, I would negotiate my way through security as if my life depended on it, travel to the fourteenth floor, wind my way through a maze of cubicles, and eventually end up in front of a converted conference room with blacked-out windows and a keypad entry system designed to keep the riffraff out. I was not privileged enough to know the code, so I would just bang on the door until Elliot opened it.

Elliot was malnourished to the point of resembling a skeleton covered in masking tape and worked for another agency, although he was less than forthcoming about which one that was. He wore a black T-shirt and black jeans that his skinny little hips could do nothing with. His eyes, behind thick plastic glasses, were always bloodshot. If I handed him a large Starbucks Frappuccino with whipped cream and a generous caramel swirl, he would let me in. If I came empty-handed, I was more likely to secure an audience with the Queen of England than gain entry to Elliot's conference room. We had our own technical experts at the USAWMD, but everyone knew Elliot was better.

But I have no Elliot now. The closest thing I have is Leonard the pot-smoking barista at the Java Luv. I lean back in the desk chair and stretch my arms above my head, kind of wishing Will hadn't convinced me that aluminum-containing deodorant was going to kill me and possibly poison all the groundwater in California. I put my arms back down. Theo reappears in the doorway.

"Are you done yet?" he whines. "I am *soooo* bored."

"Do you even know what 'bored' means?" I ask. Bored is riding on a Nepali bus full of angry roosters and burning incense for fifteen hours and covering barely one hundred kilometers in that time. That's bored.

"No. Yes. It means that you won't play."

"Okay," I relent. "I'll play." Perhaps a round of *Star Wars* or BIONICLE or NERF guns will help distract me.

I push Theo out of the office and toward the stairs and again a whiff of hibiscus floats up from his hair. I really have to get this kid a different shampoo. I'm not sure how much more I can take because here my mind goes once more, right back to Nepal.

On my hard mattress at the Hotel Kathmandu, Ayushi continued to play with my hair and hum a tune that sounded like an off-key "Star-Spangled Banner."

Suddenly, she stopped singing and stared at me with her huge brown eyes.

"You should go now," she said.

The hotel was two stories high, but they were uneven stories, and the side of the building my room happened to be on was a little lower than a normal second story would be. Which was a good thing because I was about to jump out the window.

"Ayushi, thank you," I said, clutching her face between my hands and kissing the top of her head. "I owe you one." She gave me a smile and a gentle curtsy, sitting back down on my bed to watch what would happen next. A weird little kid but as long as she was on my side, I was just fine with that. I pulled on my backpack, thinking for a second how nice a shower would have been, and climbed up on the windowsill. The cheap wood splintered under my shoes as I positioned myself to take the leap. Down below was nothing but dirt. Not even a shrub to cushion my fall. Oh, well. Broken was better than dead.

I hit the ground, not altogether gracefully, and rolled in an attempt to absorb the impact, stopping only when I bumped into a pair of worn flip-flops attached to a pair of legs belonging to Min, my tour guide.

"Come on," he whispered, pulling me to my feet. I groaned and began to sink back toward the ground.

"Let's go," he said again, tugging at my shirt. "This is not the time for slacking."

"Are you accusing me of being a slacker?" I asked, my mouth full of dust, my body feeling great sympathy for the street in Pamplona after the running of the bulls. Min gave me a disgusted look and more or less dragged me to his waiting car. There, I gamely climbed into the backseat of the disintegrating Toyota, thinking I should probably figure out which side Min was on before we went very far.

"Who are they?" I asked. "The guys back at the hotel?"

"They work for the king. Secret police. But they are more like a goon squad, if you ask me."

Min turned to face me, driving with one hand and no eyes on the road.

"I was determining a plan to come in and get you when you jumped," he said.

Sure you were.

"Do you know why they want to kill you, my friend?"

The list of possible reasons was long but distinguished. "I don't know," I said, folding my feet up under me to keep them from being ripped off by the road flying by where the floor mats should have been. I'd only been in the country for about four hours and yet I'd totally lost control of things already. I wondered how much of this I could keep from Simon and not get caught. With my luck, he was videotaping the whole affair from a polite distance and smirking all the while.

"Well, you must have done something. But I am no friend of the new king. In my mind he is nothing more than a murderer. So I'll help you. For my country. For my true king."

"Thank you. Can you look at the road now?" I said. Min swiveled his head back around and faced the road.

"What is your name, friend?"

"Allison," I said, although I couldn't be 100 percent sure without checking my passport. As I stared out the window at the dust cloud being kicked up by the Toyota, I couldn't puzzle out how they knew I was coming. Later, after many more unexpected greeting parties in every corner of the world, I started to believe I was cursed. But in Kathmandu, it was still an isolated incident, something I could attribute to bad information or bad informants and not necessarily to my own personal cloud of bad karma.

"Where are we going?" I asked.

"To catch a plane to Lukla and start walking. You still want to go to Namche for your pictures?" Boy, things must have been tough in the tour guide business for him to willingly accept a client from hell, as I was turning out to be.

"Absolutely," I said. My statement was punctuated by a loud noise coming from the Toyota's rusted-out trunk, as if a tiny jackhammer were pounding away on the back of my seat.

"Pull over, Min," I shouted. "I think someone's in your trunk." Min slammed on the brakes and I went flying over the seats, landing right in his lap.

"Oh, my, Miss Allison. My apologies." The loud knocking sound continued. I untangled myself, jumped out of the car, and tried, with limited success, to pop the trunk.

"When was the last time you opened this?" I asked. Min shrugged.

"Never?" he said.

"Great."

"Try this way," he suggested. With that, he climbed into the backseat and pushed a fist through one of the gaping holes in the upholstery. A second later, from the hole he produced the slim, tan leg of a child.

"How did you get in here?" he roared, pulling the rest of Ayushi from the hole. "This is dangerous. You could have died."

Not to mention she would have had to move at the speed of light to get from my hotel room into the trunk of the car without notice.

Ayushi took a second to stand up and straighten out the now torn and filthy skirt of her uniform. She fixed her liquid eyes on us.

"I would rather be dead than stay with Kirin for one more minute," she said with a conviction I've not often heard since

then. Min and I looked at each other. It was hard to argue with
her but it didn't explain her apparent power to teleport herself
from one place to another undetected. I put my hands on my
hips in my best imitation of an irate mother and waited. Under
my gaze, Ayushi kicked the ground. A little cloud of dust
floated up between us.

"The drain pipe," she said quietly, "through the other window, in the back."

"And you didn't mention this to me because of . . . why?"
I asked, thinking I really could have done without jumping
out the second-story window. I dreaded the bruise I'd have
by nighttime.

"You didn't ask," she said, jutting her chin out in defiance.
True.

"This is ridiculous," Min interrupted. "We'll take her to
my cousin's wife's brother-in-law. She will be safe there."

Ayushi pulled on my shirt.

"You owe me one," she said, as if I needed reminding.

My luck was now officially classified as awful. Where was
my sprinkling of fairy dust when I needed it? Hung up in customs? I was not suited to mind a child. In fact, keeping a cactus
alive was a stretch for me. But what she said was true. I owed
her for saving my life. And in my business, that wasn't something to be taken lightly.

"Listen," I said, kicking the dirt. "Min's cousin is the saf-
est place for you to be. Being with me isn't always that safe."
What an understatement. I hoped she was old enough to read
between the lines.

Ayushi crossed her arms and glared at me.

"I'm coming with you," she said. "If you leave me, I'll
follow you."

She was beginning to remind me of a baby duck that accidentally imprints on a fox or some other totally inappropriate animal. Min glanced at his watch, tapping his foot in case I missed his point.

"Okay," I said finally. "She comes with us."

"This will make things complicated, Miss Allison," Min said, already looking tired.

"If you haven't noticed," I said, "things are already complicated." Simon was going to kill me or, at the very least, send me to count snowflakes in Mongolia for six months.

Back at the airport, we headed toward a plane I think was actually a 1973 VW minibus with wings. The pilot heaved plastic chairs and irrigation tubing out onto the runway to make room for our bodies. When he was done, he shook each of our hands enthusiastically and welcomed us aboard.

"Nice weather for flying," the pilot said. "No rocks in the clouds today."

Oh, dear. I recited what I remembered of the Lord's Prayer, which was not a whole lot, and closed my eyes. The plane lurched and sputtered and eventually was airborne. All around us were steep hills covered in dense green foliage. Steel gray rivers cut their way through, pulled by gravity to an unknown sea. In a matter of minutes, we appeared to be crashing right into the side of a mountain.

"You're hurting me," Ayushi said, as I grabbed her arm in a terrific imitation of panic. "It's just the runway."

"Sorry," I whispered.

"You can open your eyes now," she said. "We're on the ground."

"Right. I was just resting."

"Okay," she said, "if you say so."

"What?" I said, assuming the nonchalance of a cat that has just fallen flat on her face.

Ayushi laughed and her small round face lit up as if she held the warmth of the sun inside her. I felt my heart constrict just the tiniest bit. She was not a cactus. Maybe I could save her.

"You were scared. You were scared," she sang, dancing between Min and me. The skirt from her school uniform twirled with a joy that seemed alien to this dark, dreary place.

As far as the eye could see, in every direction, there was nothing but mud. A few yards from the landing strip was a row of rudimentary houses, haphazardly constructed and leaning precariously on one another for support. A foul stench belched from their chimneys.

"Yak dung," Min said, turning up his nose. "No wood left to burn up here." I nodded as if it were a perfectly ordinary thing to burn yak shit for fuel and followed Min into the five-inch-deep mud. It was aggressive mud, grabbing onto my boots and requiring a Herculean effort for each step forward. Ayushi clung to my neck, baby koala style, and I said a silent thank you that she was small for her age. During my time with the Agency, I'd have many good ideas. Bringing a child into this environment was not one of them.

10

Theo dances around the kitchen. His shiny silver shin guards are strapped to his forearms, part of an imaginary superhero outfit that includes a baby-blanket cape and a child-sized San Francisco Giants batting helmet. He speaks Kung Fu, sounding exactly as he might if he were being strangled. I try to pack a bag with enough snacks to cover the morning, which isn't as easy as one might think.

"Cheese sticks?" I ask.

"Blah. Cheese sticks make me sick." An Academy Award–winning fake barfing scene follows.

"Stop that right now," I say. "And cheese sticks do not make you sick."

"Yes, they do. I'm allergic."

"No, you're not."

"Well, Zach is, at school. He turns funny colors and has to stick himself with a pen. Allergic to cheese sticks and broccoli."

"Just because you don't like something doesn't mean you are allergic to it. It's okay not to like every food. But if you don't even give them a try, how will you know?"

"Mom, I hate cheese sticks."

Okay. No cheese sticks. For some reason, this makes me

mad at Will. He shouldn't be spending his weekend negotiating the price of windmills but rather here negotiating about
cheese sticks and water bottles. And while he's doing that, I
can be . . . doing something else. Like figuring out who has
Gray and coming up with a daring yet responsible plan for getting him back, perhaps? No, no, no! Not that. Again, I tell the
nagging voice of my instinct to shut up and go away. I'm just an
ordinary person taking her normal kid to the regularly scheduled Saturday morning soccer game. It's all very mundane and
routine. But the effort required to make myself believe I don't
care is exhausting.

"Let's go, Mom," Theo says. "We're going to be late and
it's all your fault."

"You didn't just say that to me, did you?"

"What?"

"Oh, never mind. I guess it's time," I say, rolling up my
sleeves. "Assume the position."

Theo plops down on the floor in front of me and sticks
both legs straight up in the air like a cartoon character that just
keeled over dead. I take a shin guard and strap it to his leg. It's
too big and covers him from ankle to knee. I wrap the extra-
long Velcro straps around and around his skinny calf until
he resembles a modern-day gladiator, albeit a very small one. I
move on to the size XXS soccer socks, which are at least twenty-
five feet long. I roll them up as if I am preparing to put a pair of
panty hose on the Jolly Green Giant.

"Keep your toes tight," I say. "Don't bend your foot." Even
after all this time, Theo has no idea what that means and starts
waving his foot around in the air, a sail that has broken free in
the wind. I grab it and go in for the kill. The sock gets hung up
on the first set of shin guard straps.

"That hurts," Theo wails. "You're pulling too hard."

"I know," I say. "I'm sorry. Just another second here and I'll be done." I put his flat foot against my thigh and give the sock a quick tug. With that, my whole child goes skidding across the kitchen floor.

"Mom, what are you doing?"

"Almost home," I tell him, breaking out in a sweat.

The sock bunches up at his knee. I pull out all the wrinkles and fold it over and over again on itself to get it to the proper length. Theo's leg now suffers from a bad case of soccer-sock elephantiasis. We repeat the process on the other side and jam both feet into cleats that fit very nicely with normal socks but are almost impossible to get on with the soccer socks. And this is what we do for fun.

"Okay," I say as cheerfully as I can manage. "We are good to go!"

We climb into the car and I wait while Theo insists on buckling himself in.

"I can do it," he says, pulling out about fifteen yards of seat belt. "I need slack."

"Looks like you have some," I say. The minutes pass.

"I can't do it," he moans. "I hate this car. Get a better car, Mom." It's not exactly the car's fault but I agree with the sentiment.

A quick word about the car. I used to have a cool car. It was fast and sleek and shamelessly chugged gasoline like a linebacker chugs Gatorade. But one day I opened my garage and found that my cool car had been replaced by a fuel-efficient tin can. I have many names for the tin can, none of which are polite, but its given name is Prius.

"Don't worry, honey," I say. "Mommy has her eye on a

Tesla, a cherry red one, that even Daddy can love." Theo has no clue what a Tesla is but the very word makes him smile.

At the soccer field, I wedge my eco-car into a tiny parking spot. It's so tiny, in fact, that Theo has to climb over me in the front seat and squeeze out a very thin sliver of open door. I give him a quick shove with the heel of my hand to make sure he doesn't spend the remainder of his childhood wedged here between the outside world and me.

"Mom! My arm." He shoots me a wounded look and rubs his elbow.

"Sorry, kiddo," I say, trying to extract myself, "city parking." I suck in my stomach and attempt to push my too big body through the narrow space. My jeans catch on the door latch and rip clean across the thigh. I couldn't have cut a straighter line with a pair of scissors. A patch of denim that used to be attached to my pants dangles from the latch.

"Great," I say, but Theo's out of earshot, dashing toward his team, already assembled on the grass.

Any sun we had was left behind in our neighborhood. This field, closer to the ocean, is shrouded in a cold, damp fog. I zip my fleece jacket up to my chin and think about how quickly I would trade my Prius for a cup of hot coffee.

On the other side of the field, Avery, my best mom friend, waves to me. Her daughter Sophie, wearing pink cleats, pink socks, and a pink bow in her hair, runs toward Theo. I experience a sudden weird wave of love for her unapologetic girliness.

I sit down next to Avery on her blanket. Avery is the kind of woman who remembers things like a blanket and a thermos full of hot coffee and mittens, and she most certainly is not wearing jeans with a huge gaping hole in the thigh. If she weren't so nice, I wouldn't like her at all.

"How many more games are we going to be forced to endure in the name of teaching our children to be team players?" I ask.

"Four," she replies without even a moment of hesitation. See? She's that kind of mom, the one all the rest of the moms want to be, the one who remembers things. A few minutes later, Sam joins us on the blanket. It's not a big blanket but Sam is a grandfather, so the chances of him remembering a blanket and coffee are slim to none.

"Have you guys made any kindergarten decisions?" he asks as he settles in next to me. "Matt and Emily want to know." We have never met Carter's parents. They don't come to soccer games or yoga classes or the playground. Apparently they work and meet their son for the occasional late dinner. "Personally, I don't know what the big deal is but Emily's going a little crazy over it. What happened to your pants?"

"I don't want to talk about it," I say.

"Private," says Avery, covering the hole in my pants with Sophie's jacket. "I'm afraid of the public school lottery. I've never won anything in my life so I'll probably get a lousy lottery number and there goes Sophie's chance at a top-rated public school. I'd rather take my chances on applications I can actually influence." She pats the jacket in my lap as if to say, great, now that giant hole in your jeans is all taken care of.

"You aren't going to resort to bribery?" I ask, only half kidding.

"No, of course not," Avery says, "but if they need an extra wing for their library, I might consider a donation."

I laugh. True colors are often revealed in times of great stress.

"Who cares?" Sam says, obviously exasperated by the topic. "It's kindergarten, ladies. It doesn't matter that much."

Avery and I look at him as if he were a tried and convicted traitor.

"It matters," I say.

"It does," Avery agrees. "Do you want Carter to be playing catch-up in junior high because he didn't go to a good elementary school?"

Interesting. I was thinking more along the lines of it mattering because I want the school where my son is least likely to be snatched by someone I pissed off in Afghanistan ten years ago. But Avery's point is a good one, too.

A whistle blows and eight little kids in baggy uniforms huddle around their coach, who is passing on instructions not a single one of them will remember thirty seconds from now. Occasionally, these soccer games come to a screeching halt because a lone butterfly will flit across the field. All it takes is one player to spy the butterfly and off goes the team, en masse, chasing after the poor thing with a focus we thought they lacked.

"You're both crazy," Sam says. "My daughter-in-law is crazy. This city is crazy. And if we keep it up, all these kids are going to grow up crazy."

"Oh, Sam," says Avery, "don't be so cynical. These kids are great." She gives him an affectionate punch in the arm. Avery will love you even if you insult her to her face while sitting on her blanket drinking her coffee. I'd like to be more like that. But who am I kidding? I'm not even a little like that.

Theo's team, in sky blue jerseys, races down the field

looking as if they know what they're doing. The other team, dressed in red, does exactly the same thing. Somewhere in the middle they pass each other and just keep on going. The ball goes missing and one player sits down on top of the goal. Someone is crying. Another kid is taking off his shirt because it's itchy. Another child is pretending to be a robot.

Out of the corner of my eye, I see a bright yellow Porsche pull into the crowded parking lot, a fresh lemon in a bowl of moldy fruit. Sam lets out a slow whistle.

"Nice ride," he says.

"It's yellow," I say. "Who buys a yellow car?"

The passenger door opens and a tall man in a custom-made black suit unfolds himself to standing. In his left ear, a wireless headset blinks a radiant blue, off and on and off and on, lending him an odd resemblance to a Borg. He puts one delicate Italian leather shoe onto the fog-damp grass and I'm sure I see a small shiver run the length of him.

"Suit on a Saturday? Lawyer?" Avery suggests.

"No question," Sam answers. "And not the nice Save the Whales kind."

The man in the expensive suit makes his way over to the sidelines of the abbreviated field, not acknowledging a soul, and takes up a position about four feet from our blanket. There he stands with a slightly hostile look on his clean-shaven face. I sneak a quick peek at his hands. Manicured and perfect. I decide I hate him and that I'd better keep a close eye on him.

"Madeleine," he barks suddenly, his voice deep and harsh. Next to me, Avery jumps. "Faster. The point is to kick the ball, not have a conversation with it." He immediately turns his attention back to his phone, thumbs flying.

Out on the field, a little girl with two spiky brown ponytails sticking straight out of her head comes to a dead stop. She turns slowly toward the voice and when she sees the man she doesn't smile. In fact, I would swear she shrinks an inch right there in front of us. A middle-aged Hispanic woman comes running up to him.

"Mr. Colby, you're here. She is playing good. You'll see." She keeps her head down as if preparing for the verbal blow sure to be coming her way.

Mr. Colby turns his gaze on her and his eyes remind me of a shark, empty and dark.

"Are you her coach? Her personal trainer? No? You're just the nanny." He says "nanny" with a sneer and turns his attention back toward the phone. The woman, head still down, backs away.

By now, the kids are having a jolly time kicking each other in the shins and tripping over cleats that are purposefully two sizes too big.

"Madeleine!" Mr. Colby gestures toward her with the phone. "Pay attention! Get up! Are you useless? God, you're worse than your mother."

And there it is, that small twitch in the corner of my eye. It's the same twitch that shows up when Theo won't put on his shoes or eat breakfast or insists on taking all the forks out of the drawer and relocating them to the living room because he's playing "sorting," whatever that is. I rest two fingers gently on my eyelid and try to stop the frantic motion. But Colby won't quit.

"You're such a girl! Madeleine, kick the ball! Don't be so weak!"

Everyone stares at him but no one says anything. On the field, Madeleine is about to go fetal.

"Excuse me," I say, not bothering to get up off the blanket. "Can you maybe stop shouting? I think it's distracting the kids."

Mr. Colby looks down at me as if I am nothing more than a cockroach that just happened to crawl over his fine Italian loafer.

"And why would I care what you think?" he asks, a tight look on his sharp thin face.

The move itself is easy enough if you're positioned properly. It's actually one Simon Still taught me on a slow day down in the Underground. We were in the circular center of our offices where there was no furniture and an inch of industrial gray carpeting covered in twenty years of dirt because no one was allowed down there to clean. One minute I was walking beside him and the next I was flat on my back, examining the ceiling tiles.

"What the hell?" I wheezed, the air all but gone from my lungs. Simon stood over me.

"When someone isn't paying attention, that's when you take them to the ground. As you can see."

"Thanks for sharing that," I said, not moving. The world spun in fast, lopsided circles. "Maybe next time you could send a memo?"

"Get up, Sally," he commanded. I stood, my arms straight out for balance. As soon as I was upright, Simon stuck his left leg between mine and pulled. As I was going down, he fired his forearm into my throat. And there I was, back on the floor again.

"Okay," I sputtered. "I get it. If you do that again, I'll murder you in your sleep."

"Ha," he laughed, "my bedroom is booby trapped in so

many ways even I sometimes sleep on the couch." I stayed right
there flat on the ground until another a man I'd never seen before came wandering by.

"What's wrong with you, Sally?" this stranger asked, peering down on me with abstract concern, as if I were a rare species
on the verge of extinction. I groaned and a look of understanding flashed across the guy's face. "Simon got you with the ol'
scissor, didn't he? Can't believe you fell for that shit." Then he
stepped over me and vanished into an open office.

I don't even need to stand up. From my position on the blanket,
I simply shoot one of my legs out, lodge it between his, and jerk
it forward. Mr. Colby goes down hard. A small scream escapes
from his thin lips, the kind of scream he'll be embarrassed
about when he tries to recreate events later on in his head. His
headset bounces away into the wet grass, where it continues to
blink on and off as though nothing has happened. Play on the
field stops and several of the parents come rushing over.

Colby is moaning now, either from shock or humiliation.
It's hard to say which.

"I'm a doctor," says one of the parents. Of course she is.
This is San Francisco.

"He just collapsed," I say, innocently. "Maybe a heart attack?"

With the words heart attack, at least ten people pull out
their cell phones and start dialing 9-1-1. Colby continues to
gasp for air. I clutch his hand tightly in my own, the perfect
picture of concern. He looks at me with frightened eyes.

"Don't worry," I say. "An ambulance is on the way. You'll
be fine."

"You. You," he squeaks. "You can't get away . . ."

I lean in closer so my lips brush the soft flesh of his ear. "I asked you nicely to stop shouting," I whisper. "Next time I might break your neck."

He starts to gurgle something. I sit back up. "Shhhh," I say. "Better to be quiet now." Colby closes his eyes, probably wondering how a guy who drives a yellow Porsche can get beat up by a girl.

Moments later, two EMTs load Mr. Colby onto a stretcher and cart him off to the waiting ambulance. Madeleine, still on the field, wears a strange little smile as she watches her father go. She doesn't make any move to follow him. The kids resume the madness of the game.

"What a jerk, but poor guy," Avery says. "It was nice you held his hand, Lucy. I bet that helped."

"I hope so," I say. Sam gives me a curious smile.

"That car was really over the top," he says.

I nod in agreement. "Definitely couldn't fit a booster seat in that sucker."

"Well, you know how it is," Sam says, "you can't choose your family. At least she didn't inherit his beady little eyes. You see those eyes? That would have been awful. To have him as a father and get stuck with those beady little eyes too."

Sam's casual words rain down on me. It's all in the eyes. It always is. They tell you everything you need to know. Is the person going to pull the trigger or is he bluffing? Does he love you or are you merely today's entertainment? The eyes can't hide the truth.

Out on the field, a little girl scores a goal. There is shouting and clapping but I'm barely aware of it. Although no one can tell, I'm slowly suffocating to death right here in front of the soccer moms and dads, in front of my friends, in front of the world. Somewhere out there, Blackford laughs and laughs. The whistle blows, ending the game, and the kids come running over.

"We won!" Theo shouts. "Did you see my goal?" He jumps up and down, his eyes full of the thrill of victory and the promise of more to come. They're the same eyes that look out at me from the faded Polaroid. They're the reason I cannot let go of Gray's kidnapping even when doing just that is the obvious choice. They are Charles Gray's eyes. Like a flower on a one-hundred-degree day, I feel myself wilt.

Charles Gray is my father.

II

Until I was eight years old, I lived on a farm in upstate New York with a woman and a man I called Mom and Dad. I had no memory of not happily being with them on the farm with the dogs and the fields and the cold dark winters. That parts of my life sat at odd angles to the lives of normal eight-year-olds was irrelevant because I was too young to have any perspective.

Once when I was in the third grade, my teacher, a young woman fresh out of school, caught me daydreaming and called on me to answer a question about the Civil War. I gave what I thought was a perfectly acceptable answer and didn't understand why she and all of my classmates stared at me as if I had been caught running naked through the hallways.

In reality, naked would've been a fine alternative. It took about five seconds for me to realize I had answered the question well enough but I had done so in Russian. I couldn't explain why I could speak fluent Russian when I had never even met anyone from Russia. Neither could I explain how all of my scariest dreams happened in Russian. So I just sat there, my cheeks glowing crimson, and prayed for time to speed up.

Eventually the class moved on but I never forgot that feeling. I was a farm kid like all the other farm kids, wasn't I? But from the looks on my classmates' faces, the answer to that question was clearly no. I was something else, something "other." I was not like them.

On the night my parents died in a car crash on an icy stretch of the New York Turnpike, a state trooper arrived at the door of our farmhouse, hat in hand, to deliver the news. It was cold and dark outside and while he stood on the porch and spoke, all I could think was how the fat snowflakes looked like dandruff on the trooper's exposed head. My babysitter cried and cried, holding me, smoothing my hair, telling me it would all be okay. But I knew those were just words and meaningless, no matter what language I said them in. The next day my mother's sister and husband, who I had never met before, came and took me to live with them in Vermont and there I stayed until college.

An ordinary person might question the strangeness of these events but I didn't because I remembered that moment in the third grade. Outsiders were not afforded the same protections as those who belonged.

That sense of not belonging, of looking in the window but never entering the room, made me a good spy. I could be whoever I needed to be. If I disappeared in Nigeria for ten months at a time, no one would come looking for me. The assumption was I was doing my job. I was obligated only to my country and that somehow managed not to be too personal.

After Theo was born, everything changed. I found myself searching his face for a trace of the people I knew as my parents, hoping for evidence that maybe everything was exactly as it had seemed back then and that my feelings of being on the outside looking in were no more than the product of an overactive imagination.

Theo's blond hair and wide grin come directly from his father, the shape of his eyes from me. It's also possible I'm responsible for his desire to take inappropriate risks but I'm not willing to cop to that quite yet. His long fingers came from William II and his fashion sense from Rose Marie. The kid is a road map of those who have come before him and the map does not include the woman I remember swabbing my forehead when I had a fever or the man who read me storybooks at bedtime. The need to know who is responsible for my ugly feet and the slope of Theo's nose grows with each passing day. Yes, I know it's possible that Theo's nose is all his own, but in my experience, nothing stands in isolation. Everything is connected, even if that connection is fragile.

The one time I met Gray at the USAWMD, he sat in his office behind an enormous oak desk, examining me as if I were something necessary but inconvenient. He wanted to know about me only in so much as it related to Blackford. Maybe Gray really wanted a boy. Maybe he hated my mother. Maybe I was a mistake. Or maybe I was just not good enough for him to even consider.

But in the end, none of that matters. I can't let him die. He's the only one who can tell me where I come from because he was there, on that train, wearing the scratchy overcoat, taking me away from where it all began.

12

On the way home from the soccer game, I make a detour to the Java Luv. Theo's excited because it means chocolate milk for him and a chance to play with the burning incense, which Leonard sincerely believes hides the smell of other burning things.

He stands behind the counter, rearranging the muffins as if he's in a trance.

"Hi, Leonard," I say. He jumps. I feel like everything is an out-of-body experience. I see myself in the coffee shop, feel Theo's hand in mine, and yet I'm floating on the ceiling. This whole situation seems enormously unfair for a Saturday morning. Saturday mornings are made for relaxing, taking a slow stroll to the bagel shop, and buying unidentifiable produce at the farmer's market. They are not made for playing genealogical roulette as I seem to have been doing.

"Sorry, Lucy," Leonard says. "I was thinking about the war in Afghanistan. I think I have the solution."

"That's great, Leonard. Maybe you should e-mail the White House."

He considers this briefly.

"Nah," he says. "Too busy." And I think Leonard really believes that. I worry about his future.

Theo grabs a chocolate milk from the cooler and sits down on the low window seat next to the incense burner.

"What are you doing here on a Saturday anyway, Lucy?" Leonard asks.

I didn't intend to be here. I intended to drive straight home after the soccer game and lock myself in the closet until I regained my equilibrium and could think rationally. And yet here I am, pulled into the fray by the singular idea that Charles Gray cannot die and the accompanying belief that I might be the only one who can save him.

"I could ask you the same question," I say.

"Please don't," Leonard says. "Because I really have no idea why I'm here."

"So, Leonard," I say, trying to get to the point before the day is over, "I need something."

"Espresso?"

"Not exactly." In his eyes I can see him slowly processing my request.

"Oh," he says. "*Oh*. I didn't think you were the kind. So how much do you want? It's great stuff, from up north."

"Not drugs, Leonard," I say. "Don't you know what drugs do to your brain?" He looks at me blankly. See? "I need a black hat."

"Well, there's that boutique down on Twenty-fourth Street that's nice," he says.

"Leonard, look at me. A black hat."

Finally, understanding registers on his face.

"Why?" he asks in all sincerity.

"You're not supposed to ask me why," I say.

"Wow, Lucy. I'm learning so much about you today. It's really cool."

"Stay focused, Leonard. Do you know anyone?" I know he does. He runs in those circles. I can tell. Later, Leonard and all of his friends will end up either in jail or voting Republican. It's inevitable.

"Yes," he says after a pause. "She's kind of weird and I think she might live in her car. But she's got a good reputation. You know, in those circles. Plus, she wears a Rolex."

She could live in a tree house and wear Big Ben on her wrist for all I care as long as she'll do anything for money. "Call her," I say.

"Okay," Leonard says. "Lucy, what happened to your pants? You look homeless."

I roll my eyes. "Make the call, Leonard."

Within minutes, Theo and I are headed to an abandoned warehouse in the South of Market neighborhood to meet a woman named Sheila. This should teach Will to work on a Saturday. If he were with us and not at a meeting with a bunch of granola-crunching, Birkenstock-wearing, save-the-rainforest types, I wouldn't be forced to take our five-year-old son along with me while I commit what is indisputably a crime.

But before you get too upset over that, let me tell you a thing or two about computer hackers. They are, by and large, antisocial, unwashed, and exceptionally smart. They assume anyone falling outside of their immediate shadowy circle of computer gangsters is an idiot and in many cases they're right. But hackers aren't violent. In fact, most are downright squeamish. It might be because they're malnourished from consuming nothing but Starbucks Frappuccinos and weak from a lack of vitamin D because they never go outside. A swift karate chop, Theo style, would be enough to send them scurrying under the bed.

We park next to a pile of broken car-window glass on a deserted side street. I have no doubt the building was right in the middle of a condo conversion when the market collapsed a few years ago. There's yellow security tape blocking off the area where the front steps should be. Someone has stacked plastic milk crates to one side. I climb up and hoist Theo over the yellow tape and onto the landing.

"Doesn't the tape mean you can't go in?" Theo asks.

"Well, sometimes it's more of a suggestion," I say, "something to consider when you're making a decision."

I wonder at what point in Theo's teenage years this statement will come back to haunt me. "I considered the illegality of the drugs, Mom," he will say, "but decided to take them anyway." But for now, Theo nods thoughtfully.

"That's nice, Mommy," he says, indicating he has no idea what I'm talking about.

The building's front door is open, an empty hole where one would normally find the knob and lock. Inside sit mildewing boxes of tile, parts of light fixtures, and unopened paint cans. A thick layer of dust covers everything, as if the workers went off to lunch one day and just never came back.

We head to the second floor as instructed and there we find Sheila, dancing alone to one of Phish's extended jams. Two tiny speakers are attached to her iPod and the music echoes through the unfinished warehouse. From the ceiling dangle frayed utility cables and ducts to nowhere. Construction debris is piled all around in haphazard little mounds.

Sheila wears a long peasant skirt so colorful it appears she is being trailed by a lovelorn peacock. A dark blue, slightly grungy tank top is all that stands between her and the roughly fifty-five degrees of the room. Around her neck hangs a giant rusty peace symbol on a leather cord. Her dreadlocked hair is of an indeterminate color and I half expect a swarm of insects to come flying out of it at any moment. The only thing Sheila lacks is a burning joint between her lips. She doesn't look like a hacker. But I don't look like I can kill a grown man with a single strategic punch in the chest, so who am I to judge?

"You Lucy?" she asks, snapping a red rubber band at her wrist. The Southern accent she's trying to kill is not quite dead yet.

I nod. She doesn't acknowledge Theo at all.

"Why can't we live in one of these?" Theo asks, wide-eyed. "I could scooter in here!" He starts racing up and down the length of the warehouse, jumping over the piles of debris and dodging discarded panels of sheetrock.

"Theo," I bark. "No running. Nails on the floor."

"Aw, Mom, you're no fun."

I know that. Everyone knows that.

"Is it okay for him to look around?" I ask Sheila.

She shrugs. "Don't care. None of this shit is mine. Leonard vouched for you and we fuck, so I guess that's gotta count for something. What do you need?"

Normally the idea of Leonard having sex would be so disturbing I'd need a moment or two to recover. But not now. What I'm about to do is wrong on many levels but it's clear that Righteous Liberty asking for me was no fluke. And that means I need to know who Richard Yoder is. I'm not the kind of girl who likes to sit in the dark.

"There's a secure government network," I say. "I want in."

She snaps the rubber band.

"Sure. Two thousand dollars. Small bills. Up front."

Let me acknowledge up front that most moms don't walk around with two thousand dollars in small bills stuffed in their handbags and, normally, neither do I. But this morning, anticipating this little detour, I made a pit stop in the back of my closet, behind a bin of maternity clothes, where there's a small, nondescript box that's actually a safe. By sticking the safe behind the maternity clothes, I virtually guaranteed that Will will never find it. He claims he's still trying to forget about those elastic pants that came up to my armpits.

Inside this safe is ten thousand dollars in U.S. currency, a British passport that, if I tried to use it, would probably land me in a black site prison somewhere undesirable, and four stolen, disposable cell phones that I prefer not to discuss in too much detail. Some parts of the spy life are like the glitter in the floor mats of my car; no matter how much I vacuum, the glitter is not going away.

As soon as I hand Sheila the money, I can officially consider myself a rogue agent of the USAWMD. The thought sends a shiver down my spine and I'm not sure if it's the result of joy or horror. Either way, I am skating on thin ice.

"Fine," I say, digging into my bag for the pile of money. "Can you do it fast?"

She snorts. I have inadvertently insulted her professionalism.

"What's the name of the place?" she asks.

I hand her a piece of paper with United States Agency for Weapons of Mass Destruction written on it. She smiles.

"Cool. Never done them before. When I'm in, I'll text you a password. It will come from a random phone number. You will gain access but only once so don't fuck up and sign out until you're done."

"Great," I say, as if we are going to be fast friends. "Is this where you usually are, if I need to find you again?"

Slowly, she surveys the abandoned warehouse as if she has never seen it before.

"No," she says. "We're done now." She points to the exit.

Theo and I roll in our door around 2:00. His little belly bulges with three slices of pizza and what has to be a liter of lemonade, the reward for being such a good boy while Mommy indulged her criminal alter ego.

"I'm so full," he moans, lying on the floor spread-eagled. During lunch, my cell phone chirped and a message containing a password appeared. In between bites, I memorized it, deleted it, and immediately began plotting on how to come up with ten minutes alone in front of a computer. Although I hate to resort to bribery, I'm not above it. I'm about to suggest an episode of *Go, Diego, Go!* to my beached whale of a son when Will comes out of the kitchen.

"You're home," I say, startled. Rogue agents are not supposed to be caught off guard.

"Yup. All done," he says.

"I'm stuffed," Theo says, rolling into Will's legs.

"What happened to him?"

"Pizza." And by the way, my father is not actually my father but someone else entirely and most definitely not dead. At least not yet.

"Lucy, are you okay? You look funny."

He could not have served it up better if I'd ordered in advance.

"I don't know," I say. "I'm feeling a little off today. Maybe something I ate? Do you mind if I go and lie down for a bit?"

"No. Go. Theo, do you want to come to the hardware store with me?"

I don't hear the end of the conversation because, moving very fast for a sick person, I'm already upstairs planted in front of the computer. There's a small smile plastered on my face. This isn't supposed to be fun so why the stupid grin? I'll tell you why. There's no good way to twelve-step yourself out of an adrenaline addiction. I don't deserve to call myself a rogue agent. Rogue agents are way cooler than I am.

13

The USAWMD has no idea that at 2:15 on Saturday they get hacked. As much as I hate to admit it, I feel a small thrill as I waltz right through their security and belly up to the information bar. Scrolling through a number of menus that to the outsider would appear to be just this side of word salad, I search for the trail that will lead me to Richard Yoder. It takes a few minutes but soon enough I stumble on his file. It's written in code but it's a code I wrote in for nine years and I remember it as well as my own name. Okay, maybe that's not the best example, but you get the idea.

Richard Yoder is younger than me by a decade or more but from his photograph he doesn't look it. He's tired and drawn, sporting the beginnings of a beard. Dark-hooded eyes complete his expression of utter resignation, as if he just missed the last bus for joy and happiness.

I'm unprepared for what I read next. According to the file, it appears that Yoder's last employer was none other than Chemical Claude. I snap the pencil I'm holding in my right hand in two.

"Why Chemical Claude?" I ask the computer. I would take anyone over Chemical Claude, even Blackford in a pinch. The fact that Chemical Claude is even tangentially involved here makes the hairs on the back of my neck stand on end.

The story is they meet in Sudan when Richard Yoder is a child and Chemical Claude is selling weapons to interested warlords. One night, while driving back to his lodgings, a drunk Chemical Claude's Land Cruiser rams a small pickup truck and sends it careening over a cliff. In that truck, engulfed in flames at the bottom of a ravine, are Yoder's parents. They are fresh-faced missionaries from the United States, but now they're dead. Claude feels something unusual in his gut that might be guilt and takes the boy under his wing. He uses the young Yoder to run messages for him, as communication networks in Sudan are notoriously unreliable, technology's greatest enemy being sand. Yoder turns out to be well suited to the task. Even at age five, he can remember all the details of a message without having to write anything down. It saves his life a few times as he appears to be nothing more than a young boy out for some mischief.

Chemical Claude grows oddly fond of Yoder, becoming a father figure to the boy as he grows up. As fathers go, he's not so bad, keeping Yoder in pretty girls, fast cars, and expensive champagne flown in from France. All Claude expects in return is loyalty. And Yoder, now a teenager, tries hard not to let him down. But when he's alone, he fantasizes about attending architecture school at Cornell or MIT and traveling to Dubai to build towers that touch the sky. He carries a worn copy of *Architectural Digest* around with him wherever he goes.

Occasionally, Claude will catch Yoder wandering the halls of the château in France or the villa in Spain, a tormented look on his face. What more could this boy of no means and humble family want? Chemical Claude finds the whole tortured soul act rather annoying.

Things proceed more or less as usual until one night while

soaking in a hot tub full of naked girls, Yoder decides that if he just had something to bargain with he might be able to negotiate his way out of this life and into another. It would need to be something so valuable that Chemical Claude would do anything to secure its return.

Now, the casual observer might wonder why Yoder didn't decide on a more direct approach, perhaps simply asking Chemical Claude how much he would mind if the young man took off for the states to attend college, or something along those lines But Claude's answer to such a request would, more likely than not, be a bullet between the eyes and an order to remove the body from his sight. Chemical Claude does not take perceived treachery lightly.

Yoder's half-formed plan has "bad idea" written all over it but he wears the Teflon of youth. He actually thinks he can pull it off.

In the world of Chemical Claude, power comes in many forms but the most obvious one to Yoder is the little black notebook Claude carries with him everywhere he goes and never lets anyone see. Rumor has it Claude sleeps with the book in one hand and an Uzi pistol in the other. When Yoder finally works up the nerve to ask Chemical Claude what's in the little black notebook, he's met with reproach.

"When it's time," Claude says cryptically, "the whole world will know." And there Yoder was, hoping for a little more detail.

At this point, the USAWMD report indicates a conflict between sources. One source swears Yoder stole the notebook and hid it at an undisclosed location; another one swears that, although he tried, he never got his hands on it. And yet a third claims that during the wedding of Chemical Claude's dead wife's niece, while guarding the bathroom door to insure his boss could take a poop in relative safety, Yoder found himself holding Chemical Claude's dinner jacket, the black book winking at him from the breast pocket. Stepping back so as to be out of view of Chemical Claude while he sat on the toilet, Yoder had a full four minutes with the notebook before the sound of flushing startled him back to reality and he quickly returned the book to its place in the jacket pocket.

But no one knows what actually occurred as no source was willing to back down. Sources can be cranky that way.

What happens next is the result of poor planning or sheer idiocy, depending on how you choose to look at it. Yoder manages to recruit a few of Claude's underlings to go along with his coup attempt by promising them riches beyond their wildest dreams. He knows he'll never be able to deliver on his promises, but he's sure all this will be in his rearview mirror by the time anyone realizes they've been had.

But it's important to remember that Chemical Claude did not climb to the top of the bad guy heap by having a weak spot. Upon discovering Yoder's betrayal, Chemical Claude flies into a fury the likes of which people have never witnessed before. His rage is boundless. Before Yoder's sad little crew of coconspirators can even launch their attack, they're all dead and Yoder himself is running for his life. It doesn't take long for Yoder to realize he has two choices, both highly unattractive.

But the man is the definition of desperate. He calls Simon Still.

"You're going to want to take this one, sir," says the agent on duty as Yoder is patched through to Simon's Washington home, where he is happily drinking Scotch and smoking illegal Cuban cigars.

"Got in a little over your head, did you?" Simon asks without preamble. "He'll hunt you until you're dead, you understand. There are no second chances with your mentor."

Whether Yoder has been running or is just having an anxiety attack, it takes him a minute to catch his breath and answer.

"How did you know?" he asks.

"I know many things," Simon says, gnawing on the cigar.

"I don't want to die," Yoder says.

"Well, no one *wants* to die," Simon says. He pauses to take a sip of Scotch, savoring the smoky flavor as it rolls back on his tongue. "Give me something. Out of goodwill. Show me you care."

"There's a bomb being transported as we speak," Yoder says without hesitation. "It's en route from Kazakhstan to Afghanistan."

"How?"

"Fake Army transport. The papers are flawless." Yoder sounds almost proud. He was, after all, in charge of the forgery. Simon doesn't appreciate his tone, so he brings him down a notch.

"I wouldn't say 'flawless,'" he says. "'Flawless' would mean your bomb was delivered safely to its buyers. Which it wasn't."

On the other end of the phone, Yoder is speechless. He begins to think making this call was a very bad idea.

For his part, Simon has always believed Source Number One to be right about Yoder and the notebook. This is mostly because Source Number One keeps Simon in those good Cuban cigars but of course no one would ever admit to such a bias. But there's a reason Yoder ended up talking to Simon and that's because Simon set it up to happen in just that way. Since escaping all those years ago (no, I never caught him), Chemical Claude has been running around causing chaos without a hall pass and, with Yoder in hand, Simon finally sees a way to take down Claude. And to make it hurt.

To do this properly, Simon needs to know what's in the little black book. His need borders on the irrational but that's not unusual. Agents go overboard in the pursuit of critical intelligence all the time. It's expected.

"Stay where you are," Simon tells Yoder. "If you're still alive in thirty minutes, we'll pick you up."

As Simon hangs up the phone, he thinks he hears Yoder crying.

It turns out Yoder has a lot more to cry about after spending a year at a black site prison in the Czech Republic, compliments of the United States of America. A layer of thin green moss covers the thick cement walls of his cell. The whole place smells of feet.

Down in its murky depths, Simon and Yoder spend many months talking about the little black book, after which time Yoder is more a wisp of smoke than a human being. A year of black site hospitality can do that to you.

But at the end of the year, Simon is forced to admit he might have been wrong about Yoder because no one could stand up to these enhanced interrogation methods and not confess. Often, people confessed to things they didn't actually do just to make it stop. But Yoder takes it all silently, continuing to claim he knows nothing of the little black book. His uselessness infuriates Simon. He hates wasting time.

Yoder ends up in the hands of HIDE, the USAWMD's version of witness protection. When he steps out of the prison and sees the sun again, he weeps.

Several weeks later, Richard Yoder is reborn as Ronald Smith. Ronald Smith cleans office buildings at night and is never late for work. He doesn't have close friends. Those with whom he shares the occasional sandwich would describe him as a quiet, nervous young man who generally keeps to himself. A woman he takes on a single date to the movies calls him haunted, old beyond his years.

Ronald Smith is a diligent worker for a kid barely out of his teens, seemingly content to push the floor-waxing machine up and down the hallways. He drives a used Chevy Malibu and lives in a slightly run-down house of his own with a green garage door. At night, the shadows from the streetlights make him nervous. The house sits on the corner of Judah and Twenty-eighth Avenue in the fine city of San Francisco, which means that for the last twelve months, Richard Yoder has been living not five miles from my front door.

14

I lean back in Will's desk chair as far as I can go without tipping over. I glance at the time. Soon, my illegal access to the USAWMD database will expire. But the knowledge I've gained comes at a price and the one I have to pay is going back in my memory, once again, to Nepal.

By the time our ragtag crew of three reached Namche Bazaar, a tiny town tucked into the Himalayan mountainside at 11,000 feet, I was the respiratory equivalent of an asthmatic off her meds.

"Meager air," Min commented, although he seemed impervious to it. "Not much oxygen." I had yet to actually hire Min in any formal way but he didn't seem overly concerned by the detail. After saving my ass at the hotel, he acted as though he was responsible for my overall well-being as long as I was in Nepal. Try as I might, I couldn't shake him.

The intelligence report, handed to me as I set off on this mission and probably not worth a single rupee, listed a number of behaviors that were meant to give me insight into Chemical Claude's psyche. The first was that Chemical Claude paid the Sherpas to bring as many empty water bottles and oxygen canisters as they could manage down from Everest. The second was that he would then make art, little plastic animals and replicas of the mountain herself, out of the discarded bottles and canisters. Trekkers, attracted to lightweight and unusual souvenirs, would buy his mini sculptures from a little stand on the main drag of town. If you were to rank the bizarre hobbies of America's most wanted, this one would certainly be up there.

"The element of surprise, Sally," Simon Still told me before I left. "He'll never expect us to come at him in Nepal."

"If he's actually there," I said.

"Don't be cynical."

I was to uncover what I could about his operations without detection. No one believed he was really crazy enough to simply be hanging out in the mud, making plastic origami. No. He had to be up to something and we wanted to know what.

After being forced to jump out of my hotel window, it was pretty clear my mission was compromised. I should have called it a day and gone home but if I had to choose between Chemical Claude shooting me in the head or Simon Still accusing me of acting like a sissy, I thought I might pick the bullet. I was in it to the end, whatever that turned out to be.

Min settled us into a guesthouse that smelled of yak dung and unwashed armpits. The stink from the indoor latrine wafted along on the faint breeze. I pulled a scarf around my face, covering my nose and mouth, which worked well to filter the air and also hid my features. Ayushi didn't seem to mind the smell.

"You get used to it after a while," she said. "That's what we used to tell the Western visitors at the hotel."

"Is Kirin really your father?" I asked.

We sat together in a small room on the ground floor of the guesthouse. Below our feet were wide, unstable planks upon which sat a small stove. The guesthouse owner was methodically feeding hardened patties of yak dung into the fire, where they crackled and hissed. The smoke vented right into the room, filling the space between us. Around the fire were wooden benches made from plywood that no one had bothered to sand. It was important not to move too quickly lest you end up with an ass full of splinters.

"No," Ayushi said, playing with the tattered end of a prayer flag. "He found me in town. His wife wanted a child so he took me. But then she died."

Took her? "Did you have parents of your own?"

She shrugged matter-of-factly. "I don't remember."

"What am I going to do with you?" I asked. I didn't really intend the question for the girl but more for myself. Bringing Ayushi here was not only against protocol but it was completely at odds with plain old common sense. Any other agent would have dumped her on the street in Kathmandu and, not giving it a second thought, raced off to get the bad guy. But not me. No. I was just naïve enough to think my force of will could protect her. This was going to end badly for both of us.

"I will go along with you until you are done," she said with a finality that left little room for debate.

"I have things here I'm supposed to be doing," I said, coughing on the smoke, my eyes watering.

Ayushi smiled as if she knew much more about the world than was appropriate for someone her age.

"I stay with you," she said again firmly. I wondered if I could somehow transfer this problem to Min, make him take her back down to the mountain and deposit her with his wife's cousin's sister as we should have done in the first place. But when I looked around, Min was gone.

"I'll be right back," I said, leaving Ayushi in the smoke. "Don't go anywhere."

Outside, I looked up and down the street for my guide, determined to get Ayushi headed back down the mountain as soon as possible. Trekkers crowded the narrow muddy strip between buildings. Stalls were set up every couple of feet, with vendors hawking an assortment of junk, brightly colored polyester Chinese blankets, handmade wool hats with pom-poms and long tassels meant to be tied under the chin, strings of Tibetan prayer flags and jewelry bearing all sorts of incomprehensible religious symbols. There was knock-off technical gear like North Face down jackets with the labels sewed on upside down and hiking boots guaranteed to fall apart at the first sight of snow. There were blurry photocopied maps and bootleg copies of recent best sellers in German and English and French.

I took a step out into the sea of people drifting by and made my way toward the end of the line of stalls looking for Min, sure that sending him back down to Kathmandu with Ayushi was the proper thing to do. I didn't need a guide anyway; all you had to do was follow the yak poop and eventually you'd get where you needed to go.

Inside another guesthouse, through a door partly off its hinges, I caught a glimpse of Min. He was on a satellite phone, gesticulating wildly. His face was red and he seemed frantic, angry. As he slammed the phone down, he turned toward the open door and our eyes met. I immediately looked away, pulling my scarf tighter around my face and pushing back into the crowd.

A minute later, Min grabbed me from behind and swung

me around toward him. His voice was calm and serene, belying the fire in his eyes.

"Allison. Sorry," he said. "I was talking to my family. Some trouble with my brother."

"Sure," I answered. "I hope everything is okay."

"It will all be fine," he said, sounding grim. I had only a second to decide which team Min was playing for. Was he in with the men who wanted to kill me in Kathmandu? Or was he coming at this from a different angle altogether? Because if he was on the phone talking to his family back home, then I was destined for the cover of the swimsuit edition of *Sports Illustrated*. And that just didn't seem likely.

"Let's go and get your camera," he said, linking his arm through mine. "We can stroll among the vendors and get some of the shots you wanted."

"I have my camera," I said, pulling it from inside my heavy coat.

"Great news," Min said with forced enthusiasm. "Let's get to work. Tomorrow we go back down to Kathmandu and we send you home, okay?"

Why the rush?, I wanted to ask but Min didn't look like a man who was going to answer such a question.

Forgetting all about Ayushi, we slogged along in the mud, not having to work too hard to blend in with the other gritty trekkers. In his mug shot, Chemical Claude had a face that looked average at first but upon closer inspection was off in a number of ways. His eyes were too close together and his broad forehead appeared to go on for miles. He tried to hide its expanse with shaggy bangs that went out of fashion with the Monkees. His deep, saggy cheeks could have stored a winter's supply of nuts without much effort. The result made for an unattractive man but not one so horrifying as to make small children run away at the mere sight of him.

I snapped picture after picture of the vendors, hoping that Chemical Claude still resembled his mug shot and hadn't grown a long beard, dyed his hair, or gotten plastic surgery after escaping from prison. At one stall, a long cotton scarf, indigo and pale green, caught my eye. I thought it would look nice on Ayushi.

"How much is that?" I asked in Nepali, pointing to the scarf. A similar scarf flecked with orange obscured most of the vendor's face and he wore sunglasses to cover his eyes. But even so it was obvious he wasn't Nepali or Tibetan. He was not a large man but sturdy, his feet planted as if he were anticipating an attack. He paused for a moment at the sound of my voice before handing me the scarf.

"It's a bargain," he said. His Nepali sounded strange, tainted by an odd, flat accent. I ran my hands over the scarf. It was dirty and torn on one end. Fingering the frayed edge, my body started to tingle. It was either the acute onset of altitude sickness or something was wrong here.

"You hesitate," the man said. "One should never hesitate when one knows what one truly wants."

He leaned close to me. "Welcome to Namche Bazaar, Sally Sin. They told me you'd walk right in like John Wayne, like you owned the place, dragging innocent children behind you no less. So American. You people can't bear to be alone."

Time did that strange thing it does when you have but a split second to decide what you're going to do and yet the choice could use so much more consideration. My entire focus turned to Ayushi, whom I had left stupidly unattended in the smoke.

I dropped the scarf, turned, and ran back through the market toward the lodge where I had left her earlier. Behind me I could hear the man laughing. It was a high-pitched sound that bounced off the surrounding mountains and ricocheted around the valley with wild abandon.

I crashed through the flimsy front door of the guesthouse. Min was at my heels, trying desperately to figure out what was going on.

"Where is she?" I shouted at the owner's wife.

"Those men said you sent them to get her and meet you. She went with them."

I grabbed Min by the shoulders and shook him as if he were a rag doll. "Where would they take her?"

"Who?" Min stammered.

"Claude Chevalier. Chemical Claude. Notorious bad guy who likes to make origami." I didn't expect my explanation to mean anything to him but, without pause, he answered.

"Back down," he said. "To the river. The bridge. They have done it before."

"Before? What are you talking about? Oh, forget it. Move!"

I shoved him out of the way and took off at a run down the very trail we had toiled to scale that morning. Behind me, I could hear Min shouting for me to stop, but all I could see was Ayushi's face. The terrain was rocky and damp and my boots skidded around as if the whole trail were coated in ice. My ankles repeatedly gave way, bending at unnatural angles, but I kept running, not willing to slow down even a bit.

As I rounded a corner, I heard the pop of a gun. Instinctively, I dove to the side of the trail and lay flat in the yak shit and mud, completely still. A moment later, Min came barreling down the trail, a Glock 19 gripped tightly in one hand. Briefly, I registered that a Glock 19 would cost more than what the average Nepali trekking guide made in a year. And it's not like you could just drop by the local hunting and fishing superstore and pick one up at your leisure.

"Nice gun," I said from my position on the ground, "but why the hell are you shooting at me?"

Min tucked the Glock into the pocket of his puffy down jacket. "I asked you several times to stop but you did not seem to hear me."

"I need to go," I said.

"I can't let you do this."

"Listen, I appreciate your sense of obligation as my guide or whatever, but I think you're getting in over your head."

Min sighed, looking at me as if I were hopelessly naïve, which, in retrospect, was certainly true.

"I cannot let you go after the girl," he said. "My orders come from the top, Sally."

I was pretty sure he had just called me Sally. "The top of what?" I asked. There were a lot of mountains around here and all of them had tops.

"The Director," he said. "The head of the Agency. That top."

"As in Director Gray?" I asked slowly.

Min nodded.

Sitting there in the mud, I was speechless and I'm not often speechless. Director Gray and Min? Even accounting for six degrees of separation that relationship seemed impossible.

"But I picked you out of a random line of taxis," I said as if that would explain everything.

"Nothing is random, Sally Sin," Min said.

"I'm starting to get that."

"My job is to keep you safe while you attempt to carry out your mission."

Emphasis on attempt, I guess.

"You're my babysitter?" Was I really that pathetic?

"I prefer to think of myself more as a guardian."

When I woke up that morning, I'd been concerned about normal everyday covert agent things such as if I was going to die from a brain aneurysm brought on by a lack of oxygen or if Chemical Claude was going to kill me before I had a chance to complete my mission. But it was rapidly turning into the kind of day that well illustrated one of Simon Still's fundamental beliefs: Things are seldom as they seem.

From the back of my pants, I pulled my small Colt Commander. It was slick with sweat from being nestled against my skin. Before Min could figure out what was happening, I had the barrel pointed right in his face.

"I'm going to get that girl," I said.

"Sally, be reasonable. You're walking right into their trap. They want something. And then they'll kill her anyway."

If I had been Simon Still or, I suspect, any other agent from the USAWMD, I would have seen the logic in Min's argument. But I wasn't and I didn't.

"Get out of my way," I said.

"I can't do that."

"Who's in charge here? You or me?"

He shrugged. "Hard to say."

"So if I run, you shoot me. And if you won't move, I shoot you, is that it?"

"Looks like it."

"Those aren't very good choices," I said. "I hate a rock and a hard place."

And then I shot him in the foot. As he fell to the ground, cursing, pulling at his boot to remove it, I took off down the trail. I would end up spending two months in a desert in Mali for this act of reckless aggression because shooting an innocent man is just not acceptable, even according to the rules of frontier justice governing the USAWMD.

I ran over the treacherous ground until I came to a rickety wooden footbridge strung haphazardly across a raging, chalky gray river. On the bridge stood the man with the scarf and two goons, one of whom held Ayushi, a beefy arm around her slim neck. I skidded to a stop. The man began to unwrap the scarf. Gone was the giant forehead; bleached blond hair tumbled to his shoulders in stylish waves. If I had to bet I would say the nose was new, too, but no amount of reconstructive surgery could take care of those eyes, filled full of sadistic pleasure at this turn of events.

"Welcome to the party, Ms. Sin," Chemical Claude shouted above the thunderous sound of the water. "We knew you would come." I had found my man.

The time on my fake password expires and the computer screen goes dark. I push back from the desk and close my eyes. Chemical Claude's voice rings in my ears just as it did that day, floating in the thin air above the furious river. And despite his best efforts, no amount of voice-distorting software can mask the flatness of his accent. Chemical Claude and Righteous Liberty are one and the same and, when I think about it, there was never really a chance they weren't.

And to make matters worse, by staging this elaborate effort to get Yoder back, Chemical Claude has indicated to Simon Still that the boy does indeed know something, and Simon really doesn't like being made a fool of. Gray is irrelevant. Simon's on an unsanctioned one-man mission to get Yoder to confess all he knows, damn the consequences.

What a mess.

"Shit," I say, squeezing my temples, hoping if I apply enough pressure the whole world might disappear.

Back from the hardware store and sucking on a lollipop, Theo stands in the door, looking at me with a curious expression. I have no idea how long he's been watching. The fact that he's not an early reader suddenly seems a point in my favor.

"Mom," he says, "how do you spell 'shit'?"

"You can't," I say, digging my fingernails into the soft flesh of my palms. " 'Shit' doesn't have any letters."

But that doesn't mean you can't step in it.

15

Theo and I play *Star Wars* in the living room, he with great enthusiasm and me not so much. We patiently await the return of Will with our regularly scheduled Sunday night Chinese take-out from the place around the corner. Theo will eat a single egg roll but not before he has deconstructed it and organized all the ingredients into separate piles on his plate. All day, from the beach to the playground to the grocery store, the contrails of Chemical Claude's voice have floated behind me.

"I am Darth Maul and I have two light sabers," Theo announces in his best attempt to intimidate me. "I will stab you with them, you bad guy." With that, he pokes me right in the stomach with two plastic swords, left over from Halloween.

"Ouch," I yelp. When did my darling and loving child turn warlike and mean? He stabs me again.

"Come on, Mom. Be the bad guy," he whines. "You said you would play."

I never said anything of the sort. I'm twitchy, anxious, trying to put the pieces of this puzzle together while simultaneously being pursued by a foe with a double light saber. It would be a challenge on a good day.

Finally, I take my sword, cut from a cardboard box, wrapped in peeling tinfoil and slightly bent in the middle, and tap Theo on the head with it.

"I am the bad guy," I say in my "Theo-clean-up-your-toys-or-I-am-going-to-throw-them-all-away" voice. "I am here to disarm you and take your planet and, um, recycle it." With that, Theo's lips start to quiver and his blue eyes fill with tears.

"What's the matter?" I ask. "I thought you wanted me to be the bad guy?"

"You're supposed to let me win," he cries, the tears spilling over and running down his cheeks. This kid needs a sibling. He's starting to exhibit symptoms of being an annoying only child.

"Honey, I'm sorry. Here, let's try again." He looks skeptical but eventually takes up his swords and makes a halfhearted attempt at gutting me with them. I fall over, accompanying the action with a series of horrible gagging noises, much to Theo's delight.

"Is that better?" I ask from my twisted position on the floor. He nods.

"Yes. Keep doing that. Keep dying."

What a sweet kid. I lie there groaning and gasping for air and hoping Theo will soon grow tired of this and let me get back to the serious business of panicking over Chemical Claude and being the spawn of Director Gray. Overall, it's been a lousy weekend and I can't say I'm unhappy to see it end.

Will returns holding a brown paper sack already stained with grease in one hand and a bouquet of red gerbera daisies in the other.

"What are you doing on the floor?" he asks. "Are you sick? You have been looking a little pale lately." He stands over me, examining my face but not making any motion to help me up.

"I'm playing dead for Theo," I say. "Dead people are

pale." Will looks as if he's considering a follow-up question but, using his better judgment, decides against it.

"These are for you," he says.

"They're lovely," I say, still on my back.

"So are you," Will says, raising his eyebrows. "Even if you are a little pale."

I think it's a compliment but I can't be sure.

"How long did it take me to pick up the take-out?" he asks, looking around. A trailer park after a tornado has got nothing on my living room.

"Twenty minutes," I say.

"You guys work fast." He plucks a stray Harry Potter book from between the couch cushions. Theo's attempt to write his name inside the front cover in fact takes up the whole first chapter.

"And we're efficient," I add. "And thorough."

Taking advantage of his father's momentary distraction, Theo sticks Will in the back with a plastic sword.

"Take that!" he yells.

In retaliation, Will grabs Theo by the legs and turns him completely upside down. Dangling there, Theo squeals with delight. I stay on the floor, stretching my arms above my head and listening to all of my vertebrae snap and crack. When I was twenty-five, my body didn't make all this noise.

Still holding Theo upside down, Will steps over me as if I am nothing more than a fallen tree in the forest. He used to come through the door, slide an arm around my waist, and pull me to him so our bodies curved around each other. He would kiss me slowly, as if time and dinner and children and baths and storybook reading weren't important, as if the two of us together were all that actually mattered in the universe. Those were the moments that helped me over the sometimes mindless and infuriating task of caring for a small, unruly, illogical howler named Theo who appeared, at times, hell bent on self-destruction.

But over the last two years, things have cooled between us in a way that sometimes makes it hard for me to breathe. Maybe it's the weight of everyday logistics, the basic management of a family unit that leaves little time for all the other important things in life. Although it doesn't happen every night, occasionally I'll tuck myself into bed by 9 P.M., which does not leave much room for adult conversation, let alone other activities.

Or maybe it's the fact that, although we've been married for a number of years now, Will still has no idea who I am and that sort of thing can be a hurdle to intimacy once the momentum of pure lust disappears. I sometimes think I'd like to tell Will about Sally Sin and the Agency and how long a night can seem when you're trudging through the jungle or what the air tastes like when you're running as fast as you can at 18,000 feet, but I cannot risk the safety of our family for my own self-indulgence.

And for his part, Will has yet to ask. I know he sees the cracks, the inconsistencies in my stories. But he digs no deeper, indicating to me a fear of what he'll find if he does. Sally Sin has been officially dead for some time now yet she still has the power to destroy all of us.

Watching Theo and Will roll around on the floor like puppies, I remind myself that every relationship has its peaks and valleys. Or I think they do. None of my past relationships were conducted in English or lasted very long, so it's not as if I have a great data set from which to draw conclusions. But I am hopeful. Or hopelessly naïve. I haven't decided yet.

Theo tries gallantly to impale Will with one of the light sabers. Will ducks and sidesteps as if he studied fencing with the royals at Buckingham Palace. Theo giggles with delight at each failure, his blond hair falling into his eyes, flushed from a dogged pursuit of the enemy.

A strange sensation rises in my stomach, a toxic mix of nausea and dizziness.

"I'm going to set the table," I say, standing up quickly, which makes the feeling worse. I walk down the hall, holding the wall for support. Please don't let me puke on my shoes. I don't want to spend the evening picking barf out of the lace-holes with a Q-tip. That thought is so appalling I'm forced to hold on to the edge of the sink with my eyes closed, waiting for the sensation to pass. When I open them, I see my reflection in the window above the sink. I look ghostly, hollow. Can that really be me? Surely I'm dying of some terrible disease, liver cancer perhaps, or the plague.

I wipe my face with a damp dish towel that smells faintly of apple juice. There are questions I must answer and they create an off-color haze around me. The first one is, what do I owe a man who saved my life but never wanted me to know he was my father? The second is, should I be willing to risk everything for him? Is he the third person on my list of people I would willingly give my life for? But maybe I'm not asking the right question. The right question may be, is it worth risking my future to uncover the truth about my past?

I trace the outline of my face on the window. The air is

cooling outside and my fingers leave little damp trails on the glass.

"Yes," I hear myself say out loud. "Yes, it is."

And that means, according to Chemical Claude's demands, I have less than forty-eight hours to do something about it.

16

In Nepal, bridges aren't given all that much consideration. They are pieced together with whatever materials might be lying around and usually that doesn't include steel and bolts and detailed engineering plans. The bridge I suddenly found myself on didn't look like it could hold the weight of Chemical Claude, his two hatchet men, and Ayushi, let alone me. I approached the first rickety board very carefully, my Colt Commander dangling at my side. I was not nearly a good enough shot to take out the goons and Chemical Claude and miss Ayushi and grab her before she fell in the river. Later I would be, but not on that day.

"Chemical Claude," I said, trying to buy time. "Where'd you get a name like that?"

He made a face as if he were sucking on a wedge of lime. The eyes of the man holding Ayushi grew round like saucers. Clearly, my attempts at small talk needed some improvement.

"That name," Chemical Claude hissed, "does not reflect the extent of my range. I am much more than chemicals. I am warfare for the ages."

"That's a great tagline," I said, inching forward slowly. "You might want to make a commercial."

"You're ill informed," he said. Sadly, if that were true, it would not be the first time. "I come here to rekindle my spirit, to be as close to the gods as a mortal can get."

"So then you must mean that literally?" I asked, trying to gain a few more inches as he talked. His beady eyes narrowed on me. I stopped moving.

"Everyone knows I'm committed to conducting no business during my time in Nepal," he said. "You're disturbing me."

"Give me the girl and I'll go," I volunteered.

"Oh, it's too late for any of that," Chemical Claude said. "The price for what you want is to tell me in agonizing detail what Simon Still is doing in Pakistan."

Pakistan? Simon Still? I had no idea. I hadn't been with the Agency long enough to be given access to actual state secrets. In fact, the extent of my spying experience so far was limited to following various misanthropes around and taking notes about what they had for breakfast and how many people they had sex with and what movie they happened to take in. At this point, I had more in common with a golden retriever than with an actual secret operative.

"I don't know," I said honestly. "They don't exactly explain themselves to me."

Realizing that if I had known the answer to his question, I would have considered telling him in exchange for our lives, struck me in a physical way. What kind of spy did that make me? I'll tell you. A very bad one.

Chemical Claude nudged the man holding Ayushi closer to the edge of the bridge. Big tears rolled down her cheeks. All of a sudden, Min appeared, limping, on the trail behind me.

"Great," I said. "The band's all here."

"Sally," Min said, through clenched teeth. "This is not going to go over well on the home front. For either of us."

I was quite confident that if I ever got home, Simon was going to exile me to an ice floe somewhere in the neighborhood of the South Pole, so I was trying not to sweat it too much.

"Just don't shoot me, okay?" I asked.

"You have some nerve asking me not to shoot you," Min said. He took a small step and winced. Blood soaked through the laces of his heavy leather boot.

"Hello over there!" Chemical Claude bellowed. "Can we focus on the question at hand, please? What is Simon Still doing in Pakistan?" I looked at Min, who shrugged his shoulders. No help there.

"I have people there," Chemical Claude went on, almost as if talking to himself. "Good people, but Simon is slippery. I can't always get a hold of him." He seemed genuinely perplexed.

"We all walk away if I tell you?" I asked, embarrassed by the rank cheesiness of the line.

"Sally," Min warned.

"Yes, you have my word," Claude said.

I was sure he was lying, the word of a terrorist not really worth that much, but I figured I had to exhaust all possibilities and there weren't that many to begin with.

Well, if you really have to know," I said, "Simon Still is in Pakistan looking for whoever just purchased a nuclear warhead from Ian Blackford. We heard noise that it's destined to visit India in the very near future." Technically, this could have been true. I heard things, rumors mostly, floating around the Underground that Blackford was doing something particularly awful. Maybe it was selling a nuclear bomb to some fringe group in Pakistan? Why not? He'd done worse.

"You lie like an amateur," Chemical Claude said, exposing his perfect white teeth in what I think was meant to be a smile. "Blackford works for me. He knows better than to sell anything to anybody without my approval."

This was not good news and I'm not talking about my inability to lie convincingly.

"That's what you think. Blackford has no allegiance to anyone but Blackford," I said, parroting word for word a lecture Simon Still had delivered to me no less than a hundred times. All the while I continued to move forward on the swaying bridge, hoping I could get close enough to do, well, something. What that was, exactly, I had not figured out. I was making it up as I went along, a behavior that would become something of a bad habit of mine in the future.

"I was told you would know the answer to the Pakistan question," he said, taking a step toward me, examining my face. "But I think I was misinformed. You're nothing more than middle management. And this is a waste of time. I hate wasting time. Just kill them all."

For a second I didn't think I'd heard the words correctly because I was focused entirely on the man with the beefy arms as he moved to shove Ayushi right over the side of the bridge into the raging river.

"No!" My scream was useless, a dog caught in a snare with no hope of rescue. Pulling my gun, I fired all my bullets into the guy who began to fall backward off the bridge. As I ripped Ayushi from his grip, pushing her to safety, the dying man lodged a bloody arm around my waist and together we plunged off the bridge into the water. For a second, I could hear chaos behind me, Min shouting, Chemical Claude's shrieking laughter, gunfire. And then nothing but the thrashing of water in my ears as I tumbled down the river to an almost certain death.

I surfaced briefly, trying for a glimpse of shore before the river pushed me back down and forward. My lungs burned and my arms and legs were heavy chunks of ice somehow loosely attached to my body. I had maybe a minute left before I boarded the bus to hypothermic cardiac arrest, when I found myself spinning in a small, swirling eddy alongside the riverbank. With a trembling blue hand I grabbed onto a rock and held fast. There was a thin stream of blood flowing from a gash in my scalp. Every time I blinked, the world turned a shade of rosy pink.

Slowly, with great effort, I pulled myself out of the river and up onto the surrounding rocks. The sun shone brightly in a pale and washed-out sky and I sat there on a rock with my arms wrapped around my legs, shivering. There was blood from other places. A bullet hole in my arm? It didn't matter. My mind was completely blank.

At some point, Min came hobbling down the trail. With a sense of urgency, he tried again and again to pull me to my feet. But I didn't want to move. I intended to sit with my frozen body on this frozen rock forever, so what was the big hurry?

"We need to go," Min said quietly. "It's not safe."

"Is she dead?" I asked, my blue lips cracking with each word.

"No."

"Did he take her?"

"Yes."

Suddenly, I reared up as if shot through with pure adrenaline. I couldn't bear to think about what Chemical Claude would do to Ayushi.

"I tried," Min said, holding me tightly, a human straitjacket. "They're gone. They assume you're dead. You should be."

The energy surge dissipated as quickly as it had come. I had nothing left.

"You really work for Gray?" I asked.

"Eventually we all do, Sally Sin. We all do."

And that was the last thing I remember before I woke up on a cot in a completely white room in the Bangkok Airport. Simon Still sat across from me, blowing smoke rings and poking his finger through them.

I tried to sit up but an IV line kept me tethered to the bed.

"Chemical Claude works with Ian Blackford," I squeaked with what was left of my voice. "Something about Pakistan. Wanted to know what we were up to in Pakistan."

Simon flicked the ash of his cigarette right on the floor. It settled there in a little dusty pile.

"Well, that's not really any of his business, now is it?" he said. "In any case, nice work. Good girl." Those words remain the first and only compliment Simon Still ever gave me. That it was something you might say to a puppy who had finally managed to take a pee in the grass rather than on the kitchen floor was not entirely lost on me. My whole body ached and I couldn't seem to stop shivering.

"The doctors assure me you'll be fine, more or less," Simon said, lighting a fresh cigarette from the dying one.

"Should you be smoking in here?" I asked, the yellow air thick in my throat.

"It's Thailand, Sally," he said. "I can do anything I want."

As Simon watched me, I tried desperately to keep him from seeing that Ayushi's face was a drifting jellyfish across my consciousness.

"Why do they call him Chemical Claude?" I asked. I wanted more than an answer to my question. I wanted to be let in the club. I wanted to be on the inside. Simon took a few more drags on his cigarette while he decided what I deserved to know.

"They call him Chemical Claude because his first time out he botched an effort to hijack a subway in Beijing," he said. "Instead of knocking out the passengers with sarin gas and holding them hostage for a fortune, he killed them all. It was early, kids were on their way to school. It was a crowded train. The Chinese government asked for our help in covering it up. They did not want to appear weak. They've learned a lot since then."

I kept my eyes averted, afraid to look at him.

"This will not be your only professional failure, Sally," Simon said. "True, he gets this round. But maybe you'll get the next."

Inside, I was consumed with defeat and helplessness and anger. I wanted to wrap my hands around Chemical Claude's neck and squeeze until the life flowed out of him like that goddamn river. It didn't feel at all like a professional failure. It felt personal.

"In any case," Simon said, "we can talk more about it later." With one swift move, he yanked the IV from my arm. "Time to go." I covered the hole left by the line with my opposite hand, the blood seeping through my fingers.

How did I get here? Did Simon know about Min? Why would Director Gray have someone following me? None of it made any sense but even then, I knew better than to ask Simon Still for clarification. I stood up, wobbly, dehydrated, shaking, and followed Simon from the silent white room into the seething airport terminal. As I joined the throngs of people on the move, I had no idea when the next round would come and, if it did, what I would do.

That is, until now.

17

The clock reads 7:30 when Theo starts jumping on me. Thankfully, today he's not wearing cleats. I am keenly aware that it is Monday morning for a number of reasons.

It has been three days since Simon Still made me call Righteous Liberty, which means that Yoder is probably no longer living the American dream. I'm 100 percent sure that, as soon as Simon left me in the coffee shop, his first move was to call in the order to pick up Yoder. By now Yoder's new address is probably a USAWMD holding cell buried under the ground in Washington. And there he'll stay until he tells Simon what he wants to know.

But just because they have Yoder doesn't mean I shouldn't go to his house and check it out. If you don't go looking for clues, it pretty much guarantees you'll never find any. Besides, every plan needs a first step, and visiting Yoder's residence will be mine. The fact that my plan doesn't include a second step or a single chart or map or graph would be troubling if flying by the seat of my pants wasn't something I inadvertently specialize in.

"Field trip!" Theo yells into my ear. His plastic dinosaur dances a jig on my head. I have a vague recollection of a discussion involving a field trip many weeks ago but beyond that, I cannot be sure.

"Field trip later," I say, throwing my legs over the side of the bed. "Coffee now."

"Mom, do you know how to spell 'Tyrannosaurus Rex'? It's super long."

"Yes."

Maybe.

"How?"

"Can I brush my teeth before I try that one, honey?" I'm tired, weary, in a way I don't remember being a month ago. A bitter taste fills my mouth.

"Every opportunity is a learning opportunity," Theo says. The word "opportunity" comes out with fifteen syllables. "Teacher Wendy says so."

And Teacher Wendy is right but that doesn't mean I can't resent her perky smile and sweet purple chairs every now and then, does it?

"Mom, I'm hungry. Where's my spider T-shirt? I want some juice and I can't find my LEGO Darth Vader."

Downstairs, Will is in the kitchen, wearing jeans and flip-flops, his back to the door. I'm about as likely to find my husband still at home at 7:30 on a weekday as I am to find a komodo dragon in my refrigerator.

"Are you sick?" I ask, as he hands me a full mug of coffee. "Did you get fired?" I smell the coffee and that nasty bitter taste fills my mouth again. I put it aside. Really, the plague would be very inconvenient right now. Or maybe it's something else entirely, the last bit of evidence in support of the theory that I've completely lost my edge. It's possible I am now just as susceptible to stress and anxiety as the next person. I think I would rather have the plague.

"Lucy, I own the company," Will reminds me. "And

remember, I'm going to Idaho in about two hours? It's on the calendar."

"Idaho?" *Calendar?*

"The biogas project? Capturing the methane from decomposing animal waste. We talked about it."

"That sounds rude," I say. "Theo, cover your ears."

"It's not small potatoes," Will says, laughing despite himself.

"Oh, that was awful."

"I know. Apologies. The calendar, Lucy?"

Ah, back to the calendar, the one upon which I am supposed to record all the important dates and events related to our collective existence, like field trips, for example. While Will is meticulous about the family calendar, I have room for improvement. In fact, Will went so far as to threaten me with weekly staff meetings if I didn't get my act together. But I'm used to keeping everything important in my head. Anything written down can be used against me.

"Right," I say. "Idaho. When are you back?"

"That's on the calendar, too. You don't remember any of it, do you?"

"I might. If you give me a clue." There is a hint of exasperation in Will's tone, as though I remind him of a small, badly behaved child.

"Lucy, there's something else we need to talk about," he says.

Why is it that when someone says "We need to talk," it's never because they want to discuss the weather or what color to paint the bedroom or the fact that you just ran out of milk? It's used exclusively to start conversations one party would rather not be having and I get the sense I am that party in this situation. On the counter behind Will are several cardboard boxes full of plastic ziplock bags. Will picks up the snack-sized bags and holds them out to me.

Busted.

"You might be some sort of master of deception, Lucy, but I know what you've been up to," Will says.

Oh, but you really have no idea.

"So no trial," I say, "I go right to the guillotine? How medieval."

"We agreed we would try to go bag free," he says. He uses the word "we," but what he means is "me." Will would not use a brand-new plastic bag if he was told that the only way he could save the planet was to stuff Theo's free-range celery sticks into one immediately. To him, such an act would be the first step toward an insatiable need. If pot is the entry drug that inevitably leads to you snorting cocaine off a prostitute's naked ass, then the plastic bag can only end in a 10,000-square-foot house with a Lamborghini Murciélago parked in the driveway. A slippery plastic slope.

And to give Will credit, he's not completely off the mark. I'm a total plastic-bag junkie. It's infinitely satisfying to pop some carrot sticks or pretzels into one and zip it closed with a swift pull of the thumb and forefinger. And for organizing things in a suitcase or a diaper bag, there's simply nothing better. I've searched the world over for a suitable alternative to the lowly plastic bag but have yet to come up with something that gets the job done with quite the same understated finesse.

I understand that plastic bags are bad. They go straight into the landfill and take one thousand years to biodegrade. Sea turtles choke on them and they strangle birds and things.

But I'm like your garden-variety crackhead. I want to stop, I really do, and yet I keep going back for more.

"Americans throw away 380 billion plastic bags a year," Will says, waving my contraband snack bags in the air. "Less than five percent of those get recycled."

"I know," I say, "but those reusable containers, they pop open, they spill, they crack, they're way too big. I can't take it."

Will puts his arms around me. "I'll find you better ones," he says. "I promise."

This man really loves me. And he really hates plastic bags. If we had a battle to the death, the bags and me, I wonder who Will would root for?

"Okay," I say. "If you find good containers, I'll try them."

But even as the words leave my lips, I'm thinking that the back of my closet is an excellent hiding place for plastic bags. Maybe behind the big box of maternity clothes in the safe with the money and the stolen cell phones?

"Can I ask any more than that?" Will says.

I shake my head. You could, but it might not be the best idea.

"So," I say, changing the subject, "how about you blow off Idaho and all that cow poop and take twenty preschoolers to a Giants game today instead?"

Because even though I didn't put it on the calendar, this morning I'm scheduled to head across town and do a little breaking and entering. Will looks at me as if I'm insane, which clearly I am, but not for the reasons he thinks. He puts a hand on my shoulder.

"Lucy, you know I would love to, but cow poop waits for

no man." He gets that faraway gleam in his eye that always appears when he talks about any kind of recycling and I know on some level all those books about coparenting are complete bullshit. In the real world, Mom does the heavy lifting.

"Are you okay?" he asks. "You look a little pale." He keeps saying that.

"I think I'm dying of the plague," I say. "Or maybe malaria. It really could be malaria."

Will laughs. He thinks I'm kidding but I'm not. Tropical diseases are no laughing matter and I say that with an authority I'd rather not have.

For reasons I still don't care to examine too closely, I ended up in the jungle far more frequently than Agents 1 through 25 did. Down in the Underground, they got to calling me Jungle Jane. I had grown weary of the Agency's fondness for alliteration so while there was not much I could do about Sally Sin, I put a stop to that Jungle Jane nonsense with some carefully placed WWII hand grenades I'd stolen out of a locker in Moscow.

As a result of my jungle frolicking, I suffered from a whole host of illnesses with frightening names, such as dengue fever, malaria, Japanese encephalitis, and leptospirosis. I even had to do a round of rabies vaccinations, thanks to a pissed-off sewer rat. Please don't ask for specifics on that one. My mental health depends on pretending it never happened.

Once, during the rainy season, Simon and I were in a dreadful jungle in Guinea where it seemed everyone had dengue fever. Even now, I can't remember exactly why we were there but it started with a man claiming to have information about a stockpile of plutonium 239. And it ended when the meeting turned out to be a setup and Simon shot the man, which, in turn, made some people very unhappy.

My cheap plastic Timex glowed midnight when Simon sat up on his straw mat and started swatting frantically at the mosquito netting. I could see his face glistening with sweat in the faint light, a deranged look in his eyes.

"Sally," he screamed. "They're in here with me! In my bed! Get them out!"

I scrambled from under my net and crawled over to him.

"Get them out," he whispered, clutching the net as if he were a 175-pound baby with his favorite blankie. "Please."

"There's no one here, Simon. Just me," I said. "It's okay." I slowly pulled the net over his head but let him continue to hold it. I laid my hand on his forehead as my mother had done when I was a kid. He was on fire. I pulled him into my lap.

"They're coming, you know. For me. For you. For all of us. Soon."

"Shhh. We need to go to the hospital, Simon."

At the suggestion of the hospital, Simon covered his face and howled.

"No! Are you trying to kill me? I would rather die than go to the hospital in this country. I'm freezing."

He began to shake uncontrollably in my arms, his eyes rolling back in his head. It would be bad for my professional development if the boss died in my lap.

"Simon!" I turned him on his side as he proceeded to puke all over me. After having a child, being puked on is not that big a deal, but back then, in the Guinean jungle, it was still really gross.

I slid Simon, now completely limp, onto his stomach and

crawled back over to my straw mat. I seemed to remember that in cases of dengue fever, Tylenol was about the only medical response. In my knapsack was a plastic bag of just that, or so said the guy on the street from whom I'd bought it. Could very well have turned out to be LSD for all I knew. But Simon was already hallucinating so he probably wouldn't have noticed if I accidentally fed him psychedelic drugs. I dumped a bunch of the pills into my hand, hoping the dose was at least in the ballpark, grabbed a bottle of water, and crawled back to Simon.

He was trembling now and I shook him hard.

"Simon, if you don't wake up I'm going to shoot you," I shouted right in his ear. His eyes flew open.

"You can't do that!" As his mouth opened, I popped the pills in. He tried to spit but I held my hand firmly over his mouth until he choked them down, glaring at me as if I were the devil or, worse, Ian Blackford. I held the water bottle to his lips and tipped it. He sputtered and growled at me but swallowed everything. Then he collapsed back onto my lap in a shivering damp heap. Lovely.

It didn't take long for both of my legs to fall asleep and as I tried to shift Simon back onto his own mat, he woke up, momentarily lucid.

"The secrets," he whispered. "They'll drive you mad. They'll make you crazy. But still you'll keep them. Secrets about you. About me. About him."

What secrets? And who was "him"? He couldn't have delivered the lines better if he were auditioning for *Hamlet*.

"Close your eyes," I said. "Go back to sleep." Simon nodded his head and did as he was told.

The next morning, I called for reinforcements and two burly men I didn't know showed up to help me carry a moderately dead and severely bedraggled Simon out of the jungle and onto a plane to Germany, where they yelled at me for giving him so many unidentifiable pills. He never acknowledged our night in the Guinean jungle nor did he ever explain about all the secrets. And I, of course, never asked.

I dump my coffee down the sink and pour Theo a bowl of Cheerios. They smell pretty good so I fill another bowl for myself. I hear Theo kissing Will good-bye and extracting promises to build weapons of mass destruction out of LEGOS upon Daddy's return from frolicking around an Idaho dairy farm.

We eat our Cheerios side by side. Most of Theo's end up plastered to his pajama shirt.

"T-Y-R-A-N-N-O-S-A-U-R-U-S R-E-X," I say. "Two words."

Theo stops eating and grins. It's the smile that makes my heart flutter no matter how many times I see it. His eyes crinkle and his face is radiant and I forgive him all the dawdling and temper tantrums and lost shoes and beads up the nose. I just hope, when the time comes, he will forgive me for all the secrets.

18

I stare into my closet, the only place on earth that would surely benefit from a weapon of mass destruction. On one shelf, there are several pairs of jeans with holes in the knees from crawling around on the floor when Theo was a baby. Underneath is another shelf with long-sleeved T-shirts. Hanging are fleece vests, fleece jackets, fleece scarves. I'd buy fleece underwear if I thought I could get away with it. San Francisco is roughly sixty-five degrees, damp and windy every day of the year. And it's a cold wind, not happy until it works its way through to your bones. Occasionally, I find myself pining for the Sahara Desert but then I remember what it was like to be stuck there without a ride and the desire quickly passes.

When we moved into our house, Will set about hiring all sorts of people to expand things like our closets and bathrooms.

"Grown-ups don't share a single closet, Lucy," Will told me. I looked at my lone duffel bag of belongings and said nothing. In truth, I required little more than a cardboard box but I wasn't raised as Will was. His expectations were different.

"My own closet would be nice," I said, trying to project confidence that someday I might actually have something to put in it.

Of course, the closets are made of bamboo, sustainably

farmed by a family in Southern Oregon. I suggested that Will go all the way and carry the wood down here on his back but he didn't think that was funny.

Along the bottom of the closet is a shelf specifically designed for shoes, of which I own three pairs. Theo used to use the shelves as a ramp for Matchbox cars. Now it's a cave for LEGO men and plastic dinosaurs.

It's not that I don't want to wear beautiful clothes and shoes. I'm hopeful my destiny includes wearing something other than a fleece jacket every single day for the rest of my life. But the truth is I haven't figured out how to make it work. Avery once defined my sense of style as "survivalist" and I don't think she meant it as a compliment.

Right now, I need an outfit that can do double duty for a ball game and a breaking-and-entering. Good thing I don't have a dinner date to follow or I'd be facing a serious fashion dilemma. I pull on a pair of jeans but they feel too tight. I leave the top unbuttoned until they have time to stretch out. I refuse to consider the idea that the pants are fine but my body is getting bigger. No. Not today. If I need to go on a diet, it will just have to stand in line with all the other unpleasant things I need to do and wait its turn.

Near the top of the unpleasant things list is chaperoning a preschool class trip to a Giants baseball game. A few weeks ago, Teacher Wendy announced that a Happy Times family had donated enough tickets for the entire class plus chaperones to attend today's game. Did I mention it's a play-off game and this is the point in the season when riots tend to break out over a single available ticket? No? Well, don't be too surprised because this is San Francisco, where money apparently grows on trees.

After her joyous announcement, Teacher Wendy put on her sad face and said we couldn't go without parent volunteers. My hand, apparently embarking on a solo career and no longer taking orders from my brain, popped right up and I was rewarded with a big Teacher Wendy smile. I'm a reliable volunteer. I have visited fire stations, zoos, museums, and aquariums. I can find a clean public restroom in any San Francisco neighborhood. Honestly, the idea of Theo and twenty of his closest friends wandering around the city with nothing more than a bunch of overtired parents for protection is a bit more than I can handle.

"You are so involved," Teacher Wendy will say to me as I sign up for yet another chaperoning gig. "It's super and so are you."

There's no point in explaining that I'm motivated by fear rather than an overdeveloped sense of altruism. It seems harmless to let Teacher Wendy continue to believe in my overall superness. And there are benefits, such as one less day I have to hang out with Leonard at the Java Luv and watch him lose IQ points. However, when I raised my hand last week, the day was empty. How was I supposed to know I'd need it free to continue my rogue agent crime spree?

Theo wanders into my room with his Giants baseball hat and T-shirt on. Theo's wardrobe, in contrast to my own, is worth a small fortune. His grandparents don't see why a child, particularly their only grandchild, should wear a pair of jeans from Target when he can just as easily wear a pair of jeans from Ralph Lauren. When I bring Theo's hand-me-downs to the consignment shop, they treat me like royalty.

"When are we going?" Theo asks, shaking his head back and forth so fast his cheeks go slack. "I'm getting so bored."

"There are kids who never have a chance to be bored," I say, "because they're out scavenging for food all day long."

"Why would I do that?" he asks. "I have the refrigerator."

This is the perfect opportunity for a lesson on world hunger and excessive consumption but I'm not up for it. Besides, Will provides a far more dramatic delivery of this one than I do.

"We'll leave soon. We need to pick up Henry at his house, run a quick errand, and then we'll go meet your class at the ball park. Sound good?"

He sighs as if this plan causes him great emotional stress.

"How long?" he asks, dragging the words out for emphasis.

"Seven and a half minutes," I say.

He's happy with that. This kid deals in absolutes. No gray areas for Theo.

Henry Coen lives two incredibly steep hills away. We pull up to the curb in front of his house and he springs from the front door, a small brown-headed jack-in-the-box.

Judy Coen follows her son out, shouting about jackets and hats. Judy Coen's life project is maintaining herself to such a degree that she never seems to age. It wouldn't surprise me one bit to discover she sleeps in a jar of formaldehyde. I've known her now for close to three years and the expression on her face hasn't altered in the slightest during this time. She always looks surprised. Me, I'm waiting for a team of archeologists to show up and begin excavating the wrinkle developing between my eyebrows. I'm not saying my way is better, but it certainly takes less time.

"Hi, Judy," I wave. Judy scans the Prius. I think she would like to arch her eyebrows in a rather wry way but the eyebrows don't do that anymore. They are frozen in place.

"You're so *good*, Lucy," she says. "Making up for the rest of us and our naughty habits." She laughs, a wineglass dropped on a tile floor.

"Well, you know, someone has to save the planet," I say.

"Better you than me," she says. "I have no *time* for anything. I am *so* stressed out about the kindergarten decision I can barely sleep. What are *you* going to do?"

This topic must be peaking because I cannot seem to meet an adult and not discuss the kindergarten issue. It's beginning to make me tense and when I'm tense I bite my cuticles. It's disgusting. I know this because Theo tells me so.

"I'm going to look at some public and some private and then make some decisions," I say, which is more or less true.

"You seem so *calm*," she says. "How can you be so calm about something this *enormous*?"

I think Sam is right about everybody in this city being crazy. Choosing a school is big, yes, but not enormous. Nuclear war is enormous.

"Drugs," I say with a perfectly straight face. "They work wonders."

"Oh, I know," she says with a wink. "My doc will do almost anything to get me out of his office. It's great." She laughs again although I consider what she just said to be rather alarming. Mental note: Monitor all playdates at Henry's house with more than the usual level of paranoia.

"Do you mind if I take Henry out to the Sunset with me before the game?" I ask through the open window. "I have to pick something up."

"Sure," Judy says, strapping Henry into the booster seat next to Theo. "The Sunset is so *ethnic*. I love it." I'm confident that Judy could not find the Sunset neighborhood on a map if someone held a gun to her head. It's too "over there" for her. She leans in and tries to give Henry a kiss. He, in turn, leans as far toward Theo and away from her as he can with a seat belt on.

"Yuck," Henry says.

"Kissing is so gross," Theo concurs.

"Forget it," Judy says, retreating. "Have fun at the game. Thanks for driving and everything, Lucy. I have an appointment with my dermatologist today that I can't miss or I'd have gone myself."

Botox, apparently, waits for no one.

There are those who say the sun never shines in the Sunset. The fog rolls in off the nearby ocean and just stays, settling in like melted butter on an English muffin. We drive through the mist over a couple of hills and head down Judah, a wide avenue cluttered with Muni tracks and bad parallel parking that runs clear to the Pacific Ocean. In front of the house I'm looking for, just outside the green garage door, sits a sparkling clean Chevy Malibu.

And much to my surprise, Richard Yoder is climbing out of it. He holds a new Adidas duffel bag in one hand and a big plastic cup with a logo for the Luxor Las Vegas on it in the other. Under his worn leather jacket he sports a Luxor Las Vegas T-shirt that matches the cup.

There are times when I consider myself unlucky, when I feel as if there's a worldwide conspiracy meant to keep me down. This is not one of those times. This is a time when I realize that if I wasn't sprinkled with just a little fairy dust, I would have been dead long ago. Richard Yoder was in Las Vegas for the weekend and Simon Still had no idea. Simon's crew has been patiently watching the house for three days, waiting for the missing Yoder to turn up, and as soon as he does, there I am. I can't help but smile. This is really going to make Simon mad. I place a quick phone call as I pull up in front of Yoder's driveway.

Yoder stretches and yawns, popping off his sunglasses and rubbing his eyes. He probably drove all night to get home after losing his last penny. But that's not my problem. My plan has changed. It now includes kidnapping Yoder and arranging the trade with Chemical Claude, making sure I take time out to shoot the aforementioned Claude in the head at the first opportunity. Now my plan has three steps. I feel much better.

"You boys stay here, okay?" In the backseat, Theo and Henry argue about what happened after Darth Vader cut off Luke Skywalker's arm in the seventh *Star Wars* movie, which is really the second movie, but that point is lost on these two.

"Hey," I say, vying for their attention, "neither of you have even seen the movie so why the big debate?"

"Well, we will someday," Theo says.

"Probably true but for right now I need you to stay put for a minute, okay?"

They nod and immediately return to arguing about Luke's missing arm. Yoder is too tired to have noticed me yet, focused entirely on finding his house key on an overloaded key chain. He's about my height with thick, dark hair that sticks up in the back in the same way Theo's does when he rolls out of bed. Theo's teacher calls it "Good Morning Hair." The fact that Yoder has Good Morning Hair makes me squirm. Whatever this turns out to be, Yoder is too young for it.

As I draw closer, I see the sharp bones of his clavicles sticking out from beneath his thin shirt as if his body has not yet finished filling in all the empty places. In five years' time, age will make him thicker but right now he's nothing more than an overgrown child. Which, of course, complicates things but doesn't change them.

Finally, he looks up and sees me coming toward him from the curb. It takes a split second for fear to register in his eyes. He's had the sort of life where the odds are against me being a random stranger asking for directions. The way I walk toward him, he knows.

"What do you want?" he asks, his voice hoarse from long smoky nights at the slots.

Without breaking stride I grab him. His upper arm is so thin I can almost close my thumb and forefinger around it.

"You," I say. "I want you."

"You can't do this to me," he says, clutching the big plastic cup to his chest. "I'm an American."

Why do people always say that? Citizenship doesn't come equipped with an invisible force field. Maybe it used to back when everybody liked us, but not anymore. In fact, these days you might consider holding your passport face down and pretending to be, say, Swedish. Nobody seems to want to kill the Swedes while everyone seems to want to kill the Americans.

"I don't care," I say. "Mr. Yoder."

He hasn't heard his real name in a while and it has the intended effect.

"I have friends, important friends," he stammers. "They won't allow this to happen."

"The same friends who put you down in that dungeon for twelve months?" I ask. "Those friends?"

He physically recoils at the thought. Whatever Simon did to this man in the name of peace, love, and the American way, it sure stuck with him.

"If you want to live, come with me," I say. It's the worst line ever. I'm embarrassed for myself.

"Why would I do that?" he asks.

"Because I'm armed," I say, which is a complete lie but effective.

"Where are you taking me?" he asks. "Where are we going?"

This is a question I should have answered in my planning stage, perhaps under the heading of "contingencies." The truth is, I'm far more afraid of what would happen to me if I were to blow off my chaperoning responsibilities than I am of what will happen if I bring a known terrorist along on a preschool field trip. I have four Giants tickets burning a hole in my pocket.

"We're going to a Giants game with twenty five-year-olds," I say. "It's a play-off game but try to stay calm."

Yoder smiles grimly.

"You people and your codes," he says. "Why can't you just say what you mean?"

"I'm not kidding about the baseball game," I say. "Put your bag back in the car and let's go."

As I escort Yoder to the waiting Prius, I feel the eyes on us. They watch from the roofs, the sidewalks, the cars parked across the street. But they can't do anything. Three San Francisco Police cruisers provide my cover and while I feel a little guilty for calling 9-1-1 about nonexistent gunshots at the bodega across the street, the alternative somehow seemed much worse.

I shove Yoder into the front passenger seat, taking a second to stick the stolen cell phone I used to call the police under the front wheel of the car. The boys stop trying to stab each other with light sabers long enough to register the scene unfolding around them.

"Mom," Theo asks. "Who's that? Look at all the police cars! Cool!"

"Hey, Theo's mom," Henry says, "how do you spell 'police'?"

It's an epidemic, this spelling thing. Someone should call the Centers for Disease Control.

"P-O-L-I-C-E. This is Richard, a friend of Mommy's." Yoder cringes at the reckless use of his name, as if it has the power to turn him into a toad.

"Hi, Theo's mom's friend," says Henry. "Do you want a light saber?"

Yoder does not turn his head to acknowledge Henry's offer. I give him a nudge.

"Henry offered you a light saber," I say. "It's a big deal when you're a five-year-old boy. Be kind enough to answer him. Good manners are important."

Glaring at me, Yoder turns to Henry. "No thank you," he says.

"Okay," says Henry cheerfully.

"It was nice of you to offer, Henry," I say. "Good sharing."

"Thanks, Theo's mom." I've tried to get Henry to call me Lucy or even Mrs. Hamilton but names seem to have a problem sticking to me. "Everybody strapped in? Richard, seat belt, please. Okay, who wants to go to a ball game?"

Yoder does as he's told. His expression indicates that he believes he might be experiencing very realistic hallucinations, the result of driving all night without a break. For a second, I worry the Prius is not actually heavy enough to crush the cheap cell phone wedged under the front wheel, but after a satisfying crunch we begin to head east, back toward the bay, passing alongside Golden Gate Park and through Haight-Ashbury.

"Tomorrow, this will all be over," I say, not taking my eyes from the road. Raffi sings "Willoughby Wallaby Woo" in the background and Richard Yoder sways to the music.

"But it will not end well," he says, "not for you or me. Not for anyone." His tone is unnervingly matter-of-fact. He seems ready to close his eyes, lie down on the yellow line, and get run over by whatever is coming down the pike.

In the driver's seat, an unfamiliar unease settles over me. When I used to be a spy, I never considered the life of the bad guy. A folder, usually stamped TOP SECRET, would arrive on my desk with the bad guy's name on the inside, sometimes accompanied by a blurry snapshot, sometimes not. I never thought about the guy's mother or sister or who would pay his gardener after I deposited him stateside. To end up in a folder, you had to do something wrong and that was all there was to it. The void such a person would leave behind was not my problem. I never looked beyond the obvious because even if I did, there was no choice to be made. I had orders and I followed them.

But this is different. I'm not doing this for national security or because the safety of the free world depends on it. My motives are entirely selfish. Charles Gray is the only person who can answer the questions of my past and because of this, I have deemed his life to be more important than the life of Richard Yoder.

And that kind of moral authority fits me about as well as a fluorescent pink mini and platform heels.

19

As we drive toward the ballpark, Yoder mutters verse about the end of time. Or maybe it's a Springsteen song, it's hard to tell. He appears to be in a self-induced trance and I sincerely hope he doesn't collapse in convulsions or something. That would really set the boys off and "convulsion" is a difficult word to spell

"Mom, can we have juice boxes?" Theo asks. "We can do the straws."

"Yes," I say, "but don't tell Daddy, okay?" Daddy hates juice boxes. They're not a good use of resources. I reach between Yoder's legs for my bag. He stops chanting long enough to recoil like I'm about to pass him a raging case of the cooties. I pull my hand back.

"Fine, then you do it," I say. "There are two juice boxes in my bag. Pass them into the backseat. And there's nothing in there to bludgeon me to death with, so don't get your hopes up."

Yoder digs out the juice boxes and spins them around slowly, examining them.

"You don't have children, do you?" I ask.

"No," he says. "No, I don't." And he looks sad all of a sudden, as if he forgot to do something important.

"Well, don't worry," I say. "You're young. You have time."

"Let's not kid ourselves," he says. I want to tape his mouth shut. He's too young to say things like that. Somehow, if he were an old man, wrinkled, with a shock of white hair and bifocals, this would be easier. But he's a kid. I want to button up his coat and give him a plastic bag full of Cheerios to munch on. Okay, maybe not a plastic bag. Maybe a reusable glass container. But either way, he could use a megadose of calories and a good night's sleep, neither of which I'm prepared to provide.

We park in a lot that costs forty-five dollars an hour and guarantees it will return to me a car that's both dirtier and dented, but it's not like I have a lot of choice down here by the stadium. The parking-lot attendant pockets my cash and gives me a smile full of gold teeth. I envy him because, even if he's a bank robber by night, I'm 100 percent sure his life is less complicated than mine right now.

We pile out of the car. Yoder's eyes are restless, darting every which way, looking for an escape route. Theo and Henry hold hands and start singing "Take Me Out to the Ball Game." I think it's cute. Yoder looks ill.

"Don't run," I say.

"Okay," the boys say.

"I was talking to you, Richard," I say, pulling him along with us, struggling not to lose Henry and Theo in the swelling crowd of fans. "Your friends aren't your friends anymore. You've become a liability and you know what happens to liabilities, right?"

He shakes his head.

"They disappear," I say, patting him on the shoulder. "But for now, let's try and have fun. And please don't say or do anything too weird if you can help it."

Most of Theo's class is already assembled in the stands.

They climb over the stadium seats like the place is the world's biggest jungle gym. I'm profoundly sorry for anyone sitting within a ten-row radius of us. Half of the kids are eating popcorn. The other half are eating tasty whole-wheat, low-sugar snacks lovingly prepared at home by overinvolved moms and snuck into the stadium in concealed inner pockets. Those kids don't look as happy as the kids eating popcorn. Within seconds, Theo rolls his baseball program up in a tube and uses it as a makeshift light saber to attack Henry who, in turn, does the same. It could be a long day.

Plopping down in a seat next to Avery, I announce, "This is Richie. He's the younger brother of a friend of mine in town for a few days. You know, job-hunting and things." There are lots of nodding heads and hellos.

"I prefer Richard," he says as Avery leans across me and shakes his hand.

"I don't care," I whisper, a big fake smile plastered on my face. Finally, Yoder has the decency to appear surprised by his new reality. I hand him an extra baseball program.

"Here," I say. "Brush up on your baseball stats."

"Do you think I should be looking at the public schools?" Avery says, twisting and untwisting her baseball program like makeshift worry beads.

I'm pretty good at changing lanes, at thinking about one thing while talking about another. But today, I can barely keep up.

"No," I tell her. "You're fine. Don't worry about it."

"Are you ready for your interview at Country Day tomorrow?" she asks.

Well, that sounds like something I should remember. I bet Avery has a very tidy calendar that she checks each morning while eating a freshly made croissant and drinking a home-made latte. I'm not bitter, just jealous. Of course, my jealousy is tempered by my knowledge that she's married to a closeted college professor. And while I feel for my friend, I sympathize, in a strange way, with her husband. Marriage isn't easy in the best of circumstances; and it's not made any easier when one partner is pretending to be something he is not.

"Sure," I say. "I'm ready. It's going to be fine." By using the word "fine" over and over again, I'm more or less guaran-teeing that nothing will even be close.

"They're going to love Theo," Avery says. I agree although I'm less confident about them loving me. "We take Sophie for her interview next week. I'm already nervous."

"It's all going to be fine," I say again, craning my neck around, looking for Sam. He seems to be the only person in San Francisco who has not drunk the Kool-Aid. "Superfine," I add.

"You're probably right," Avery says quietly. "Is your friend okay? He's awfully quiet."

"Pathologically shy," I say.

Next to me, looking resigned to his fate in hell, which is sure to last longer than nine innings, Yoder pulls his coat col-lar up practically to his forehead. He will not be good for my reputation as a normal, everyday mom unless his attitude improves, and we may not have enough time together for that to happen. I accept that it was incredibly stupid of me to take him from his driveway, but the alternative was handing him directly over to Simon and never seeing him again. And that also seemed incredibly stupid.

"It's a play-off game," I whisper to him. "Do you know what certain people would do for these tickets? As far as kid-nappings go, I think you're doing pretty well."

Yoder turtles down further into his collar. "I know nothing of this game," he says, "this great American pastime."

Well, that makes two of us but at least I'm making an effort.

The game is excruciatingly slow but the kids love it. I have a really hard time sitting and watching guys with beer bellies in tight pants do absolutely nothing. Instead, I try and pretend that Director Gray is not my father and that none of this is actually happening. My attempts at total denial fall flat, as usual.

"Mom," Theo says, tugging on my sleeve, "can we have popcorn? Can we have a corn dog? Can we have . . . soda?" Normally, I'm one of the overinvolved moms with the snacks that taste like cardboard. But today I'm distracted.

"Sure."

"Really? We can?" Theo says with surprise. "You just said yes, right?"

"Yes. I said yes." True, I'm processing a few seconds slower than normal but I'm not totally dead yet. "To the popcorn. Not the corn dog or the soda."

"Okay," says Theo. "We'll take that deal."

"Is your mom okay?" Henry asks.

"I don't know," Theo whispers, staring at me with big blue eyes. "But we're getting the popcorn."

I lean over and whisper in Yoder's ear. "I'm going to get popcorn. Don't move. If you do, bad things will happen to you."

"Like what?" Yoder asks,

"I don't know. Bad things."

"Whatever," he says, waving me off. He deserves a time-out for being unpleasant, in addition to the unnamed bad things I haven't thought of yet, but I remind myself I'm his captor, not his mother, even if the two roles kind of overlap in certain circumstances. I go in search of the popcorn guy.

In exchange for all the money in my wallet, the popcorn guy hands me three overflowing bags. Yoder probably doesn't deserve one but I know what happens when young men become calorie deficient and that is something I don't need right now. To hedge my bets, I get a corn dog for him, too.

When I turn to head back to our seats, I bump smack into a woman in a long black cashmere sweater. The hood elegantly conceals her features. The sun glints off the black wool, making it iridescent and I'm struck with an urge to reach out and pet her like a cat.

"Excuse me," I say, in a feeble attempt to juggle my popcorn bags and corn dog and not fall down the steep stadium stairs.

She stops and turns to face me. Her silver hair is striking against the black and hangs loosely to her shoulders. Her deep blue eyes scan my face with a sense of urgency, almost of longing. I suddenly feel as if I've lost my balance. She steadies me with a delicate hand.

"Do we know each other?" I ask, feeling oddly out of sync with my own voice.

Her smile is not one of joy or resignation but rather of acute pain. She leans in close to me, holding my shoulders tightly. The position is awkward and panic floods my central nervous system.

"It's a trap," she whispers. "Don't fall into it."

"Mom," Theo yells from his seat. "Hurry up!" My head turns immediately toward the sound of my impatient son's voice and by the time I swing back toward the woman it's too late. I catch a glimpse of black cashmere disappearing from the stands.

Every impulse tells me to drop the popcorn and run after her, but I can't do that. Mothers come back with the popcorn and sit nicely and chaperone and things. They don't abandon their children so they can chase down mysterious, well-dressed women who mutter incomprehensibly in passing.

"She probably was singing to herself," I say to the popcorn. "Or talking on the phone. Yes. Probably she was on the phone talking to her broker and commenting that the latest silicon valley IPO is nothing more than a money trap."

Right. And now I'm going to head out onto the field, smack a homerun into the bay, and win the game.

"Theo's mom!" Henry yells. "What are you doing?"

"I'm coming, I'm coming," I say, trying to gather my wits about me because clearly they've scattered on the wind.

I hand out the popcorn. Yoder peers into his bag with suspicion but the boys convince him ballpark popcorn is nothing short of awesome. However, the corn dog is another story.

"Just eat it," I tell Yoder. "It'll make you less grumpy."

"What is it?" he asks, his brow furrowed in confusion.

"It's a hotdog," I say, "with stuff on it. On a stick."

If I were him, there's no way I would eat it, but to his credit, he takes a tentative bite. As the corn dog fills his mouth, his eyes light up in the same way Theo's did when he first tasted ice cream. I turn back toward the field, not wanting to watch any more of the simple pleasure in Yoder's eyes. There's a player on second base. He's itching to steal third but at the last second loses his nerve.

"Don't you want to know why you're here?" I ask Yoder, quietly so the people around me don't stand a chance of hearing. Yoder shovels a fistful of popcorn into his mouth and squints in my direction.

"Probably not because you had an extra ticket," he says, little bits of popcorn spraying every which way.

"If I hadn't shown up when I did, you'd be en route to D.C. right now with a black sack over your head and no chance of an in-flight meal. I kind of did you a favor."

"That's your interpretation."

"Righteous Liberty wants to trade Charles Gray for you," I say. "Does that surprise you?"

Yoder gazes out at the bay. "What does it matter?" he says without emotion.

How come in the movies rogue agents are always sexy and always right, no matter the methods they employ to see justice done? In real life, being a rogue agent isn't turning out to be all that much fun.

We watch a few more swings. Nobody seems to be able to hit the ball. If I were making forty million dollars a year, I would try harder to hit the ball.

"This guy stinks," I say as the batter swings wildly at a terrible pitch.

"Well, not according to the numbers," Yoder says, his popcorn bag resting on the closed baseball program in his lap, his half-eaten corn dog poised in midair. "In 470 at bats this season, he has 148 hits, of which 32 were doubles, 3 were triples, and 27 were home runs. In fact, he has a batting average of .315 and an on-base percentage of .381. He's actually had quite a regular season. The opposing pitcher, on the other hand, is quite formidable. Over 33 games and a total of 212 innings pitched, he has thrown 231 strikeouts—more than 1 per inning—and permitted only 81 earned runs for an earned run average of 3.43. Although he has given up 92 walks. Perhaps the batter should stop swinging and hope for the best."

I suddenly remember what source number two, in the USAWMD's report on Yoder, claimed happened in the bathroom. Yoder alone with the little black book for four minutes. Four whole minutes. We stare at each other over Yoder's half-empty popcorn bag. Yoder's eyes shine. Finally, he shrugs.

"Maybe he does stink. What do I know about baseball?"

Without warning, a fly ball comes falling out of the sky right on top of us. Yoder sticks out a hand and the ball sails right into it as if attracted by a very powerful magnet. Immediately all the kids pile on top of Yoder, wanting to see the ball, to touch it, to beg to take it home. Underneath the mountain of little bodies, Yoder flashes a brief smile and for a moment he seems utterly regular. This kind of day is as American as apple pie for certain socioeconomic groups. However, to enjoy it you must embrace the illusion that we are all the same, heads down, striving for the dream. And that is just not the case.

20

I t is a good thing your average citizen of the world goes around with blinders on. People are quite skilled at seeing what they want to see rather than what is right in front of them. Over the years, I've successfully masqueraded as a number of different people and I'm fully aware of the fact that if anyone had bothered to take a closer look, I would have been dead in a ditch long ago. Simon Still is the master of misdirection. He can look you in the eyes and lie with the greatest of ease. I was never as good as he is but that doesn't mean I couldn't get by.

Take me being here chaperoning a ball game with a surly twenty-something sitting beside me, stuffing his face with everything on the concession menu. If you really examined the details, you would see it was off. Or better yet, take the burglar.

We live in a relatively safe San Francisco neighborhood. It's easy to believe that crime doesn't exist here, that it only happens in other neighborhoods where there are fewer golden retrievers and thousand-dollar strollers cluttering up the sidewalk. Such belief creates a nice bubble of complacency that's quite comfortable if you can manage not to pop it.

It was winter and the rain pounded down on our roof with a vengeance. A few months into married life, I was in the peculiar position of trying to figure out what to do with the rest of my life. Will encouraged me to take as much time as I needed but it was turning out not to be such an easy question to answer. So, rather than waste valuable time focused on an unpleasant task, I took to reading magazines.

Oh, what I had missed while racing around the world trying to catch bad guys. There were party dresses to consider and accessories and skirt lengths and the hair question, of course. There were quizzes to help determine if I was a nymphomaniac or a wallflower or a Type-A bitch. There were diets and exercise regimens designed to make me sweat off ten pounds by summer! Eating whatever I want! Taking these pills the FDA swore would grow me a nice bushy tail in no time at all! There was decorating advice to help me achieve a successful living room, whatever that was. There were recipes with spices that could only be obtained in the jungles of Burma or from the mountaintops of Peru or, in a pinch, at the Whole Foods one neighborhood over.

I devoured it all, the meaningless noise that helps us to ignore the chaos outside our collective window. If you can concentrate on the perfect golden highlights, the kind that make your blue eyes pop and enhance your not-quite-defined-enough cheekbones, well then, who gives a shit about bombs?

I was most of the way through an issue of *Cosmopolitan* that promised the secret to a happy marriage was frequent blow jobs and nipple-exposing lingerie when I heard a sound coming from the front door that I was fairly certain wasn't the rain.

It's important to note that our house, while utterly charming, had as many security holes as a wheel of Swiss cheese. I realized that to bring it up to what I considered a most basic standard would raise some eyebrows, so I was trying to be

Zen about it and relax in my non-secure environment. I even thought the experience might help me grow into a better person, someone able to live in a house with a single deadbolt on the wooden front door. However, I was having a hard time getting over the glass panels in that same front door. Glass. In a door. With a lock. How did people live like this?

Sitting at my kitchen table, I heard the distinct sound of wood splintering, followed by the creak of hinges. The front door was opened and then closed.

The man, dressed in dark clothes and soaking wet, was in my living room, busily making a pile of Will's coveted electronics.

"You're dripping on my floor," I said. "It's sustainably farmed bamboo and apparently harder than diamond, but still, it's rude. Plus, who breaks into a house in the middle of the day? Aren't you at least supposed to commit these sorts of crimes in the dead of night?"

The man slowly stood up. I wondered for a brief moment if he had a gun and, if so, what exactly I would do with that information.

"You're not supposed to be home," he said in as menacing a voice as he could manage. "Turn around and I'll forget I ever saw you."

He had a point. San Francisco was hardly doable on one income. Every able-bodied person needed to work to keep the whole thing afloat. The only people ever at home during the days were the nannies and the babies.

"The last time I checked, this was my house," I said. "Maybe you should leave. Or better yet, maybe you should plug all that stuff back in first. Do you know how complicated it is to set up a sound system these days? It practically takes a Ph.D. Do you have one of those?"

The man looked confused.

"A what?"

"An engineering degree. Because I don't want to spend the rest of my day putting this all back together. I was reading. It was nice."

In his eyes, there was the first flicker of realization that this was not going as planned.

"You can't keep doing this," I said. "There's no future in crime."

The man stood up, took a few steps toward me. His fists were clenched.

"What are you going to do about it, lady?"

"I haven't decided yet," I said. "I would consider letting you go, but you'd have to promise me you'd reform your ways."

The man started to laugh and drew closer to me.

"It's hard out there, man," he said. "This is the only way."

"There are always options," I said, planting my feet.

"Not for people like me," he said. It was a little sad but he had broken into my house and that was not allowed.

He never considered, even for a moment, that a person like me could be dangerous. In his eyes, I was just some girl blocking the door. He'd already accepted the fact that he wasn't getting out of here with his haul but he was certain he was getting out of here, and tomorrow he'd just try again down the block. This was too good a neighborhood for wide screen TVs and electronics and laptops to move on.

He thought he'd punch me and that would be plenty. But I

caught his fist mid-flight and twisted his arm around behind him. As he spun, I clamped my arm around his neck and squeezed. With both hands, he clawed at my arm and his feet ran in place on the wet floor as if he were a gerbil on one of those wheels. He was heavy and I felt the weight of him dragging me to my knees. Resting on the coffee table was a Steuben glass globe a little bigger than a baseball. It fit comfortably in my hand and didn't seem to sustain any damage when I clocked my burglar in the head with it. He immediately slumped into a boneless heap at my feet.

At the Agency, I would have called for a clean-up crew and eventually a few men I had never seen before would show up and take the person in question, mostly alive, away to be debriefed. I wasn't usually privy to where they ended up. I didn't do interrogation. That job belonged to people even more shadowy than myself. But this was my living room and I was unsure as to the protocol, so I called my newly minted husband for advice.

"So I was sitting at the kitchen table reading a magazine," I began, "and some guy broke into our house."

There was silence. Perhaps my approach was too casual?

"He didn't get away with anything," I continued, hoping to reassure Will, "but he did unplug a bunch of stuff."

"Lucy, hang up the phone and call the police." Will's voice was measured and still within his control, but it teetered right on the edge. "Do it now. I'm on my way."

"I'm not in any danger," I said. "The guy is unconscious on the floor. I hope his wet coat doesn't stain the wood."

That was it. Will lost it. "Lucy," he screamed. "Why are you still in there? Get out of the house! Get out right now!" I was touched that he cared. It was sweet.

"It's okay. Really," I said.

"Hang. Up. The. Phone. Call. The. Police," he said, obviously taking deep breaths in an effort not to sound hysterical. No one likes a hysterical man. I could hear him out on the street. I thought he must really love me because he was hailing a cab and Will never takes cabs. He thinks they're a symbol of wasteful human consumption. We have feet. We have public transportation. We have bicycles. Ergo we ought not to have taxis. Or something along those lines.

"Okay, okay," I said. "I'm doing it now. I'm going outside. Just let me grab an umbrella."

The police detectives arrived round about the same time as Will. Martinez was a short stocky guy. He looked profoundly uncomfortable in his clothes, the shirt under his sport coat straining across his broad chest. His partner, Walters, a tall stringy woman, had the opposite problem. She was a human clothes hanger and her shapeless suit hung accordingly. They made an odd couple and for some reason that made me smile. I wondered who got to drive the cruiser. Did they rock-paper-scissors every time they got in? Will wrapped his arms around me.

"Jesus, Lucy," he whispered. "You just scared the shit out of me. Please don't do that again." Walters poked at the damp criminal on my floor with a gloved hand.

"Better call for an ambulance," she said. "Ma'am, can you explain to us what exactly happened?"

It was then that I realized the rules I was used to playing by didn't apply in the so-called civilized world in which I now lived. My story, however supported by the evidence, was not going to be well received by this audience.

"Well, I was in the kitchen when I heard a sound, like the

splintering of the front door lock, so I came to see what was happening and, well, this guy was in the house trying to take, you know, things. I guess I startled him because he slipped on the wet floor and knocked himself out. Isn't that lucky?"

The silence was so loud I swear they heard it down at police headquarters.

"That's your story?" Martinez asked.

Yes. Is there something wrong with it?

"Are you saying you don't believe me?" I asked, putting an incredulous look on my face.

Walters tapped her pencil on her open notepad.

"Most people would be, let me see, how should I put it here? Upset? Yes, maybe that's the word. Most people would be upset to find a guy like this in their living room. But you seem fairly relaxed."

I shrugged. "I do a lot of yoga and practice intense biofeedback when confronted with stressful situations." Translation: I'm just another kooky San Franciscan and no matter how hard you try to understand me, I will never make any sense to you.

I was saved by the arrival of the ambulance and several medics rushing in to deal with the guy on the floor.

"We aren't done asking questions," Martinez said, although he did not sound completely committed to that position. "There has been a rash of burglaries in this neighborhood. If this turns out to be the guy, we'll need you to testify."

"Regardless," Walters interrupted. "We'll be expecting you down at headquarters sometime tomorrow. To chat." She handed me a card with her number. As I studied it, I could feel her watching me. I knew that look. Her radar was up.

It's a good thing that most of the world's terror is perpetrated by men. In general, men aren't as observant as women. They're much more focused on great shows of strength and violence than on the subtler approach that subterfuge provides. And it's this very focus that makes bringing them to their knees even a possibility. When we start to have a surplus of female bad guys, then we're in serious trouble. There will be no stopping that tide.

After everyone finally left, the police, the EMTs, the photographer, and the evidence collector, Will sat down on the couch. He looked exhausted.

"Tell me that's what really happened," he said quietly.

"That's what really happened," I said.

"Lucy, did you ever see any of those horror movies where the heroine goes into a house that is clearly possessed by a demon carrying a machete, just so she can have a look around?"

I nodded my head.

"Well, normal people don't do that," he yelled. "Normal people run away! What the fuck were you thinking?"

In the back of my mind, I saw Walters plugging my name into her database and coming up with something that didn't look quite right. I saw her digging deeper, pulling in favors, stretching her resources to their logical limit. After which I saw her captain calling her into his office and shutting the door.

"Cease and desist," he would say. Walters would protest, demand an explanation, and the captain would sigh and tell her it came down from the top and there was nothing he could do. Walters would experience a small shiver then, the kind that makes the hair on your arms stand straight up. And she would stop poking around because she would be suddenly and painfully aware that they were watching her.

But my husband was not so easy. I had to bring out the big guns.

"I have something to tell you," I said, sitting down next to him on the couch, taking his warm hand in mine.

"I'm not sure I can take any more surprises today," he said, pulling me closer.

"It's a good thing," I said. "I'm pregnant."

As far as misdirection goes, that one worked like a charm.

21

By the fourth inning, the kids are antsy and I'm busy working on a theory that involves four minutes and baseball statistics. Teacher Wendy is trying to get everyone to sing a round of "Take Me Out to the Ball Game" but all the kids want is more junk food. Richard Yoder has hit me up for a Coke and a box of Cracker Jacks in addition to the popcorn and the corn dog, so I'm no longer feeling that badly for him.

I pull out my cell phone and dial the number for Chemical Claude and his Righteous Liberty pals. I don't have a special cell phone like Simon but we civvies have to make do with what we've got. Chemical Claude answers after the fourth ring.

"Put Gray on the line or no deal," I say. Claude chuckles. He'd make the perfect evil Santa Claus.

"Sally, you didn't say hello," he says.

The noise of the ballpark fades into the background and his voice fills the entirety of my head. The experience has all the qualities of a bad sinus infection.

"She was a lovely girl, you know," he says. "Compliant. Pretty. A shame you couldn't protect her."

It's ill-considered to have this conversation in broad daylight, surrounded by a bunch of children. They're certainly going to wonder what's up when I crush the cell phone into dust with my bare hands.

"Put Gray on," I whisper, each word a chore. My heart pounds in my chest and I'm aware of Yoder's eyes on me. I dig my nails into his thigh, indicating that now is not a good time for him to make a break for it. On the phone, there's shuffling and the sound of wind.

"Sally?"

"Is this Director Gray?" Calling him Dad will take some work. The voice is muffled and soft and doesn't sound like the Gray I used to know. But maybe that's because I never really knew him and for some reason he's speaking Russian.

"Don't come. They want you . . ." He is cut off before he can finish. Chemical Claude comes back on the line.

"I'm pleased you were able to make this happen," Claude says. "I knew you would."

A vote of confidence from Chemical Claude is not necessarily heartwarming. Plus, if we start talking about it I might feel compelled to admit that skill had nothing to do with it. Mostly, it was dumb luck.

"We trade tonight," he says.

"Nights don't work for me," I say. Can you imagine the hoops I'd have to jump through to get an overnight babysitter on such short notice? "Tomorrow afternoon. Ferry building." I'm already excited about a post-hostage-exchange Blue Bottle coffee.

"Sally, why do you think you get to make the rules?"

"Because I have your guy," I say.

There is silence. Chemical Claude doesn't like being told what to do.

"We will see you there at two o'clock," he says finally.

I agree, although I'm already sweating the logistics of such a venture. As soon as I hang up, my phone rings again. I'm sure it's the CIA curious to know why I'm chitchatting with a terrorist wanted in all 192 countries of the world recognized by the United Nations. But the number that flashes up is Will's office.

"Hey," I answer. "Aren't you supposed to be in Idaho up to your knees in shit?"

"Well, when you put it that way, it makes me kind of sad I'm missing out."

The sound of Ian Blackford's voice, even coming through the air, is enough to make me cold.

"Are you in Will's office?" I ask. Next to me, Yoder is getting into it, on his feet cheering a two-base grounder.

"No," Blackford says. "I just really like the element of surprise, don't you? Keeps life interesting."

"I liked you better when you were dead," I say.

"You don't mean that."

"Yes, I really do." We couldn't have a party and invite Simon and Chemical Claude and not have Blackford crash. His presence is somehow inevitable.

"Oh, Sally, don't be so melodramatic," Blackford says. In the background, I hear a police siren. He could be in Will's office. He could be anywhere. "You should have known the minute I gave you the Polaroid, but you decided to stick your head in the sand like an ostrich. And for my purposes, that wasn't helpful."

I hate that he just compared me to a big dorky bird that can't even fly but even more I hate he's playing an angle that's not immediately obvious to me.

"And those purposes are what, exactly?" I ask, not expecting an actual answer.

"Oh, you know, me, rising like a phoenix from the ashes."

I have no idea what he's talking about but his cryptic statement sends an old familiar tremor of fear through my body.

Had you asked me at any point over the last year or so, I would have proclaimed myself finally inured to Blackford's dark magic. The fact that he occasionally showed up in my dreams looking indistinguishable from the cover of a bad romance novel was utterly beside the point. I might even have taken it a step further and said I was no longer scared of him. But here I am shaking in the pale sun like one of those pathetic little dogs that needs to wear a sweater in the wintertime. Yes, the feeling is part fear but also part fury. Blackford will do what he wants and I will sit back and take it because I haven't yet figured out an alternative.

"Are you here?" I ask, assuming he knows exactly where I am.

"No. Baseball is dull," he says finally. "I like games where the players bleed."

"That's nice," I say. "Really."

The smell of garlic fries wafts by on the breeze. The Cheerios I had for breakfast crawl back up my throat. I sound as if I am being strangled.

"Sally, are you okay?" The genuine concern in his voice strikes me as completely hilarious.

"I'm great," I say. "Really fabulous. The Giants are winning. I'm thinking they go all the way this year."

Through the phone, I hear a familiar sound, the horn blast of a container ship gliding into the Bay. I look out toward the water and there it is, riding low with cargo from China, destined for places like Toledo and Albuquerque and Des Moines. The horn blasts again.

"I wonder what your husband thinks about all the fuel being dumped into the Bay by those tankers?" Blackford asks. "Surely it's an environmental no-no."

Down on the field, a player shouts at the umpire. He spits on the ground and kicks at the dirt, an angry bull about to charge. The umpire gestures violently. In a flash, the dugout clears. All the players spill out onto the field and begin swinging at each other with big fleshy fists. Theo and Henry and the rest of the Happy Times Preschoolers are rapt, mouths open. They've never seen adults act this way. Teacher Wendy, looking shocked, launches into a speech about not letting anger get the best of you and then she starts to sing a song about sharing our toys. The kids could not care less about singing. It's important to remember that, not long ago, for pleasure, we'd fill the stands of Roman arenas to watch lions tear unarmed men limb from limb. Violence is fascinating as long as it's happening to someone else.

Without answering Blackford's question, I press the End button on my phone because there's nothing else to talk about. I get it. He's here and he's close. I don't know why or what he wants but I have no doubt that at some very inopportune time in the very near future, he will let me know.

Meanwhile, the umpires struggle to regain control of the field. There will be multiple fines and penalties and reprimands when this is over. Sitting beside my very own personal hostage, watching the scene unfold below, all I can think is how I would sell my very soul for a chocolate cupcake with a thick layer of frosting, which is an odd thought, considering the circumstances.

22

Fear is a funny thing. For me, it usually shows up after a near-death experience, be it a shooting, a near drowning, or some other general kind of ass-kicking. I get a strange sensation in my stomach that is best described as four hundred butterflies and a quart of motor oil. Usually, the feeling passes quickly and I keep on going.

But I've noticed that fear makes other people, normal people, behave erratically, as if all logic got off the bus at the last stop. I suppose this shouldn't be surprising. Half the reason I was recruited for the Agency in the first place is that I rarely let fear get a stranglehold on me. Although that time in Laos, it came pretty close.

The flight was short, from Vientiane to Luang Prabang on Laos Airlines, which wasn't the sort of outfit to give you peace of mind on its best day. In five months, sixteen days, and ten hours I would no longer be with the Agency, but at the time all I knew was that going overland in Laos to our destination was out of the question. Simon Still had made it clear he did not intend to spend the day crammed into a rickety open-air bus traveling at five kilometers an hour in the mud. When I suggested to him that overland was always safer than air travel in these circumstances, he looked at me as if I were an unwelcome hallucination.

"I do not recall asking your opinion," he said dismissively. In reality, it probably had more to do with his white suit and how it would look after ten hours on a bus than with the overall safety of the mission or those of us on it.

The turbo prop sat on the cracked runway, the roar of the engines and rotating propellers indicating that the plane, for now, was at least operational. It was already hot and damp even though the sun was just beginning to rise in the sky.

Sitting next to me, Simon ran a tentative finger down the slightly grungy leg of my khaki pants.

"There's a stain," he pointed out, a disgusted look on his face. I nodded. The stain was tea or bike grease or mud, all of which seemed better than the blood, someone else's, that was covering my other pair of pants.

"I don't have any more," I said. "These are the last ones."

"We just spent four weeks in Vietnam," he said. "They make clothes there, Sally. Did you not notice?"

I did notice but I was working, following a guy who was supposed to reveal the secrets of the universe to me but did little more than kibitz with his friends over thick Vietnamese coffee and cigarettes. My feet were tired from all that shadowing. I had no idea where Simon had found the time to dash off and pick up a few custom-made suits. I was clearly doing something wrong.

"I was busy," I said, "following the guy. Remember? What were you doing?"

He waved me off, trying to fasten a broken seat belt.

"Things," he said, which meant I could tie him to the rack and torture him and he still wouldn't tell me what he was up to while I was sweating it out with the coffee klatch.

I didn't even bother with my seat belt, a frayed and faded piece of orange webbing that was probably cut from a rice sack and stapled to the seat. In the cockpit, a young pilot kept wiping his damp forehead. Almost as if he could feel me looking at him, he turned and our eyes met. His face was pale and bruised-looking. Even from fifteen feet away, I could see his hands were shaking. On the right, the copilot's seat was empty. The pilot turned away quickly, swabbed his forehead with the back of his sleeve, and slammed the cockpit door shut with his foot.

"The pilot looks unwell," I said.

"Sometimes you just fly with God, Sally," Simon said, not looking up from his newspaper.

But I didn't want to fly with God. I wanted to fly with a pilot who didn't resemble a dead fish. I felt the tingly fingers run up my spine, challenging me, but as the plane began to race down the runway, I did nothing more than sit back and close my eyes.

There were twelve people on the plane, including us. You would think people would stare at Simon Still in his white suit and hat but it was as if he didn't exist. If asked later on what they remembered, none of the passengers would mention a thin man in a white suit reading a current edition of the *Wall Street Journal*. They would remember my stained khakis and dusty white shirt but Simon was a ghost. To this day, I'm not sure how he did it, disappeared like he did in plain sight.

"Where are we going?" I asked.

"Anonymous tip," he said.

"That usually means I get shot at."

Simon shrugged. "It happens," he said.

"Not to you," I say. You always seem to be out getting a suit made when it starts raining bullets.

I never defied Simon Still in the nine years I worked for him. I never purposefully lied to him or misled him or set him up to take the fall. And, believe me, there were times when doing so would have made my life easier. I was loyal even though Simon never treated me as anything more than an inconvenience.

The plane struggled to gain altitude, doing its best imitation of a salmon swimming up a stream of dark molasses. Gravity nipped at our heels, not willing to give up on this one quite yet. Simon read his newspaper. All around me, people slept peacefully. Maybe my sense of impending doom was misplaced? No one on this plane looked interesting enough to die in a dramatic fiery crash.

My head bounced uncomfortably against the small window when suddenly I seemed to rise out of my seat a few inches. My stomach lurched into my throat. Simon looked over the top of his newspaper at the cockpit door.

"Feels a little bit like Space Mountain in here," he said. The noise and the wind outside grew steadily louder. The plane rolled right and began a rapid descent. One by one, the other passengers woke up to a troubling new reality. As we hit what felt like a speed bump, the cockpit door swung open, revealing the cause of this troubling new reality.

"You may have been on to something about the pilot," Simon said calmly, while leaping from his seat. Inside the cockpit, the pilot slumped over the yoke, arms dangling at his sides, neck twisted at an unnatural angle, a rag doll abandoned by a child. Moving fast, Simon elbowed his way through the now screaming passengers and into the tiny cockpit. Trying to follow, I was surprised to suddenly find the huge man from across the aisle in my lap, with his arms wrapped around my neck. It took me a second to realize he wasn't trying to suffocate me but instead clinging to me, baby-monkey style.

"We're going to die!" he shrieked in an Australian accent. "There's no one flying the plane." He was right about that, so I didn't see any point in trying to convince him otherwise. What was Simon doing? I tried to untangle myself from the man around my neck but it was a no go. We continued to plummet together, wrapped in a strange embrace.

"Sally, get up here!" Simon shouted.

"I cheated on her twice," the Australian sobbed into my neck. "And then I lied about it. I wrecked her car and said I wasn't driving. And it was me in those naked photographs on the Web, even if you can't see my face."

My companion was starting to remind me of a bad country song. At least if we crashed, I'd get some relief. I tried again to wrestle free but he hung on tighter.

"Sally!" Simon shouted again. "Now would be good!"

"Um, excuse me. I know you're scared but I have to go and help make sure this plane doesn't crash, okay?"

"Don't leave me!" he wailed.

"I'll come back in a minute," I said, even though we didn't have as much as a minute left before we were all pudding.

"I can't let you go," he cried. He was a big, strapping Australian with Wolverine-sized hands and he was not letting go. I could have killed him but that seemed harsh, considering the circumstances. It took all of my strength to rotate us around so my feet were now in the aisle.

As Simon pulled back on the yoke, trying to level the plane and bleed off the excess speed, it was as if we'd arrived at the bottom of Space Mountain. I stumbled and landed right on top of the Australian. Our faces were centimeters apart.

"Please don't take this the wrong way," I said. "But this relationship is not working for me." With that, I leaned hard with my elbow on the pressure point between his neck and shoulder and watched as his eyes immediately rolled back in his head.

In the cockpit, I found Simon sitting in the copilot's seat, shoulder-to-shoulder with the dead guy. As soon as he saw me, he started to get up.

"Sally, take the controls," he said. "I need to move the pilot out of the way."

"Are you sure that's a good idea?" I asked.

"Yes," Simon said, shoving me into the now vacant copilot's seat. "We need room to work up here."

I'd been thinking more along the lines of, is it a good idea for me to fly the plane?, but it was too late for discussion because Simon pulled his hands from the yolk and placed mine on it.

"Keep the nose on the artificial horizon," he said.

I knew next to nothing about how to fly planes and thought "artificial horizon" could just as easily have been the name of a pop band, but I did as I was told and tried to aim the plane right for it.

"So it could be dysentery or poison that got him," Simon said as he tried to pull the dead pilot from his seat. "My bet is on poison. Do you have an opinion?"

I might have if I hadn't been using my force of will to keep the plane aloft. Simon gave a final heave, pulling the pilot out of his seat and shoving him through the narrow cockpit door. Then he slammed the door shut, muffling the terrified screams of the passengers.

"There," Simon said. "That should help. Are we level? How many feet?" He slid into the pilot's seat and fastened his harness securely. We were shoulder-to-shoulder in the cramped cockpit. Next to me, Simon was sweating and tapping his foot in an erratic rhythm. The idea that he might be nervous was something I was afraid to even consider. Simon didn't get nervous.

"I think we're level," I said. "And at around sixteen thousand feet. That's pretty high, right?"

"Well," he said, "that's from sea level. And what do we know Laos has many of?"

"Mountains," I said.

"Correct. Try not to hit any."

"Right. Sure."

Quickly, I surveyed the horizon and was relieved to find no obvious mountains in our way. I was starting to feel better about my piloting skills, as long as no one asked me to land. Or turn.

"So?" he said.

"Poison," I said. But we didn't have time to reflect on this for long because just as Simon got comfortable, a red light in the panel of instruments started blinking frantically. Naturally, it was the fuel gauge.

"Look out the window on your side, Sally. Look back toward the engine. What do you see?"

I saw clouds and blue sky and the sun reflected all along

the silver wing. I also saw a stream of iridescent fuel flowing out of the plane and into the atmosphere. In the bright light, it was pretty.

"We have a situation," I said.

"I suspected we might. This is their backup plan, Sally. Just in case the dead pilot didn't get the job done."

"What do we do?" I asked, letting go of the yoke as Simon took control of the plane. He seemed oblivious to the passengers howling in the cabin behind us.

"We crash," he said, "as gracefully as possible."

Interesting. I had never been in a plane crash but for some reason it didn't scare me. Sometimes the odds are so much against you that fear seems an utter waste of time.

Outside, the engine on the right side cut out. I scrambled into my seat harness, pulling the straps as tight as they allowed.

"Well, that's inconvenient," Simon said, tightening his grip on the yoke. Moments later, the other engine went silent.

"Now what?" I said, trying to keep the panic from my voice. I considered reminding Simon that if we'd taken the bus we would not, right now, have front row seats to an unscheduled plane crash. But I kept my mouth shut. No need to die angry.

"Find a field," Simon said, without looking at me, "some open space, something without trees or jungle or water. Somewhere we can land."

Appreciating his optimism, I pressed my face to the side window. The world below rushed by in a green blur. We were losing altitude as Simon struggled to keep the plane level with no working engines. A few miles ahead, I saw a temple surrounded by a few clear-cut acres dotted with statues. Not much, but it would have to do.

"Hard right," I said. Wrestling the forces of gravity, Simon slowly turned the plane. "There," I pointed. "The temple."

Simon nodded thoughtfully. "When we're down and out of the plane," he said, as if survival was a real possibility, "move. Don't stand around waiting for someone to take a shot at you."

"But there are people back there in the cabin," I said.

"And one of them probably has a bullet with your name on it and very little regard for life. Let's not be here to see what that looks like."

That would be the backup, backup plan. Whoever they were, they were serious.

"Boy, these guys must really hate you," I said, wanting to close my eyes as the sound of air rushing past the plane grew ever louder.

"Me?" Simon said. "Why do you think they want to kill me?"

In normal circumstances, I'd have wanted to spend a few minutes pondering what Simon said because it seemed important. But that was not going to happen because, before I could manage it, we fell out of the sky like a brick.

It was the middle of the rainy season in Laos and the ground was a thick casserole of mud and grasses and rocks. As the wheels of the plane plowed forward, the straps of my seat belt cut through my skin and knocked the wind out of my lungs. Back in the cabin, the passengers were nothing more than dice being tossed around on a craps table.

Simon held fast to the yoke, trying to keep the plane headed straight but it was a losing battle. The nose swung to the left and the wing went down into the mud, causing the plane to tumble. Sounding like a train barreling through a tunnel, the fuselage broke apart and drowned out what might have been me screaming. I caught a glimpse of an enormous stone temple as my pilot's seat came unmoored and I went flying, still strapped in, out of the collapsed side of the plane. I hit a crop of trees seat-side first and came down sideways in a broken heap. An unnerving silence filled the air as what was left of the plane slowly came to a stop alongside the temple. Monks in orange robes flowed out and down the steps like fiery comets moving every which way, emitting a low chant.

With my right hand, I undid the seat belt and fell directly into the mud. Blood ran freely from a gash in my upper arm.

"Get up," I heard coming from behind me. I rolled over on my hands and knees and tried to stand up but everything was spinning. I wiped the blood from my eyes to see Simon emerge from the trees. His suit was dirty and torn but his hat was still on.

"How did you not lose your hat?" I asked, still on the ground. "We just crashed a plane."

"Are you delirious?"

"I'm not sure. Are you wearing a hat?"

Simon put a hand on his head. "Yes, I am. What's wrong with your wrist?"

I looked down to see my left hand twisted at a very odd angle. "Oh, that's not so good."

Without asking, Simon grabbed my hand and pulled my wrist back into its proper alignment. Bright pain flashed before me.

"I wish you hadn't done that," I said, my jaw clenched so tight the muscles burned. But Simon was already heading back into the jungle.

I looked again at the wreckage, which was now crawling with monks searching for survivors. Slowly, I pulled myself to my feet, cradling one arm in the other, and took a tentative step forward. It was the first time I'd been in a situation where I felt the hopelessness of our fight, how small and ineffective I was in the face of the big sprawling enemy. But it would not be the last.

23

For some reason, I am thinking about the Australian's country song confession as we ride the escalator out of the ballpark. I hold Henry in one hand and Theo in the other, in case the escalator decides not to let them go at the bottom. I've heard the urban myth about plastic sandals and being eaten alive by escalators and I'm not taking any chances. Like I said, fear makes you do funny things.

In light of that, what happens next should not be a surprise but somehow it still is. Yoder is afraid. He sees this ending badly for him. The second his feet hit the sidewalk, he makes a run for it. And I'm not in a position to chase after him, exactly.

"Mom, why is your friend running away?" Theo and Henry stare after Yoder sprinting through the crowd as if he's being chased by a swarm of angry bees. "How's he going to get home?"

"Public transportation?" I suggest. "Maybe the bus or the Muni?"

I'm trying to formulate some sort of plan that gets Yoder back and gets Henry home before his mother starts to freak out, when Yoder stops short, frozen in place among the bronze statues of baseball legends surrounding him. Standing about ten feet in front of Yoder, looking like a rock star at a hoedown, is Simon Still. Of course I knew Simon would eventually be coming for Yoder, but I'd banked on him at least waiting until it was dark, thus buying me some time to figure out what to do. Besides, trying to kidnap a hostage who is rightfully mine in broad daylight seems the sort of plan I would come up with and is therefore highly suspect.

Yoder gives an audible yelp and begins backpedaling. He reminds me of a cartoon character and I grin, which is totally inappropriate. This is not funny. This is bad. Simon, moving forward, mirrors each step Yoder takes as if they are hostile dance partners.

"Mom, me and Henry want a baseball hat," Theo says, pulling on my jacket. "One of those black-and-orange ones." He's feeling cocky after pulling off the popcorn. I'm lucky he hasn't asked me for a Maserati or the Death Star LEGO set.

"Do you plan on trading it back and forth?" I ask, eyes still focused on Yoder and Simon, moving closer.

"Huh?"

"You asked for a single baseball hat. Don't you each want one?"

"Yeah," says Theo, rolling his eyes. "We want two. Matching ones."

"We can wear them to school! We can show Teacher Wendy!" says Henry.

"Teacher Wendy will be so excited to see our hats," Theo says.

"Okay," I say. "If you can spell 'baseball' for me, you can each have one."

Yoder turns and starts to run toward me. Simon doesn't

break his stride. Meanwhile, the boys have a conference about how to spell "baseball."

"Do we get more than one try?" they ask.

"No. It's all or nothing," I say, not sure to whom exactly I'm speaking.

Yoder skids to a stop behind me, hands on my shoulders, breathing hard from the exertion.

"Help me," he whispers. "That man is the devil."

I don't entirely disagree. Simon stops in front of us with a twisted smile on his face.

"Isn't this nice?" he says. "Did you have fun in Vegas?"

"It's that guy again," Theo says, incredulous. "The one who wouldn't play cars with me when I was a baby."

"And what are you now?" Simon asks in a voice meant to terrify small children and furry household pets. But Theo jumps off buildings. He's not easily intimidated. I have an inappropriate proud parent moment.

"Mom, can we get our hats now?" Theo asks, ignoring Simon.

"You didn't spell 'baseball' yet," I remind them.

"Yoder belongs to me, Sally," Simon says. "You know that."

"What does it start with?" Henry asks. Neither boy seems at all concerned by this other conversation in which I am presently engaged. To be that secure is kind of a fantasy of mine.

"Please," Yoder whispers again. I can smell his desperation and it makes me a little ill.

"B-A-S-E-B-A-L-L," Simon says.

"Awesome! Thanks!" Theo says, now looking at Simon in a whole new light. "Does that count? Can we get our hats now?"

"How will they ever learn if we don't let them figure things out for themselves?" I ask. "Why do you want him? Are you going to make the trade for Gray?" Out of all the possible scenarios, this one seems the least likely, but I have to ask.

"I can't share the details with you," Simon says coyly. "But the United States government would like you to turn him over and back off. They have everything under control."

"They said that about Hurricane Katrina," I say.

"Mom, the hats," Theo reminds me.

"Kill me first," Yoder says. His yearlong stay at the Hotel Simon must have been memorable for all the wrong reasons because people don't ever really ask you to kill them. That only happens in bad movies about sixteenth-century England.

"So where are they?" I ask Simon.

"Who?"

"The United States government, your muscle?"

"Sally," Simon says. He's losing patience.

"The United States government does not acknowledge my existence, remember? All those rules they told me I had to live by when I left, that was a big part of it. I was never there. Which means I'm not really here, either."

"You're not thinking clearly," Simon says. "Give me Yoder and go back to the life you so desperately wanted. Remember, you're just one person now. How much can one person do?"

"Forget it," I say. "Yoder is coming with me." To stick to my three-step plan, the one where at some point I get to shoot Chemical Claude in the head, I need Yoder. Simon narrows his gaze so we're now the only two people in the world. I squirm, filled with sympathy for all those poor ants burned up by kids with magnifying glasses. Who needs that kind of attention?

"When you joined the Agency, Gray asked me to make sure he did not ever have to see you," Simon says. He's going in for the kill and I have no doubt it's going to hurt. "He never wanted you there in the first place."

But I lasted nine years. "I have to buy hats," I say.

"Think about the odds of success here, Sally," Simon says.

"They're pretty slim," I say and that's my honest answer. But it doesn't mean I'm excused from trying.

"Give me Yoder," Simon says again. I shrug my shoulders.

"No." You cannot choose your family but you are responsible for them nonetheless.

In this game of chicken, I wait for Simon to blink. He looks at the crowds milling around, not yet ready to leave the stadium. His hands are tied.

"The human shield," he says, almost to himself. "It's working now, but eventually you'll be alone and when that happens, I will be there."

He's not threatening me, merely stating the facts.

I walk slowly toward the hat kiosk, holding a boy in each hand. Yoder stays pinned to my back. I cannot imagine how strange we must look but it's San Francisco so no one stares. Simon melts into the crowd, keeping his eyes pinned on me until he's swallowed up by Giants fans.

Step four of my plan is me being completely screwed.

24

had been on a total of five missions and kidnapped once by Ian Blackford when Simon Still walked into my cramped windowless office and, dropping a folder on my desk, announced it was time for me to go to the Ranch. I heard laughter in the hallway, bubbling out of a pair of grizzled old agents who had been wearing the same clothes since the Cold War.

"Poor Sally," said the one with the permanent five o'clock shadow. "Hope Lee is retired." This was followed by more raucous laughter from Simon and the others.

"No," Simon said. "Lee's still there. That's why I'm sending her now. Can't miss the opportunity. If Lee goes, so goes the Ranch." The three men were now so tickled they could barely stand up. I leaned forward and kicked my door shut, which didn't even register with the occupants in the hallway. The Ranch? I had never heard anything about a ranch. Was this a joke or was I being punished for some unknown crime committed against humanity or, more specifically, Simon Still?

Tentatively, I flipped open the folder. Inside was an itinerary with a flight to Midland Airport in Texas, approximately south of nowhere. I was definitely being punished. Upon arrival, I was to look for the man in the photograph clipped to the inside cover of the folder.

"I'm dead," I said to the empty office. From the looks of it, Lee was about six feet six inches and 350 pounds of solid muscle. Each finger alone was roughly the circumference of my waist and his nose was flat as a pancake. His smile was full of missing teeth; those that remained were stained and crooked.

In real life, he was actually bigger. A peacock on Fifth Avenue would have blended in better than this Lee did at the Midland Airport. I resolved to be tough, squared my shoulders, and marched toward him with purpose. The top of my head was level with his armpit, which was unpleasant in so many ways.

"Do we know each other?" he asked in a booming voice. I cringed. Was a coded exchange really necessary when I was the only other soul in the terminal?

"Yes," I said. "We met last year in the Hamptons." I wanted to smash whoever was in charge of this ridiculous code. Lee, covered in naked-lady tattoos and wearing a Harley-Davidson tank top that was two sizes too small, would be arrested in the Hamptons simply for the crime of being unfashionable. "Yes, we met last year in prison" would have been easier to believe.

"Great to see you again," he said, taking my hand and pumping my arm up and down so hard I thought it might detach from my body. "There are just two of you this round and the other guy is waiting. Let's go."

I followed Lee into the blinding sunshine to a waiting pickup truck with an extended cab. In the front seat was a man with a twenty-inch neck and forearms that reminded me of Popeye. Lee plugged his iPod into the jack and the sounds of Celine Dion filled the cab. If I lost some weight I could escape through the window. Or I could strangle both men, wrestle control of the vehicle, toss the iPod, and escape. Things were looking grim as I racked my brain trying to figure out what I'd done to Simon to deserve this. So I was slow with my paperwork and he didn't think the mousetrap in his desk drawer was funny, but was that reason enough to send me to Texas to be beaten to death by two meatheads?

"Kevin Cairns," Popeye said, extending a hand over the back of the seat. "I can't wait to get started." Who was this guy? Had I ever seen him before? Was he Agency? Did it matter?

"Sally," I said, offering no last name. I could definitely wait to get started. I thought about asking Lee to stop for coffee but in no time at all, we had turned onto a dirt road that seemed to run straight and empty right to the horizon.

"So, Lee," I said after a while, "where are we going?"

"Lee?" he said, a toothpick dangling out of the side of his mouth. "I'm not Lee. You thought I was Lee!" He laughed and laughed as if I'd just said something outrageously funny. "I'm not even close to Lee."

Popeye laughed right along with him. He was clearly in on the joke. I slid down in my seat and for the next two hours I didn't say anything, concentrating instead on inventing elaborate scenarios of my impending doom.

It was hard to make out the ranch until we were almost upon it. The low outbuildings and the main house nestled into the scrub as if they had grown there from seeds. The afternoon sun was high in the sky, baking the earth to a lovely well-done.

Popeye chattered away about the heat and the ranch and how excited he was. He was going to get killed someday for the simple crime of being annoying.

"Madame Li will meet you both in the main room in five minutes," the big guy whose name was not Lee informed us. He pointed to the house and hopped back into the truck. Where was he going? Why was he leaving us here? Who the hell was Madame Li? I wanted to run and hide but the only thing to hide behind were tumbleweeds. Instead, I marched up the stairs, trying to look as cocky and confident as Popeye.

The main room was a huge empty space. There were floor-to-ceiling mirrors on the far wall reflecting the blinding sun. In the rays, dust hung in the air, barely moving. We stood to either side of the door and waited.

Five minutes later, Madame Li floated into the room, her feet barely touching the floor. She was dressed in black yoga pants and a tank top and carried a bamboo cane that she spun in slow circles. She was tiny and compact and the only signs of her age were the crisp white streaks in her black hair, and even those were all lined up, ready to obey her every command.

Popeye hopped to it. "Madame Li, Kevin Cairns. I'm so excited to be here."

Madame Li held a delicate finger to her lips.

"Silence," she said in a fairy princess voice, "is a virtue." With that, she did something that I haven't seen again since that day. Reaching up with her knuckles, she tapped Popeye in the center of his chest. Just a quick thump and he was flying across the room. He smashed into one of the mirrors and slid down into a heap, gasping for breath. She turned her back to him.

"You can call me Madame or Madame Li," she said, giving me an impish smile. "Whichever." Popeye tried to pull himself up to standing but all his attempts ended with him back on the floor.

"How did you do that?" I asked finally, hoping my question would not send me sailing across the room next.

"Practice," Madame Li said, examining her hair in one of the mirrors, "and skill." Taking my arm, she led me over to Popeye. With the other hand, she yanked him to his feet and turned so all three of us now faced the mirrors, looking at ourselves.

"Things are never as they appear," she said. "I am a small person, quiet. I mind my own business. And yet . . . what is possible?"

She poked Popeye in his six-pack stomach and she squeezed his bulging bicep.

"Puffy muscle is good for nothing. It will not save you if someone tries to kill you in an elevator or in an airplane lavatory. Good for the ladies, maybe, but not much else."

Popeye looked defeated. I was willing to bet he was no longer excited. Madame Li tapped her head.

"This is what you must use to survive, to defeat the enemy. You must see the future and then act upon that knowledge. You must know what someone is going to do before he does it. Use the unexpected."

She was starting to remind me of Yoda, without the big green ears and the odd sentence structure. Popeye nodded his head as if she were preaching the Gospel from on high. Although he had no way of knowing at the time, in ten years a slimmed down, tightly wound, mean-ass motherfucker named Kevin Cairns would join Madame Li at the Ranch, terrorizing all those unfortunate souls who stumbled across his doorstep. But for now, he was a humiliated nobody hoping to pass muster.

We remained under Madame Li's care for six weeks, during which time we saw nobody else. For three hours in the morning, before the sun came up, we would train, which basically involved Madam Li kicking the shit out of us, followed by her taunting us as we tried to do likewise. After our daily beating, we would work cleaning out stables, scrubbing toilets, peeling potatoes, sweating our way to dehydration in the scorching Texas sun. This was followed by five more hours of training after which Popeye and I collectively begged for mercy and went to bed.

After a while, little muscles started to show up on my body that I had never seen before. And every last one of them ached. Through the thin walls of our rooms, I could hear Popeye groaning in his sleep. He would shout out things like "Anticipate!" and "See the future!" and sometimes he cried.

On our last day, as I packed up my few belongings, Madame Li showed up in my doorway. She ran her fingers over the items I had spread out on the bed—a clean shirt, a book of short stories, a small notebook and pen.

"You are the first, you know," she said, flipping the pages of my notebook.

"The first what?" I asked, hoping she wouldn't say "Failure." If nothing else, I was confident I could kick Popeye's ass or at the very least call him names and make him feel bad about himself.

"Girl," she said. "We get lots of boys out here but you are the first girl. Are you something special, Sally?"

I shrugged, not wanting her to see I was surprised by her revelation.

"I think you must be," she continued. "You don't cry. Everyone cries. Especially the big fancy men, they cry quickest and longest. But you stay quiet. Why is that?"

Her questions caught me off guard. Since our arrival, she had delivered many long lectures in her tiny voice about balance and focus and the weakest parts of the body, but she had not asked a single personal question of either of us. She never referred to us by name and showed no interest in our thoughts on any subject. We had no idea where she slept, what she ate, if she did anything when she wasn't beating us up.

"I just don't cry," I said. There was a story to it but even I was unsure how it went. She nodded, as if that explanation was satisfactory.

"You are so alone, aren't you? But you can't see it. You believe you are married to the Agency, Sally Sin. You are not."

But she was wrong. I was married to the Agency and it wasn't until I saw Will Hamilton standing on a dive boat in Hawaii that I even considered the idea of a divorce.

Six weeks after I left the Ranch, on a moonless night in Freetown, Sierra Leone, I found myself caught in the house of a local businessman who was also the head of a number of regional terrorist cells. Rumor had it he was busy assembling the components for a nuclear weapon. Cornered in a narrow hallway, I listened as the man waved his gun around and explained in Krio what he was going to do to me before he took mercy on my soul and shot me in the head. He was so close, grinding his hips into mine as he pushed me back against a wall, taking my Colt Commander from the waistband of my pants and tossing it aside. His breath was hot and smelled of rancid spices.

The energy has to be focused, like a laser, Madame Li said. It has to flow from all the parts of your body to this one controlled point. It must be lightning fast. Keeping my eyes averted, I pulled my right elbow back as far as the wall would allow and fired my fist forward, striking the man right in the heart. He did not fly across the room as Popeye had but he was suddenly silent, even as his lips continued to move. After a few seconds, he collapsed at my feet, his face the color of a blue Popsicle.

"I didn't think you could," he wheezed, white foam appearing at the corners of his mouth.

I had never killed anyone before. A mixture of delight and horror surged through my veins and I felt instantly sick. Even in the moment, I knew I had passed over into a place from which I could never return. But before I could spend any time contemplating the power Madame Li had literally put in my hands, I heard footsteps in the courtyard. Sixty seconds later, I was running down a dark, empty alley littered with garbage and crawling with rats. As the distance between them and me opened up, I thought about the dead guy's last words. What he really meant was, sometimes you just aren't expecting it from a girl.

25

Even though I don't see anyone, I know they're following us. We pull up to Henry's house and I honk the horn. Judy pops out of the front door, her face tight as a spring and slightly puffy.

"Thank you so much for driving," she says, leaning in the driver-side window. "Did everyone have fun?" She notices Yoder. "Oh, hello."

Yoder gives her a half smile. He's behaving better now that he's realized the alternative to me is Simon Still.

"Say hi to Judy, Richie," I say, giving him a nudge. "I'm giving Richie a ride home." Theo and Henry high five in the backseat and Henry reluctantly climbs out, his oversized baseball hat sliding down over his eyes. I wonder if he recognizes his mother. Can you reach a point in plastic surgery where your own child would have a hard time picking you out of a lineup? I suppose if Theo continues to hang out with Henry, I'll have ample opportunity to field-test my theory.

"Bye, Henry," I say. "We'll see you at school tomorrow."

"Thanks for the hat, Mrs. Theo's Mom," he says, waving to us as he runs up the front steps.

Judy lingers by the car window. Hard as it is to believe, I think she might be flirting with Yoder.

"Are you still interviewing at Country Day tomorrow?"

Judy asks, twirling a lock of hair around her finger. How come everyone seems to know about this interview tomorrow except for me?

"Yes," I say with complete confidence. "I can't wait."

"We *loved* it," she says. "Absolutely fabulous and *so* diverse." By which she means there's at least one student who is not blond. She's very close to Yoder now. He backs away from the open window but the seat belt won't let him get too far.

"Oh, it would be so much fun to have the boys together again next year, don't you think?" she continues. "We could carpool." Yoder is practically sitting in my lap now.

"Mom, I want to go to school with Henry," Theo says.

"Great!" I say. "We have to go now. See you soon, Judy!" I roll up the window, forcing her to pull her head out of the way or face decapitation. I think she might still be talking to us as I pull away from the curb.

"It's just school," Yoder says. "Why are you all so hung up on it?"

"You overhear two conversations and now you're an expert?" I snap. "Your intel is rather sparse."

"I had tutors," Yoder says. "Never went to school."

"You see?" I say. "I don't want my kid to turn out like you."

"That was mean," he says.

"It was," I agree, "and I meant it to be." I'm clearly more troubled by the idea of kindergarten choice than I'm willing to admit. I stomp on the gas and the hybrid roars to life, closing in on roughly forty miles per hour. We can almost hear the wind rushing past the rolled-up windows.

"Hey, Mom?"

"Hey, Theo?"

"I feel funny." I glance in the rearview mirror just in time to see Theo projectile vomit popcorn, illicit bites of corn dog, and something that might have been nachos all over the back of the car.

"Oh, no," I say, pulling over to the curb. Yoder is covering his ears and whimpering when he should really be holding his nose and praying.

"Theo, honey," I say, pulling him out of the backseat. "Are you okay?" I want to avoid getting vomit on me but he seems so pathetic that I pull his head to my chest. A clump of vomit jumps onto my fleece jacket. I turn my head into the fresh, cold air and take a few gulps. It will make everything worse if I end up puking on Theo's head. Usually, I'm a pro with bodily fluids but today I'm close to coming undone.

Theo nods, wiping his mouth with the back of his hand. It comes away covered with stringy slime. Seeing no reasonable alternative, he runs his hand through my hair and, just like that, it's clean.

"Theo!" I shout. "Please. Let me get some wipes." But it's going to take a whole lot more than wipes to make this right. It surprises me that Theo's little stomach could hold this much food. I stand him on the sidewalk and strip off his jacket, turning it inside out on itself and throwing it in the trunk. I pull off his shoes and pants while he stands there in his Spiderman underwear, looking like a newborn calf. I shake out my fleece jacket and wrap it around him. If I were Yoder, I would choose now to run. But when I look up, he's still in the front seat, hand over mouth, eyes wide with horror.

"What?" I ask. "You've never seen anyone throw up before?"

"The smell," he says, through his fingers. "It's awful."

I point a finger at him. "If you puke in my car, I will hold you prisoner until you clean it up."

"You're already holding me prisoner," he says. True. But still.

"Mom, I'm freezing," Theo says. His legs look skinny and pale under my long jacket.

"Okay," I say. "Almost there." I peel off my long-sleeved T-shirt and put it over the soaked booster seat. It won't do much but it gives me the impression of being in control of the situation, which counts for quite a bit at the moment.

We drive the rest of the way home with all the windows rolled down. I now wear only a thin cotton tank top and my teeth are chattering wildly by the time we pull into the garage. I tell myself the elaborate plan I was developing to keep Simon from taking Yoder back was derailed by the puking. But who am I kidding?

"We just leave the car like this?" Yoder asks, climbing out.

"You want to clean it?"

"No."

"Well, neither do I," I say. All I really want to do is wash the vomit out of my hair.

We file into the house. It's cold and gloomy now and I go around and turn on all the lights because Will isn't home to yell at me about wasting energy so I can see. Next, I crank up the heat to a pleasant 75 degrees. I pull my hair up in an elastic band and sit Yoder down at my kitchen table.

"Do you drink coffee?" I ask. My time is limited. I know Simon meant what he said and they will be coming for Yoder soon. It's inevitable. I have no cards to play, no way to hold Yoder for long enough to trade him for Gray without risking all of our lives.

"Yes," Yoder says. "Coffee would be nice."

Although it's not obvious, the gears in my head have been turning, grinding up the question of why Simon wants Yoder back so badly. And sitting here with him, I catch a glimmer of the truth and I hang on.

"How long did you need?" I ask.

"What?" Yoder asks. There's a scar on his forehead that turns a deep red. Unconsciously, he rubs it with his forefinger.

"Did you even need the full four minutes, while your boss was in the john? Is it possible you would have been fine with only two minutes?"

Yoder buries his head in his hands. "I don't know what you're talking about," he says. His shoulders are tight and up near his ears. He rocks gently in his chair. "Why are you asking me these things?"

I stir my coffee with a spoon that has been lying on the table since breakfast. It's coated with a thin layer of dried milk.

"In Sudan, when you were young, Chemical Claude used you as a runner," I say. "It was dangerous work but we both know Claude has no real respect for mortality, especially someone else's. You were good, better than the other little boys, because you didn't need to carry paper. It wasn't something you ever talked about; no kid wants to be labeled a freak, does he? But the truth was you could remember everything a document said by reading it just once. There were a couple of times the so-called police caught you but they could find no evidence that you were anything other than a kid out for some dangerous fun."

Yoder keeps rubbing at the scar, faster and faster. I slide a piece of paper and a box of crayons in front of him.

"Start writing," I say.

"Why would I do that?" he says defiantly.

"I can't save you if I have no leverage," I say. How did step five of my plan become saving Yoder? What happened to step four? I want to kick myself.

Slowly, Yoder picks up a purple crayon and positions the paper horizontally. I watch upside down as he starts to scratch out a series of seemingly unrelated words and symbols. My throat goes dry. It's not what I was expecting but it's very clearly what Simon was after.

"That's enough," I whisper, pulling the paper from him.

"But there's much more," he says.

"Do you know what any of this means?" I ask.

"No."

Well, I do, and at this moment I kind of wish I didn't.

There are always leaks in the intelligence business, small ones that are merely irritating and big ones that are dangerous. Sometimes they embarrass the government and other times they bring it to its knees. Simon hated leaks. He took every single one personally.

After a few episodes in which Gray had to attend closed-door meetings at the White House, he and Simon got serious about a solution. They came up with a code that would render leaks useless, at least those originating at the USAWMD. If information is leaked in an utterly incomprehensible format, then it doesn't really matter who sees it. It remains meaningless unless you happen to have the right Rosetta stone.

The code was instituted during my second year at the Agency. It was meant only for the eyes of Director Gray and Simon, but to me it was just another language and easy enough to understand after a moderate amount of late-night snooping. The code was used to secure the most sensitive information, primarily an agent's identity and all of his known assets in the field. Simon could look at a spreadsheet littered with symbols and letters and numbers and know immediately where all his people were and what they were doing. He could add and subtract and reorganize as necessary. When someone died or disappeared, their symbol was deleted and their assets were redistributed among all the other symbols. It was a game unless you were the deleted symbol. Then it was as if you woke up dead.

"You never told Simon Still about this?" I ask Yoder.

Yoder casts his eyes down. "No."

"Even after he saved you?" I say.

"It was not an act of kindness," Yoder says. It's clear he might have bared his soul to Simon if Simon had thought to skip the torture part of the daily schedule.

"No one is ever the same after spending time with Simon Still," I say. And I mean that on many levels.

"You said you would save me," Yoder says bluntly. "You don't know me. Why would you do that?"

I suddenly remember Simon Still berating me for being soft.

"You're the kind of person who takes home all the kittens from the pound to save them from being drowned," he had said. "No one wants the fucking kittens, Sally. That's why they're at the pound to begin with."

There are probably many reasons why I feel the need to save Yoder, but the only relevant one has to do with the pound kittens and the drowning bucket. I cannot change who I am.

"I believe in second chances," I say. "And sometimes thirds and fourths, if absolutely necessary." It's only what I hope for myself.

Yoder's face flushes. He swirls his last bit of coffee around in his mug.

"Three minutes," he says. "I memorized the book in three minutes."

"It's a gift," I say.

"No," Yoder says, shaking his head. "Without it, Claude would have thrown me away years ago. I could have been another person."

Are we nothing more than the sum of our baggage? Before I can get too depressed about this idea, Theo wanders in holding the box for Connect Four.

"Can we play?" he asks. He is bright-eyed and wearing clean clothes, smelling as fresh as a daisy while I still have puke in my hair.

I am just about to say yes to the game when the glass in the back-door window explodes and three men dressed entirely in black crash into the kitchen. As I throw myself on top of Theo and Connect Four, forming a protective shell, I can't help but think this is overkill. Two of the men grab Yoder, who is screaming once again about being an American, and drag him by the armpits through the glass and out the door. The third guy jabs me in the ribs with the barrel of his M6A2 assault rifle, which is no way government issue, and whispers in my ear.

"You weren't invited to this party, Sally," he says, digging the gun in deeper. "Simon says you should remember that." He sniffs the air. "Something smells bad in here."

"Fuck you," I say. More desperately than I want a shower, I want to reach up, slide my hand behind this guy's puffy-muscle neck, and slam his head into the floor, but that would leave Theo exposed and I will not take that chance. I stay completely still, listening to his heavy combat boots crunching the broken glass as he leaves.

I expected Simon to wait until dark, knock on my front door, and demand I turn Yoder over immediately, which I would have done now that I have what I need. Sending his goons to smash up my house and scare the shit out of my kid delivers the message that he is not playing games quite effectively. And I get it. But now I'm mad.

Theo squirms out from underneath me, still clutching the Connect Four box, his eyes glittering with a strange sort of glee I didn't anticipate. He should be hysterical, clinging to me out of pure terror, but he is anything but.

"That was just like The Warriors that we play on Xbox at Andrew's house. Totally cool, Mom! I can't wait to tell Teacher Wendy!"

Oh please, don't tell Teacher Wendy. And Andrew and his house are now part of the no-fly zone as far as I'm concerned.

Theo dances around in the glass in his Thomas the Tank Engine slippers, as if this is the most fun he's had all day.

"Who were those guys?" he asks, hopping on one foot. "Why didn't they knock?"

People with guns never knock. "They were friends of Richard's," I say. "Please stop jumping. The glass is flying everywhere."

"Boy, they must be mad at him."

Yes. Something like that.

"Go in the playroom while I clean this up in here," I say, lifting him up and beyond the glass.

When I join him ten minutes later, he has all of his LEGO people lined up in two rows. They have tiny plastic guns and helmets and light sabers and they appear on the verge of battle.

Theo provides a dialogue that is part *Star Wars* and part Elmo and in different circumstances I might find it creepy.

War used to have simple rules. Soldiers would meet on a nice grassy field in the middle of nowhere, form orderly rows, and then run at one another with swords drawn. They would even bring a band and guys to hold their flags. Whoever had the most men standing at the end won the battle. It was almost civilized when you looked at it from a certain angle.

But now everything is complicated. The difference between the good guys and the bad guys is blurry, changing moment-to-moment depending on circumstances and personal gain. There is no black and white. There is nothing but a dark place in between, where just about anyone might show up to stab you in the back.

26

I wouldn't want you to get the impression that I was always on the top of my game. Spying is not that different from parenting. There are days when you kneel down next to the squabbling kids on the playground and in a calm mom voice explain why it's not okay to hit little Susie over the head with a plastic shovel, and all the kids nod solemnly and promise to never ever perpetrate such a crime again. And when you stand back up, dusting the sand from your knees, you feel like you know what you're doing, that the lesson you were trying to impart actually got through.

And then there are days when you kneel down in the sand and the kids actually hit you over the head with the shovel and it's all you can do not to hit them back. Everyone can have a bad day.

I only needed an official rescue once, which was not really an official rescue, being as we didn't exist. But that didn't make it any less humiliating.

It was the middle of the night when Simon called me. He was in Washington, sitting in front of a crackling fire with a glass of fifteen-year-old Macallan Scotch, cooking up ways to ruin my life. I was someplace I'm still not allowed to mention in casual conversation.

"There's a package for you at the hotel down the street," he said. "It has instructions. Follow them."

"Simon, I've got four operations ready to go here and now. Critical operations. Am I supposed to just drop them?"

"Yes. Disappear into the night like a bad romance," he said. "S.K. is coming in your place."

"S.K. is hopeless. He can't even speak the language. I don't think he knows how to brush his teeth."

"He would be hurt to hear you say such things."

"How about Gunther?" I asked.

"He's dead."

"What? How?"

"Doesn't concern you. Hit the road now, Sally. That's an order." I could hear the ice cubes tinkling in his glass and it made me homesick, although in a very abstract way. I had not seen an ice cube in the flesh for months. I had missed Thanksgiving, Christmas, and Presidents' Day, not that they missed me.

"Okay," I said, already collecting my few belongings from the floor of the rented room. "I'm gone."

Without saying good-bye, Simon hung up. He never said good-bye. Come to think of it, he never said hello, either. It was as if we were having one continuous years-long conversation interrupted by the occasional trip to a war zone.

As I stuffed my knapsack with a toothbrush and a T-shirt, a strange tingling started in the low of my back and slowly worked its way up to my neck. I shuddered, all the hair on my arms standing at full attention. Something was off about this situation. Simon had never pulled me out of an operation when I was this far in. But an order was an order. I had no choice but to march on over to that hotel, retrieve the package, and see what sort of crappy hand I'd been dealt this time.

Two hours later, I was on a flight to Belgrade as instructed. The flight was surprisingly long and only a third full, Belgrade not being a vacation hot spot this time of year. Or any time of year, really. I stretched out across three empty seats and dreamed about Ian Blackford trying to drown me in a sea of hostile pelagic fish. In the dream, he grinned while a ten-foot-long barracuda ate my leg.

I think the dream was an omen because before I could even take a pee at the Belgrade airport, a pair of ill-fitting handcuffs were slapped on my wrists by customs officials in faded uniforms. They barked at each other in Serbian about me being a terrorist and a bomber and possibly even a prostitute, but they couldn't seem to decide which offense was the worst. They dragged me backward into an interrogation room that was approximately the same temperature as my refrigerator and about as comfortable.

"I'm an American citizen," I said, as they turned my backpack upside down, shaking the meager contents out on the rough concrete floor. The name on the passport Simon had sent me in the envelope at the hotel was drifting in and out of my mind with the consistency of a cloud. Sporting multiple identifies can be complicated at times. Who was I? Susan? Claire? Bella? Katherine?

"Why you travel on a fake passport?" one of the officers said, throwing the document onto the steel table between us. Like a skipping stone on a flat lake, it bounced twice and landed open in front of me. Well, that answered one question. Claire Simmons.

"I don't know what you're talking about," I said. But even

from my position, trying to sit forward and not crush my bound wrists, I could tell something was wrong with the passport. The blue was too bright and the soaring eagle imprint was not so much soaring as crashing. I mentally chastised myself for not examining my documents before trying to pass them off to customs agents.

"Help her remember," the guard said.

The man who hit me wore a signet ring about the size of a quarter. It raked across my face as if he had spent the morning sharpening it on a stone. The blood oozed out of the wound and dripped down my face, little red raindrops landing on my white shirt.

"Why are you here?" they demanded.

"I'm an American citizen here to take pictures for a magazine. I'm a photographer." One of the guards picked up my small digital camera from the floor.

"With this?"

I shrugged. "Low rent," I said. "I'm not the kind of girl to sit in a snow cave for six months in the Uzbekistan mountains waiting for the elusive snow leopard to show itself. If you know what I mean."

"Who said anything about a snow leopard?"

"I did. I'm not who you think I am." My cheek stung and every time I opened my mouth, the skin felt oddly loose and detached.

"Put her in a cell," the head guy said, suddenly bored with this whole affair.

My new accommodations were underground. The cement block walls were tinged green with mold and a slow trickle of water came down from the ceiling, pooling in the middle of the floor. I sat down on the wooden platform I assumed was meant as a bed, pulling my legs up tight to my chest to conserve what little warmth I had left. I concentrated on keeping my face still, allowing a scab to form over the slice in my cheek.

"Hey. Hey, you," came a voice. "On the other side of the wall. Is someone there?"

"Yes," I said, standing at the bars, trying to see into the next cell. "I'm here. Where are you?"

"I'm next to you. I don't think there is anyone else down here."

"Where are we?"

"The dungeon."

Fabulous. Really, an actual dungeon was just what I needed. Now, if they could arrange for a purple dragon or two, things would be looking up.

"How long have you been down here?" I asked.

"Oh, I don't know. Years maybe."

Years? I'll admit I started to panic a little bit with that news.

"Why are you here?" I asked. A burst of laughter came from the other side of the wall.

"I can no longer recall. Made someone angry. Killed the wrong person. It's not so bad down here once you get used to it."

"And how long did that take?"

"A few years. At the most."

"Lovely." It was dark but I got the feeling not even Martha Stewart could do all that much with the place.

"So how about you?" my new cell block friend asked from the other side of the wall. "What did you do?"

I wasn't big on confessions. Besides, the list of things I'd done was so very long it might take the rest of my life to get it all out and I sincerely hoped I wouldn't be here quite that long.

"I'm innocent," I said. "A case of mistaken identity."

The man laughed and laughed as if this were the first joke he'd heard in a decade, which might actually have been the case. Being in this dark damp cave was punishment enough. Being down here alone was just plain cruel.

But his question was a good one that I could not answer even to myself. I had no dealings in Belgrade. I had no assets. I had no interests. The whole thing started to feel like a setup to me, from the badly forged passport to the waiting guards at the airport. It was as if someone arranged for events to unfold in this fashion and was now standing back and watching what happened.

In my limited life experience thus far there was only one person with that kind of power. That we were supposed to be playing for the same team did not seem to matter.

The next day, two wiry men in flannel shirts hauled me into a room lit with a single bare bulb. There was a metal chair, rope, a generator of some sort, buckets of water, and a variety of tools not available at the local Home Depot. Knowing I would die before I gave up any information, I took a deep breath and tried to clear my mind for the inevitable questions and pain that would soon rain down upon me.

And rain down it did. I tried to disassociate from the pain as I had been taught to do but the men in charge of dispensing it were chattering away incessantly about the World Cup, distracting me from my attempts to disappear to my happy place. And to make matters worse my happy place on this day turned out to be an image of me building sandcastles with a small blond child, clearly of my own design. My normal happy place was indeed a beach but with swaying palms and warm white sand and a giant fruity cocktail in my tanned and manicured hand. My normal happy place did not include a child of any sort.

Through it all, the two men in charge did not ask me one single question. There was no shouting in my face, no degradation, no rage on their part. They were just a couple of guys doing a day's work that happened to involve the torture of another human being. They were oddly detached, as if working from an agenda they didn't quite understand nor care particularly about.

After five hours of this business, I'll admit I was feeling rather low and would have happily considered trading state secrets for a little relief. But then one of the guys glanced at his watch and nodded to his partner.

"We're done, looks like," he said.

"Went fast, didn't it?" the other said.

Speak for yourself. They dragged me under the armpits down the deserted hallway and chucked me back into my cell. I don't know how long I lay there moaning before my dungeon friend called out to me.

"Are you okay?" he asked.

"That depends on what you mean by 'okay,'" I groaned. I was alive but beyond that, I wasn't willing to say.

"What do they want from you?" he asked.

"I don't know," I croaked. "They didn't ask me any questions."

There was silence from the other side of the wall.

"Nothing?"

"No."

"Strange."

"Yes," I said. "And now if you'll excuse me, I'm going to go ahead and die."

I must have fallen asleep right there on my cell floor because hours later when the approach of heavy footsteps woke me I was still facedown on the couch. The steps had a familiar cadence, an urgency that the guards who'd tortured me earlier had lacked. Sure I was hallucinating, I rolled over so I could look through the cell bars at whoever was coming. Everything hurt. My very skin seemed to scream out in agony.

"Jesus, Sal. You look like shit." Simon stood outside the cell, a curious expression on his face.

"Well, it's not like I've been spending company time at a spa or anything," I said, trying to sit up. Simon gestured to several of the men, dressed head to toe in black and carrying automatic weapons, standing behind him.

"Open the cell," he said. A small charge was rigged to the lock and almost silently blew it open. A puff of white smoke floated into the dank prison air. Simon pulled open the door and squatted down in front of me. He poked at my face and at the open wounds across my shoulders.

"You'll live," he announced. "But there might be some scarring. Help her up." Each man grabbed me under an arm and hauled me up from the bed. I wanted to cry but I'd die before doing so in front of Simon.

"Wait," I groaned, freeing myself from the two agents. I wobbled over to the next cell but it was empty. "There was a man in here. What happened to him?"

Simon looked at his watch. "Sally, it's not as if we have a whole lot of time here. Can we move it along?" Before I could protest further, I was carried off down the hallway and pushed through a hole in the concrete wall. Outside, they stuffed me into the back of a waiting black Mercedes and away we raced, lights off, into the night.

A week later, still limping and generally pathetic, I was back to work. Shuffling slowly toward the stained Mr. Coffee machine in what passed for our lounge, I heard two agents talking behind a partially closed office door.

"So he let it go for five hours?" one of them said.

"Yes," the other answered, "but the Serbs are a tough bunch. It had to look legit."

"An experiment. First time I ever heard of it. And I've heard a lot of crazy shit."

"Simon had to know how long it would take Gray to order her removal."

The sudden intake of air at these words hurt my cracked ribs. The conversation behind the door stopped. I didn't move.

"Anyway," the one guy went on, "it took less than a day. That's what I heard."

"But when was the last time Gray ordered a retrieval of anyone?"

"Never. That's when."

The two agents burst out laughing.

"Our sorry asses would have been left for dead."

"No shit. But did you see her?"

The laughter faded.

"Yeah. She's pretty messed up."

Dragging myself back toward my office, I pressed the palm of my hand hard into the dark bruise covering my rib cage. The pain flashed brightly before my eyes, pushing all thoughts of Simon and Gray and why I was really sent to Belgrade from my mind.

At least for the moment.

27

Hunched over in a squat that's making my inner thighs burn, I sweep shattered glass I missed earlier carefully into a dust pan. Theo sits at the kitchen table with a green crayon in hand, poised like an artist in front of a blank canvas. He looks thoughtful. I need to talk to him about what just happened but I'm at a loss as to how to explain it and make it real and yet not terrify him at the same time. I somehow doubt there's a parenting book for this kind of problem.

"There's some more glass," he says, pointing to a glimmering shard under the refrigerator. "How do I spell my other name?"

I sit on the floor and marvel at how beautiful the light is, bouncing off the shard of glass, and also at Theo's ability to so easily turn his attention to the next project, in this case writing his last name. He seems remarkably unfazed by the fact that a bunch of machine-gun-toting lunatics dressed in black smashed up our kitchen and took away Richard Yoder before he could even finish his coffee. Theo's ability to compartmentalize reminds me of my own, which is indeed disturbing. I had, possibly naïvely, hoped for Will's genes to overpower mine.

I spell "Hamilton" and Theo writes it in green crayon. Part of the name is on the paper; the rest is on the table. I gave up on the table long ago. If he carved his name into the kitchen table with a pair of scissors, my main concern would be that he spelled it correctly. There are things in life you need to let go of. My lovely kitchen table is one of them.

"That's a great 'T,' Theo," I say, now standing over him. "Nice work."

"Mom, did you know in *Star Wars* there's a guy with two light sabers? He's a bad guy."

"I didn't know that," I say. "That's very interesting. Is pasta okay for dinner?"

"Yeah. And plums. And strawberries and cheese sticks."

"I thought you hated cheese sticks."

Theo looks at me as if I have lost what little remains of my mind.

"I love cheese sticks, Mom. Me and Henry love cheese sticks."

Now if I were a gambler, I'd bet my life savings one hundred to one that when I suggest including a cheese stick in Theo's snack tomorrow the idea will be met with shock and outrage. After which I will happily retire to Maui on the proceeds of my bet.

Cheese sticks aside, there's no escaping the fact that I have made a giant mess of things. I have no idea where Simon will take Yoder and therefore no possibility of getting him back. I could call Simon and offer to trade what I know about the black book for Yoder's life, but Simon made it a point to take back his one-button cell phone from me that morning in the coffee shop. I guess I could try the Bat Signal, but it might attract the wrong sort of attention.

The situation fills me with despair. I pour about half a bottle of wine into a glass. It reaches right to the lip and I have to bend down and slurp it up as it sits on the counter. It makes a loud sucking sound, the kind I'm always telling Theo it's impolite to make when he's eating soup. I'm out of the game. I lose.

I really hate to lose.

"You know, there's a LEGO set with that guy with the two light sabers," Theo says. He draws a rocket ship on his paper that looks as if a purple penis has been set on fire. "I have to pee. When's dinner? I'm starving."

Without waiting for an answer, he runs off to the bathroom. I remind him to wash his hands and flush the toilet. Inevitably, he'll stop on the way to the bathroom to collect a bunch of LEGO guys to line up on the sink while he pees, after which he'll get to playing with them and forget all about hand-washing and toilet-flushing. When he comes back to the kitchen, I'll remind him and he'll get mad that I keep telling him things he already knows. We've had this conversation about three hundred times. He does not yet accept that the difference between knowing and doing is wide and deep and often everything.

As it is right now. If I were a good agent, I would be analyzing the situation and reformulating my plan accordingly. But I'm not a good agent; I'm a rogue agent and I have no idea how they go about things. My solution is to make pasta.

I fill two bowls, sprinkle some Parmesan on top, and call it good. A plate of sliced plums sits in the middle of the table. Theo aims his fork like a spear and stabs a plum.

"Gotcha," he says, shoving it into his mouth.

"So, Theo," I say, "what happened this afternoon, those guys who broke the window, they were bad guys. They wanted to take something that wasn't theirs. And we had to let them because it wasn't safe for us to do anything else. Does that make sense?" Quite frankly, Mommy would love to have shown you how to kick puffy-muscle ass, but you can't always do what you want to.

Theo attempts to squeeze an enormous amount of spaghetti into his mouth. Bits of it hang out at the sides so he could be a blond walrus. He says something but while I speak many languages, I do not speak spaghetti.

"Swallow your food," I remind him. He rolls his eyes. I'm so annoying. It's hard for him to handle.

"You should have karate-chopped him," Theo says.

"Well, no. In that situation, fighting was the wrong choice," I say. "Fighting is almost always the wrong choice."

"I would have done the karate chop." He hops down from his chair to demonstrate, giving me a whack right in the arm.

"Ow. That hurt. Sit. Eat," I command. "No karate-chopping."

"Why? It's cool. Conroy's mother lets him karate-chop." Okay. Conroy is now relegated to the no-fly zone, too. I'm concerned that if this keeps up, Theo is going to be left with only me as a playmate and the jury is still way out on what sort of influence I'm turning out to be. The best I can hope for is that when Will comes home tomorrow, Theo has completely forgotten the assault on our kitchen. Or that, while explaining it to his dad, he throws in a few references to Han Solo or Luke Skywalker and Will just naturally assumes it's an extension of Theo's ongoing internal *Star Wars* dialogue, which shows no signs of abating.

"Hey, Mom?"

"Hey, Theo?"

"How do you spell 'bad guy with two light sabers'?"

I get up from the table, my overflowing wineglass now tragically empty. Cardboard secured with duct tape covers the two gaping holes in the door. The other two panes are cracked but functional. It is through those broken panes that I see a shadow, an arm snaking in under the edge of the cardboard, a hand grasping the doorknob and pushing the door open with an almost silent nudge.

"Mom, how do you spell 'bad guy with two light sabers'?" Theo asks again, growing impatient.

"B-L-A-C-K-F-O-R-D," I say, filling my wineglass right back up to the brim. But perhaps I'm not thinking broadly enough. Perhaps the solution in this situation is to skip the glass altogether and drop a straw right into the bottle.

28

As Ian Blackford steps into the room, I automatically scan for suitable weapons. Anything with a point will do. I pull the big carving knife from the wood block and lay it flat on the counter. My heart plays staccato in my chest. When did my kitchen become Grand Central Terminal for uninvited guests? It's starting to wear me down.

Amazingly, Blackford looks older than the last time I saw him. I swear I see a single gray hair mixed in with his famously dark coif. But I know better than to point out its presence to him.

"Sally," he says with a slow syrupy smile. "I'm so pleased to be back here."

Theo licks the last bits of Parmesan from the bottom of his bowl, apparently unconcerned about the terrorist in his kitchen. My fingers close around the knife handle.

"Hi," Theo says to Blackford. I watch for a reaction, some evidence of recognition, but there's none. Whatever Theo remembers of this man is buried in his subconscious and seems only to reveal itself in his artwork.

"Hi," Blackford says, giving Theo a little wave. Children freak him out. It's something I might enjoy watching if I didn't feel on the verge of a heart attack any second now.

"Can I be excused?" Theo asks politely.

"Yes," I say, my fingers sweaty on the knife handle.

"Should I clear my plate?" he asks.

"No, I'd say you can leave it for now." I talk to Theo but my eyes are on Blackford. Any sudden moves and I will pin him to the wall with the steak knife. "Go and play for a few minutes and then I'll read you some stories."

Theo is gone before I finish my sentence. Blackford eyes the knife, a look of detachment on his face.

"Put that away," he says. "You should know better by now."

He's right. There is no point. Slowly, I slide the knife back into the block and pick up my wineglass. The red liquid sloshes over the rim, running down my hand as if I accidentally severed an artery. I gulp down half the glass in one swig. Blackford watches me, amused. I hate that look.

"I'm not offering any to you," I say. "You weren't invited so I don't need to be polite."

"I don't drink," he says.

"You lie."

"About many things. Yes."

"Theo is drawing little evil stick figure Blackfords at preschool. The teacher thinks he's growing up in a house full of psychotics." I don't know why I feel compelled to tell him this.

"Is he?" Blackford asks. "You know what they say about the apple not falling far from the tree."

"Will is completely sane."

"Except he married you."

"What do you want?"

Blackford pulls out a chair and sits down. Reaching across the table, he helps himself to what is left of my pasta.

"Could use a little flavor, Sal," he says. "Maybe some sauce? Salt and pepper?"

I lean against the sink because sitting down with him would be an act of treason. Blackford scoops out the last bite of pasta and wipes his mouth with my napkin.

"Thanks," he says as if this is a casual dinner among friends, "I was hungry."

"It's been really fun for me too," I say. "Can you go now?"

"You don't understand what you did, do you?" he says, a hint of something not so friendly in his tone. "My reputation. What happened after I couldn't deliver the Death Lily to my customers who were waiting on it."

I remember, two years ago, the look on Blackford's face as I threw the resin from the last remaining Death Lily into the ocean. It was not a happy face. In one swift move, I'd ruined years of work on a new sort of WMD that would have turned all us humans into zombies, making the science fiction of mind control a reality.

I didn't care that Blackford would then have to go off and explain to his clients—North Korea, Iran, those sorts of calm and understanding types—why he'd failed to keep his end of the bargain. I didn't care about anything but getting my son as far away from Blackford and Simon Still and the Blind Monk as possible.

"I lost credibility, Sally," he says. "Do you know what that means to a man in my position?"

I shrug.

"It means everything goes to shit. Your competitors start

to move in on your territory. Deals go bad. People don't call you back. Work becomes hard."

I throw back the rest of the wine. I'm dizzy but it's comforting in a way.

"I'm sorry I rained on your parade," I say.

"I could have killed you," he said. "I wanted to kill you. It took a great deal of willpower on my part not to kill you."

"Is this the part where I say thank you?"

"You?" he scoffs. "Not likely." Well, at least he knows that much about me.

"Why are you here?" I ask. "Other than wanting dinner."

"I'm here to help you," Blackford says in all seriousness. The only thing scarier than Blackford wanting to hurt me might be Blackford wanting to help me. I'm confident our definitions of help vary widely.

"Just so I'm clear," I say, "what exactly are you going to help me with?"

Clean the house? Kill my neighbors? Haven't you done enough already with your photographs and your refusal to stay dead? What more can a girl reasonably ask for?

"Clawing my way back to the top has required some sacrifices," Blackford says. "I've had to do favors that in the past would not have been necessary."

The phoenix rising from the ashes. I am filled with a sense of dread.

"What sort of favors?" I ask.

"Well, for example, I tipped Claude Chevalier and Righteous Liberty off about your relationship with Gray," he says "They were pleased to confirm that the stories of your demise were fabricated. I said I thought you could be motivated to help uncover Yoder's whereabouts. They had tried a number of times to find him but one thing the U.S. does very well is hide people. I knew if Claude shook the family tree, you'd step up. And I was right. As I usually am."

My face goes slack. I stop my jaw just before it drops. A phoenix rising from the ashes, while standing on my head, is more like it.

"Sacrifices, Sally," Blackford says defensively. "Getting back on top requires sacrifices."

That's it. The wineglass disintegrates in my hand, the tiny pieces of glass covering the kitchen floor like yesterday's confetti. A shard sticks right in the meaty part of my palm but I refuse to look at it.

"Why didn't you just do it yourself?" I hiss. My chances of actually being able to stab him with the carving knife are slim to none, but right now I love the idea.

"That's not the sort of work I do," Blackford says and he is completely serious. The last time I saw him there was a moment when I thought it could be over, that he might go and spend his free time wrecking someone else's life. But that would be an act of kindness from a man who does not acknowledge the difference between love and control. I'm speechless at his betrayal but I don't know why. He is, after all, the enemy.

"Oh, don't take it all so personally," Blackford says. "I will admit things got unexpectedly complicated when Claude called Simon Still. I thought I made it clear to him that he should call you directly and not the Agency but you never can tell if a terrorist is paying attention, now can you? And I thought you'd come up with a better plan for holding on to Yoder until the scheduled trade tomorrow. But I suppose I should have expected that, too. You've been out of the game a good long time now. Hard not to get rusty." He relays all of this as if he's having just the nicest time hanging out in my kitchen chatting.

"You're a bad person," I say.

"Remember," Blackford says, pointing after Theo. "You *owe* me for saving that kid. Don't forget it."

I couldn't forget it even if I tried. Which I do. Often.

Blackford pulls the half-full bowl of sliced plums toward himself with the end of the fork.

"You're sitting in my house eating plums," I say, sounding daft even to my own ears.

"They're out of season here, you know. Does Will know you bought them?"

"Don't say his name. Not now. Not ever."

"Touchy," Blackford says.

"You said you're here to help me," I say, now only wanting to end this meeting as quickly as possible.

Blackford takes a drink of Theo's milk. "Yes. As I said, I have a certain stake in seeing you complete this task. Right now, Simon has Yoder. Chances are if Yoder doesn't give Simon what he wants, Yoder will end up dead. And when you fail to live up to your end of the deal with Righteous Liberty, Gray will end up dead. A lot of dead bodies by nightfall."

It's very quiet in my kitchen. The muffled sounds of Theo talking to his LEGO men down the hall seem far, far away.

"But what if I told you where you could find Yoder?" Blackford says, licking his fingers. "Alive."

There are moments when being a modern-day mother feels a little bit like being a piece of Silly Putty. Your child is demanding something, your husband is demanding something, your boss is demanding something, and your cat wants food. You're stretched in so many directions that your center, the very core of your being, becomes so thin you can almost see through it. Right now, my center is very thin. I'm a mom with a sink full of dishes, a floor covered in glass and red wine, and a man whose face is on the MOST WANTED posters at the post office sitting at my kitchen table snacking on leftovers. I'm not Clint Eastwood. I don't know how to do this. I take a swig from the mostly empty wine bottle. Blackford looks horrified.

"Where is he?" I say, wiping my mouth on the back of my sleeve.

"There's a safe house in the Presidio," Blackford says. "Simon's reasoning is, if Righteous Liberty is going through all this trouble to get Yoder back, then Yoder must know something. And Simon will not be fooled twice. He won't stop this time until he gets what he wants. You know Simon. Anything for the safety of the United States. Anything at all."

"So this is what we've come to? We torture people here?"

"Interrogate, Sally," he says. "There's a difference."

"Only in how they're spelled," I say.

"Save your disillusionment for later. Yoder will be there. You still have time. Go and get him."

If given a choice, I would not willingly help Blackford smooth the way back to his former glory and domination of the illegal arms trade. But Gray's life hangs in the balance and I don't see that I have any option other than to do as Blackford says.

"You do want a chance to get back in the game, don't you?" he asks, smiling as his question settles over me.

Of all the people in my life, past and present, it's rather unsettling to consider that Ian Blackford may be the one who knows me best.

29

The house is quiet, not even the sound of a Muni street car rumbling by to interrupt the peace. Theo is asleep upstairs and the seat Blackford occupied not an hour ago has cooled. There is no evidence he was here other than in my own memory, which is a bit fuzzy on account of the completely empty bottle of wine.

I scribble a "to do" list on the back side of a preschool glitter-glue masterpiece of what I think is a cat. Call about new glass for the back door, get milk, wash Theo's soccer uniform, go to the Presidio and kidnap Richard Yoder back from Simon Still, who kidnapped him from me, stop taking orders from Blackford when I am pretty sure his intentions are less than wholesome. Regular people never have kidnapping on their "to do" lists. It's just not done. But the fact remains that at some point tomorrow, possibly following Theo's interview at the very proper San Francisco Country Day or maybe after lunch, I have to get Yoder back. If I fail, Gray dies.

I put my head down on the table. It's cold against my burning skin. From the beginning, I knew it wasn't going to be easy, living as if the past never happened. All it took was a long weekend in Paris, almost exactly six years ago, to wipe away those delusions for good.

It was our first trip together as a couple and I desperately wanted to believe I could start anew, that we could be just like any other couple heading off to Paris for a romantic interlude. And there are few things more romantic than autumn in Paris. The air is crisp and cool and most of the tourists have gone home. It's perfectly acceptable to throw on some Jackie O. sunglasses and spend the afternoon cruising up and down the Champs-Élysées, feeling fashionable and stopping for fluffy little pastries every twenty-five feet. However, for me, Paris was a mental war zone. I'd been there many times but never as a wife. Only as a spy.

One afternoon soon after I'd moved to San Francisco, Will came home waving an itinerary for a surprise long weekend in Paris.

"I want to see you there," he said.

Just the mention of Paris was enough to turn my brain to the spin cycle, with French as the laundry. The words and phrases and mechanics raced around in there with abandon, so much so I was afraid to open my mouth.

"Say something," Will said. "Aren't you excited?"

"Thrilled," I said, concentrating on the English.

As we boarded our plane and settled into our enormous first-class seats, I felt almost relaxed. When I worked for the government, I never got to travel in luxury. If they could have gotten away with it, they would have stuck me in the cargo hold with only the dogs and the suitcases for company. Sometimes I'd buy a first-class ticket on Simon Still's personal account but that usually ended up with me back in economy the very next day, on my way to someplace like Yemen. And I'll be honest, I never much liked Yemen. Too much sand.

As I handed my passport over to the French Immigration

officer, my hand trembled. I continued to remind myself I was a regular old person now and the name on my passport was the name on my life. As the officer returned my passport, he wished me a pleasant stay and, although he spoke English, my answer came out in flawless French. It must have been something in the air; I was powerless to stop it.

Will, standing beside me, took a step back as if I had shoved him.

"I didn't know you spoke French," he said.

That's the cherry on top of the things you don't know.

"College," I said dismissively.

"It sounded good," he said. "Really good. Say something else."

Ever obliging, I launched into a description of how good-looking he was despite the fifteen hours of travel time he wore on his face.

"Keep talking," he whispered, nuzzling my ear as we slid into a cab. The cabby rolled his eyes in disgust but I just laughed like a debutante with the bass player's hand up her skirt.

On our first day, we wandered through the Tuileries and I complimented a painter on his watercolor landscape, which was really quite awful. As the French flowed out of me, Will's eyes glazed over with lust. Who knew foreign language could be an aphrodisiac? I started to consider what sort of sexual bonuses I could expect when I finally got around to whispering sweet nothings in his ear in Urdu.

After about twenty-four blissful hours in Paris I had the strange sensation I was having a good time. Of course, I didn't heed that as the warning it was and things immediately began to go to shit.

She was vaguely familiar, like someone you met in a dream.

I recognized the idea of her before the rest came into focus. We were in the Louvre with a million other sweaty tourists trying to catch a glimpse of Mona Lisa's mysterious smile, when I knew I was being watched. It was hard to turn around and I took a few elbows to the ribs as I scanned the crowd. She was tall and French, with black hair piled elegantly on her head in a way I could never pull off. She stared at me intently as if she were the eagle and I the mouse. But I didn't want to be a mouse, in Paris or anywhere else for that matter. When I met her eyes, I expected her to look away, to show some sign she'd been made. But no. Instead, she began to push her way through the crowd right toward me.

"I heard they have a room with a handful of Monets and Degas and things up on the second floor," I said to Will, pulling him by the hand. "Might be less crowded." Will was still lost in Mona Lisa's smile.

"What do you suppose she was thinking about?" he asked as I attempted to part the crowd, a tourist version of Moses and the Red Sea. "Lunch?"

"Maybe the perfect meatball sub," I said, trying to find a balance between dragging him by the hair caveman-style and being overtaken by the eagle lady. "You had to sit for a long time in one position for those portraits. They had a lot of patience."

"Lucy, why are you in such a rush? Slow down."

"I'm positively desperate to see those Degas," I said. "Desperate." Over Will's shoulder I saw a flash of the woman drawing closer. "Let's take the stairs."

I pulled Will into the stairwell and gave him a shove to get him started going up. In a moment, he was going to accuse me of being deranged and I was going to be forced to concur.

As we rounded the top of the stairs, I heard the door slam one floor below us.

"I think this is it," I said, pushing open the door to the second floor. "Come on."

"Lucy, you're acting a little strange," Will said, a puzzled look on his face. "Is this really about Degas?"

"Yes!" I said. "I worship him. He was a genius. Those ballet dancers? My god!" I had us at practically a run down the corridor, the whole time babbling about my love affair with the master Degas. I needed to get Will away from me.

"I'm going to make a quick stop in the bathroom," I said, propelling him with a push toward Room C. "Meet you in there."

The bathroom was mercilessly empty. I tucked myself behind the door and waited. Sixty seconds later it opened. In the mirror I could see her reflection. She wore an expression of determination that went very nicely with her chic hair. Before the door closed again, I had her around the neck. I dragged her, struggling and kicking, into a cramped stall and locked the door.

"Why are you following me?" I whispered into her ear. "Who do you work for?" She grunted and squirmed. I squeezed tighter and she went still.

"Who sent you?" I asked again.

"Serendipity," she gurgled. Which was not exactly the answer I expected from her. In the pocket of her coat was a small vial of what I assumed must be chloroform. She wanted me alive.

" 'Serendipity' implies a random occurrence that's happy in nature," I said, dangling the vial in front of her. "Are you happy? Because right now I'm not feeling that happy."

She laughed, digging her fingernails into the sleeve of my coat. "There's not enough in there to kill you," she said. "Just enough to make you sleep."

"It doesn't take much, you know," I said. "People miscalculate all the time and then you've got all sorts of problems. I'll ask you one more time, who sent you?"

"No one," she said. "But that same no one will be infinitely grateful I stumbled upon you in the Louvre. Sally Sin is supposed to be dead, after all."

"She *is* dead," I said. "Who are you?"

Now that the woman had stopped struggling, she was simply heavy. I leaned against the wall to prevent us both from falling into the toilet.

"I accept death first," she said, almost with relish.

"Oh, come on," I said. "You're not a guy. No need for the macho bullshit. Can't we just have a conversation? Aren't women supposed to be good at that?"

In response, she pressed her lips into a stubborn thin line and I knew I would get nothing from her, especially tucked away in a bathroom stall at the Louvre.

"I was having a pretty nice day," I said, taking a wad of toilet paper and the chloroform vial in a single hand. With a quick tap on the bathroom wall, the vial cracked and the chloroform leaked onto the tissue.

"Hope you got the measurements right," I said as I held it over her mouth and nose. Her feet kicked frantically for a few seconds and finally went still. Her eyes rolled back in her head and she went completely limp. Not without effort, I propped her up on the closed toilet seat, leaning against the wall, hands folded neatly in her lap. She would wake up in about thirty minutes with the headache of a lifetime and no memory of where she was. If anyone happened upon her in the mean-time, she'd be dismissed as a young woman who'd had one too many over lunch and was passing the hours in a warm museum bathroom.

As I washed my hands and straightened out my clothes, I caught a glimpse of myself in the mirror. And there was Sally Sin, looking back at me.

Will was walking around Room C with his hands clasped behind his back like an absentminded professor.

"I can see why you love these, Lucy," he said. "I've never seen them before except in pictures."

"Let's go," I said.

"But we just got here. What about the Degas?"

I ran a hand down his chest. "I was thinking it might be time for a siesta," I said, subtle as a truck. "Back at the hotel."

Will gave me a slow smile, the one that still turns my knees to Jell-O.

"I like the way you think," he said. We walked, arms wrapped around each other, out of the room and right past the bathroom door, behind which my mysterious stalker slept off the hit of anesthesia meant for me.

It was the middle of the night and a rhythmic rain fell out-side our hotel windows. Drenched with sweat, my heart pounding in my chest, I climbed out of bed and stood look-ing at the dark shadow of the Eiffel Tower. I'd made a terrible mistake believing I could live a normal life, that I could come and go like any other citizen of the world. I could not. I was not.

But now it was too late.

30

Sometime around 2 A.M., I hear Will's key in the door downstairs. Or at least I hope it's Will's key. I'm too tired to deal with any more intruders. Whoever it is, he's welcome to steal all our stuff as long as after he's done, he leaves quietly. Will drops his suitcase in the hallway and takes off his shoes. I can barely hear his footsteps on the stairs as he comes closer. I pretend to be asleep because that's what most people do in the middle of the night. Will strips off his clothes, dropping them in a heap on the floor, where they will remain indefinitely, and slides under the sheets next to me. His body is warm but his hands are freezing. I recoil from their touch.

"Sorry I'm late," he whispers, clearly not convinced by my imitation of sleep. "We got hung up in Idaho. Weather."

"Weather," I mumble. "You don't smell so good."

He nuzzles my ear. His hands grow warmer, stealing my heat. "You should see my shoes."

"What are you doing here anyway?" I groan, pulling a pillow over my head. "The calendar doesn't have you back until tomorrow." Or that's what I expect the calendar would say if I actually ever looked at it. I'm suddenly overcome with gratitude I didn't try to hide Yoder in the guest bedroom based on my sketchy memory of the calendar.

"I wanted to be here for Theo's interview tomorrow, otherwise I'd have just stayed over in Idaho." His answer causes a sharp, small ache right in the middle of my chest that catches me off guard. He used to rush home from New York or Washington or Boston because he couldn't wait to be back in San Francisco with me. But our priorities have shifted. Children will do that to you.

"I missed you," I whisper, curling myself into him. He doesn't hear me because he's already snoring lightly in my ear but I'm wide awake now, thinking, for some reason, about Ian Blackford with his shirt off.

In the beginning of my relationship with Will, there were not enough hours in the day. We couldn't get out of bed without having sex and we couldn't have dinner without having sex and we couldn't watch TV without having sex. There were times when we had to run home from a restaurant because we were sure dropping to the floor and doing it right there in front of everyone would get us arrested. Overall, it was a pretty satisfying way to live.

If Will was on the road for more than a day, I experienced his absence as pure agony, as if some important part of my body had been ripped off and nothing could staunch the bleeding. I was in a new city with no job and no friends and I would wander around looking stoned, wanting nothing more than for the hours to pass and for Will to come back to me. There were moments when he was gone that I doubted his very existence. Was any of this real? Had I finally lost my marbles, as Simon Still liked to say?

But if San Francisco and the fog and my new husband were all part of a larger nervous breakdown, it was not altogether unpleasant. I thought I could just keep on going in this manner for quite some time.

Eventually, in a marriage, things have to slow down if you ever plan on getting anything done in life. And I do mean anything. It's hard to concentrate on something as basic as reading the newspaper when you're busy pining away for someone who crawled out of your bed not ten minutes earlier.

One way to slow down the twenty-four-hour sexual buffet is to get pregnant and have a baby. Yes sir, that works very well to bring things to a screeching halt.

At first, Will treated me like I was dying, opening doors, helping me out of the car, not letting me walk on the outside of the sidewalk. He brought home a stack of baby books I couldn't have finished reading even if the gestation period for a human baby were closer to that of an elephant. The books led to conversations I wouldn't have expected to have if Will and I were locked in a room together for a million years and forced to talk to one another for the entire time.

"Did you know in some cultures they practice placentophagia? That's when the new parents eat the placenta," Will would say.

"No. Why on earth would I know that? I don't even want to know that now. Please take it back."

Meanwhile, I watched with horror as the body I had grown accustomed to living in stretched and strained in ways utterly alien to me. I was used to a body that did as it was told. When I said run, it ran. When I said hide, it hid. When I said duck, it hit the deck as if life depended on it, which it usually did. But now I struggled simply to get my shoes on. I kept bumping into doorjambs and almost setting myself on fire on the stove. A man actually gave me his seat on the bus and I was so grateful I almost wept. If this was what life felt like being a whale, I was extremely happy to have been born a human. I was no good at being a whale.

"It's such a remarkable experience," Will would say, resting a hand on my enormous stomach. "I'm just in awe of it."

"If you think it's so amazing then why don't you carry him around with you for a while?" I'd suggest. And Will would laugh because it was easy to marvel at pregnancy from the male side of the gender divide when there was absolutely no risk of being forced to take it up yourself.

Toward the end, I didn't want to stray very far from the house. The unnamed baby was sitting on my bladder and every six minutes I had to run off and find a bathroom. And while my doctor assured me this was perfectly normal and happened all the time, it didn't make it any more dignified.

In a way, I was grateful Simon Still wasn't able to see me in this condition. Because even though his job was to protect the roughly 7 billion human inhabitants here on earth from mass destruction, he didn't really like people very much, and pregnant women held a special place in his mental ranking of things that disgusted him.

Nothing was normal. The smell of my husband made me sick to my stomach. I could no longer even enter my favorite coffee shop and it wasn't solely because the doorway was shrinking. I kept meeting women who talked about the glowing and the empowerment and how they appreciated themselves in a whole new way. They munched on nutritious snacks and carried bottles of filtered water around with them everywhere they went. They read parenting magazines and talked about baby gear with an intensity I had thought was reserved for trying to make peace in the Middle East. I marveled at their ability to shut out the world and all evidence that suggested it was going completely to hell.

I tried to follow their example and not think about the world but the world wasn't willing to cooperate. In every direction, I was confronted with the downward spiral. In New York, two heroin-addled parents locked their two-year-old in a bathroom with scalding hot water running in the tub. They couldn't hear his screams through their drug-induced haze. In Detroit, a six-year-old girl was traded to a child pornographer for drugs. When they found her, it was almost as if she had been turned inside out. In Los Angeles, a four-year-old boy was removed from his teenage mother and her boyfriend after they'd insisted upon using him as an ashtray. The detective on that case broke down and cried on the local news station. The reporter didn't know what to do.

There was no shortage of bad in the world and that didn't even take into account things like the nuclear warheads no one seemed to be able to keep track of. It was hard to believe you weren't committing crimes against humanity simply by perpetuating its existence.

In the last month of pregnancy, when I weighed almost as much as my husband and had taken to wearing his T-shirts, I declared I was never doing this again.

"If you want another baby," I announced, "you'd better find a different wife or work it out mail-order somehow."

"But you're doing so great," Will said. It really is impossible to empathize with a whale so I shouldn't have been so hard on him. "I picked up some things you might need today."

What he was doing cruising the baby aisles at CVS rather than sitting in his office contemplating trash was beyond me. But I didn't have time to ask because my eyes came to rest on a tube of nipple cream and I could no longer speak. I picked up the purple tube and held it in front of Will's face.

"Apparently, nursing mothers sometimes need this stuff. That's what the lady said at the drugstore." He shrugged. After all, he wasn't the one who invented the human body. Maybe if he had, he would have done women the world over a great service and made nipples out of titanium.

"So, I'm to understand that this baby is going to suck the nipples right off my body?"

"Something like that," Will said. "You should read the books."

I *did* read the books, at least what I considered a fairly aggressive assortment of them, and not one mentioned the need for nipple balm. They were holding out on me like a critical asset who wants more money. I started to sweat, which seemed to happen with alarming frequency. My internal thermostat was desperately in need of a tune-up.

"I don't think I can do this," I said. "Really. I mean it."

"Of course you can. There is nothing to worry about. It's all going to be fine."

Nothing to worry about? There were melting ice caps, dying coral reefs, droughts, floods, tsunamis, terrorists, mad scientists, angry man-eating ants, and a variety of nipple creams for sale at the local drugstore. In my opinion, nothing good could come from any of it. Seeing the panic in my eyes, Will sat me down on the couch.

"Listen, our job is to keep this child safe, to make a happy home for him, to help him to grow into a passionate, responsible adult. That's our mission. And we're going to be good at it. It's all going to be okay."

There was something about the way he phrased it that

calmed me. There was a goal and that was something I could get my head around. I could carry out the mission of keeping this baby healthy, happy, and safe. Two weeks later, Theo was born and I found I had nothing near the energy to contemplate my potential failure as a parent. I was in survival mode and deep thinking suddenly seemed a luxury I could no longer afford.

Will, whose life didn't seem to change quite as dramatically as mine, kept careful track of the passing days. Part of it was to marvel at how quickly our little lump of red flesh turned into something resembling a baby boy and part of it was to know exactly when he could get back in the saddle and to be ready when that day rolled around.

"The doctor said six weeks, Lucy," he said, lying next to me in bed, stroking my arm. "We seem to have made it that far."

I, well into my second tube of nipple cream, stared at him blankly.

"You want to have sex with this?" I asked, pointing to my body, which didn't actually resemble my body but must have been because it was attached to my head.

"Yes," he said. "Very much."

I thought about his request for a few minutes. He waited patiently, hopefully, for my answer.

"Well, okay, I guess. But you can't actually touch me. Is that possible?"

"Sure," he said, reaching to pull off my shirt.

"No!" I howled. "The shirt stays on. I said you weren't allowed to actually touch me."

He sighed. This was going to be a challenge, but Will never backed down from a challenge.

"Fine. No touching."

I have to hand it to him, he managed to pull it off by leaving most of my clothes on and indulging in the liberal use of unflavored lubricating gel.

"That was different," he said afterward.

I'll say. Before we could dissect the new nature of our relationship, Theo, sleeping in a bassinet not twelve inches from my head, began to bawl.

Eventually, sex tipped the scales back toward pleasure rather than obligation and I think we were both relieved. It would have been terrible to face a lifetime with someone who turned you on about as much as a pair of argyle socks.

But there were a number of things that stayed permanently skewed. The minute Theo was out of his crib and into his big boy bed, he discovered the joys of showing up in our bed at 6 A.M. He would sneak in the door, glide around the foot of the bed on padded feet, crawl up and over Will, and snuggle down between us. He would always bring his blanket and a stuffed animal that had to share my pillow. And most of the time it was sweet. But sometimes it wasn't.

"Wait! Stop!" I'd whisper, barely able to keep my voice down.

"What? Are you okay? Am I hurting you?"

"No. Get off me. Quick!"

"What's going on? You're acting really weird."

"Kid in the doorway."

"Oh, shit. I mean, Hi, Theo."

Yes, the old Theo interruptus. Theo would look at us strangely and shake his head as if he couldn't understand why he'd gotten stuck with such odd parents. He was a good kid, after all, he ate most of his vegetables. So why the karmic payback of the wacky mom and dad rolling around on their bed like fish out of water? Once I got over the sheer horror of being caught in the act, I kind of felt sorry for him.

After a while, I realized Theo filled my thoughts. He might be in the background, like elevator music, but he was still there. Even in the honest throes of passion, there was a part of me that stayed with my child. I would do anything for him, even when he was screaming like a banshee on the checkout line of the supermarket, even when he overturned his dinner onto the floor or showed up in our bedroom when I would rather he didn't. I no longer belonged to Will. I no longer belonged to myself.

For now, I belonged to Theo.

31

The first rays of sun creep into our bedroom, illuminating the dust hanging in the air in a way that's almost beautiful. If yesterday was a full frontal disaster, today promises more of the same. First, we have an interview for Theo at San Francisco Country Day. I had planned on a rather casual approach but now Will is accompanying us, and I may have to reform my ways.

San Francisco Country Day is the sort of private school Will attended as a child where everyone wears navy trousers, maroon sweater vests, and white button-down shirts. Each student is required to have a blazer with the school emblem sewn neatly over the left breast pocket. Right there, I'm already in big trouble. I can sew a button but only at gunpoint. The classes at Country Day are small, the teachers have a collective 400,000 years of classroom experience, and when you talk about squash, everyone knows you mean the game and not the vegetable.

I didn't go to private school. The very thought of it terrifies me. However, while the idea of my child growing up in such a rarified atmosphere with actual princes and the offspring of extremely rich media tycoons is not ideal, San Francisco Country Day employs a staff of seven private security guards. Normally, the presence of private security guards would do little to ease my fears. They tend to stand around reading magazines, talking on the phone, or texting. Plus, most of them are so out of shape that chasing down a criminal would inevitably lead to cardiac arrest.

However, I checked out San Francisco Country Day's security company and it seems they're a subsidiary of a much larger private security company that works with the United States government, specifically in war zones. Shockingly, they're wholly owned by the family of a student in the third grade.

Public schools don't have money for crayons, let alone gun-toting paramilitary cowboys who are surely covered in tattoos under their official-looking jackets and ties. For most people, that's just fine. But I'm not most people. The criteria I use to judge a school's appropriateness isn't something I share with my mom friends. There's no need for them to think I'm that weird.

So it seems I'm willing to put up with diversity being defined as a child with brown hair and dressing my kid up like an accountant in exchange for a campus patrolled by a bunch of ex-marines. I mean, I'm pretty good but I can't be everywhere at once, can I?

For the privilege of sending my five-year-old into such an environment, I will pay $27,000 a year in tuition. No, you did not misread the number. And that's for kindergarten. The price increases as the child advances through the grades. After all, a sixth-grader is bound to eat more than a first-grader. Whether he can eat $10,000 more is up for debate.

When I first opened the brochure to a smiling bunch of kids sitting attentively in a classroom, absorbing knowledge like wee sponges, I felt the difference between Theo and me as a blow to the gut. Theo will move in these circles with these people as his friends. But he won't be pretending. It'll really be him, not some invented version of himself meant to confuse and distract the other side. Staring at the brochure, I wondered if there was a real version of me lurking around somewhere and what she might be like.

"Can we really justify spending that amount of money for kindergarten?" I'd asked Will. "They read storybooks and decorate pumpkins and things."

"They have a strong reputation for math and science," my husband said. How did he know this? Was he doing his homework on the side, stepping into my territory? "They also recently installed solar cells on the roofs of all their buildings. They're sending the right message, doing the right thing, and I want to support that." Ah, I knew it had to be more than great test scores in algebra.

I let Will continue to sleep and slide into the shower. The last time Will was out of town, I took a pair of pliers and removed the water-saving device from the showerhead. I stand under Niagara Falls and enjoy how it pounds my head. It won't last, so I relish the temporary luxury of all that water.

Before I can rinse the conditioner out of my hair, I hear a wail coming down the hallway. I give it a minute to see if Will is going to wake up and attend to his howling son. From the shower, I can see he has pulled the comforter up over his head, so I guess the answer is no.

"Mom, I have to go to the bathroom!" I stand in Theo's door, a towel wrapped around me, my hair dripping all over the wood floor.

"That's why you got me out of the shower?" I ask.

"Can you carry me? The floor is really cold."

"Theo," I say, now freezing, "you're five years old. Five-year-olds can walk themselves to the bathroom. Maybe put on some socks?"

"Please, Mommy?" I have stared down nervous terrorists with their fingers on the trigger but I'm somehow powerless against Theo's quivering lower lip.

"Come on," I say. He stands up on his bed and I pick him up. He takes a deep inhale of my wet hair.

"You smell like French fries," he says. That's unfortunate for many reasons.

Fifteen minutes later, we're down in the kitchen, where I spend the bulk of my life. I plop Theo on the counter and put him to work scooping coffee into the French press. Six or seven scoops in, I reconsider my decision.

"What do you think about taking a walk in the Presidio today after we visit that school?" I propose. "Just you and me? It will be fun. Maybe we'll play on the beach?"

And Mommy can do a little reconnaissance. And hope no one notices.

"What are we going to do besides walking? I want to do more things."

"We can play on the beach," I say again. There are clocks everywhere, on the stove, on my cell phone, on the wall. They are all telling me the same thing. Gray is running out of time.

"Can Henry come?" he asks.

"I don't think so. Not this time."

"Please, Mom? I never get to do anything with Henry." I don't point out that just yesterday we spent the entire excruciating length of a ballgame with Henry. However, what happened yesterday is utterly irrelevant when you're five. Only right now counts. You get no points for before.

Scouting for a secret safe house isn't exactly an appropriate outing for Theo, let alone his little friend. I should do what any sane mom who used to be a spy would do and call a babysitter, leaving Theo at home, safe and cozy and out of harm's way, while I go off and try to infiltrate a bunker presumably guarded by armed government agents, and attempt to steal back my terrorist. But for the same reason I sit outside Theo's school, I don't do babysitters. They make me anxious, chatting away on their cell phones, backs to the monkey bars and swing sets. It would be so easy to snatch a kid without the sitter even noticing. It might take minutes for her to realize her charge is gone. I start to sweat just thinking about it.

Early on, I decided I didn't want to force Theo to have all his playdates at our house because I suffered from an overdeveloped sense of paranoia. I wanted to say yes to little Matthew or Luke or Joe and let my son go and play with someone else's toys, which is what it's really all about anyway.

I also decided there was no need to confess that as Theo and Matthew or Luke or Joe drive home from school, I'm never far behind.

I park somewhere close by where I've a decent view of the house and I watch. Fortunately, I've had years of practice lurking around undetected so I have yet to be caught in the act, which is good because I haven't worked out an appropriate cover story to explain myself if I did. You think I'd take care of that, come up with something during all those hours sitting and staring at closed doors.

Theo sits on the counter, pouting, his face scrunched up in displeasure.

"I really miss Henry," he says.

And I really need to get Yoder back. It might not be

possible to satisfy everyone's needs today. Sometimes mothers have to make hard choices.

"I know, sweet pea. I'll see what I can do." But it doesn't matter because Theo's no longer listening to me. Daddy has entered the kitchen. Will looks tired and incredibly gorgeous in faded jeans and a white T-shirt. I almost give in to the urge to set Theo up in front of the TV and drag Will back to the bedroom for a few minutes of X-rated behavior.

"Good morning," he says with a yawn. He takes a sip of coffee and spits it in the sink. "What the hell?"

"I made the coffee," Theo pipes up. "Do you like it?"

"Yes," Will says, recovering. "But I might add a little milk."

"Treat it like espresso and you'll be okay," I suggest. Will wraps his arms around me. Theo squeezes in between us.

"You smell good," Will says.

"Please don't say like French fries."

"Huh?"

"Never mind."

"Are we ready for this interview?" he asks.

I was unaware I was meant to prepare.

"Theo," he says. "Are you ready to dazzle these people?"

"Yes," Theo says, although I'm pretty sure he didn't even hear the question. He's thinking about something else. He's thinking about yesterday. "So the guys who broke the windows last night are now on the bad-guy ship with Darth Vader and Darth Maul. The good guys are on the good-guy ship. In the playroom. Come on, I'll show you."

Will's eyes drift toward the back door and the tape and cardboard. I freeze. I also failed to prepare for this scenario. However, it's clear I owe a karmic debt to Darth Vader as Will doesn't even flinch at Theo's story.

"Accident," I whisper in Will's ear. "I slammed it pretty hard and it broke. The panes were cracked on the edges anyway. I'm not surprised."

"And then Mommy lied on top of me and crushed the Connect Four box!" Theo says, tugging on Will's arm. "It was totally cool. Come on!"

I give Will a weak smile. At least Theo didn't mention the guns.

"Yesterday was a little crazy," I say.

But I can tell Will has already mentally moved on to other things, like the thirteen thousand unanswered e-mails in his inbox and an afternoon meeting with a company that wants to mass-produce home composters. "A composter in every home!" As a tag line, I think it needs work.

"Oh, I almost forgot," Will says, untangling from us. "My parents are coming today."

My shoulders immediately tense up at the thought.

"Are they staying the night?" I ask.

"Yup," Will says.

And there it is. The final bit of evidence that I am indeed cursed.

32

Will stands at the mirror, knotting his tie. Theo, dressed in a dark blue sweater and khaki pants, watches intently. I stare into my bamboo closet with a feeling that can only be described as despair.

"I think you'd better take Theo on this interview without me," I say.

"You can go like that," Will says. "You look good in your underwear."

"I'm not sure the folks at San Francisco Country Day would agree."

"You're probably right. It's pretty much guaranteed that no one there will have a sense of humor."

So why are we even considering this for our only child? I mean, I'm well aware of my own irrational reasons but what are Will's? Are solar panels really that compelling?

I settle on a pair of black pants. They have a bleached-out streak on the left leg that I fill in with a Sharpie permanent marker. The color is slightly more brown than black but if I cross my legs in just the right way when I sit down, I might get away with it. As I struggle to button the pants, I feel another wave of the nausea that's been plaguing me lately. Could it be the malaria, contracted during an unfortunate visit to

Guatemala, that seems to flare up whenever I have something really important to do? Right after this interview I promise myself I will see the doctor, go and take back Yoder, escape Simon Still, rescue my father, and rid the world of yet another complete lunatic. No big deal if I were actually five people instead of one. And it would be helpful if the other four were Navy SEALs without previous commitments.

To enter San Francisco Country Day, one must pass through a set of concrete pillars etched with various Latin phrases: "BE BOLD IN YOUR INTELLECT." "DO NOT BACK DOWN IN THE FACE OF ADVERSITY." "STUDY HARD." "PAY YOUR TU-ITION ON TIME." "GIVE GENEROUSLY TO THE ANNUAL FUND." Things like that. I smile at the security guard standing beside one of the pillars. He ignores me as if he were a guard outside of Buckingham Palace protecting the Queen of England. He thinks I'm perfectly innocent.

Beyond the gates is a world that's the complete opposite of urban. Green lawns resembling Augusta National, inter-rupted only by majestic trees or bursting flowerbeds, roll right up to the sturdy brick buildings that practically ooze knowledge. I may have added ten points to my IQ just by proximity alone.

"Where are the toys?" Theo asks, holding tightly to Will's hand, looking skeptical.

"Probably inside," I say. But he has a point. The school is shrouded in an unnatural stillness. It's the kind of stillness that, in my experience, always predicates complete chaos. A trickle of cold sweat runs down my back. Something about this place is slightly creepy. Even the ivy climbing up the out-side walls seems sinister.

Our footsteps echo along the main hall as we make our way toward the admissions office. I'm curious how they're going to go about interviewing a five-year-old when all he wants to talk about is Darth Vader and the wholesale slaughter of clone troopers.

"Welcome, Hamilton family!" trills Frances Claiborne, the admissions director, who wears a proper navy suit with matching pumps. A dainty string of pearls hangs around her thin neck and her gray hair is pulled back so tightly it looks like a poorly executed face-lift. She offers a dead-fish handshake, which makes me immediately suspicious. I don't trust people who can't properly shake a hand because how hard is it really? These are the sorts of people who, when they encounter something truly difficult in life, immediately begin looking for a way to blame it on you.

"We're so thrilled you're interested in our little school," Ms. Claiborne says without much emotion.

"It's nice to meet you, Frances," Will says.

"Oh, everyone calls me Mrs. Claiborne," she corrects.

"Of course, Mrs. Claiborne," he says. He doesn't punch her in the face. Interesting.

"The way we work this is we send Theo off with one of our evaluators, giving us adults a chance to talk."

She has yet to look at or acknowledge Theo, who hides behind my legs and pulls at the sleeve of his cotton sweater. The trickle of cold sweat running down my back expands into a river. Will is smiling, nodding, as if this process is right as rain.

"Where exactly will he be going?" I ask, trying to keep the mounting hysteria out of my voice.

"Oh, to one of the lower school rooms, with the evaluator"

is what she says. What I hear is "to the underground prison cell, with the interrogator."

"And this is necessary why exactly?" I ask.

Mrs. Claiborne pulls herself up straighter as if someone just stuck an iron rod up her ass.

"It's the way we do things here, Mrs. Hamilton," she sniffs.

Will lays a hand on my arm. "It's fine, Lucy." But it doesn't feel fine to me. It feels all wrong.

"Gretchen, can you take Theo down to room 4C for his evaluation?" The assistant behind the great mahogany desk nods her head. She's a little afraid of Frances Claiborne. I'm guessing everyone is.

Theo gives her a big smile, takes her hand, and heads off to find room 4C, where some man in a Jimmy Carter mask will probably torture him until he confesses I once let him watch an episode of *SpongeBob SquarePants*.

Stop it, Lucy, I tell myself. You're being ridiculous. Sadly, it's not the first time I've had this conversation with myself.

Mrs. Claiborne's office is covered in dark, serious paneling and populated with red upholstered furniture. On the walls, there are paintings of horsemen heading out from their English estates with dogs in tow for a day of jolly fox hunting. Which is great fun, unless of course you're the fox.

She scans our application, making little *tsk tsk* noises to herself. And then she turns to me, her sharp eyes flashing above the half moons of her reading glasses.

"Tell me, Mrs. Hamilton," she says, "what exactly did you do before Theo was born?"

This is a story I've told a number of times. I try not to

vary it for fear it'll come back to haunt me at some inopportune time if I do.

"I was an analyst for the United States Agency for Weapons of Mass Destruction," I say.

She practically sneers at me. "You worked for the government?" Everyone knows that only people seriously lacking in ambition work *for* the government.

"Yes. I did." I hate the way Mrs. Frances Claiborne's pearl drop earrings bob up and down as she talks. But if I get right down to it and really examine my emotions, it might be I just hate Mrs. Frances Claiborne.

"She left that job when she moved out here," Will adds. He's trying to please her and that strikes me as strange.

"And your family?" she continues. "Do they remain in the East? The information about you on the application is rather . . . thin."

That's because I don't want to go to school here. I already went to kindergarten and I'm pretty sure it didn't cost $27,000.

"I have no family other than the one that you see," I say.

"Well, now, how can that be? We all have families."

"I don't come from money," I say flatly, "if that's what you want to know."

My statement ruffles her feathers. Will shoots me a look, telling me in no uncertain terms to keep my mouth shut. Rich people don't talk about money. The assumption is everyone has it and it'll always be there. So while Mrs. Claiborne pretends to be interested in me, what she really wants to know is what she can expect me to cough up during fund-raising. Am I going to build a new wing on the library or am I more the twenty-five-dollar check kind of a gal?

"Well," she sniffs. "We consider ourselves a big family here, so we like to know as much as we can about applicants before making any decisions. Are you going to fit into the family or not?"

If I leap across the desk and stab her in the heart with one of her faux fountain pens, my husband will probably get upset. And telling her the truth about my family is out of the question because the only way I could really discuss that in any detail would be after I saved my father and he confessed all, and I haven't gotten around to any of that just yet. So I go for plan C.

"Actually, if you want the truth, I came from a test tube," I say. "Anonymous donors. It's not the sort of thing I like to talk about."

"Lucy!" Will is horrified. Mrs. Claiborne is horrified. I feel a little more relaxed. Will and Mrs. Claiborne collectively decide to pretend I'm no longer in the room, which is fine with me. It's too hot in here anyway. My husband is talking about his firm. He's telling Mrs. Claiborne exactly what she wants to hear. But the damage is already done. I'm becoming just the kind of loose cannon that used to terrify me, a person who doesn't know when to shut up.

After the interview, we drop Will at his office and head for the playground. Our visit to San Francisco Country Day has made me long for fresh air and the reasonable voices of my mom posse.

In the backseat, Theo flips through a *Star Wars* "EZ Reader" book. He's been strangely silent since our visit to San Francisco Country Day. I know how he feels.

"What did you think of that school?" I ask him. Moments before, when Will asked him the same question, Theo plastered on a fake smile and said it was good. But I didn't believe it for a minute. I can tell when someone is lying.

"The lady didn't want me to get paint on my pants," he says. "And I wanted to do the painting on the floor to make a bigger rocket but she said no. I like Teacher Wendy."

I like Teacher Wendy too and kind of wish we could stay in preschool forever. But at some point, making art out of toilet paper rolls would no longer be the developmental challenge it once was. Kindergarten is going to happen to us no matter what.

As we drive, I remember what Avery once told me about the San Francisco public schools lottery system. She swore those families who listed a foreign language as the primary language spoken in their home often got their first choice of schools in the lottery although she had no explanation for why that would be.

"So maybe we should practice Spanish at home now?" I mutter in Spanish to myself. "Maybe then we'll get a decent lottery number. Or maybe I can figure out a way to bribe the people who run the lottery? Free solar panels?"

The Spanish sounds as it always did, fast off the tongue, no rust. I'm suddenly depressed by all our schooling options. And home schooling is out because the only subject I'm any good at is foreign affairs and my approach might not be appropriate for a kindergartener.

"I don't know, Mom," Theo says. "Then Daddy won't understand us and that would probably drive him crazy." I spin in my seat, practically crashing us into a parked car. My son just answered me in perfect Spanish.

"Theo, are you doing Spanish in school?" I ask. Please let the answer be yes.

"No," he says, still in Spanish. "I listen down in the Mission and to the ladies at the playground sometimes. I like the way it sounds."

Oh, my.

33

As we pull into the parking lot of the playground, I pepper Theo with questions in Spanish. What color is the sky? How old are you? What's your name? He answers each in a grammatically perfect complete sentence. It feels as if someone has sucked all the air out of the car. Will is a normal guy, maybe a little evangelical when it comes to the environment but still, overall, nicely American. I was counting on his normalness to counteract my weirdness in our child. Apparently, that theory is full of holes.

Dancing along beside me, Theo sings his ABCs, counts to fifty, and starts reciting *Green Eggs and Ham,* all in Spanish. I tell him to be quiet but he's clearly enjoying my discomfort at this unexpected turn of events. Assembled on the benches is the mommy posse that helped me survive the first two years of Theo's life more or less intact. I'm overcome with relief at seeing them here, same as always.

Sam and Avery occupy one bench, sipping coffee and talking, of course, about kindergarten. Next to them sits Belinda, holding four-month-old Cooper, and Claire.

They stop mid-conversation and stare at me. I wonder if I have snot in my hair or food on my face.

"Well?" says Avery.

"Well what?" I ask.

"The interview," she demands. "How was it? Did you like it? Did they like you? Did Theo do okay?"

"Fine," I say. "And no, definitely not, and yes to the other questions."

"It was awful," Avery rightly concludes.

"Worse than that," I say. There is a collective sigh from the group as they see another option slip away from them. Now, if they decide to send their sons and daughters and grandsons to San Francisco Country Day, they will inevitably be plagued by my negative assessment of the school. They'll forever wonder if I saw something they missed.

"Will liked it," I offer.

"I'm telling you," Avery says, "I'm rethinking the whole thing. I need to send Sophie to public school. I don't know why I was even considering the privates. That environment is all wrong."

"You need a vacation, that's what you need," says Sam. "Or a good case of amnesia."

Claire laughs. "Or you need to be poor like us," she says. "That makes the decision easy."

I look at Claire with shock. Her definition of poor is an annual income of marginally less than seven figures. Claire shrugs. "It's all relative," she says in her own defense.

"That's it," Avery says. "I can't take it anymore. We're moving out of the city."

A dramatic hush descends upon us. Avery just spoke the words that shall not be spoken: "move to the suburbs."

Mothers have their own language and this group is no different. It took me a little while to figure it out but once I did,

I was in. All you need to do is ask how old another person's child is and how potty training went and bingo, you've got yourself at least a full hour of conversation while you tirelessly push your kid on the swings. When I explained this to Will, he accused me of pimping out our child to make friends. I wanted to argue but the idea was basically true, even if I took issue with his choice of words.

A mommy posse has certain unwritten rules. First, we aren't going to talk about anything that falls outside the home sphere. Politics, old jobs, current events, and extramarital affairs are off-limits. Stress about school choices, Halloween costumes, picky eaters, and sales at the Nordstrom shoe department are acceptable. Well, we do give some leeway to Sam when he attempts to broaden the conversation but that's only because we feel sorry for him, having to masquerade as a mom and all.

We live in a nice happy bubble and no one is pretending otherwise. But the bubble has a shelf life and it's getting closer to its expiration date. Our days of sitting on benches, watching the kids play in the sand and slide down the slides, are limited. Recently, Claire said her old company asked if she would consider a small consulting gig during the week.

"Nothing serious," she said, already on the defensive. "Some mentoring of the new recruits. A few hours a week. That's all."

She was met with silence. Finally, Avery spoke up.

"That's really great, Claire."

"Well, I didn't say I was going to do it. I never said I would do it." With that, she burst into tears and Sam looked like he wanted to die or at the very least go find a bench occupied by professional football players or anyone more masculine than crying mothers. Reinventing yourself is not without issues. I should know, having done it a number of times.

My last personal reinvention began one night in the slums outside of Manila. I was chasing a woman who used an orphanage as a front for her far more lucrative business of selling feedstock chemicals for nerve agents to the highest bidders. I mean, who would ever suspect the Sweet Caress Home for Children as being anything other than what it appeared to be? And even if you did suspect, you'd never admit it. People would simply dismiss you as being cynical and angry and who wants to be called cynical and angry? Davina Castillo had the moral high ground, dedicating her life to saving these poor rejected little souls, so it was next to impossible for the local authorities to pin her down as a hard-core criminal. She was Mother Teresa gone to the dark side.

And, of course, she knew I was coming. They always knew I was coming. If you used that as a criterion upon which to judge my career as a spy, I would certainly warrant a check mark next to "needs improvement." It left me little choice but to chase after her and she, smartly, headed straight into the slums of Quezon City, where a person could uncomfortably disappear for decades. My Filipino was perfect but I had blue eyes and pale skin and I might as well have been from Mars as far as the locals were concerned.

The streets were snarled with traffic and the air thick with a yellowish pollution. The dwellings were constructed of cinder blocks and discarded pieces of corrugated metal. Tattered sheets and tapestries thrown over bits of twine stood in when the residents ran out of scavenged building materials. As I walked down the center of an alleyway littered with empty plastic bottles, Styrofoam packaging, and mildewed cardboard boxes, a handful of children watched me with intense dark eyes. Eventually one would come up and offer information in exchange for a handful of money.

"Lady, you want help?"

"I'm looking for someone," I said. "Her name is Davina."

"Oh, yes. I know her. Mrs. Davina. Her brother lives near here."

Nice. She's making millions dealing in illegal chemical weapons and she won't even buy her brother out of the slums.

I handed the boy a pile of small bills and, grinning, he gave me very specific directions to Davina's brother's shack.

She was surprised to see me but tried not to show it.

"You seem to be leading a double life," I said to her in English, my finger loosely positioned on the trigger of my gun.

"Aren't we all?" she said, with a brief nod of her head.

There were three of them and they obviously took their jobs as bodyguards seriously. And then there it was, that split-second hesitation on my part.

I don't want to die here, whispered a voice pushing up from the dark recesses of my consciousness. *There are so many things left to do.*

I remember that moment as the beginning of the end. An elbow jab to the throat of one bodyguard, a knee to the skull of the second, and a foot to the groin of the third saved me, but I could've lost everything in that split-second pause. Now Davina and I stood, guns drawn, staring one another down.

"I have nothing to lose," I said. But I was still rattled by the voice and I didn't sound convincing. "You've all that money. And think of the children."

"Who cares about the children?" she said with a smirk that

I resented on behalf of the kids. "And I won't be able to do much with the money if I'm in an American jail, now will I?" I saw her clench her teeth, ready to absorb the kickback from firing her gun. But I was faster, I was trained, and that had to count for something.

My bullet hit her dead center in the forehead. Her bullet hit the roof, putting a hole in the tin panels and letting rays of light burst through as if I were receiving a message directly from God.

Simon was really mad I killed her.

"We needed her," he said, when I returned to Washington. "She knew things and now her brains are all over the floor of some Manila slum. Good work, Sally."

"She was going to kill me," I pointed out.

"That really isn't my problem, is it?" he said, leaving me to contemplate what horrible locale he'd send me to next to make his point that I shouldn't have shot Davina in the head.

I never told anyone about the voice that made me pause in a Quezon City slum. But I didn't have to. The seed had been planted and I was already beginning to reinvent myself.

Belinda, holding Cooper and bellowing for Amanda to stop beating up Carter, looks exhausted. Cooper is four months old and demanding. She swears she isn't going to make it. It is our job to assure her she'll be fine even if secretly we're horrified by what we see. Her eyes are sunken into her head and her skin is the color of a fresh bruise. She hasn't brushed her stringy hair in what looks like weeks and I can only guess about her teeth.

"Amanda is acting out her hostility," she says, trying to nurse Cooper, who is kicking and screaming and turning red as a beet. "She covered his head with a blanket yesterday and when I caught her she said she thought he was cold. And I wanted to hit her. I really did. Is that wrong?"

Well, yes, but confirming the worst to someone on the brink is unkind in lots of ways.

Avery steps in to give the perfect answer and we all nod our heads in agreement and thank the heavens we aren't Belinda. After a few afternoons on the playground with Belinda and Cooper, Claire announced that Owen would be an only child. Fortunately, Belinda was too tired to take offense.

I watch Theo and Carter rolling around in the sand and laughing. I never had siblings. I have no idea what it's like. Would you be hitting each over the head with metal Tonka trucks in an attempt to secure the bulk of limited parenting resources for yourself or would you love and protect one another no matter the cost? Amanda has apparently decided the resources are rightly hers and suffocation is a perfectly reasonable way to get them back. The guilt at having ruined Amanda's life is written all over Belinda's face. She is nothing short of a tragedy at the moment.

Avery takes the little bundle of Cooper and begins bouncing him around, cooing sweetly in his ear in a way I never managed to pull off without looking ridiculous. Cooper immediately stops shrieking, nuzzles down in his fuzzy green blanket, and goes to sleep.

"He's so beautiful," Avery whispers. She desperately wants another child but can't seem to make it happen even with medical intervention.

Sam rolls his eyes. He demanded a promise from his son

that if he agreed to be Carter's nanny and hang out with the likes of us all day there would be no more babies.

"Two is enough," he told us. "I only have two hands. A third baby would require me to grow another arm and I'm too old for that nonsense."

His son, having no alternative but to meet his father's demands, went off to the doctor the next day. Such is the way families are made in the modern economy.

I'm undecided on the idea of a second child. There's no denying the ticking grows louder every day but sometimes I'm still able to ignore it. Could I love another child the way I love Theo? Is it possible to have that much love and not be crushed by its implications? I rest a single hand on my mostly flat stomach and wonder briefly what such a child would look like. Would he have my hair, my eyes? Would he come out speaking Tagalog? Would he be a she?

My reverie is interrupted by the silence. Everyone is staring at my son, who's involved in an animated conversation with a nanny.

The nannies sit on the other side of the playground. We would never consider sitting on their side of the playground and they would never sit on ours. It's perverse playground etiquette that makes no sense whatsoever. The nannies all speak Spanish except for one who speaks Russian and she sits alone. Occasionally, I hear them ranting about an employer or a charge and when they catch me staring, I look away.

Theo is gesturing with his arms. He is telling them something about Luke Skywalker and C-3PO but I'm too far away to catch the details. The nannies are laughing.

"Lucy?" Sam says accusingly, as if I have been holding out on him. "When did Theo learn to speak Spanish?"

I can't exactly say I don't know so I lie. "The cleaning lady speaks to him and she has been, um, coming a lot these days."

"Wow," says Avery, still bouncing a sleeping Cooper in her arms. "He's really got it down. Can you keep up?"

Oh, yes. And later I plan on teaching him Mandarin.

"Sort of," I say. "Theo, go play! We don't have much time."

He waves good-bye to the nannies and heads back to the sand pit. My cheeks are red. Lying is about to become a whole lot more complicated.

"That's fabulous," says Claire, her brow furrowing in concentration. "I'm going to sign Owen up for lessons immediately. He should know a second language by now. How is he going to get into Yale if he can't speak a second language?"

Poor Owen. Someday I'll owe him an apology.

As we sit on the benches, watching the kids, listening to baby Cooper's little snores and basking in the familiarity of the scene, the conversation turns back to the issue of where to send the kids to kindergarten. We'll beat it to death and when we are done we'll start all over again from the beginning. It's what we do and, for now, it allows us to ignore what is just on the horizon, the call to reinvent ourselves yet again. But the truth is, I'm starting to wonder if I have what it takes to pull it off one more time.

34

My in-laws are sitting on the front steps when Theo and I pull up from the playground. Is it time for me to give them their own key? That's a thought too horrifying to contemplate with any seriousness right now. But they should be happy because this is the day when the earth is going to move, the heavens open up, and William II and Rose Marie are going to be asked to babysit. I'm confident that William II's reaction will be nothing short of jubilant. The jury is still out on Rose Marie.

Part of William II's acute obsession with grandfathering after his brush with death was a desire to take Theo places. He was tickled by the idea of a trip to the zoo or the aquarium or the beach or the ice cream shop two blocks away.

"How wonderful!" he'd say. "I don't think I've ever been to an aquarium."

"Of course you have, dear," a tortured Rose Marie would answer.

"Well, not with my grandson," he'd counter.

He thought he might take up skiing.

"Will never has time to take Theo skiing but I do," he'd say. "We'll rent a house. Slope side! I have *time*." And he would pause for a moment to savor the idea of time, of being alive instead of being dead. "I love skiing."

"You've never been skiing, dear," Rose Marie would remind him.

"So we'll take lessons together. It'll be fun!"

My mother-in-law has taken to accessorizing her St. John suits with a look of permanent resignation.

If there were an alternative, I'd take it, but I'm in a situation and I don't see any other way. I took Theo along on one of my misadventures before and learned my lesson. I will not make the same mistake twice.

Yes, it's time to begin letting go even if the idea leaves me weak in the knees. Theo has to live in this world and not the one from which I came. I have to trust that others can keep him safe and love him as much as I do. I have to believe it even if on some level I know it's not possible.

"Theo," I say, opening the garage door, "how would you like to go to the zoo with Grandma and Gramps this afternoon?"

"Can I ride the train?" he asks, apparently unaware of the world shifting beneath him.

"Of course," I say. "Gramps loves the train."

"He loves everything!" Theo says with wonder. "Are you coming?"

"No."

"Okay." He's unfazed. I have clearly overestimated my own importance. "I can show them how to get there. I know the directions."

"I have no doubt about that," I say. "Now hop out and say hello. In English, please."

William II squeezes Theo so hard it looks as if Theo's eyeballs might pop out of his head. Then he tosses him up in the air without any look of strain on his face. Rose Marie, who visibly blanches every time she hears the name "Grandma," air kisses me and then looks disapprovingly around the living room. It's a disaster but certainly not the only one on this fine San Francisco day.

As Rose Marie settles them into the guest bedroom, which includes replacing the 100-percent-recycled toilet paper with something softer than sandpaper, I float the plan to Gramps, without getting into the specifics, of course.

"I have a few things I need to take care of this afternoon so I was wondering if you would be willing to take Theo to the zoo without me?"

My father-in-law takes a step back as if I just whacked him across the chest with a two-by-four.

"Are you ill?" he asks. "Because you look a little washed out to me."

I wish everyone would stop saying that. I'm starting to take it personally.

"No," I say. "I'm fine. Just a few errands to run and I thought Theo might have more fun with you two than being dragged around with me all afternoon."

"I love that boy," William II says in a deep voice. "I love him more than anything." The Laurence Olivier vibe comes through strong and steady. "We can do whatever he wants. Oh, and I want to pay for that San Francisco Country Day that Will was telling me about."

I'll leave it to Will to explain how Theo will probably not be accepted because he has a loud-mouthed, overly paranoid mother.

"That's very sweet," I say, "but unnecessary. Let's start with the zoo."

Over the course of the morning, I've convinced myself that,

logistically, it would be difficult for anyone to sneak up and snatch my kid at the zoo. Too many people milling around eating cotton candy and popcorn and feeding the giraffes. But that small fact does little to help my stomach, now located somewhere down around my shoes. I feel as if I just jumped off the Empire State Building without a parachute.

I begin to pile various snacks on the kitchen table for the zoo expedition: cheese sticks, crackers, yogurt tubes, apple slices, unsalted almonds. It must appear like I'm having a snack-related seizure because William II takes me by the shoulders, forcing me to look at him.

"We'll be fine, Lucy," he says with a genuine smile that did not exist B.C. "Just go on and have a nice afternoon."

I have heard mothers talk about a sense of liberation, the sense of freedom they get when they walk out the door alone. It's as if they're walking back in time to the person they were before little Johnny or Mary Sue showed up to complicate things. But I don't feel that. I feel nothing but dread.

I stop at the Java Luv to fortify myself with a few shots of espresso. Leonard is behind the counter, staring into space, a completely vacant look on his face.

"Leonard!" I yell. "Come back to us."

"What? Oh, hey, Lucy. It's the middle of the afternoon. What are you doing here?"

Getting ready for battle. Some people meditate. I drink coffee.

"Can I get an espresso for here and a coffee to go?"

"Loading up, are you? Wait a minute. Where's Theo?"

"At home with his grandparents," I say. I wait for a tear in the space-time continuum to occur or something equally dramatic. But nothing happens.

"Holy shit, Lucy," Leonard says. "What gives? Are you dying?"

"Of course not," I snap. "I just have some stuff to do. What's so weird about a kid spending time with his grandparents?"

"You're the only weird thing in that equation, Lucy," he says with perfect kindness. "For anyone else, it would be completely normal."

I toss back the espresso. "Thanks, Leonard. You're a real pal."

He smiles. He likes compliments of any sort. I pull out my cell phone and dial my old pal Chemical Claude.

"I'll be ready to make the trade in ninety minutes," I say. "If you're not at the Ferry Building with Director Gray at that time, you don't get your prize. No second chances."

I hang up before he can answer. Leonard stares at me.

"What?" I ask.

He shakes his head. "Nothing. Too much acid maybe? Gotta lay off that stuff."

"Drugs are bad for you, Leonard."

"Sure they are. Yeah. Here's your coffee." I take the container, give him a wave, and head out into the afternoon. The fog is rolling in fast and steady. I can feel the cool lick of its tongue on my face as I slide into the front seat of my car.

It's time to get to work.

35

On my way back toward the Presidio, I take a quick detour to a big, anonymous bank in the financial district. Parking there is hell but the chances of anyone recognizing me in that neighborhood are slim to none. Downstairs in the bank's vault is a safe deposit box registered to Maggie Wilson and paid for with cash. In the box, nestled in a bed of newspaper, is a gun. It looks almost exactly like the Colt Commander I dropped off the bridge at Point Bonita a couple of years ago. Except it's not. I have never run through a jungle with this gun nestled against my back. It has never been soaked with my sweat, squeezed tightly in fear. This gun has never killed anyone. The ridges on the grip feel unfamiliar and new. It's really clean.

It's also stolen. It's generally not a good idea for a girl like me to purchase a weapon through normal channels. The required background check would send up all sorts of red flags guaranteed to confuse the poor dumb guy behind the counter at Walmart. And eventually a note would pass over Simon Still's desk and there would be questions I don't want to answer.

Instead, I went to visit the guy who did some after market work on my old fun car and asked him bluntly to sell me a stolen gun. That he did not expect such a request from me, wearing yoga pants, hair in a pony tail, and driving a shiny new Prius, worked in my favor. The situation was so outside the norm that, to his mind, there was no way I could be a cop and he willingly threw open his store of stolen guns for my perusal. When I picked up the exact Colt Commander I'd lost, he even went so far as to berate me for picking a small, sissy gun. But I ignored him and stuck to what I knew.

I don't know why I felt the need to go out and get a gun on that particular day. Nothing of interest was happening in my life but as soon as I woke up I knew it had to happen. There was no way around it. If I didn't need it today I would certainly need it tomorrow. And here I had arrived at tomorrow.

I tuck the gun into the back of my pants. I put a handful of bullets in my jacket pocket and close up the box. I have to get this whole thing wrapped up by 5:00 so I can get back here before they close. Can't have a gun in the house. There are too many children wanting to hide in my closet so they can see their glow-in-the-dark light sabers.

No one tells you when you have kids that you'll completely lose control of your life. In your life before, you were probably able to maintain a semblance of order, chart a linear path through your days. But motherhood does nothing if not hone your ability to bob and weave. Any plans you make have probably gone to shit before breakfast is even over. It can be very disorienting.

Here it is just after lunch time and I've already read Theo four or five books, made a mess of an interview for private school, had some playtime on the playground, had at least six cups of coffee, passed Theo off to his grandparents with many instructions and snacks, all of which will be ignored, retrieved my gun from a safe deposit box, and headed off to get my terrorist back. I'm tired. I could use a nap but I just don't see that happening today.

It's a beautiful day down on Crissy Field. This is one of my favorite spots in the city of San Francisco. A long stretch of coast running from the Marina to Fort Point, great efforts have been made to return it to its natural state. The results of those efforts is a long walking path through restored habitat with incredible views of the Golden Gate Bridge, accompanied by the salty air and the ever-present wind. When Theo was a baby, I'd regularly walk him up and down this route in his BabyBjörn, breathing in the sea and letting the natural beauty clear my foggy mind. I have so many fond memories from this place, playing in the sand, watching the surfers, seeing Ian Blackford for the first time since he died. Okay, maybe not that one.

I drive west on Mason Street. Very few empty warehouses remain along this stretch of road with unobstructed views of the Bay and Golden Gate Bridge. Most of them are rented to swim clubs or gymnastics studios or rock-climbing gyms. S&S Outsourcing appears to own its whole building. Although I'm sure it wasn't intentional, it turns out the Presidio is perfect for a clandestine effort like this one. Federally owned land meant a minimum of questions if the Agency paid off the right people. And the Agency, as with all intelligence-gathering organizations, functioned as if laws did not apply to them, so that was not an issue.

The S&S Outsourcing building has been converted to what looks like office space to the casual observer, a hulking mass refinished in light-colored shingles meant to pay tribute to its industrial roots. The windows are all new and, from the way the sun glints off them, I can tell the glass is bulletproof.

The building looks ominous, the kind of place that does not guarantee your eventual exit. And if you turn out to be one of the fortunate souls who does earn an exit pass, you might come out and not recognize the person you see in the mirror.

I pull the Prius into a space in the tiny parking lot near the door. When considering a getaway car, I doubt the Prius would float to the top of anyone's list. Of course, what it does have going for it is the element of disbelief. Slap a FREE TIBET bumper sticker on that sucker and no one in their right mind would ever believe the driver could be a criminal. It's simply too far-fetched. I leave the car unlocked. I'd leave it running but I don't know how to do that with a Prius.

Standing outside S&S Outsourcing, I don't have even the slightest semblance of a plan. I have nothing but a gun, a fleece jacket, and the element of surprise. Fleece jackets are warm and dry and easy to clean but they aren't intimidating like the Bat Suit or Spiderman's get-up. But I have the gun and the surprise thing so while neither of those will vault me to superhero status, they're better than nothing.

It's possible Simon Still, two stories underground, is right now watching me on the security cameras. And if he is, his complete confidence in his state-of-the-art security system will keep him from getting too excited about it. But I know something he doesn't know. And that is what they say is true—you *can* buy anything on eBay.

For $250, I scored an electronic key card the prepubescent thirteen-year-old seller assured me could break any security system. And it worked just fine at Nordstroms so I'm hopeful my luck will continue.

I slide the card through the slot and the door opens. Inside, about ten feet away at a desk, is a receptionist in a navy suit, bent over a printer, her back to the door. In a split second, Simon will be barking orders at her through her headset, telling her to shoot me. He probably won't even take the time to tell her to shoot to injure, not kill.

I cover the distance between the door and the desk in a few big strides. The receptionist, turning toward me with a dazed look on her face, is none other than Nanny Pauline. I should have known by the navy suit and sensible matching pumps. Putting a gun to Nanny Pauline's head is harder than putting a gun to an anonymous fake receptionist's head. I do it half-heartedly.

"Sally!" Pauline says. "How did you get in here?"

"Do you remember what I told you about calling me 'Sally'?" I ask.

"Yes," Pauline replies, shrinking back from the gun barrel. "Your name is Lucy."

"Very good."

"Simon said even if you happened to find us, which was impossible, you'd never be able to get in. This place is a fortress, he said."

I like that I made Simon nervous enough to mention me at all. I'll take all the points I can get.

"Sometimes Simon is wrong," I say. Actually, this might be the first time Simon's been wrong but she doesn't need to know that.

Pauline clears her throat. "How's Theo?" she asks, turning her head so my gun rests on her temple. Her eyes are squeezed shut. No matter how good you think you are, having a gun pointed at your head is never a relaxing experience.

"Great," I say. "He's in his last year of preschool. Choosing a kindergarten is turning out to be more difficult than I expected but we'll figure it out."

What's wrong with me? Why do I feel the need to yammer on about my kindergarten woes to anyone with a pulse? I give myself a mental kick in the ass. Stay focused.

"Wow," Pauline says, opening her eyes and inhaling deeply. "Time flies."

"How many agents are down there with him?" I ask. A lot depends on her answer. "And don't lie. I can tell if you're lying. I'm good at that."

Pauline nods and licks her dry lips.

"None," she says finally.

"You sure about that?" I say. "Remember, it'll be your body between me and them."

"I'm not lying. He's alone down there with the prisoner."

So my sprinkling of fairy dust hasn't worn off just yet. Good for me.

"Get up," I say. "Let's go see him."

Pauline wipes her palms on her skirt. I imagine they're slick with sweat.

"Don't worry," I say. "Just do as I ask and everything will be fine."

"Whenever anyone says things will be fine," she says, "they always turn out awful."

"Look at you," I say. "You're finally getting it. Way to go!"

I march her at gunpoint toward the elevator.

"Enter the code," I order. Pauline punches in some numbers and I detect a small tremor in her hand. I'm not supposed to be here. The door wasn't supposed to open. She was unprepared to deal with me just walking in like I owned the place.

Later, when Simon ships her off to Siberia for being weak, she'll feel betrayed. It's not her fault I got through the door and it's not her fault that having a gun to her head made her scared. She'll consider once again whether Agency life is for her but will stay in the end because Simon inspires that kind of twisted loyalty. Your hatred of him is matched only by your desire to have him love you. And Simon does not love anyone.

We step into the elevator as if we are one person. I catch a faint whiff of lemongrass rising off her. The smell makes me instantly ill. I close my eyes and take a few quick gulps of air. Now is not the time to go around throwing up on hostages.

"What do they call you?" I ask her as we descend.

"Nanny Pauline," she says, with some hostility. "Simon thought it fit."

"I'm sorry," I say.

"Hard to get taken seriously with a name like Nanny Pauline."

Tell me about it.

The elevator doors open on a dark corridor. Simon Still stands in a circle of light thrown off by a single ceiling bulb. He looks at me with a half smile, his Magnum pointed right at my face.

"Sally," he says.

"Simon."

"The door?" he asks.

"I'm just that good," I say. If I tell him about the kid on eBay he's likely to launch into a speech about the private sector versus the public sector and who's better suited to make really cool spy gear. From experience, I know it's a long speech and our schedule today is a bit too tight to allow for Simon's rambling.

"Admit it," I say. "You're surprised to see me."

"Sadly, nothing surprises me," he says.

"Um, excuse me," Nanny Pauline interrupts. "Are either of you going to kill me?" There's something about the question that makes me laugh. I'm aware I sound like a lunatic.

"No," I say, trying to regain my composure. "I can't speak for your boss, though. He's pretty casual when it comes to other people's lives."

"Pauline, stay calm," Simon commands. "Everything will be fine." I hold her against me, my personal human suit of armor. She's softer than I expected. I wonder if she's been to the Ranch yet.

"I wish you wouldn't say that, sir," Pauline says quietly, "about things being fine."

"Sally," Simon says, looking resigned, "the United States government thanked you for your help in making that phone call and then asked you to please stay out of it. That's the way this works."

"The United States government," I ask, "or you personally? Are you really willing to sacrifice Gray just to find out what Yoder knows? Have you lost your mind or is the idea that a mere kid held out on you too much to handle?"

Simon grips his gun. The blood drains out of his fingers. It's the only evidence of how furious he is at what I said. If we were alone, I'd be dead by now.

"I think," he says, "you just questioned my loyalty."

"You want Yoder to tell you what's in the little black book and I want Yoder to save Gray. I think my reason is better."

"You never learned the lesson that one person is less important than one million people."

"I tried," I say. "It didn't stick."

"Rogue doesn't suit you," Simon says.

Yes. This is something I've figured out all on my own.

"So now what?" I ask.

"How about I shoot you, you shoot me, and Pauline here goes somewhere hot and sandy to learn how to be a bit more aggressive," he suggests.

Pauline hangs her head. I begin to move us closer to Simon, who holds his ground in the dim puddle of light.

"Maybe Yemen," Simon continues. "You liked Yemen, didn't you Sally?" The only way you can tell he's not made of stone is one index finger tapping ever so gently against his thigh.

"Yemen was lovely," I say, inching forward. "Gray came for me in Russia, you know, when I was just a baby, younger than Theo is now. I can remember the smell of his coat and the snow and how he seemed very tall. I can't let him die."

"Sally, I will say it again, your affection for mere individuals is a weakness," he says.

It's not a weakness. It's the only thing.

"I tried to teach it out of you," he continues, "but apparently I failed."

Simon's trigger finger is loose and that lack of tension will give me the split second I need to duck.

"I learned some lessons, Simon," I say. My left leg shoots out like a bullet and catches Simon somewhere between the knees. His gun fires into the ceiling as he goes down hard. A shower of glass from the light above rains down on us. I land on Simon's stomach with my knee, pinning him to the ground. I still have Pauline around the neck.

"The scissor," Simon groans. "Nice one."

"I've been practicing," I say, "on lawyers."

A small trickle of blood runs from the back of his head and stains the concrete floor. I drag him a few feet and handcuff his one wrist to an exposed pipe. The handcuffs are covered in a fuzzy leopard print but sometimes a girl has got to make do with what's lying around, unused, in her bedroom.

"I didn't think you were the type," Simon says, stroking the fuzzy handcuffs. Then his eyes close. I roll him over just a bit. The split on his head is small but head wounds bleed a lot, making a big cakey mess of your hair. It won't take Pauline long to break the silly furry handcuffs but a small head start is all I need.

"I know what's in the black book," I whisper to Simon. "You're not going to like it. Someone in your organization is a rat." But his eyes are already closed. My words fall on deaf ears. I notice Pauline is gagging.

"Sorry," I say, releasing my grip on her throat so she can breathe. She sputters for a few seconds and the color returns to her cheeks.

"Have you been to the Ranch?" I ask. Pauline sits on the floor and rubs the red mark rising on her neck.

"The where?"

"When Simon wakes up, tell him two things. One, he has a rat, and two, you want to go to the Ranch. Trust me. It'll be fun."

She looks at me skeptically. Okay, maybe fun isn't the right word but definitely useful. If she'd been to the Ranch, I never would have gotten this far.

"Lucy?" Pauline asks tentatively.

"Yes?"

"The last time, when I was babysitting Theo, when I went back to the Underground, no one there believed I'd met you. They thought I was crazy."

"I'm in kind of a rush here," I said, pulling the keys from Simon's pocket. "Gotta spring the prisoner and all."

"Well, before you go, can I get a quick picture of us as proof, to show the guys back in D.C.?"

You have got to be kidding me.

36

As we step out into the daylight, Yoder does a solid imitation of a vampire and recoils as if he is at risk of bursting into flames. His wrists are red and raw from where the cuffs dug into his flesh. I hand him my sunglasses and a Clif Bar. Yoder murmurs a thank you.

The Prius is right where I left it. I shove Yoder into the passenger seat and slam the door. As we make our way toward the bay, the car is silent except for the deep rattle coming from Yoder's lungs. I find it hard to believe he contracted tuberculosis in the short time since I saw him last. More likely he has seasonal allergies or a cold. The mother in me wants to put him to bed with a dose of Tylenol and a bowl of chicken soup. The spy in me just wants to get this over with.

I park in the small lot on the north side of the San Francisco Ferry Building. The attendant explains in detail how I should go about getting my parking ticket validated but I don't think I'm going to have time to catch even a quick bite, and that makes me sad. There's a place here that makes the world's most amazing fish tacos. You can sit outside and eat them while gazing up at the wretched Bay Bridge traffic. It's the kind of experience that makes you grateful to be where you are rather than wishing you were somewhere else. Theo and I are regular customers although he prefers to stick with the chips.

While the Ferry Building is in fact a place where you can catch a ferry, that is really inconsequential. Its long main hallway and side corridors are a marketplace overflowing with every sort of culinary delight imaginable. From exotic mushrooms to the perfect· cappuccino to avocado ice cream to Vietnamese food so good you'd sell your mother up the river for it in a heartbeat. It's also overflowing with tourists from all corners of the globe. And that's exactly what I want, a reliably dense crowd. Witnesses. The last time I made the mistake of setting up a meeting in the middle of nowhere. I'm not sure this time is going to actually go any better but I'm proving I can learn from my mistakes. At least some of them.

I hold Yoder under his arm and drag him along with me. He's anxious, his eyes darting every which way. His skin seems to jump and twitch like a cat with a bad case of fleas. I get a whiff of anticipation off him that doesn't seem to fit the situation. If anything, he should be scanning for an opportunity to escape. As we maneuver through the tourists, my cell phone rings. It's Will.

"Hi," he says. "I was just thinking about the interview this morning."

I can barely remember the interview. It seems to have occurred a lifetime ago.

"I thought it went fine," I say, scanning the crowd.

"Where are you?"

"Downtown," I say. "I have a doctor's appointment later. Theo is with your folks."

The silence is not to be ignored.

"They seemed really happy," I go on. I hold Yoder around

the waist as if we're lovers, me in the role of cradle-robber and him in the role of baby.

"Good for you, Lucy," he says eventually, the shock of my revelation wearing off. "I'm glad you feel like you can trust them."

Oh, I don't trust them. I'm just desperate and a desperate woman will do strange things. A man approaches us. He could be a tourist or he could be part of Chemical Claude's pack of wolves.

"I have to go," I say. "If I'm running late, order pizza for dinner. You know how doctor's offices can be."

"Sure," he says. I hit End and stick the phone in my pocket with my car keys. In my other pocket is my gun and I make sure Yoder can feel it in his ribs. But he doesn't care. He stares at the man approaching us. I guess he's more of the wolf variety and less of the tourist.

The man blocks our way, grinning. The other visitors flow around him to both sides as if he were a boulder in the middle of a stream.

"You come with me," he says.

"Where are we going?"

"We don't trade in here," he says. "We trade out there." He points to the piers.

"No," I say.

"If we bring your guy in here, we all spend the night in the slammer."

He has a point. Gray can't be looking his best right now.

"Let's go," I say and follow the man out of the Ferry Building.

Moored to a pier south of where we stand is a gleaming white yacht with the name *Everest* painted on the side in enormous black letters. The "E" is designed to look like the mountain herself. A rubber-coated ramp runs from a floating dock to the deck above. Our guide gestures we're to board the vessel. This is just what I was hoping to avoid.

"Forget it," I say. "We're staying right here." Next to me, Yoder hums to himself. He seems oddly happy and relaxed all of a sudden. I wonder where Blackford is and why, if he insists on meddling in my life, he can't choose now to do it.

The man points to a turret on the yacht. Sticking out from a window on the turret is the barrel of a gun and it's aimed directly at me.

"Get on the boat."

I have a number of choices here. The first is, I can scream for help. The second is, I can jump in the Bay and swim to Hawaii. The third is, I can do as they say and hope that everyone is still alive come dinnertime. I choose number three, cross my fingers, and board the boat.

37

The moment Yoder and I are on deck, the ramp comes up and the engines roar to life. The yacht backs smoothly away from the dock. I reconsider the option of swimming to Hawaii. This has all the telltale signs of a disaster in the making. And of course as soon as I think that, it gets worse.

Standing on deck above us is Chemical Claude himself. He wears a jaunty red beret and a thick matching scarf and looks as excited as a kid on Christmas morning.

"Welcome aboard the *Everest*, Sally," he booms. "In a way, I named her for you."

Somehow the hat and the scarf and the name of the boat really make me want to kill him. I reach around to my pocket, pull out the Colt, and aim it at his head. Instantly, three machine gun barrels are pointing at mine.

"So emotional," Chemical Claude says as he slides down a set of stairs and comes to a stop right in front of me. He taps me on the head with a gloved finger. "You should think before you act. But I know you have other talents. Languages you shouldn't know but somehow do because you're so very curious. Remember what happened to George when he was so curious? The difference is, you don't appear to have a man with a yellow hat to save you. Now give me the gun."

I hand it to him and he tosses it overboard directly into the Bay. Well, there goes that.

Tucked into a leather shoulder holster, he carries a SIG P226 handgun. This particular gun bears a "Blackwater USA" logo on the slide.

"It's a nice gun," he says. "A trophy. I won't tell you the details of how it came to be in my possession."

"I didn't ask," I say. "Where's Gray?" But I have lost Chemical Claude's attention. He has turned his eyes to Yoder, and they're hard eyes, dark little pieces of coal in a snowman head.

"You stayed too long in Vegas," Claude says. "You probably lost all your money and came home with a case of herpes from that girl. That was not part of the plan."

"Neither was my year with Simon Still," Yoder spits back. He shakes with apparent fury, his thin fists balled up and ready to strike.

"Plan?"

"Yes," Chemical Claude says to me. "The difference is I follow through. Richard here, he apparently likes to freelance. Lock her up until we get to the island."

As Chemical Claude's henchmen drag me across the deck of the yacht, I remember something Simon once told me. The obvious answer, he said, is usually the right one. And the right one is usually the one directly in front of your face.

"We think people are so clever, coming up with complicated schemes and lies and plans," Simon lectured as we walked the endless corridors to Director Gray's office. "But they're not. For the most part, they're hopeless, struggling to overcome the simplest complications. Imagine the harm they could do if they were thinking people. If they were smart. We owe the hopeless morons a huge debt of gratitude."

Simon didn't care if I answered. My job on that day was to walk with him so he didn't end up talking to himself all the way to Gray's office, thus appearing totally batshit. Once we arrived at the office, I would turn around and trudge back to the Underground. I was merely the inbound entertainment.

"So if all the evidence points to party A having just purchased a pile of nuclear componentry then . . ." He turned to me to fill in the rest of the sentence.

"Then they're probably going to build a weapon?"

"Yes! You're a genius, Sally. You'll go far." These exchanges always served to remind me that I wasn't necessarily one of the morons Simon was talking about but I was damn close. Yet every once in a while, Simon had a point.

"Oh, no," I say. My wrists are bound and I'm locked in a cabin down below deck. It's so obvious it's almost impossible to believe. "How could I have missed this? What was I doing?" The answer is easy. I was busy playing LEGOs.

It's the code, stupid. Chemical Claude is after me.

Setting up Yoder to be taken in by the Americans, kidnapping Gray, forcing me to show myself in order to get him back, it's all part of a much more complicated plan that has been in the works for some time now, probably since the Louvre, when Claude found out I was still alive and pretending to be a civilian. It makes me shudder to imagine what he went through in an attempt to find me after that, my only protection being that the United States hides people better than anyone. In retrospect, I should have drowned that Frenchwoman in the toilet and enjoyed the Degas.

Blackford's revelation that Director Gray could be used to motivate me was the last piece of the puzzle. Chemical Claude finally had a way to flush me from my hiding place.

Chemical Claude's goal is simple. He wants me to translate the code in his little black book. I am his Rosetta stone.

38

Through the tiny porthole, Angel Island looms off our bow, shrouded in wispy fog. The largest of the Bay Area islands, on a cold and windy day such as today, Angel Island is likely to be an empty and isolated 740 acres in the middle of a metropolitan region with seven million people. At this hour of the day, with the last ferry already departed, it'll be me and the lunatics. Why does this keep happening to me? Am I being punished for being a warlord or an independent voter in a former life?

As the yacht swings around, I catch a glimpse of what's most certainly our destination. Right on the shore of the island sits a three-story, faded red warehouse. The water laps practically to its door. A partially collapsed wooden pier looms in the shadows directly in front of it. All the windows are boarded up. What a perfect place to perpetrate a crime. I hear an anchor splash down.

The door to my cabin pushes open and the barrel of a gun attached to a very large man pokes through. There's a grunt I interpret to mean "Please follow me topside. Thank you."

Seated in a rubber raft bobbing next to the *Everest* is Chemical Claude. He has a fleece blanket draped over his shoulders and an odd grin on his face. Next to him sits Yoder, looking peevish.

"I BASE jump the KL Tower in Kuala Lumpur each year," Claude says as I climb down into the raft. Yoder rolls his eyes.

"Not this story again," he says.

"You shut up," Chemical Claude says to him, turning to me. "It's a thrill to jump, the rush of the wind in your ears, the cold on your face. Such bodily freedom seems almost divine."

"That's nice," I say.

"I want you to know that it's awesome. But I anticipate I'm going to enjoy this, too."

Why is it these villain types can't seek out reasonable entertainment like the rest of us? See a movie, have dinner at a fancy restaurant, go fishing? Why do they act as if we're all still living in ancient Rome?

We're completely enveloped in the fog. A few seagulls bob in the water beside us. All sound is muffled.

"I can't believe I thought you deserved a second chance," I say to Yoder. "I even took you to a play-off game and bought you popcorn." He keeps his eyes forward but I see a tremor at the corner of his mouth.

Chemical Claude gazes across the water at the lonely warehouse. A person stands on the narrow stretch of beach out front, legs planted firmly. Her pants are rolled up to her ankles and her dark hair blows in the wind. She's been waiting on our arrival. The little raft bounces through the waves and gradually evens out as we enter the protective zone of shore.

"She has a son," Yoder says, out of the blue. Chemical Claude sits up straighter and actually looks surprised. His eyebrows shoot directly up toward his hairline before he can regain control of them. I wait to see what will happen next.

"Didn't know, did you?" Yoder continues, sticking the needle in a little deeper and wiggling it around just for fun.

"Your pal Blackford knew but he didn't tell you. That's gotta chafe. The kid is actually kind of cute, if a little bit spoiled."

My eyelid twitches furiously. Is it because Yoder just outed me as a mom or because he obviously thinks I lack discipline as a parent? Whatever the reason, I have lost control of the eyelid. I rest a finger on it to calm the madness, keenly aware of the shotgun pointed at my chest. Chemical Claude's lips form a tight little line.

"You paid Blackford all that money for information and he held out on you," Yoder says. "I told you, you can't trust a man like that, but do you listen to me? No. She knows the code. If she won't do it, just snatch the kid." I want to leap across the boat and squeeze the life out of Yoder with my hands but before I can get too far along in that fantasy, the raft runs aground on the beach. Chemical Claude and Yoder each grab an arm and toss me out of the boat and onto the sand where I land, face first, right at the feet of Ayushi, all grown up.

For a moment, I think I might be dreaming, that maybe the stress has finally overwhelmed my resources and all the circuits in my brain have gone haywire, leaving me to live out my life as a blithering idiot. As a blithering idiot, I would certainly not have to contemplate how it is I came to be here, facedown in the sand on an island in the middle of San Francisco Bay, looking up at Ayushi, whom I'd assumed died at the hands of Chemical Claude many years ago.

Chemical Claude watches me closely, curious about the effect seeing her will have. With an air of ownership, he slides an arm around Ayushi's waist and pulls her toward him. He kisses her long and hard and from my position on the ground I cannot tell if this makes her happy or not. What it does to me defies description.

Ayushi is tall and willowy with miles of dark hair blowing in a tornado around her lovely face. The little girl who saved my life in Nepal is no longer.

"Ayushi," I say. It's the first time I've said her name out loud since I fell in the river and was swept away from her. It comes out as a grateful prayer. Ayushi stares down at me with a curious expression, the same one she wore while sitting on my bed in the Hotel Kathmandu.

"She has worked out very well for me and I have you to thank for that," Chemical Claude says, pulling me to my feet by the back of my jacket. "Now, let's go and see your father, shall we?"

The building is old and concrete, a relic from the days when this was a military fort guarding San Francisco from Confederate invaders. There's no glass in the windows and an icy wind blows through with impunity. There are several folding chairs scattered across the vast open space but little else. In a far corner, guarded by two husky men with guns, sits Director Gray, loosely tied to a chair with nylon rope. His chin rests on his chest, which rises and falls ever so slightly. He wears a torn button-down shirt that was once white but is now stained with streaks of blood, dried to the color of rust. His ripped suit trousers expose a deep wound on his right thigh that will make it difficult for him to walk. His feet are bare. From across the great empty room, he's nothing more than a beaten old man, and if he was ever a master of the free world, those days are now just a memory. I feel something break off inside of me and float freely in my bloodstream. It's a stripped-down version of what I feel for Theo but with jagged, unfinished edges.

"Don't do it, Sally," Gray says, without raising his head. "No matter what happens."

That's easy enough for him to say, but they kind of have me over a barrel here. I don't translate for them and they kill Gray. I don't translate for them and they kill Theo. I don't translate for them and they kill me. The order in which they choose to proceed doesn't matter, as the results will be the same. Dead, dead, and dead.

"This sucks," I say.

"Sit," Chemical Claude commands, pulling the small black notebook that has caused all these problems from his inside pocket and shoving me onto a metal folding chair. "You translate and everyone walks away. I'm a man of my word."

"No, you're not," I say.

"Well, I could be if I choose to," he says with a sniff.

"That's reassuring," I say. "Thanks."

Claude grabs me by the neck. His strong fingers dig deep into my windpipe. I see funny little stars swirling around his head, as if he wears a halo.

"You'll read now," he says. Not seeing an alternative, I nod in agreement and he releases me. I gasp. Claude slams the book into my hands. On the upper right-hand corner is engraved the number 17. He's been filling these little black books for quite some time, waiting for me to show up and read them to him.

I flip open the book. Inside is page after page of code, recorded in pencil, revealing the secret workings of the USAWMD.

It's not complete; big sections are missing but I'm shocked at how current it is. The latest entry is from a mere two days ago, which confirms Simon has a sewer-sized rat in his organization.

Chemical Claude circles me, running his gun along my

cheek and through my hair. The barrel is cold and I shudder despite my best efforts not to.

"Finally, the means to bring you down," he says, half to me and half to Gray, "to put an end to your ridiculous crusade to save the world. If any of you paid closer attention, you'd discover the world doesn't want to be saved."

"I don't think it wants to be blown up, either," I say. In response, he whacks me on the head with the butt of his gun. I see a brief flash of light and colors and my eyes water.

If I had a gun, which I don't, could I even kill all these people? Claude, the two men guarding Gray, Yoder. Wait a minute. Where is Yoder? Not one minute before he was standing behind Ayushi, but now he's gone and no one else seems to have noticed.

"It's all useless, you know," mumbles Gray. "That code is false. The real code never gets recorded." Gray looks worse up close. His parchment skin is papery and blueish, as if the blood in his body is sticking close to his heart. I notice his long toes and I gasp in horror. Those are my feet, my ugly awkward feet. Finally someone to blame.

"It was created to mislead people like you," Gray continues. "People who aren't too smart."

Chemical Claude doesn't like Gray's commentary. He backhands him across the face but Gray barely winces.

"You lie, old man," Chemical Claude snarls.

"Just because you believe it," Gray says, "doesn't make it true." Chemical Claude hits him again.

"Wait a minute," I interrupt, hoping to draw Claude's wrath in my direction. "If world domination is what you're after, and I think we're all in agreement on that point, why don't you just have him translate the code?" I say, gesturing to Gray. "He's the one who wrote it, after all."

"Do you think us fools?" Chemical Claude shrieks. "Gray and I are enemies, yes, but we're both from an age of respectability, when a man giving his word stood for something." I have no idea where he's going with this but as long as he prattles on about old-school techniques and respectability, he isn't killing anyone.

"You kids think you can do anything you want and get away with it," he says, standing over me. "Just change your minds when it suits you, change sides like you change your socks. It's reprehensible." He walks over to Gray and places a hand lightly on his bruised shoulder.

"It's clear this man would die before revealing the code. There's nothing he cares about more than his country." For a second, I think he might give Gray a big wet kiss on the lips but instead he turns back to me and says, "You are not that man. You won't be able to hold out while watching your father scream for his life. You'll translate the code. Girls are like that."

"He won't scream," I correct. "He might sing 'The Star-Spangled Banner' but he won't scream. And you, Claude Chevalier, are nothing like him."

"Well," Claude says, leaning down to whisper directly into my ear, "I imagine your son will scream if your father won't. Now read."

My blood pressure surges and it takes every ounce of my willpower not to reach out and strangle Claude, consequences be damned. The only thing that stops me is a gentle pressure on my shoulder, a small hand holding me in place.

Ayushi stands very close to me. The smell of her laundry detergent is familiar and I'm suddenly overcome by a sharp longing for home. I want to be sitting at my kitchen table, building wampa snow creatures out of LEGOs with Theo.

The pressure I feel against my shoulder turns out not to be Ayushi holding me in my seat. Rather, it is the butt of a SIG P226, barely visible peeking out from the long sleeve of her oversized down jacket. She must have lifted it off him when he hugged her on the beach. Quickly, as Claude fumbles with a recording device, I take the gun and slide it into the pocket of my fleece jacket. Ayushi gives me a small smile and squeezes my shoulder.

"Sally," she whispers. "Sally."

In all my time at the Agency, I never knew if I was good enough. No one ever slapped me on the back and said, "Nice work." I never got a gold star on my report card or a year-end bonus based on outstanding performance. But eventually, you have to grow up and judge yourself. And today, right now in fact, I decide I might just be okay. Maybe not the best there ever was but good enough.

"Girls are unreliable," Chemical Claude says, returning to his earlier theme as he sets up a microphone in front of my face. "They're ruled by emotion. They don't think clearly. Girls can never close the deal."

"Some girls maybe," I say, whipping the gun from my pocket, "but not this one." The first two shots are clean and the men go down immediately. I hear their submachine guns skitter across the concrete floor. The third guy starts to run and my bullet goes through his neck. Not pretty but no less effective. Chemical Claude grabs Ayushi and hides behind her, the length of cord from the microphone wrapped tightly around her neck.

"You take one step and she's a goner," he hisses. "Don't want to lose her a second time, do you?"

"Kill him, Sally," whispers Gray from his seat. He looks up now, a twisted smile on his swollen face. "You were the best shot in the place, although no one ever told you. You put those boys to shame. Do it now."

And that's all it takes.

I lower the gun just a millimeter and fire without pausing. Ayushi dives to the left as Chemical Claude crashes to the floor in a spray of red. His face is frozen in surprise, a gloved hand halfway to where the side of his head used to be. And while I expected seeing Chemical Claude finally die would fill me with relief, I find I'm filled with nothing more than a deep, cold fatigue.

Quickly, I untie Gray. He can barely stand, leaning heavily on my shoulder for support. We start to shuffle off to our getaway.

"Not so fast," comes a voice from up above. Yoder stands on a catwalk above us with a grenade in each hand, pins pulled. "Put down your gun, Sally, and pick up the book. We're not done yet."

And there I was, kind of hoping this wouldn't happen. I lean Gray against the wall and hold up my gun for Yoder to see.

"I'm putting it down," I say, placing it on the floor at my feet. "Don't do anything crazy, okay?" I position myself in front of Ayushi and Gray. "I'm going to pick up the book now."

The book is floating in a puddle of blood. I fish it out and hold it up for Yoder to see.

"Here it is," I say. "I'm opening it."

My brain, which ought to be going full throttle figuring a way out of this mess, is instead thinking things along the lines of "Gee, I hope the grandparents remembered to bring Theo's snacks" and "I wonder if it's foggy out at the zoo and if Theo is wearing his jacket?" and finally, "Oh my God, what am I doing here? What was I thinking?"

Fortunately, before I can break into full-scale panic, I see a look on Gray's face that can only be described as shock. Considering nothing is supposed to shock Gray, it gets my attention.

He looks up at the catwalk but not at Yoder. His eyes fix on a shadowy figure behind Yoder, a figure holding a very large weapon. He is looking at Ian Blackford.

In a flash, I understand Gray thinks Blackford works for the now dead Chemical Claude and is here to help Yoder finish what Claude started. And Gray knows if Claude had Blackford on his roster, the game is over. We're all dead.

So what can I say to that?

"It's the Man with the Yellow Hat," I whisper in his ear. Gray shakes his head at me. He doesn't understand the reference but it's all I can give him right now because the ride is about to get bumpy.

Up on the catwalk, Yoder flexes his scrawny biceps, all hopped up on power and hand grenades.

"Claude promised me if I did this, went along with his plan to find you, he would set me free," he says. "Then I could go to school and build buildings and be somebody real."

Like a cat, Blackford moves silently forward.

"But he never mentioned a man named Simon Still. He never told me what they would do to me. Claude took everything and I'm not leaving here without getting some of it back."

"You don't need to do this," I say, trying to keep Yoder's focus on me. "Tell me you don't want to do this and I'll come up there and get those grenades and we can end this."

I'm not even done with my speech but Yoder is already vigorously shaking his head no. He looks like Theo when I try to get him to eat Brussels sprouts.

"I'm done taking orders," he says. "I'm done being a pawn."

I sympathize with him in an abstract way but there's little I can do about it if he insists on dropping grenades on our heads.

"Please," I say again, in one last effort, "let me help you. I can help you. You're just a kid, Yoder."

The last part makes him mad.

"Read or die," he says with renewed determination. It's a terrible line.

"If you do this, you'll end up being nobody, just as everyone thought," I say. I'm straining to hold up Gray, even with Ayushi's help.

"That's not true," Yoder howls. "You watch and see. I *am* somebody." At that moment, Blackford slides up behind Yoder and puts the barrel of his gun to his head.

"Not anymore, you're not," Blackford says and pulls the trigger.

The grenades, spoons released, fall from Yoder's dead hands like overripe apples from a tree. But Blackford always has a plan and, as I see this one unfold, I think for a split second how nice it would be to be that sure of myself. As if he is playing a high stakes game of urban handball, Blackford strikes an armed grenade and sends it sailing out a glassless window.

He almost gets the other one but gravity pulls it just beyond his reach.

"Grenade," I shout, in case anyone missed it.

Ayushi and I grab Gray and push him toward an open door. He groans in agony. On the other side of the door, we huddle down against the thick cement wall. Then I pull them both to me, hold tight, and wait for the inevitable big boom.

39

The car that comes screeching to a halt in front of us is government issue and black. Although the windows are tinted, I have a pretty good idea who is inside. I hold Gray around the waist. He leans on me and, although he looks frail, he's surprisingly heavy.

Slumping down, his breath is warm on my ear. I can barely make out his words, my head ringing from the explosion.

"You look so much like her," he whispers in Russian.

In an instant, I'm back in the one room, her beautiful young face inches from mine as she holds me up so I can look out the window at the desolate landscape of Norilsk, Russia. It's winter and there's nothing but ice and snow for as far as the eye can see. When the men came for her, she locked me in a special compartment under the floorboards.

"Do not come out," she said. "No matter what you hear." She hugged me hard and I thought I heard a jagged sob escape from her throat. Above my head, she quickly replaced the planks.

She was a spy, they said. I could hear their boots, someone rearranging the chairs around the table. A double agent, they went on. A traitor. And the punishment for that was death. The gunshots were loud and I covered my ears. Moments later, there was silence. But I stayed under those boards, hardly moving, until Gray came for me. I did as I was told.

"She loved you," Gray says. "But in the end, it wasn't enough. It never is."

I hear her voice in my head, the little girl on the train, and I think Gray is wrong. Love was enough because here I am. Still alive. Still moving forward. In the end, love might be the only thing that matters.

"Who was she?" I ask. But Gray closes his eyes and shakes his head. It's too late for that question. Simon Still has arrived.

Simon climbs out of the car along with three other indistinguishable men. They're all armed and appear quite serious. My instinct is to run, fast and hard, in any direction.

"Sir," Simon says, limping up to us. "I'm so relieved to find you alive." Using me for support, Gray attempts to straighten up. He raises an inquisitive eyebrow at Simon and clears his throat.

"Are you really?" he asks.

"Of course." Simon elbows me out of the way, acting as though we have never met, as though we hadn't tried to kill one another just a few hours earlier, and takes the weight of Gray onto his own shoulders. The other men form a tight protective circle around the Director, hustling him off to the warm car.

It seems now would be a good time to take a minute and reflect on my relationship with Gray and what it all means, but that will have to wait because right now I need to see to something else.

Before the car doors slam shut on the armored sedan that will spirit Gray back to the safety of Washington, I run for the warehouse. Ayushi yells after me but I can barely make out her words.

There is, of course, no body. At least not the one I'm looking for. The explosion proved too much for the ancient catwalk and it dangles at a right angle to the floor. Yoder is stretched lifeless beneath it, a permanent look of surprise in his unblinking eyes.

We have less than a minute before the Agency clean-up crew arrives and attempts to sweep us out with the trash. I identify a faint trail of blood leading to a door on the far side of the building but it disappears before the exit. Blackford is gone.

Ayushi tugs on my sleeve. "Come now," she says in the same singsong voice I sometimes hear in my nightmares. "We need to leave." I stop long enough to take her face in my hands. There's something important I want to say but the words don't form. Ayushi places her hands over mine. They're warm and soft.

"Do not worry, Sally Sin," she says. "We do the best we can."

By tomorrow afternoon, someone will report a fancy white yacht, called the *Everest*, illegally moored to a San Francisco pier. The police will spend hours trying to figure out who owns it but to no avail. Eventually, the yacht will be auctioned off by the city and the new owner will have no clue he is cruising the bay in a boat that used to belong to a terrorist.

Ayushi, with only a small backpack thrown over her shoulder, hails a cab. She seems oddly at ease in her own skin, a survivor in a world that makes absolutely no sense.

She claims she has plenty of money, stolen slowly over the years and hidden in various locations.

"Claude taught me to be a thief," she says. "I practiced on him." She won't listen to my apologies for having left her to a madman and when I ask her where she's going, she says only "home" before kissing me on the cheek and sliding into the taxi.

"We will see each other again, Sally," she says as she pulls the door shut. "I am sure of it."

As Ayushi's taxi becomes lost in a flood of taillights, I think about all the paths I could have taken in my life, the different people I could have been. The thought makes my throat constrict. Any other path would have led to a life without Theo, without Will, without the things I value above all else.

I cannot save any of us from what has already happened. I cannot undo the past nor, I realize, would I, if given the chance.

40

I arrive home to Theo, Will, and his parents sitting around the table eating pizza and laughing about the howler monkeys at the zoo. They look so content, so connected to each other, that I stop short before entering the kitchen.

"It was like he was talking to me," Will II says. "We had an understanding, me and that monkey. It was a relationship."

Rose Marie covers her mouth with a manicured hand in horror at the memory. "I have never been so embarrassed in all my life," she says. "Honestly. Grown men do not talk to monkeys. At least not in public."

"You were so funny, Gramps," Theo says, spontaneously hugging him. "Do the monkey voice again. Do it for Daddy."

It's as if I am watching them through frosted glass, as if I am already playing back the memory of this moment.

"Hi, guys," I say. The nonchalance of my greeting almost makes me laugh. It doesn't fit with the rest of my day.

"Hi, honey," Will says. "I didn't see you there." He jumps up and puts his arms around me. "We got pizza. Good day? You look kind of washed out."

There is, I suspect, a reason for that but it requires confirmation.

"No, I'm fine," I say, kissing Theo on the head and Will on the lips. "Save me a slice. I'll be right back."

It's been a long day but I take the stairs two at a time. In my pocket, I hold two possible futures. The plus sign means everything changes once again. The minus sign means it's probably the malaria. I find myself praying for the plus sign, suddenly filled with an unfamiliar yearning.

I stand in the bathroom, holding the white plastic stick. I watch the little window on the stick change. I wait for it to reveal the future. Downstairs, the business about the monkey is ongoing. It's sure to become one of the stories Theo begs me to tell over and over again. But I'm about to send the conversation off in another direction entirely.

I fill my lungs with air and exhale in the way my yoga teacher tells me is helpful in aligning my chakras. And with what I'm about to do, I can use all the aligned chakras a person can get.

"There's something I want to tell you all," I say. "There's something you need to know about me."

An odd silence descends upon the kitchen. Will puts his glass down and rests a protective hand on Theo's thigh. Theo holds his pizza slice still, in midair, and stares at me.

"I'm pregnant," I say.

Like I said, it's the mother of all misdirection.

Epilogue

My white sunhat is about the size of a beach umbrella and I hold it on my head to keep the brisk wind from snatching it away and sending it on a one-way trip to Africa. The warm sand massages the arches of my feet with each step I take. I am sure the walking will alleviate my caffeine headache and if it doesn't then I reserve the right to drown myself right here in this lovely Hawaiian surf. A life without coffee is hardly worth living. I won't even get into how I feel about alcohol, soft cheese, and sushi because if I do we could be here all day and you might not enjoy watching me cry like a baby.

About a mile behind me, Will and Theo build sandcastles outside of our beachfront rental. It's been a pleasant week full of sun and late afternoon showers that leave everything smelling fresh and new.

The beach is almost empty. He's still far away but that hardly matters. I'd know the man who walks steadily in my direction anywhere.

We stop about five feet from each other. He wears a baseball cap and sunglasses, his T-shirt emblazoned with a San Francisco Giants logo, which I know is meant ironically.

"Blackford," I say, wiggling my toes so they sink deeper into the sand. "You're still alive."

"Apparently. Are you disappointed?"

"You're beginning to remind me of a cat," I say, in an effort not to answer his question.

"You look different," he says. I rest a hand on my growing belly.

"Yes," I say. "I am different." In a number of ways.

"It suits you." He seems so benign standing here, the water lapping at his bare feet.

"I came for a reason," Blackford says, fidgeting with the brim of his cap, playing with a belt loop on his jeans. If he were a three-year-old, I might suggest he go to the bathroom. I've never seen Blackford nervous; it's too human an emotion for a man like him.

"I didn't know you were the target, Sally," he says finally. He's now completely still, all the tension dissipated. "I never would have made the deal with Claude if I had."

Blackford has come a long way to tell me this. It's as close to an apology as I'm likely to get from him and I should be grateful for that much. I know, too, by admitting Claude played him, Blackford will turn into yet another man but I fear that man won't be kinder or gentler. The steeliness is already evident in his cold, blue eyes.

"I know," I say, instead of all the many other things I would like to say. We stand in silence for a few moments. My head throbs in perfect rhythm with the waves.

"There's one more thing," he says, his tone indicating he's not yet done with me. "A grave in Norilsk. You know where that is, right? You might want to visit."

My toes and feet are no longer visible in the sand and it looks as if I'm balanced precariously on two stumps. The pounding in my head is relentless.

"Why do you do this?" I ask. It's a big question, stretching across a number of years.

"Just helping you along on your path to self-discovery," he says. "You may find we're more alike than you think."

"I'm nothing like you," I say, but it's a whisper blown out to sea.

Blackford doesn't say good-bye. He doesn't tell me who is supposed to be in that grave in Norilsk or if it's empty. He just walks away, leaving a trail of smoke and mirrors behind him.

It is true I may not know where I come from. And I have no doubt that one day, maybe soon, I will need to fill in all the blanks. But right now, in this moment, I know exactly who I am.

I am a wife. I am a mother. And once, I was a spy.

Acknowledgments

A big thank-you to Leigh Feldman, who not only keeps everything moving forward but makes me laugh when, really, I'd rather just quit.

To Barbara Jones, for helping me find the heart of this story, and to Christine Pride, for stepping in and bringing it home.

For their technical advice, good humor, and willingness to answer bizarre questions without taking steps to have me committed, I owe thanks to: Sheri Belafsky, Joel Den Dulk, and Joseph Dumont. Any technical errors in this book belong to me alone.

I owe a debt of gratitude to my first draft readers—Sheri Belafsky, Debbie Anderson, and Charla Kordana. They are kind and supportive and don't require any bribe money whatsoever. I hope I can hit you up again on the next round.

To Mike, Max, and Katie, there is no place I'd rather be than where we are, and I'm grateful every day to all of you.

And finally to you, dear readers. Once again, I have so enjoyed living in the world of Sally Sin. My greatest hope is that you will too. Thanks for reading.

Beth McMullen graduated from Boston University with a degree in English Literature and received an MLS from Long Island University. After landing a gig with *Reader's Digest,* she eventually realized she'd rather write books than condense them. She lives in Davis, California, with her husband and their two children. She divides her time between writing and, well, we're really not allowed to say.